THE KOZLOV
BODYGUARDS

SYN BLACKROSE

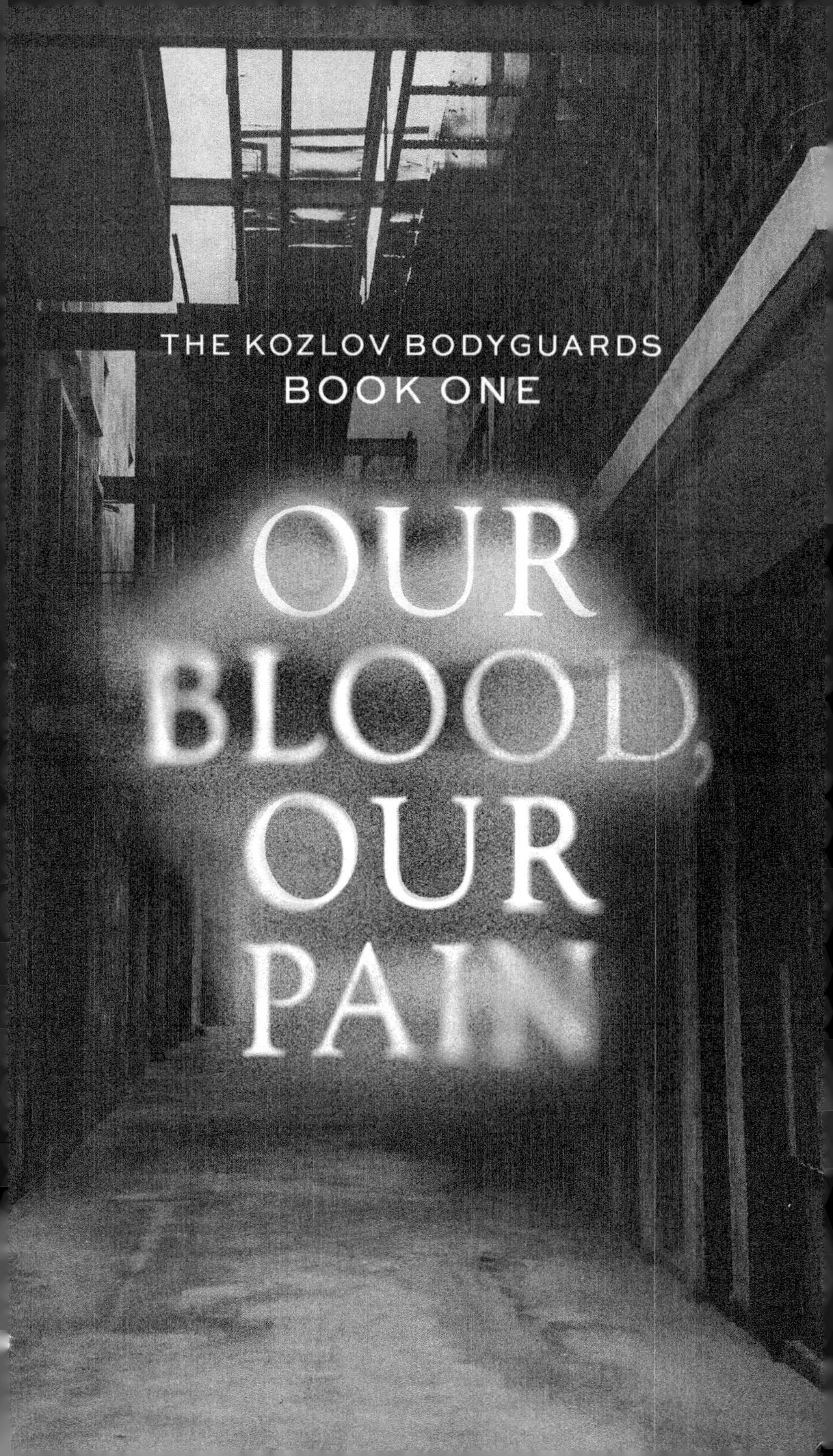

THE KOZLOV BODYGUARDS
BOOK ONE

OUR BLOOD, OUR PAIN

Copyright © 2024 by Syn Blackrose

All rights reserved.

No part of this publication may be reproduced, distributed, or transmitted in any form or by any means, including photocopying, recording, or other electronic or mechanical methods, without the prior written permission of the author, except as permitted by law.

The story, all names, characters, and incidents portrayed in this production are fictitious. No identification with actual persons living or deceased, places, buildings, and products is intended or should be inferred.

Cover Design and Formatting by Katelyn at Design by Kage

Proofreading and Editing by Jen Sharon at Fiction Editing and Proofreading

CONTENTS

COPYRIGHT
DEDICATION
BLURB
PLAYLIST
NOTE FROM AUTHOR
PROLOGUE - KAI

CHAPTER 1 - KAI	1
CHAPTER 2 - JULES	9
CHAPTER 3 - JULES	23
CHAPTER 4 - KAI	31
CHAPTER 5 - JULES	43
CHAPTER 6 - KAI	53
CHAPTER 7 - JULES	59
CHAPTER 8 - KAI	67
CHAPTER 9 - JULES	75
CHAPTER 10 - KAI	85
CHAPTER 11 - JULES	93
CHAPTER 12 - KAI	101
CHAPTER 13 - JULES	111
CHAPTER 14 - JULES	121
CHAPTER 15 - KAI	129
CHAPTER 16 - JULES	141
CHAPTER 17 - KAI	149
CHAPTER 18 - JULES	159
CHAPTER 19 - KAI	169
CHAPTER 20 - JULES	179
CHAPTER 21 - KAI	185
CHAPTER 22 - JULES	193
CHAPTER 23 - KAI	203
CHAPTER 24 - JULES	213

CHAPTER 25 - KAI	221
CHAPTER 26 - JULES	229
CHAPTER 27 - KAI	241
CHAPTER 28 - JULES	247
CHAPTER 29 - KAI	257
CHAPTER 30 - JULES	265
CHAPTER 31 - KAI	277
CHAPTER 32 - JULES	287
CHAPTER 33 - KAI	295
CHAPTER 34 - KAI	307
CHAPTER 35 - JULES	317
CHAPTER 36 - KAI	329
CHAPTER 37 - JULES	341
CHAPTER 38 - KAI	349
CHAPTER 39 - JULES	365
CHAPTER 40 - JULES	375
CHAPTER 41 - JULES	391
CHAPTER 42 - KAI	403
CHAPTER 43 - JULES	407
CHAPTER 44 - KAI	427
CHAPTER 45 - JULES	437
CHAPTER 46 - KAI	445
CHAPTER 47 - JULES	451
CHAPTER 48 - KAI	465
CHAPTER 49 - JULES	473
CHAPTER 50 - KAI	487
CHAPTER 51 - JULES	497
AFTERWORD	
ACKNOWLEDGEMENTS	
ALSO BY SYN	

To my girls who have stuck by me from the very first day.

Amy V & Sadie

Love you both and thank you xx

Jules

Kai. He's become my weakness. My purpose in life. I knew I was never a good man, but Kai has tipped me over the edge for the lengths I'd go to for him.

He's a mess, a beautiful mess, and he wants me. I've never been attracted to a man before, so this is new territory for me. But it won't take long for me to break. I want to fight him, punish him, and adore him.

Oh yeah, and most importantly, he's my step-sister's son. I may not be his Uncle in blood. But this is wrong.

So wrong.

But we can't help ourselves.

Kai

It's been years since I last saw Jules, and when he shows up to right the wrongs in my life, the crush I had years ago hits me tenfold.

Jules is not who I remembered. He's controlling and suffocating.

But he's everything I want in a man. Protective, rough around the edges. Pure dominance.

OUR BLOOD, OUR PAIN

I don't care about our family. It's not like we're blood-related.
My need for him erases all logic and moral decency. I need him to breathe. I need his marks all over my skin.
I don't care about anything else. I would give up my entire life and everyone in it to have him.

OUR BLOOD, OUR PAIN
PLAYLIST

DOOMED | BRING ME THE HORIZON

OUR BLOOD | MORIAH WOODS

ONE OF THE GIRLS | THE WEEKND, JENNIE, LILY-ROSE DEPP

ADDERALL | SLIPKNOT

CELEBRITY SKIN | HOLE

KILLING IN THE NAME | RAGE AGAINST THE MACHINE

I MISS THE MISERY | HALESTORM

WHEN I'M GONE | DIRTY HONEY

NA NA NA | MY CHEMICAL ROMANCE

BLEED THE FREAK | ALICE IN CHAINS

SEXTAPE | DEFTONES

BREATH | BREAKING BENJAMIN

CRUSHCRUSHCRUSH | PARAMORE

DO YA FEEL MY LOVE? | STEREOPHONICS

ATLANTIC | SLEEP TOKEN

BAD GIRL | AVRIL LAVIGNE
FT MARILYN MANSON

NOTE FROM AUTHOR

This story takes place between Tied to You and Kill for You. If you haven't read those books, you can still read this as a standalone, as long as you don't mind missing the detail and backstory of the other characters, as there are major spoilers, especially from Kill for You.

This is a forbideen love story between two consensual adults. They are step-uncle and step-nephew through marriage. No blood relation.

This story is fiction, and not meant as a guide to sexual kinks or relationships. You should always seek advice when it comes to any of the topics I hit on in this story, whether it be to do with sexual kinks, or mental health. I do not condone any behavior in this story. It's a fictional world where we can lose ourselves without worrying about the rights and wrongs of real life. I highly advise reading the trigger warnings on the next page, as this book may not be

OUR BLOOD, OUR PAIN

for you as my stories tend to be on the upper scale of dark and graphic.

Hope you enjoy!

TRIGGER WARNINGS

Dominance

Hickey Kink/Hand necklace

Breathplay

Controlling behavior

Violence/Torture

Unaliving

Dare you to touch or look at him

Possessive

Self loathing

Morally gray MC

Forbidden

Suicidal ideation

"His love was forbidden, but he risked his life for it, because without it, he had no life."

– Valorem

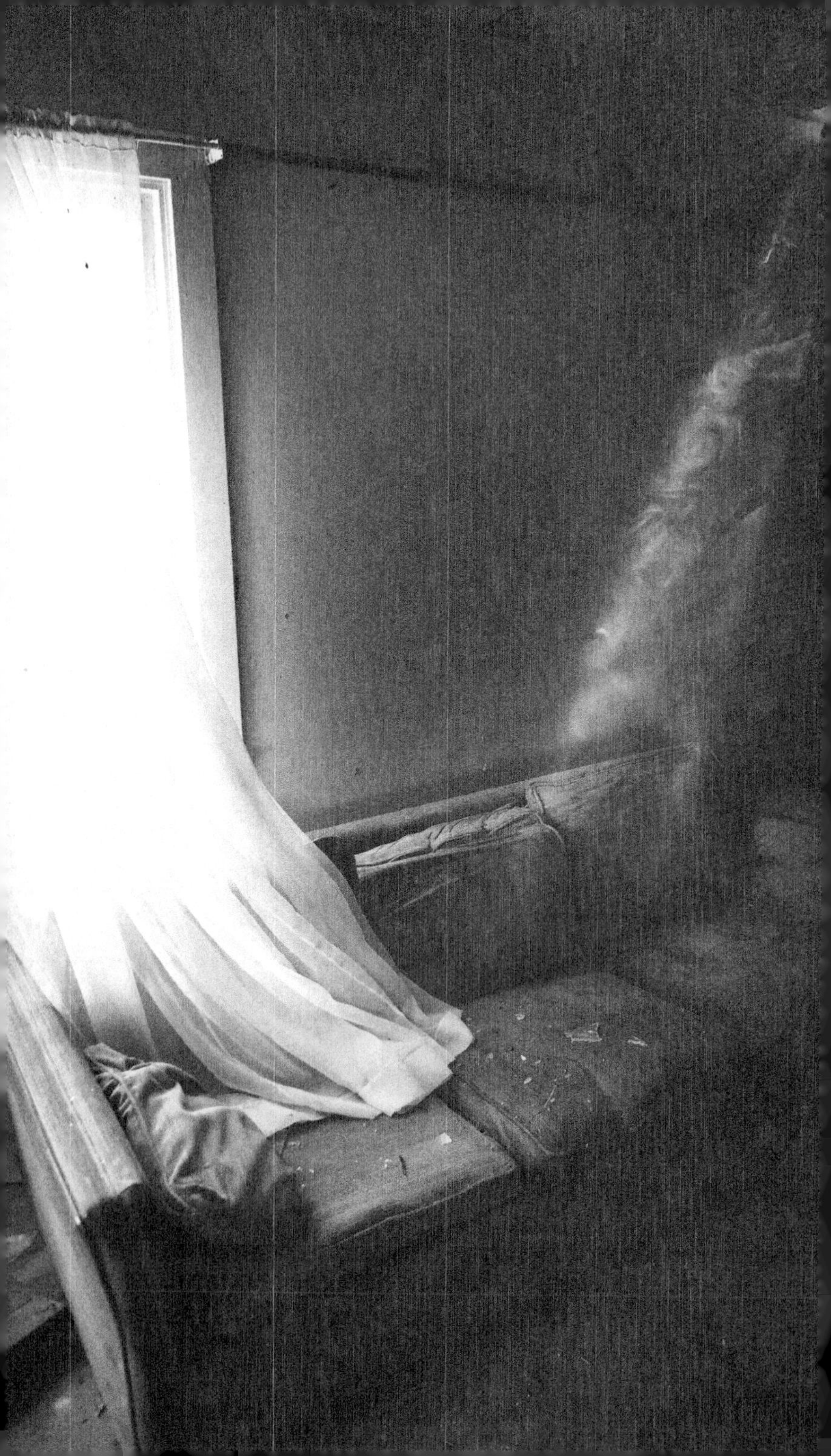

PROLOGUE
KAI

18 YEARS OLD

"Kai, you remember my brother, Zac. These are his asshole friends, Dean and Tex," my best friend Jez says. We're currently standing in his brother's apartment, which stinks of weed and body odor. To say this place is a dump would be putting it mildly.

"Hey," I say, nodding in acknowledgment to the three dudes sitting on the most obnoxious green sofa, which is covered in cigarette burns and stains that I don't even want to know about.

Jez was the first friend I made when me and my mom moved to the area when I was fifteen. School has been a complete failure, as I've spent most of my time hanging around with Jez and a few others at school, where learning is not as important as it may be in other schools. The teachers couldn't give a shit, the school is on its last legs, and every student runs with the attitude of 'what's the point.' Jez and I, along with a lot of others, didn't graduate. My mom wants me to retake a year, but I'm not gonna do that. Jez assured me that now we're eighteen, his brother will have work for us. I've only met Zac a handful of times, but I'm not under the impression that what he wants from us will be anything good, based on the vibe that I'm getting from him and his friends.

Zac and Jez look nothing alike. Jez has shoulder-length brown hair, hazel eyes and is tall and thin. He dresses like a skater boy and takes nothing seriously. His brother is also tall and has a little more muscle but is bald and edgy. He has large gauges in his ears, dull brown eyes, and dresses like he's in a biker gang. He also has a hygiene problem, but I sure as shit ain't gonna say anything.

The other two dudes don't say anything other than to give us a chin up in greeting. They are similar to Zac in height and build, Dean is blond and Tex a brunet. Nothing to write home about in the looks department. I'm bi, and a hot guy never passes my notice. Which never happens in this small town because finding another guy that likes dick and is semi-attractive is as likely as finding a leprechaun at the end of a rainbow.

"So, you ready to work with us, Kai? Jez says you're up to the task," Zac says.

I quickly glance at Jez, who smiles in reassurance. He hasn't told me what we would be doing, only that we can earn some money working with his brother.

"I think so, although I'm not sure what work it is," I say. Zac smiles at me, and it makes me fucking uncomfortable. It's predatory, shark-like, all teeth and grit before it goes in for the kill.

"Don't worry about it. Just go along with it and all will be good. Besides, it's not as if you both have many options, and college will never happen. You still living with your mom?"

"Yeah."

"Well, won't it be nice for you to be able to pay your way and help her out?"

"I suppose. Hadn't really thought about it."

"We got this, Kai. Don't worry, Zac has our back," Jez says to me as he rubs my shoulder.

I take a moment to study him. His eyes plead with me to go along with this. But when I look at Zac and the other guys, my internal panic alarm goes off, telling me that this is a bad idea. Then I think of my mom and how tired she is, working all hours with our heads barely above water. Maybe this is a good thing. That I can finally help my mom and take some of the responsibility, because Zac is right, what the fuck else am I going to do?

"Okay."

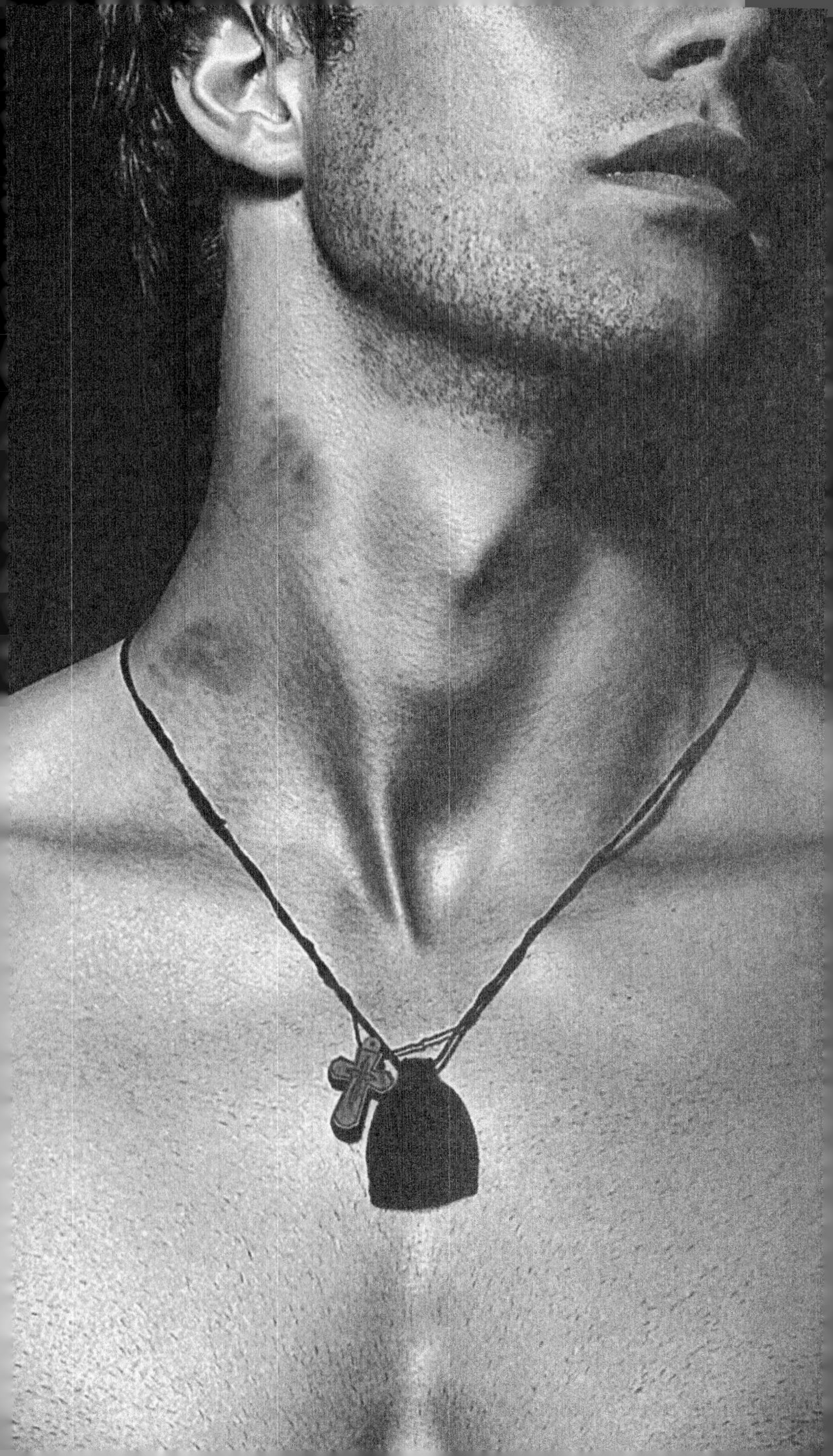

CHAPTER 1
KAI

PRESENT DAY

A swift blow hits me in the gut, forcing me to my knees, landing on the sticky, dirty floor of this shitty bar. Fuck, it hurts when your stomach feels like it's been repositioned into your chest. Clutching my stomach, I curl over, coughing, trying to get my breath back before slowly rising to my feet, grabbing onto the chair beside me to gain my balance. This always happens. Trouble follows us everywhere we go. Actually, that's a lie. My best friend, Jez, along with his brother Zac and his gang are always the ones to find trouble wherever *we* go. I've lost count of the amount of times I've been arrested and thrown into a cell for the night, only for my mother to have to come and collect me and read me the riot act. I'm lucky I haven't ended up in prison. The only reason I haven't is because of Officer Tim Lovell, who has known my mom for years and has the most obvious crush on her. I refuse to allow myself to like him, even though he's a nice guy and he's saved my ass more times than I could mention. He just makes me feel worse. He's the good guy, Mr. Fucking Perfect, and I'm the screw up.

Stop with the pity party, dumbass.

Living in a small town like this is double sided. The positives are the good people within the local community who look out for one another. They seem to see good in me that I'm not sure exists anymore. I'm numb to most things in life when it comes to expectations. The negative is that you get stuck in the bubble, staying with the same group of people who influence your routine, and you find yourself landlocked into bad decisions. A huge part of me wants out of here, to find a good path to set my life on, but it's so hard. Hard to push myself. The disappointment I see in my mom's eyes is a daily thing, and it's easier to live up to that than try to make it better.

Outside of my mom, Jez is all I have, and that's not a good thing. Over time, his brother, Zac, has had a growing number of cronies that started to hang with us and they now refer to themselves as 'The Skins'. A small-time gang that steals, deals and causes havoc with anyone who even looks at them in the wrong way. Like tonight. Same old shit, we have a few drinks, play some pool and start a bar fight with another group who accused Zac of stealing drugs from one of his guys. I'm so fucking over this life that all the energy in my body I had to try and change has been sapped out.

"Kai, we gotta go, cops are here!" Jez shouts back at me as he lands his fist into one of the guys that lunged over at us, when Zac was goading him.

My feet don't move. I just stand and watch Jez beat the shit out of these guys like it's nothing. His long ratty brown hair, tied into a small scraggly bun, looks like it's about to come undone. He has blood on the corner of his mouth where someone must have got a hit in, his hazel eyes are like slits, what you'd imagine everything evil in the world to look like in human form. As I stand here, zoned out from the shouts and crashes of broken glass, it dawns on me that he isn't my friend, or even someone I particularly care about. He is my routine. To be honest, he's kinda like a boss. He tells me what we're doing every day and I follow. Why have I only just caught onto that?

"What the fuck you waiting for, man? Let's go!" Zac shouts at me and pushes me from behind. I fucking hate him. Not only is he unaware of basic hygiene, his hardened face tells a thousand stories of a fucked up life that's never gonna change. The guy lives for violence and destroying people's lives.

I stumble when he pushes me just as the door to the bar flies open and in walks the local cops, guns out and yelling orders that don't reach my ears. Zac and Jez with the other guys are nowhere to be seen. Did I miss them leaving? All activity around me is happening in slow motion, but my body still doesn't react. Am I in shock? Or is this an epiphany?

"Kai, get down. Hands behind your back, you know the drill," one of the officers says to me. I recognize him but I don't say anything. The familiar look of disappointment is written all over his face, similar to my mom's. Fuck. My mom. She's gonna kill me.

An hour later after being processed at the local station, they allow me my phone call, which I tentatively take as the buzz from the booze earlier has officially left my system, replaced by nausea and apprehension of putting this shit at my mom's door. Again. You'd never have guessed I'm a twenty-two year old adult.

Biting the bullet, I make the call, hoping that she is awake and not too pissed.

"Hello?" Mom answers, voice slightly groggy from sleep.

"Hey, Mom."

"You're fucking kidding me. You've been arrested again, haven't you?"

"How'd you know that?"

"Call it intuition or call it a habit." She sighs into the phone. Tears fill my eyes, which I put down to exhaustion. I'm a fuck up. Who would be proud to call me their son? I want help. I need help, but I'm too afraid to ask for it.

"I'm sorry," I whisper, fighting the urge to regress into a child and cry hysterically.

"I know, but I can't do this anymore. I'm calling your Uncle Jules. See if he can help get you out of this mess."

My body goes rigid at that name that hasn't been uttered for months, maybe even years. Jules. I don't even want to entertain his name being spoken, but the excitement that's swirling in my stomach, similar to a washing machine, needs to get the message. We don't think of Uncle

Jules anymore. He isn't my real Uncle. Jules and my mom are step siblings through marriage. I barely know him as he didn't spend a lot of time around us, especially after we moved, only visiting a handful of times a year. But I do remember when my hormones started regarding him differently and he became an obsession. I'd just turned sixteen and he'd visited for my birthday. He then visited for Thanksgiving the same year and after that he left, he just disappeared from our lives. I was equally devastated as I was relieved. Does Mom still talk to him? She must, or why would she call him to help out? Why has she never said anything and why has he never wanted to talk to me?

"Jules? Why call him? We don't know him and how could he ever help me?"

"I don't know, but I'm out of options. Try and rest tonight and I'll talk to you tomorrow."

"Okay. I love you, Mom."

"I love you, too."

It takes a few seconds to notice the dead dial tone on the other end of the line, signaling that she ended the call.

As I get placed back in my cell, I spend the whole night staring at the ceiling. I let the tears fall freely, wishing this would just all end, and accepting that I'm not worth shit to anyone or anything. I'm worthless—a piece of trash. My grandparents didn't want me even before I was born so they kicked my mom out, Jules high tailed out of our lives, and now my mom is not far behind washing her hands of me. Maybe I'm the problem. I don't add anything to society, I just aimlessly drift through life, only thinking of the consequences after I've done something inevitably to fuck up. It's exhausting. I've never felt more alone than I do right now. Lost in the dense fog with no way out, nobody who can hear me silently beg for help.

Then the saddest thought passes through my mind, plummeting me into the dark depths of sleep that a small part of me hopes I won't wake from. The thought that…would anyone actually miss me?

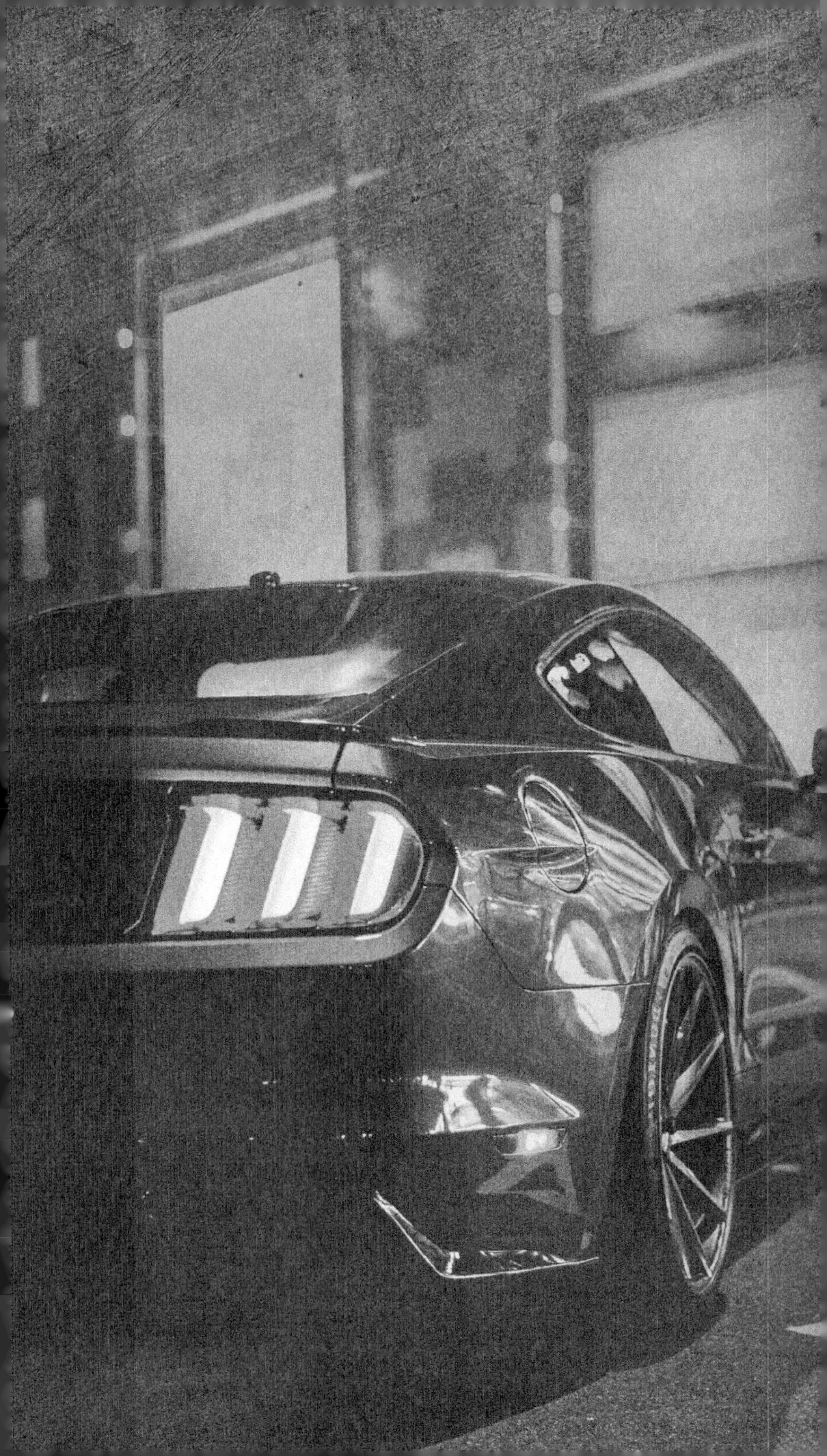

CHAPTER 2
Jules

What a night. I love this side of the job, the interrogation, the violence, but I fucking hate clean up. I'm covered in sweat and blood, with the tangy aftertaste of the dead body left lingering on my tongue. So fucking gross. I want my shower and my bed, but Dima will flip his shit if we don't get this done before morning.

I've worked with the Kozlov brothers, Dima and Lev, for years, since we were teenagers. They had a pretty chill set up going on with their drug business that has kept us all in good living. Then as time has gone on and the more notorious our names have become, that chill life has turned to multiple problems and fucking clean ups, leaving the runt jobs to fall to me and another guard, Simon. I have to be honest, I'm not loving it. Thirty years old and cleaning up this shit is not what I had planned for myself, but we're a family in this house. I owe my life to Dima and Lev. They gave me a job and home when I had nothing. A teenager scrambling to make something of myself, because I sure as shit wasn't going to go to college. My mom and step-dad tried their best, but we were dirt poor, living in a town where there were zero opportunities. I have an older step-sister, but my parents kicked her out when she got pregnant at eighteen. She's ten years older than me and always looked out for me since she and her dad came into our lives when I was four years old. But as she grew older, the age gap became more noticeable when she started hanging out with boys, and not the best kind of boys my parents would have wanted for her. I didn't see her again until I was sixteen, when I found her contact details in my mom's old shoebox that she had hidden in her closet. I was snooping one day, looking for cash, and found the old tattered thing, shocked to see my step-sister's name and cell number. I'd missed Jenny so much and decided to reach out. We may not be blood, but I'd always considered her my big sister. I called her and arranged to meet her in secret, along with her son, my step-nephew, Kai. It was odd having a nephew who was only eight years younger than me, but it was great having my sister back in my life, especially as life at home got harder.

The distance between myself and my parents grew after they kicked Jenny out in such a cold manner, I couldn't get past it. Seems like they didn't either as their indifference to my existence just pushed me further away. So predictably, I started hanging around with the wrong crowd, getting into trouble along with my friends. It's not like I had anything else to do, plus they were a welcome distraction to keep me out of the house. After I turned eighteen, I met the Kozlovs when I got tangled up in a drug deal gone wrong. I won't say they pitied me, as they don't give a shit about anyone, but I think they saw themselves in me. Dima and Lev were looking for help dealing and offered me money and a home. I took that shit up without even thinking.

My mom and step-dad both died not long after I moved out, my mom first from an aneurysm, my step-dad a year later from a heart attack. It was such an odd and confusing point in my life as I felt nothing. In the years leading up to that I grieved the loss of them, their steady neglect after Jenny severed that tie. I didn't blink an eye when they passed. The damage was done long ago, and I wasn't the same boy, a fortress built so tightly around me that not even an atomic bomb could destroy it. People are shit.

Love is bullshit. Have no expectations and nothing can disappoint you.

I'd stayed in sporadic contact with Jenny over the years, lessening when they moved away. While on the surface we appear to care for each other as siblings do, we never acknowledge that underlying tension that exists. The older I got, resentment set in on my side as the teenage me had decided that if Jenny hadn't gotten pregnant, our family would never have blown apart. And I know she resents me to a certain extent, this perception that because I remained at home I had the perfect parents that she was so desperate to be a part of, which couldn't be farther from the truth. Just like I know that I can't blame her for our parents' response to her pregnancy. Now, it's only the occasional text around the holidays or birthdays, not like the one I received this afternoon from Jenny, asking me to call her.

"You going to Desire tonight?" Simon asks me, pulling me back from thinking about Jenny and why she's contacted me. Desire is a strip club run by the Kozlovs, in addition to their burlesque/cabaret bar called Starlight. While Lev oversees Desire, I spend most of my time there making sure things run smoothly for the brothers. I must admit, it has its perks, with most of the dancers having sampled my dick at some point, but like anything else in life, the monotony gets old. Sex is just a release for me, and I'm selfish when it comes down to the act. I know it makes me sound like a dick, but I've never gotten pleasure in someone else's enjoyment when fucking. I actually find it annoying, especially loud girls. Half the time it's fake as fuck, but that part doesn't bother me. Sex has always felt like something was missing.

"Yeah, I need to stop by to check things over. Why? You tagging along?"

"I'm tempted. Just hope that fucker Carlos isn't there," Simon grumbles. Carlos took over the supply of Dima and Lev's imports earlier this year. He spends a lot of his free time at Desire, and I've noticed he takes great pleasure in winding up Simon at every opportunity. Simon, for the most part, is the quietest one out of our group, but Carlos stokes a fire in Simon of such epic proportions that it's hard not to notice.

"Come on, man. Just ignore him. The more you rise to his bait, the more he'll do it to get a reaction from you."

"I suppose. Let me get cleaned up, and I'll head out with you," he says as he puts away the hose he's been using to clean the flooring in the holding pen. The room is now spotless, the black shiny floor sparkles, and there is no sign that anything bad happened in here. I remove my gloves and disposable overalls that we wear when doing the clean-ups and follow Simon out the door.

We don't live in the mansion with the brothers, but we all share a single-story building that Dima built on the property grounds for us guards. It's a decent size, and we all have our own rooms. Lev and Dima frequently discuss expanding and building individual properties for each of us on the land. There's so much space, but it's just something they've never gotten around to.

As we both head to the rear door, Lev calls out to me, as Simon continues out of the property.

"All done?" Lev asks as he approaches me.

"Yeah. We're just gonna wash up before heading out to Desire."

"I'll come with you. Those two are already fucking and my ears will start bleeding if I have to hear princess Seb cumming again," Lev says, rolling his eyes. Dima and Seb are definitely in your face when it comes to PDA. I don't mind it too much but it pisses Lev off, which I find more than amusing.

"Don't be jealous," I tease.

"I'm not jealous. I just don't enjoy hearing my brother get the little shit off, it's fucking annoying."

I chuckle and shake my head, before turning to leave.

"I'll meet you out front in twenty," I say over my shoulder as I head over to the guards' house. When I enter the single story open plan home, I can hear the shower running from Simon's room as I pass it, heading towards my own room, which is at the end of the corridor. I quickly wash off in the shower and dress in our standard attire of black shirt and black pants. As I pick up my cell phone from the chest of drawers in my room, my eyes drift back to the text from Jenny. I'm not sure why I'm hesitant to reply, but she hasn't reached out in forever, and it makes me panic. Has something happened? Is Kai okay?

Before I know it, I've pressed the call button next to her name, and I'm taken aback at how fast she answers, barely on the second ring.

"Jules," she says, followed by a sigh that is full of exhaustion and relief.

"Jenny, what's wrong?"

"Well, hello to you too," she quips, but I'm not a fool.

"I know you. Now, what's wrong?"

"It's Kai. I just can't deal with his shit anymore, Jules. He was arrested tonight, and I just don't have it in me to deal with his bullshit again. I'm tired. He's a grown man, and I've had enough. You're my last hope of getting through to him."

"Hold on, arrested? For what?"

"Fighting. He was out drinking with those dumb friends of his at a bar, and they got into a fight with another gang."

"He's in a gang?" I'm shocked. Kai was always such a sweet boy, kind and funny. It's been years since I've seen him, and I know he's a man now, but it still rocks me to the core that he's caught up in shit like this. Then I remember who I work for and the term hypocrite comes to mind. Jenny doesn't know the full extent of my work. She thinks I work in security, which has some truth. A grain of truth.

"Yes. He's been hanging around with them for a while. Nothing I say or do is helping. I know he doesn't want this life, Jules. My sweet boy is still in there, but around here, I think he thinks he has no choice. I don't know; maybe it's my fault for moving," she says, her voice cracking on the words.

"You just did what you thought was best. You're a great mom."

A small sob comes through the phone. My instinct to make things right for them both takes over, so I decide to take charge of the situation.

"Look, let me talk to my bosses and I'll head over in the morning to the station. Text me where he is and I'll try to talk some sense into him."

"Really? You'd do that?"

"Of course. I'll head over to you after. I just need to run it past the boss here first. We'll sort this out. Trust me."

"I trust you. Thank you, Jules. I know we've drifted apart, and I'm sorry for being a shitty sister."

"Stop. We're good. I have to go now, but I'll text you later. Get some sleep."

"Okay. Night."

As I end the call, my heart starts to race. A slight twist of unease rises in my belly at what I'm letting myself in for. But I'm determined to help them.

"You ready, man? Lev is pacing around like he's about to lose it, waiting on us," Simon shouts through my bedroom door.

Placing my phone in my pocket and grabbing my jacket, I follow Simon out to be greeted by a scowling Lev. I ignore him and his broody ass as we get into my car and drive off in silence to Desire.

As we enter the club, the base of 'When I'm Gone' by Dirty Honey vibrates beneath my feet, and the smell of perfume and lust fills my lungs. It's pretty packed in here tonight. The girls are on stage, their gorgeous bodies rolling to the beat of the music. Simon wanders off to the side of the room to talk to one of the girls, his flirty smile in place. Lev and I head to the bar and grab a soda each before we make our way through the packed tables towards the back where Lev's office is situated. I scan the crowd as we move, always checking for potential threats. That is my job, after all. As Simon predicted, Carlos is here, sitting in the corner with a couple of his men, watching the show. Well, his men are leering at the girls on stage, Carlos is currently watching Simon with narrowed eyes like he's about to run over there and beat the shit out of him. I may not be gay, but I know when a guy wants to fuck, and I'm convinced Carlos wants not only to beat the hell out of Simon but to fuck him while he's doing it. I could be wrong, but I'll keep my thoughts to myself.

I close Lev's door behind us as we step inside his office. The room screams masculine dominance: the sumptuous leather chairs and large mahogany desk, the lingering scent of cigars, leather, and aftershave fills the space.

"What's up with you?" Lev says, as he sits behind his desk, and I take the seat in front of it.

"Nothing's up with me," I say. He watches me closely with those vivid green eyes, detecting bullshit, no doubt.

"You're acting like a kid. Moody and silent. Should I beat it out of you?"

"Fuck off, Lev."

Lev quirks a brow at me, taking my words as an invitation to fuck me up. Such a dick.

"Fine. My nephew is in trouble, and I need to go to collect him from jail tomorrow as my sister is freakin' out."

"Isn't he in his twenties?"

"Twenty-two."

"Why can't he sort his own shit out?"

"Because he's caught up in some gang, and Jenny can't deal with it anymore."

Lev rolls his eyes like this is the most ridiculous thing he's ever heard.

"Fuck, it's like listening to a fucking soap opera."

"I want to bring him here to work with us," I say, and I have no clue when that became an idea. Lev just continues to stare at me, and the silence forces me to continue talking to fill in the awkwardness.

"Now that Zayn's dead, we're a guard short. I can train him up. It's a win for us all."

"How do you know he'll be good enough? I don't even remember the last time you mentioned him or Jenny. He's a stranger."

"He's my sister's son, and that's good enough for me."

"Step sister," Lev corrects.

"She's still my sister, and they're family. Please, Lev. It's just a trial. If you don't like him, then I'll send him back home."

"Please stop begging. It's embarrassing."

"Is that a yes, or do you need to run it past Dima?"

"Shut the fuck up, I don't need to run anything past D. Kai can come on board, but it'll be on trial. He's your responsibility, and I'll hold you accountable for any trouble. Got it?"

"Got it."

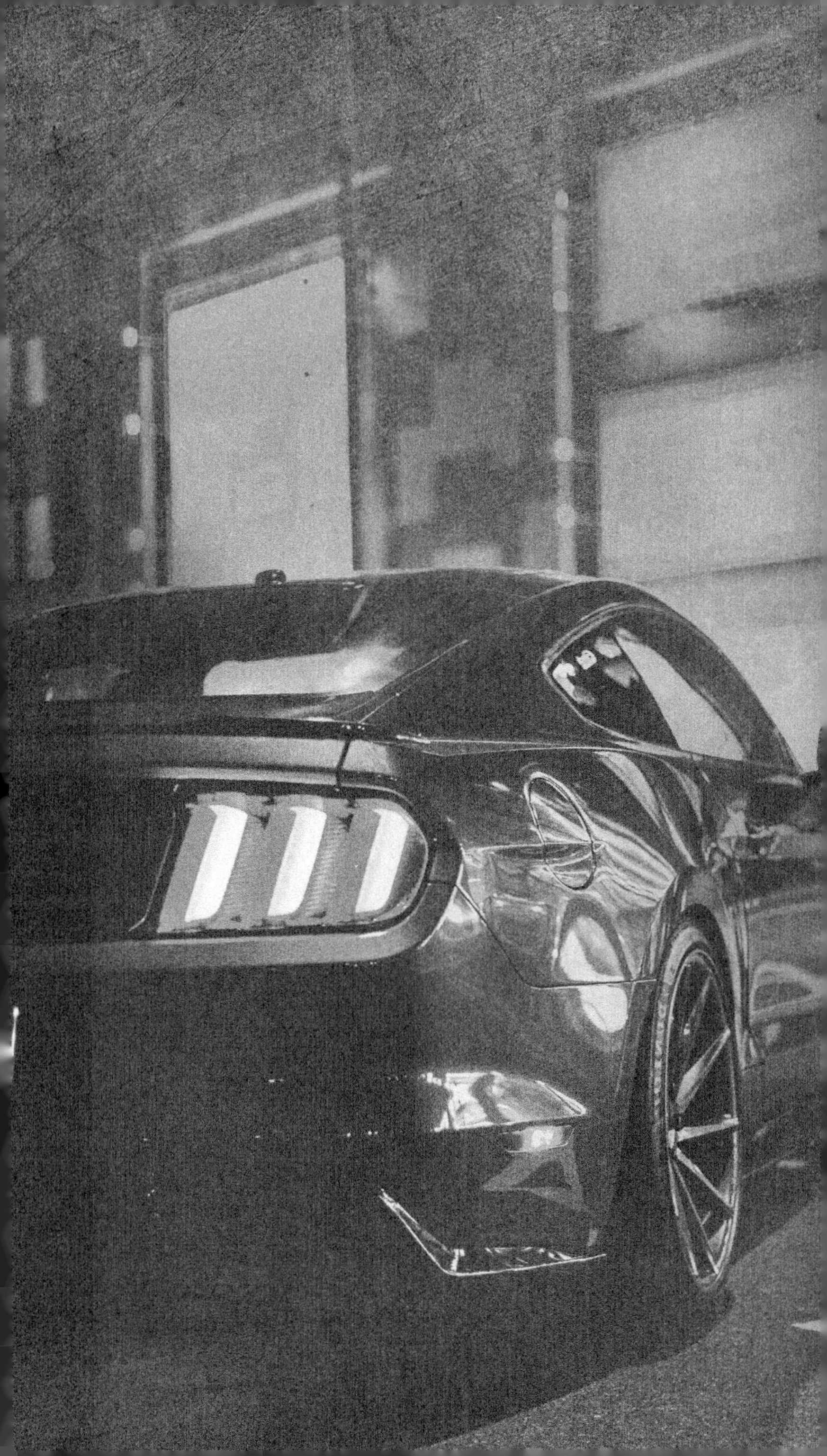

CHAPTER 3
JULES

Three hours of driving and overthinking later, I'm sitting in my car—*which happens to be the love of my life*—staring out of the window at the local police station, questioning if this was a bad idea. Jenny texted me the address last night, and I plan to go straight to see her after I pick up Kai. I have no idea what to expect from him. Will he be an asshole? Difficult? Or will he be embarrassed? Shy? Who the fuck knows. I barely knew Kai as a kid, so I have no idea how this will go. As Lev pointed out, I'm technically about to collect a stranger. Guilt builds at the years I've missed in his and Jenny's life. Maybe I could've made a difference, but I'm hardly the best role model.

Exiting my car, I enter the police station and take in the worn-down building. Faded yellow-stained paint peels off the walls and scuffs adorn the floors to the point that you can no longer tell what color it actually was when it was first laid. The air smells stale, like old coffee and sweat.

The constant sound of phones ringing and loud chatting makes my head ache instantly. This place is enough to make anyone insane. I approach the desk where the plexiglass panels separate me and the disinterested cop that is sitting behind it, waiting for me to speak first.

"I'm here to collect Kai Miller," I say to the balding cop who looks like he wants to be anywhere but here.

"His mom finally given up?" he says as he pulls out some paperwork before grabbing his keys.

"No. She's just busy," I say defensively, not liking the insinuation that my step-sister has given up on Kai.

"Not judgin' ya son, but you gonna have to keep him on the straight and narrow. He comes back here again, and he'll be facing time."

"Don't worry. He won't be back," I say with misplaced confidence. How the fuck do I know he won't be back? But baldy ignores me and disappears out of the door at the back of the office.

About twenty minutes later, a buzz on the door leading into the reception area has me jumping up out of the uncomfortable plastic bucket seat to be greeted by baldy and a tired looking Kai. Butterflies dance in my stomach as I take in the man standing in front of me. The boy I remember has gone and in his place is this tall, broad, and handsome man. I would never have recognized him. My mouth feels like it's full of cotton as we stare at each other, as I try to work out what to say. The cop clears his throat, urging this little reunion along.

"I don't wanna see ya back here, Kai. Get away from those fuck-ups you hang around with and make a life for yourself."

Kai ignores him as baldy leaves us both alone in the waiting area, assessing me from top to toe, his big blue eyes filled with weariness and curiosity. I move forward toward him, and follow my instincts and pull him into a hug. A hug that immediately connects my soul back to the family I've missed, the ones that mattered the most, that I let down.

"Good to see you, Kai," I say into his hair as his arms grip around my waist, melting into my arms like it's the first time he's been touched. A soft sigh leaves his body as he snuggles into my neck. I'm only an inch or so taller than him, so we fit together well. Why does this feel so natural?

"Good to see you too, Uncle Jules."

I pull away and smile at him, memories of when he used to call me that as a kid. For some reason it doesn't fit anymore, him calling me Uncle. I haven't earned the right to be called that. I mean, Christ, we don't know each other.

"Call me Jules. We're too close in age for you to be calling me Uncle. Makes me feel like a fossil."

Kai grins at me, highlighting a boyish charm that's both captivating and endearing. He's definitely hardened over the years, but his eyes still carry the angelic light of purity. A deep dimple in his right cheek grabs my attention and I get a strong urge to touch it. *Weird*.

"Come on, we need to go see your mom before we leave."

I pull away and take in the frown of confusion on Kai's face.

"What do you mean, leave?"

Shit. I thought Jenny had told him.

"You're coming back to Grinston with me. My boss has agreed to take you on, on a trial basis. We thought it'd be a chance for you to start afresh."

"And I get no say? I'm a grown man, not a child," he says, his tone scolding and stubborn. The light in his eyes is replaced by a dullness that I hate to see. While I can sympathize, his attitude is not welcome. I don't do well with dramatic behavior or having my orders questioned and ignored. I clench my fists as I try to hold onto my composure. In other circumstances, his response would have me go nuclear on him.

"Well, if you acted like an adult, your mother wouldn't have called me. You *will* come with me, Kai, and we *will* sort your life out. If not for yourself, you *will* do this for your mom."

"I don't have to do shit," he spittles into my face, hardly an inch between us. I tense my jaw, trying hard to remain calm, but the rising annoyance of his tone has my temper flare. I like to be in control, to be the problem solver, and this kind of bitchy behavior flips my switch from composed to irate. It's fair to say I'm a control freak. I'm the boss here and he needs to fucking respect that.

I grab him by the back of the neck and forcefully push my forehead into his, asserting dominance. He needs authority, guidance, rules, and a firm hand.

"That's where you're wrong, *little nephew*. You either come willingly or screaming as I tie you up and put you in my trunk. Don't fuck with me, I've dealt with way worse than your bitchy attitude," I whisper harshly, putting more pressure on his neck to get the message across. I move back a little and wait for his reaction. His wide blue eyes are glassy as he glares at me. The desperation to argue with me is clear from the tension in his jaw, but he doesn't.

"Now, are you coming? Or shall I get some cable ties?"

If I didn't know any better, I would say that Kai was tempted to stamp his feet. But he manages to contain it and grits his teeth, with a glare that could kill.

"*Fine*. Let's go."

Kai pulls away and barges past me, knocking my shoulder with his as I grin at his attitude and his caving to my demands. I'm not sure why, but it feels like an achievement. A simmering bubble of excitement rushes through me at his compliance, when the doors slam behind him.

I follow him outside and lead him over to my car.

"Wow, nice wheels," he says in an excited appraisal of my baby, a total shift from his shitty mood. He gently glides his long slim fingers over the hood. My car is my pride and joy. A beast of steel and chrome, the sleek black body glinting in the winter sun. The aggressive grill and long hood give it a predatory look, an unmistakable presence on the road.

"Thanks. So, is there anywhere we can grab a coffee?"

"I thought we were going back to Mom's?"

"That can wait. Probably best for you to relax a little before we go back, and we can catch up."

"That's gonna be one long catch-up, Jules. I haven't seen you since I was a kid."

"I know. But now's the time for moving forward."

"I suppose. There's a decent diner on the other side of town we can go to."

"Awesome."

We get into the car and relax into the sumptuous black leather sport seats as the V8 engine revs to growling life, and Kai directs me to the diner.

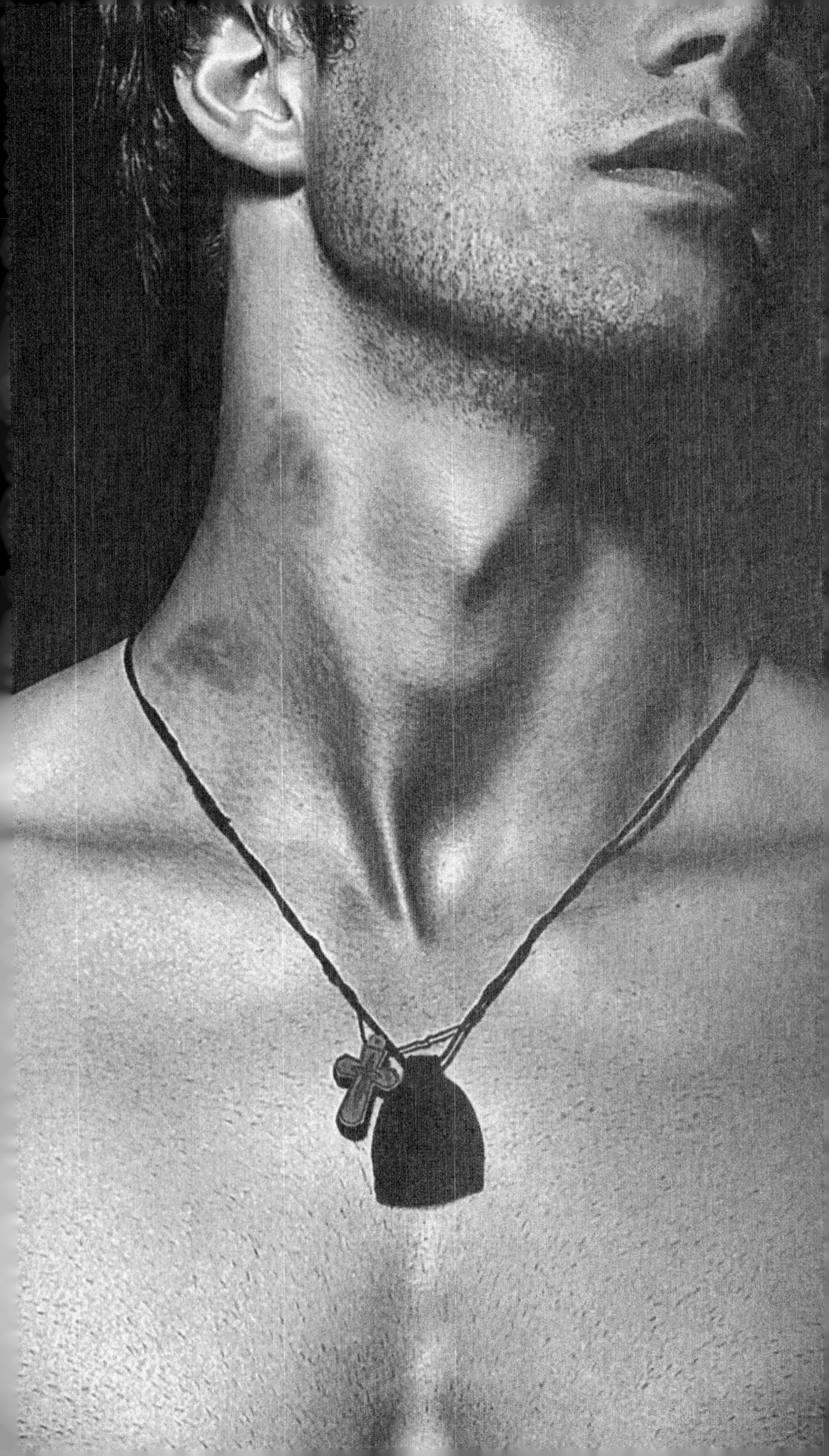

CHAPTER 4
KAI

I want to slap myself around the face to convince myself that this is real right now. That I'm sitting in this hot ass car with Jules. *Jules*. When I spoke to Mom early this morning, she told me that he was coming into town to pick me up from jail. I thought it was a joke. Well, I guess the joke's on me. And why, you may ask? Because the teenage crush that I'd had on him, which I convinced myself was hero worship, turned out to be bullshit. As soon as my eyes landed on him at the station, I felt the air leave my body. I'm bisexual and my desire for men started with Jules. I thought it was just him at first, but over the years I've enjoyed the occasional fuck around with guys. But Jules is in a league of his own. Now that I'm a grown man, the term uncle feels not only ridiculous but wrong in a dirty way. We're only a few years apart in age and the way he spikes my want for him is certainly no familia feeling although it does feel taboo. Forbidden. I don't even want to assess for a second how I felt when he threatened me just now. I shiver even thinking about it.

Christ, I should be worrying about the fact that he informed me that I'm leaving home to work with him, rather than overthink how the crush I had on him is now back in full force. I'm so pissed that Jules and my mom arranged this behind my back, like I'm some child being passed around the family. I suppose in my mom's eyes, I am a child. A complete disaster and failure that she always has to bail out of trouble. It's not that I want to be like this. I don't. But life isn't easy around these parts. I have no qualifications to my name. All I have is the long list of fuck ups since I started hanging around with Jez. After we both failed to graduate, it led to us spending more time with his brother, Zac, and trying to earn some money—days bled into one another, drinking, stealing, causing trouble with other guys like what happened last night. The cycle is never-ending, but what options do I have?

I let out a self-deprecating sigh, leaning my head back against the headrest and closing my eyes. Maybe leaving with Jules is the best thing. It would break all ties with this town and allow my mom to have some form of a life without worrying about me.

"You okay?" Jules asks from beside me as we wait at a red light. I turn my face to the side and watch him for a moment. His short blond hair makes him look like he's part of the military, and his lightly tanned skin and bulging forearms look veiny from how tightly he grips the steering wheel. As I run my eyes over that perfect body, I meet those icy blues staring into my soul. Even though we aren't blood related, it's quite comical how similar we look in some ways. My hair is a darker blond, bordering brown, and my blue eyes are softer than his icy. But we're similar heights and have the same complexion. He is slightly more built than me, but our matching features are subtle. Or maybe that's just my imagination.

"I'm tired, and not looking forward to the lecture from Mom."

The light changes, and we drive off. Jules's attention is back on the road.

"She just wants what's best for you, Kai. As do I. Just give it a shot, and come with me to work."

"What is it you do, anyway?"

There's a long pause as Jules thinks over his answer. I vaguely remember he worked in some kind of security, but it's been so long since we've seen him that his job could've changed.

"I provide security to a family in Grinston, which is on the outskirts of New York. We're a guard down, and my boss agreed to give you a trial run."

"What happened to the guard?"

"He got laid off. It wasn't working out," he says, and I don't miss how he avoids eye contact when he responds. Call it a gut feeling, but something seems off in his reply. As I'm about to confront him, we arrive at the diner and park up. I picked a place that I know Jez and the guys never visit, because the last thing I need is them swarming around me and Jules, asking questions.

As we get inside, the waitress leads us to a booth next to the window that overlooks the rundown parking lot out front. The diner needs a makeover. I don't think it's been touched since the 1980s. But the coffee is good here. The waitress leaves us with menus and scuttles off to seat other customers.

Jules is looking at the menu, so I take the opportunity to watch him greedily. He's even sexier than he was all those years ago, the boyish image gone, replaced with this mature, intense, and intimidating man. I really can't believe he's here, that he's come here because of me. What did Mom tell him?

"So, why'd you come?" I ask.

Jules looks up and drops his menu onto the table before clasping his hands together, leaning on the worn surface.

"Because your mom was worried, and despite what you may think, I do care."

"Why did you go silent on us for all those years?"

Jules rubs his chin with his hand, watching me as he formulates a response.

"There are things you don't know or understand about my life, Kai. It was better for you and your mom if I just kept my distance. But I was always a phone call away."

"Did Mom stay in touch?"

"Yes. Not regularly, but we messaged on birthdays or Christmas. Why? She never tell you?"

"No, she didn't."

Why didn't she say anything? I didn't think she kept secrets from me. I've kept many secrets from my mom, about the things me and the guys did, but it doesn't stop the hurt that she never mentioned being in contact with Jules, and never included me.

"Stop sulking. It was never more than a quick text. Me and your mom have a complicated past. It's worked out better to just keep contact simple."

"I'm not sulking," I say, in a sulky voice.

"If you say so."

"What happened between you and Mom?"

"I think she resents me for being at home with our parents after they kicked her out. She's made a story up in her mind that I had the perfect childhood, which is bullshit. But I was no better. I blamed her for the family falling apart."

"Because of me?"

"Yes, but I was an angry teen needing to find someone to blame. Which was our parents. But the tension will always be there as Jenny will never let it go, and that's all I'll say."

"Ever heard of tact?"

"No. Now I'll ask you a question."

Before he gets to ask the question, the waitress arrives, notepad in hand, ready to take our orders.

"What can I get ya both?" she asks.

"I'll just take a coffee, thanks," Jules says.

"Same."

She doesn't speak as she wanders off, and returns back with the coffee pot and fills two large mugs. The smell of caffeine triggers my thirst, as I remember I haven't had a drink of any kind this morning.

Feeling eyes on me as I fill my cup of coffee with the creamer that the waitress left, I look up to meet those blue eyes that only ever lived in my dreams.

"What?"

"You're nothing like I remembered. I wouldn't have recognized you if you'd passed me on the street."

I scoff at that.

"How nice of you to say."

"It's true, no need for the sarcasm."

"Sarcasm is my middle name," I say, before taking a sip of my coffee.

"And punisher is mine, so watch it."

"Relax, can't you take any teasing, Frank?" I laugh to myself at The Punisher TV Show reference. Such a geek.

"No."

My eyes shoot up to meet his, is he for real? From the indifference on his face, he's serious, as the joke has gone over his head, which horrifies me. How has he not seen that show? I'm about to come up with another retort, but get distracted when he licks his bottom lip, highlighting how plump it is.

"Getting back to what I wanted to ask you. Why were you in a gang?"

That question makes me chuckle, but it's without humor. I just don't know the answer and it's embarrassing. He's been in my presence for an hour and I already don't want him thinking about how dumb I am.

"I wasn't intentionally in a gang. They never said I was part of the gang. My friend Jez just took me to meet his brother and friends, said that I could earn some money and we started to hang out. A lot. Then everything spiraled and got worse and I got stuck."

"What about college?"

"I flunked high school."

"Why didn't you retake?"

"Why the fuck does it matter? What's with all the questions? I'm a fuckup. You haven't been here, Jules. This place swallows you whole. What am I supposed to do? Just find a job? Leave with no money? We can't all run off and be successful like you and leave everyone behind."

The words fly out of my mouth before I have a chance to calm myself. His intrusive questions have pissed me the fuck off. So easy to judge when he has no idea. But that doesn't matter as Jules looks at me with such contempt I want to sink down into the seat. He said earlier he wouldn't recognize me...well, the same goes for me at this moment. Jules isn't the nice guy I remembered as a kid. This guy in front of me looks like a hardened asshole that could fuck you up with one punch. Before I get a chance to apologize, his leg under the table tangles with mine as he secures it in a tight hold that I can't move from. Jesus, how can his legs be so damn strong?

"If we weren't in public right now, I would beat your ass for that little outburst. Don't play me, Kai. You don't know me anymore."

I can't stop spewing words that aren't helping the situation.

"And you don't know me. *Asshole.*"

I'm freaked the fuck out when Jules grins at me. The smile is so large, I start looking around the room for exits. Why is he smiling?

"I do know you. You just told me. You're a fuckup, right?"

As I said, he's an asshole, so I refuse to say anything back even though it's killing me not to have the last word.

"Time to go see your mom," he says, as he stands and leaves money on the table before walking away, leaving me to trail after him, completely confused by what just happened.

The drive is quiet, and I spend most of it looking out of the window. I could sense Jules looking at me from time to time. It's so strange having his attention on me, and I'd love to know what's going on inside his head and why he keeps staring. Knowing my luck he's probably planning my death and sizing up my body for a casket. We arrive back at my mom's and before I have a chance to open my door, it swings open with Mom glaring down at me. If looks could kill. She looks defeated, and I hate that it's always me putting that look of worry on her face. She deserves better.

"Get your ass inside, Kai," she yells at me. I want to roll my eyes but decide just to take whatever it is she says and do what she wants. I owe her that much. Damn it, I owe it to myself.

She completely ignores Jules and storms into the house as we both follow after her.

Fuck my life.

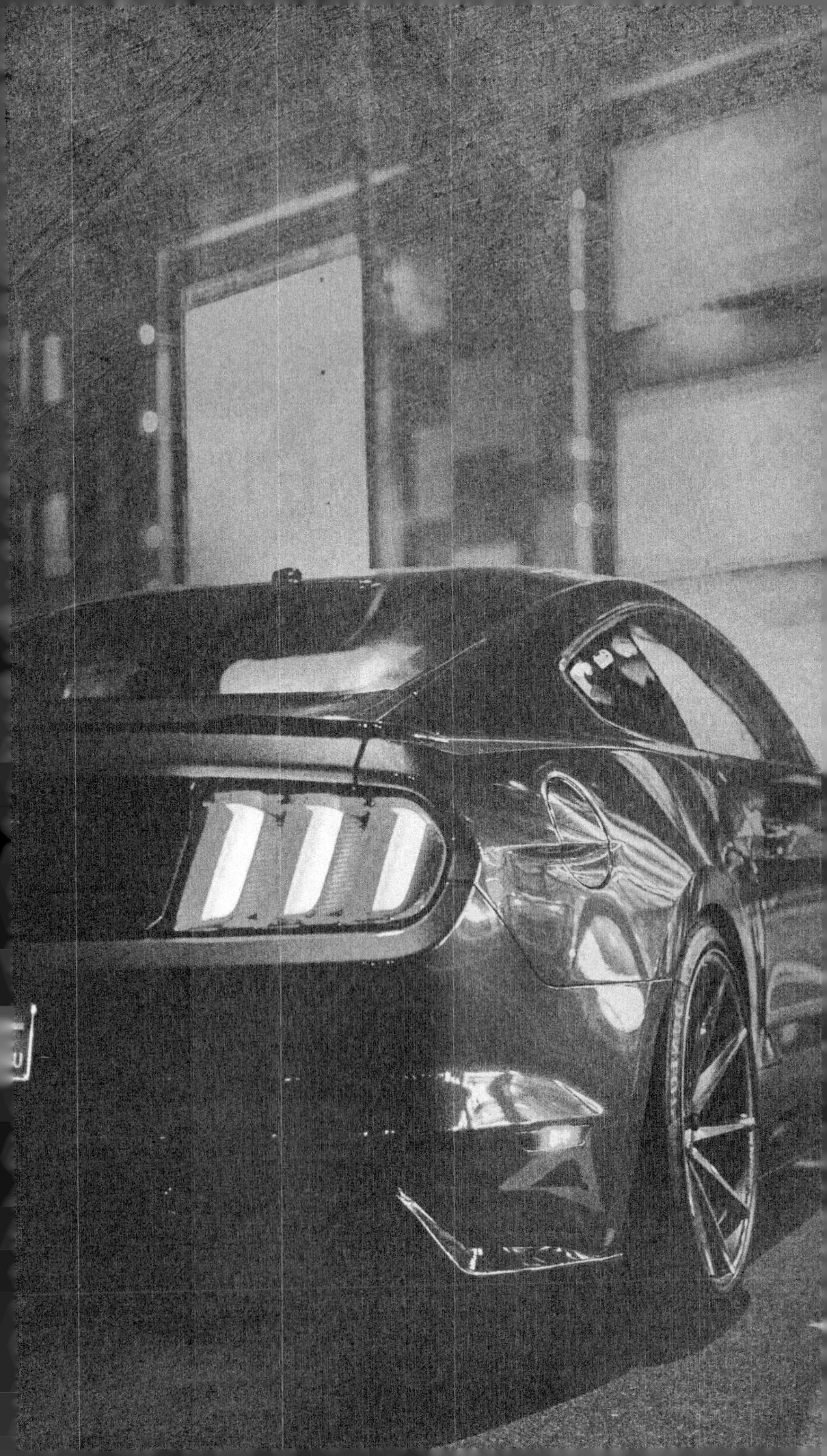

CHAPTER 5
JULES

Kai's shoulders slump as he enters the house before me. This is obviously a frequent occurrence, and again, I feel bad for not being around.

"No hug from my big sister?" I ask Jenny with wide open arms and a grin stretched across my face. I never realized how much I missed her until now, as she throws herself into my arms. For a brief moment, we can forget the past that has tarnished us, focusing on getting Kai's life in order. I've spent so many years consumed by my work and meaningless fucks, that I'd forgotten what affection felt like. This hug is like being revived back to life, memories from our childhood surging through my mind. Kai needs me. He's a purpose. A purpose that I swear to never defer from, to love and protect the only family I have left, even if it kills me.

"Thank you for coming back," she whispers into my shoulder, and I feel the wet from her eyes seep through my shirt. I squeeze her harder, reveling in the warmth that my big sister always provided when I was a child, but was then torn away because of our asshole parents.

Jenny pulls herself back and grabs my face with both of her gentle hands. She looks so tired. She's forty years old now and still has her beautiful mane of dark hair and perfect pale skin. The lines around her eyes tell the story of sleepless nights and worry that has taken over her life. But I'm here now.

"Look at you. A grown man. Always knew you'd be handsome."

"Stop trying to embarrass me." I laugh as I playfully slap her hand away. She grins at me with that hint of playfulness in her eyes that used to be a daily thing when we lived at home together.

"Gotta make up for the missed years of teasing you," she says with a weary giggle.

A loud thud grabs our attention, and I turn to see an irritated Kai slumped in one of the wooden dining table chairs. Such a pouty little brat. His arms are folded across his chest as he glowers at his mom like she's the one who has done something wrong. I can understand some of his frustration, but the little fuck's sass from back at the diner still has me wound up tight. I detest that kind of attitude and sense of entitlement. He's gonna be harder work than I thought. I also didn't miss the little glances he threw my way when he thought I wasn't aware. Little does he know I'm always aware, even when I'm not looking. It's how I'm programmed to survive. But fuck does he intrigue me. I spent most of the journey over here trying to work him out, while also admiring what a handsome man he's become. I'm not gay, but I can appreciate an attractive guy. Really appreciate it. Christ, why am I arguing with myself about this? Do I find him attractive or am I attracted to him? *Hmmm, interesting*.

"Get that petulant look off your face, Kai. You're in no position to be pissed off," Jenny scolds him.

Kai scoffs and shakes his head, looking between us both like he can't believe what he's seeing.

"After all these years, he comes back like he owns the place, and you plan to send me off with him. Of course, I'm pissed. I'm sick of being treated like a kid."

"You are a fucking child! Every goddamn week I get a call from the cops or someone in town about you. Do you know how much they let you get away with? You should be in prison for the shit you've pulled over the years. It's the end of the line now. You're twenty-two years old. It's about time you acted like it."

"Let me get away with? Oh please. Officer Tim scumbag only does it 'cos he wants in your pants."

Jenny is so fast I don't process that she has hit him until the loud slap from her palm against his cheek echoes around the room. Complete silence follows and I'm stunned. What the fuck has been going on here?

"You little shit. I've been friends with Tim for years. He cares about me, about us, and sees what you could achieve, but you're so fucking happy playing victim that you can't see it. I'm done, Kai. Leave with Jules or don't. But I'm done. No more bailing you out. I love you, but you're slowly killing me."

Tears fall down Jenny's face while Kai stares at her with eyes so wide in shock and regret as the red handprint on his face darkens. Fuck, what a mess. As I go to speak, Kai stands and storms down the hallway and slams what I assume is his bedroom door behind him.

"What the hell was that?" I ask. She scoffs at me, a small sneer tries to work its way onto her lips. The unspoken tension we never mention rearing its ugly head.

"Always forgot how perfect the golden boy was."

"You know nothing, Jenny. You asked me here. And for the record, I was far from a golden boy in our parents' eyes. Them kicking you out ended that."

Jenny breathes deeply before hiding her face in her hands, her face softens as she looks at me. The mask back in place.

"Oh *god*, Jules. I'm sorry. I shouldn't have said that and I shouldn't have hit Kai. I'm a bad mother. Our parents were right, I was never going to be a good parent," she cries. I want to reach out to her, I do. But it feels like I'm walking on a tightrope of emotions that neither of us is ready to face, as I stop myself from reacting.

"Listen to me, I'm sorry we drifted apart for a while. But I'm here now, and I promise to help make this right. This isn't Kai and I bet he's in there regretting what just happened," I say.

"I should've had more control. I've never hit him before."

"No, you shouldn't have hit him. But what's done is done. Let me go talk to him."

"Okay."

"And who is Officer Tim? Is it the bald guy at the station?" I ask, intentionally trying to lighten the heavy mood.

Jenny chuckles, and a slight flush of pink tints her cheeks.

"No, that was Larry. Tim is away visiting his daughter at college. And no, we aren't together. We're just friends."

"I didn't say anything. Although, it's good how he's trying to protect Kai. And you."

"He's a good man," she says, refusing to discuss this Tim guy any further. I won't give her any shit.

I make my way down the hallway to where Kai disappeared, and knock on his door before opening it and closing it softly behind me. I'm saddened at how bare his room is. I wouldn't have thought this was anything other than a guest room with the lack of pictures or anything personal. A small double bed is pushed against the middle of the far wall, with just a small chest of drawers next to it and a small closet on the other side of the room. Devoid of any life or hint of who Kai is.

The young man in question is standing at his window, looking out into the backyard.

"Go away," he says, croaking on the words. I ignore him, and move over to stand behind him.

"Kai. Look at me."

I rest my hands on his shoulders, and after a few moments of hesitation, he turns to me with tears running down his face. His beautiful eyes are so open and lost. Vulnerable. I gently rub the wetness away with my thumb. His breathing slows as he closes his eyes, calming at the touch. Zaps of electricity cover my skin as I touch his face, a connection that I don't want to acknowledge because it's as foreign as it is concerning. After only being in his presence for a few hours, I'm questioning certain things about myself. This sensation of desire blankets me as I look at him, akin to meeting a mysterious stranger in a darkened corner of a bar. I don't understand it. Ugh, this is stupid. Even having these thoughts feels like I'm taking some kind of advantage of him while he navigates the whirlwind he has himself swept up in. Jenny would have my head if she knew I was even thinking like this. I need to focus. Focus on getting Kai away from here, then maybe he can move on in his life and all this confusing shit that's starting to fill my head will shut the hell up.

"You're going to come with me, and we'll make this right. Your mom didn't mean it," I say with a gentleness to my voice I never knew I possessed. Years of being violent and angry, toughened to deal with the scum that is embedded in my life with what I do, has erased all memory of when I was loving and affectionate. Life stopped being full of color when Jenny left home, all I see is a world covered in different shades of gray.

"I deserved it. I've never spoken to her like that. I hate myself, Jules. I don't know what to do," he sobs, and I grab the back of his neck and pull him into my chest. His hair smells of coconut, and it settles into my soul, creating a core memory that signifies comfort—a drifting sense of peace. The soothing scent has my body automatically relaxing into his arms.

I'm surprised how he clings to me. We're all fucked up. The three of us hardened to affection that has slowly destroyed us piece by piece in some way. As we stand locked together, all I can think is that I will protect him with everything I have.

"Pack only what you need, go make peace with your mom, and then we're leaving," I say, regretfully pulling away from him and leaving the room. Like a mantra, I remind myself that he's family, and it's my job to look out for him. I completely ignore my hard dick that's been begging for attention since I smelled his hair. And his equally hard dick that was pressing into my thigh.

Don't go there, Jules, you sick fuck.

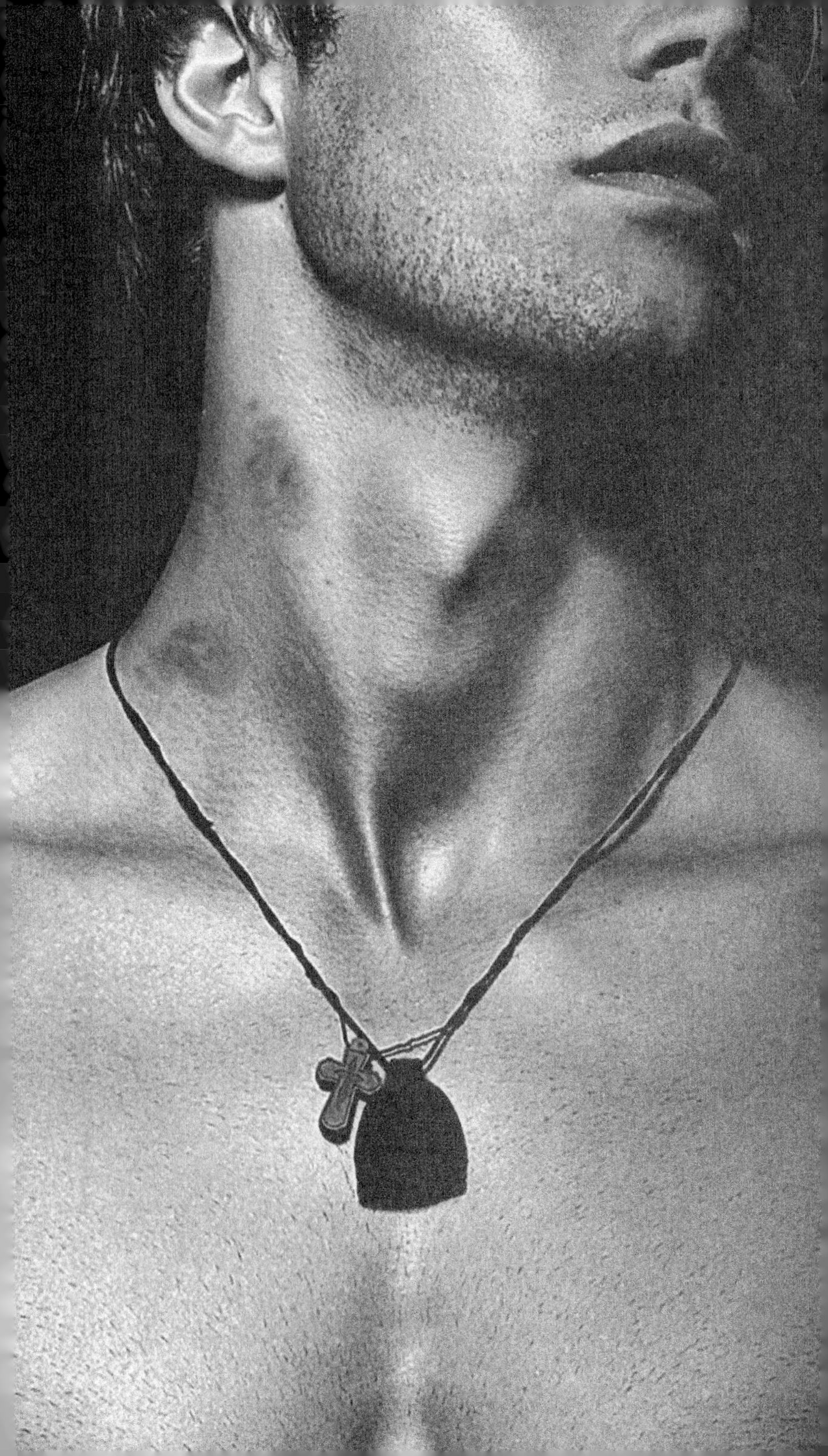

CHAPTER 6
KAI

So many emotions are running rampant in my mind right now, and I don't know which to latch onto. I can't believe she slapped me. But I deserved it. It was needed. That slap knocked some sense into me as the reality of my bad decisions suddenly weigh heavier on me than they ever have before. I'm not only destroying my mom, but I'm destroying myself.

I didn't mean what I said about Jules. Him coming back to us has forced action and I can't be mad about it, even if he is a blunt asshole. To be honest, I'm more terrified of how that hug made my heart swoop to the ground and bounce back up into my throat. I've never been touched like that before. A tranquility enveloped me when he held me in those huge arms. He smelled so good. Too good, if the hard dick in my jeans is anything to go by. While I can take care of myself, the needy part of my brain wanted him to pick me up, swaddle me in blankets, and take me away to protect me from the world. How fucking weird is that? It was painful when he pulled that secure feeling away from me to leave the room. I want him back here. Being in his arms, things just felt right for the first time in forever. Everything in my mind became balanced.

Grow the hell up, Kai. You're so twisted.

Shaking myself back to the reality that I just want to leave, I grab my duffel and pack some necessities: a few items of clothing, toiletries, and my passport. You never know.

Begrudgingly, I slowly walk back out to the living room, where Jules is sitting with my mom. She looks up at me and rushes over, kissing my forehead and hugging me so tightly that I find it hard to breathe.

"I'm so sorry. Please forgive me, Kai. I never should've hurt you like that. There's no excuse. I just want you safe and happy and I'm scared for you."

"It's okay. I get it. I do. I promise you don't have to worry. I'll give it my all when I go with Jules. I'll make you proud to call me your son."

"I *am* proud to call you my son, Kai. I just want you to find your way again," she says as she holds me like a precious baby. We're both emotional as we soak up the apologies and promises. I have to make this right.

After a couple of minutes locked into this maternal embrace, we pull away and smile at one another. That hug was the full stop to my bullshit and this smile we share is a new start for us both. While today has been taxing, there is a lightness now that we have bared ourselves, and I've stopped hiding from the truth. I look over to Jules, who wears a small smile and gives a slight nod of the head.

"Time to go, Kai. We got a few hours on the road," Jules says, and walks over to give my mom a quick hug before he walks out of the front door.

"Text me when you get there, Kai. And keep in touch."

"I will. Love you, Mom."

"I love you too."

Walking outside, Jules grabs my bag and places it in the back of his car as I get into the passenger seat. My mom stands at the door and waves us off as we leave.

"You good?" Jules asks.

"Yeah. I'm sorry for being a dick back there," I say as my phone chimes, alerting me to a text message. Jules chuckles.

"It's fine, this time," he says as I smile and pull my phone out of my jean pocket. Shit. It's a message from Jez.

> **Jez**
> Went down to the station, and they said you'd been released. You coming over?

> No. I'm in the car with my Uncle Jules. I'm leaving town. He's taking me to work with him. Mom is over my shit.

> **Jez**
> What do you mean leaving? Fuck, man, you can't just leave. Zac won't allow it.

Fuck. I never thought of that. The Skins is Zac's gang and I didn't think it would matter if I left. It's hardly a big time group.

> He can't force me to stay. I've already left. You don't need me.

> **Jez**
> I'm supposed to be your best friend. You've fucked up, Kai.

I ignore that last message, along with the heavy roll of nausea in my stomach. They'll just be upset that I didn't talk to them, Jez is just making a big deal out of it. Right?

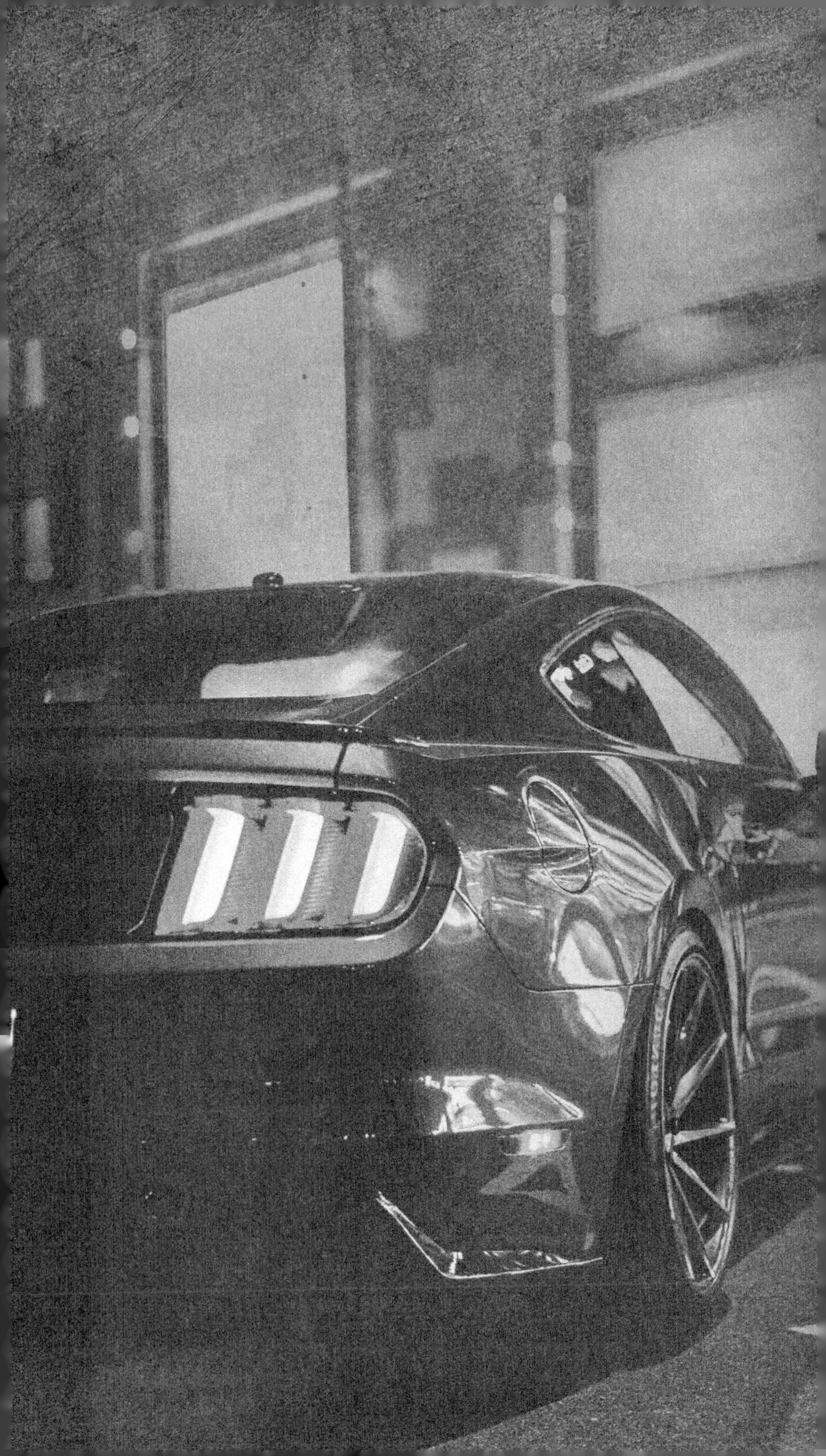

CHAPTER 7
Jules

Kai remained quiet most of the journey back, and I'm having to fight with myself not to pin him by the neck and ask him what's wrong. Ever since he received a text message just after we left his mom's, the tension in the car has had me on edge. Not to mention how irritating it's been to be sitting next to someone who has bounced their knee for nearly the entire journey.

We arrive back in Grinston, and it doesn't take long for us to arrive at the Kozlov residence. Driving through the gate, I notice that most of the cars are not here, and Seb's motorcycle is gone. Only Simon's car is left outside the property.

"Holy shit, you live here?" Kai gasps in awe as his eyes widen like a kid in a candy shop. I pull to a stop, hop out, and grab his bags from the backseat. Kai is just standing next to his open door, taking in the beauty of this house. I've gotten used to it, but I remember when Dima and Lev purchased the property, how foreign living in such wealth was for me at the time. For all of us, really, because the brothers came from as little as I did.

"Our bosses, Dima and Lev, live here, along with Seb, Dima's husband. The guards live out back in another property."

All of the rigidness that Kai held onto during the drive over has completely disappeared, replaced by excitement and eagerness to get inside. While it's endearing to see him smile and look happy with that damn dimple on full display, I'm still contemplating how to explain what really goes on here, and I need to do it fast. The last thing I need is for him to meet the brothers without being prepared.

"Come on, let's get you settled, and then we can go over the job."

I lead the way around to the side of the property that only the guards and I use to access our home. For the first couple of months, either myself or one of the other guys will have to accompany Kai in the main house, until the brothers feel they can trust him enough in their home. We don't tend to be in the main house on our own without the brothers, only if they request it. But one of us is in the house when they are home as added security. It never used to be much of an issue, but since the drama with Seb's ex and the shitshow from the guard Zayn who betrayed Dima and Lev, the brothers are now looking to secure the house better and extend the property, along with hiring extra muscle.

I hold the door open for Kai to enter our home, then lead him down to his room. It's Zayn's old room, but we cleaned out all his shit after we ended the fucker. His deceit still gets my blood boiling, how he helped Seb's ex try to get one over on the brothers.

"This will be your room. Mine is at the end of the corridor, and Simon's is across from you. Our rooms are private, so you never go into them without permission. We share food that we buy, and you can use everything else in the house that you like. You can only go into the main house with either one of the guards or the brothers until Dima and Lev are convinced you are trustworthy. They have a gym we all use, so you can go with me or one of the others."

Kai swallows hard and looks around the room, until his eyes land on mine. I shove away the memory of his hard dick on my thigh when we hugged before. It's confusing as fuck. A long silence ensues as we look into each other's eyes. This is so damn weird, why does he keep looking at me like that? I've seen that look in women's eyes before we fuck, it's full of sexual charge, but he doesn't like guys, does he? Fuck, he has such beautiful eyes, as blue as the ocean on a still sunny day, inviting and warm. I find myself drowning in them, getting lost under their hypnotic spell. Kai is just as fixed on my eyes too, his eyelids become heavy, confirming my previous suspicion, arousal is lurking in the depths of those blues, which pulls me up sharp. He definitely feels something too. This is dangerous territory and I need to back away. I clear my throat, ridding the raspiness I know would be there if I spoke.

"When you're settled, meet me in the living room, and we'll go over your role."

"Okay."

Damn it, was this a mistake? He looks and sounds so young and innocent. Completely lost, but also lustful if that moment was anything to go by. I can't second guess this, he's here now, and there's no turning back.

Leaving Kai to take in his new surroundings, I walk into the kitchen and grab a bottle of water from the fridge. I drink nearly the whole thing, quenching the thirst that has had my throat feeling like sandpaper, as I wrack my brain for ways to explain to Kai what the Kozlovs are about.

Footsteps on the hard floors behind me alert me to Kai's presence. I turn and see him standing awkwardly, his baby blues flitting around the space, his hands fidgeting, picking at the cuticles of his nails. I don't know why, but this meek version of Kai is difficult to process. The vibrant and confident Kai I had glimpses of in the past is nowhere to be seen, but I'm determined to bring him back.

"You want something to drink?"

"Uh, yeah, I'll take a water. Thanks."

I nod and grab him a bottle from the fridge and pass it to him. He unscrews the top and drinks the water in long, slow swallows. My eyes are fixed on his throat, watching the movement as if it's the most magical thing I've ever seen. I've never thought about a man's throat before, how sensual it looks when the Adam's apple moves, it's as mesmerizing as the fluid moves of voluptuous hips on the most beautiful woman dancing to an erotic beat. *Fucking hell, am I really comparing Kai's throat to hips?* Also, I really need to stop staring before I give myself away, especially now that I've sensed a mutual attraction. Mutual, as in, I think I'm attracted to him too. Me. Since when does someone realize they like dudes at thirty? Or is it just Kai related? Could I suck a dick? *Could I just shut the fuck up.*

"So, there are a few things you need to be aware of while working here—first, you never repeat anything that happens here outside of these grounds. Anything Dima or Lev orders you to do, you do it. I really need you to remember that for your own safety."

"What kind of orders?"

"Anything."

"That's pretty vague, Jules. Why are you looking at me like that?"

"Like what?"

"Like you're about to tell me someone died."

Fuck, he's perceptive. Screw it—time to tell him the truth.

"Let's sit down for this. There are things about what I do that you and your mom aren't aware of."

"O-okay," Kai says hesitantly as he follows me to the living room.

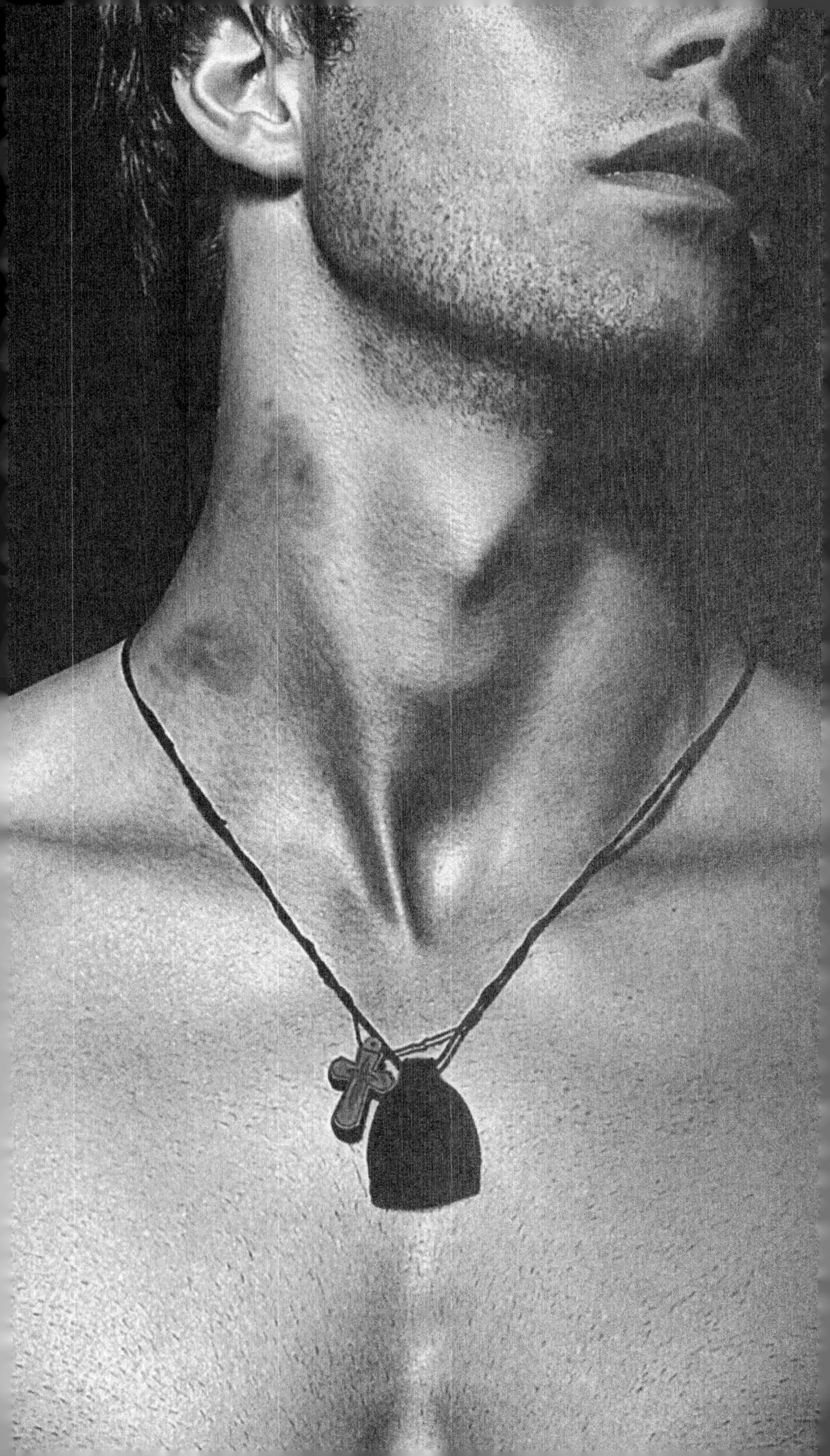

CHAPTER 8
KAI

Sitting across from Jules on the sofa, my eyes do a tour of his strong form. I'm honestly surprised his arms haven't burst out of his shirt with how obscenely it stretches across his body. Tight and muscular. When I was younger, I was in awe of his body and strength, and it was what motivated me to get in shape as I got older. I fantasized frequently about those strong arms holding me down as he destroyed my body. I wonder if his skin tastes sweet or salty?

"Kai, you okay?" Jules asks, abruptly removing me from the sexy dream world I was just in. I need to get a hold of this crush before I lose him. After that intense eye contact in my room, I'm pretty sure he can read the crush I have on him all over my face. I never could hide my emotions. For a brief moment I thought he was feeling it too. Wouldn't he break eye contact if he was straight? Or was he staring me down? Most likely I've made this up in my head because I'm tragic.

"Yeah, sorry. I'm just tired."

"I get it. You've had a lot of changes today. But we need to talk about what we do here. Lev and Dima run a business that puts them in danger, and we need to make sure they're protected at all costs."

"What kind of business?"

"Drugs. Lev and Dima are dangerous men, Kai. If you fall out of line, you don't want to end up on their bad side, or even worse, in their holding pen. Loyalty is the code you must live by, in order to be in this family. You follow that, then you'll have a family that would kill in your honor. Do you understand?"

"Hold on. You work for drug lords?"

Jules sighs like he's dealing with an idiot.

"Not that dramatic. They have crews around the city with their own patches that they run. We just make sure no trouble spills out into other territories and that the brothers are safe."

Is he for real right now?!

"Fucking hell. You and Mom lectured me on life and the trouble I could get into. And your answer is to bring me into a drug cartel? Are you fucking serious?"

I'm shaking in anger, and I'm half tempted to jump over and punch Jules in his gorgeous face.

"This is different."

"How the fuck is this different?" I yell, and stand to hover over him. Is he actually giving me shit right now?

"Calm the fuck down, Kai, and watch your tone," Jules warns as he stands to his full height to stare me down.

"Or what?"

"Or he'll put you in your place," a voice that's not Jules comes from the other end of the room. A tall guy with black hair who looks like a damn model scowls at me as he prowls over.

"I got this, Simon," Jules says to him. Simon. This must be the other guard Jules mentioned earlier.

"Simon, this is my nephew, Kai. Kai this is Simon, one of the other guards," Jules says as he moves to stand beside me.

'*Step*-nephew," I say, but I have no idea why I feel that the statement is relevant.

"I don't give a fuck if you're his brother. You show some fucking respect in this house. You get me?"

Shit. This isn't good, pissing people off before I've even started working. Simon's eyes are literally piercing a hole through my skin, he's seconds away from punching me in the face. But fuck, I hate being manipulated. Jules blindsided me, and I'm not okay with it.

"I get it. But he lied to me," I say in defense.

"I didn't lie. We are *technically* security, I just didn't tell you who we worked for. You were upset, and I thought it would be best to be honest when you had a chance to come to terms with leaving home," Jules says.

"You can paint it however you like. You manipulated me into coming here by hiding the facts. Not to mention what a hypocrite you are," I say, and stomp out of the room toward my bedroom before either have a chance to respond. Slamming the bedroom door behind me, I deflate. Yep. I'm definitely living up to the child image that my mom and Jules have accused me of.

I fall back onto the bed and stare at the ceiling before grabbing my phone from my back pocket and doing a quick internet search on the Kozlov brothers. I regret it almost instantly. The guys are for sure hot as fuck, but damn, do they look sinister. Especially Lev. He looks like the kind of guy who would enjoy fucking you up. *Of course he would.* They're criminals. Not that I can find anything about their dodgy dealings online. All I can see is that they own a strip joint, Desire, and a cabaret/burlesque bar called Starlight. I scoff to myself. Both businesses are obviously fronts for their shady dealings.

My phone chimes and another text from Jez appears. *Could today get any worse?*

J: Zac is pissed. He says you're not to come back here, or he'll kill you. You'll get no help from me, Kai. Consider yourself an enemy if you step a foot back into town.

You've got to be kidding me. Death threats? What about my mom? The assholes can't mean it, they do some shitty things, but they aren't killers. The term I'm damned if I do, and damned if I don't comes to mind. As if the threat of the Kozlovs and potential threat of Zac isn't enough, my bedroom door flies open, nearly coming off its hinges. Jules stands there, his chest rising and falling with heavy breaths, his eyes honed in on me. I've never seen him look this angry before, especially at me.

"Get up," he growls, his voice all gravelly and hoarse. Threatening. So why the hell is my dick responding?

I rush up to my feet and stand, awaiting whatever fate has in store for me.

"Come here."

Slowly, I walk over to him until we are just a foot apart. How can I be so scared and excited at the same time?

With lightning fast speed he grabs me by the throat and slams me back into the wall next to the door. Dizziness takes hold from the force of the push, before the inability to breathe has me grappling at his hand to let go.

"Never question me or speak to me like that again in front of the others. You *will* do as you're told, Kai. The brothers are not a joke. That so-called *gang* would've hurt you, or you'd be doing time. Here, you're protected."

"Jules, let go," I rasp, still trying to free his hand from my neck. He loosens his fingers, but only slightly. I greedily swallow down the air that now fills my lungs like I've been submerged underwater. But fuck me is it a rush, adrenaline lights up my body, the feeling of freefalling from the sky takes me on a high that I've never experienced before. Oh my god, what's wrong with me? Do I have a choking kink?

"Don't make me do this again, Kai. Be good, and there will be no problems. No matter what you think, I don't want you to get hurt."

"That's rich. You don't want me to get hurt, but you nearly just choked me to death."

Jules pulls away from me and stares at my neck. His perusal lowers, and warmth blooms on the back of my neck as I realize what he's staring at. I'm hard—*a hard freak.*

"Doesn't look like I've hurt you from here," he smirks, and goes to leave.

"Be out front in five; you're meeting the brothers."

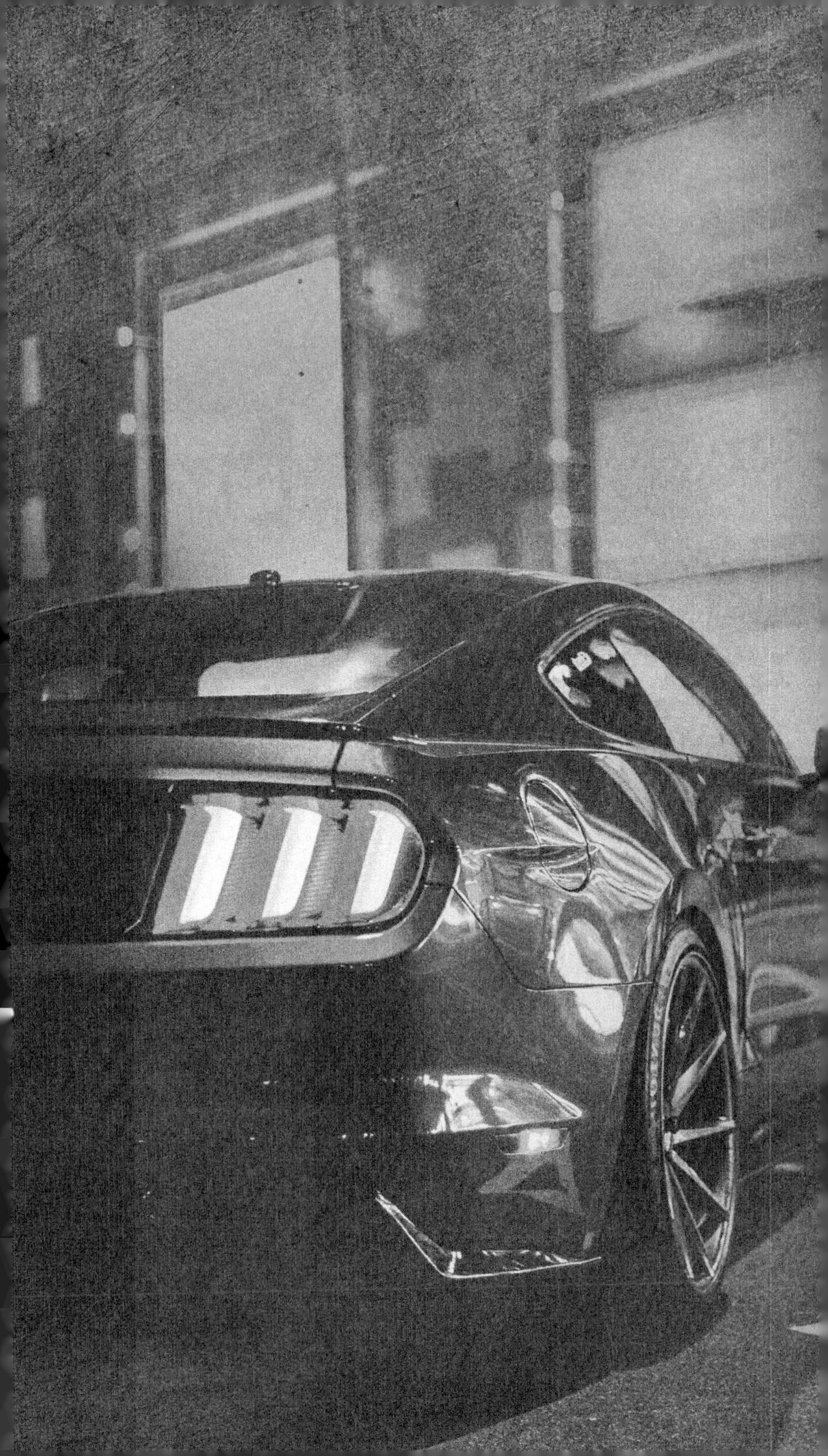

CHAPTER 9
JULES

What the fuck was that? Did I just flirt with Kai? Why the hell does it matter? The little shit is getting mouthy, and going by his reaction to being strangled, I'm not sure if that will be more of a reward for him than a punishment. Images of choking him while fucking him play like a reel in my head, tying him to the headboard where he can't break free as I destroy his body piece by piece.

Where the fuck is this all this coming from? I'm straight. Plus he's Kai...my sister's boy.

I can't wait for today to be over. Talk about exhausting. I kinda get where Kai is coming from, but he doesn't understand that whether or not you agree with the Kozlov's dealings, it's a legitimate business. Very different from being in a stupid ass group of thugs who have no rules or direction and just want to cause harm and chaos. I don't want him to piss off Lev and Dima as I didn't predict Kai needing such an attitude adjustment. Simon was ready to knock him out earlier, and Kai will need all the support he can get while he settles into life here. I want it to work out for him. Going back home would be the worst outcome for him right now.

Kai strolls out of his bedroom and meets me at the door, avoiding eye contact, and I'm not sure if that's because of how I made it awkward by mentioning his hard dick. Still no idea why I did that, but here we are.

"Come on. Let's introduce you. Be polite and keep the attitude at bay."

"Yeah, yeah. Otherwise I'll be taken to, what was it called? The holding pen? Do I want to know what that is?"

"It's a room below the house where we deal with problems."

"*Problems*. Code for torture chamber."

I look over my shoulder at him as we walk to the main house.

"Yep. Although many don't leave alive. And I mean bad people."

"Great. How the hell did you get into this? You talk about violence and death like it's normal."

I come to a stop and turn to face Kai. It's easy to forget when you live amongst the scum of evil that others on the outside still have light in their life. Striving to be good.

"I had nothing when Lev and Dima took me in. I was nothing but a resentful and angry abandoned kid, who would've ended up either dead or locked up if it wasn't for the brothers. Even at my worst they're beside me. All they ask for is loyalty."

"Do you enjoy hurting people? Have you killed anyone?" Kai's question is asked with both innocence and intrigue. I don't detect any disgust, but his tone is judgemental.

"Yes I have and I don't feel bad for it. It's not like we pick up strangers, Kai, and kill for fun. It's a job. It keeps us safe. Do I enjoy it? Now that's a very different question."

"Well answer it then. I'm not going in there until you tell me who you are, because to be honest, you sound like a monster," Kai says as he stands there with his arms crossed like he can intimidate me.

"Fair enough. The brothers taught me how to fight, how to use guns and knives. I'd watch them work until they felt I was ready to be more involved. The first time I interrogated anyone in the holding pen, it was with my fists. Hurting someone with my bare hands has been my preference since that day. When I punched that fucker, the loud crunch of his broken nose did something to me where the heavy weight in my chest disappeared, replaced by a clarity that I didn't need to think or feel anything but the raw power of my hands, and the adrenaline rush it gave me."

Kai is staring at me wide eyed, surprised by my brutal honesty. But for some reason, I don't stop. Exposing myself for who I am is necessary for him to be here. To accept this life.

"Then after the adrenaline dropped like a passing storm, an intense relief filled me where everything was calmer and quieter. As time went on and the more people I hurt started to mount, the more I craved that feeling. It replaced all the shit your grandparents threw at me and it was the best thing to happen to me because I wouldn't be where I am right now. Does that answer your question?"

Kai swallows hard, letting his arms fall to his side before he puts them in his pockets and lowers his head, looking at the ground.

"You really are a stranger."

"In some ways. Don't be naive, Kai. This place will eat you up too, and you won't even realize it. Or even feel bad. Believe me, the fuckers we bury deserve to be there."

"You're not God, Jules. None of you are."

I smile at that response. So sweet.

"We're gods here, Kai. Nothing that you or anyone else says will change that."

"You've taken me from one bad situation into a worse one, Jules. I'm in more danger here than I was back home."

I can't help but laugh. "Nothing will happen to you here because I won't allow it. They'd have to crawl over my dead body to get to you, Kai."

I don't wait for a response, and turn to walk into the main house via the kitchen patio doors where Kai follows me.

"Wow, this house is awesome," Kai says behind me.

"Yeah, it is."

"I've never seen a kitchen like this," he mutters under his breath.

"You cook?" I say, stopping to turn to him.

"Yeah, I can cook. Mom taught me, and it always relaxed me. Stop looking at me like that," he snaps.

"I'm not looking at you like anything. I'm just surprised."

"I'm not a total failure."

"I never said you were, Kai."

Kai is so damn defensive, it's painful to watch. I hate seeing that insecurity in his eyes. We all make mistakes, but Kai can't seem to move past it, and berates himself. Compared to the shit me and the brothers did when we were younger, he really needs to accept it's not a big deal.

"Who the fuck is this?" is demanded behind me. Dima. Subtle as ever.

"This is Kai. My step-nephew."

Dima frowns like that isn't an explanation. Lev follows in behind him and walks over to the kitchen island and leans against it. A smirk crosses his lips as he slowly appraises Kai, and my protective instincts kick in. I want to punch him for looking at Kai like he's a piece of meat. Lev fucks anything that moves and is willing. Plus Lev is popular with both men and women, he's built like a greek god, tattoos cover his arms and chest, and his black hair is cut into a tight military cut which makes those vicious green eyes of his pop. Dima is built the same, but has thick black hair and a cropped beard. Every fucker wants to bed these guys, and believe me, they have taken advantage of that.

"Kai, these are the brothers, Dima and Lev," I say, pointing to them so he knows who is who.

"Yet I still don't know why he's here?" Dima complains.

"He's Zayn's replacement," Lev says, with his eyes still on Kai. I can feel Kai tense beside me, shifting from foot to foot. Today couldn't get any worse.

"Err, since fucking when?" Dima asks Lev.

"Since I said Jules could bring him on."

"Why wasn't I informed?"

"I'm informing you now, brother."

"I'm the head of this family, Lev. It goes through me, I make the decisions," Dima snaps at Lev, who just smiles at him.

"I would if you didn't have your cock up Seb's ass twenty-four-seven. And I don't blame you, it's a hot ass. But I made a decision. Deal with it."

"I'll fucking deal with you, fucker," Dima says.

"No, you won't. Now, let's get to know the new boy."

Dima and Lev turn to Kai, who looks like a hunted animal that wants to run as far away from this house as possible. I'm not sure who to look at as Lev stares at Kai like he wants to eat him up, and Dima seems to want to tear him apart for answers. Awesome.

"So, Kai. Has fuckface here explained who we are and what your job is?" Lev asks.

"Yes," Kai replies faintly. The lack of confidence in his reply has me regretting momentarily my decision to bring him here. Is he strong enough for this life? I was too impulsive ripping him away from his home, assuming he would slot into this world like I did. I can only hope it works out, otherwise he's toast. And it would be my fault.

"Yes, what?" Lev asks.

"Yes, *sir*?"

"Hmm, *hell yeah*, I like the sound of that," Lev groans.

"Lev. *Stop*," I say, as he pins me with a death glare.

"Protective much? He needs to hold his own here," Dima says, still assessing Kai. Kai adjusts his body, stands taller, shoulders back, shedding the unsure version of himself. *Good*.

"I can hold my own. You have no worries here."

"Do you know how to use a gun? Knife?" Lev asks, excitement lacing his voice. He loves being down in the holding pen. While Lev gets off on the violence and fear, Dima loves the blood. Sick fuckers.

"Yes. I was in a gang, and they taught me."

"Really. What's the gang called?" Dima asks.

"The Skins. I hung around back home with my best friend. We were in a bar fight; that's why I got arrested."

"They sound like amateurs. Okay. We'll take Jules's word that you're trustworthy. But take this as a warning. You fuck us over, and we won't only end you, but Jules too. Understood?" Dima says.

"I won't let you down," Kai says, with a firm resolve.

"Interesting as this is, I need to head over to Desire. Jules, bring Kai so we can get him caught up on the business. I want him to cover the club with Simon. I think eventually it will be best that you two work apart," Lev says, and the way he is looking at me with a raised brow says he's goading me. He saw it. My protectiveness and underlying sick lust for my nephew. Fuck. *Step*-nephew. Who is also a guy, but that's another detail that doesn't seem important to my eager dick.

"Fine," I grit out, which earns me a satisfied grin from Lev. The bastard.

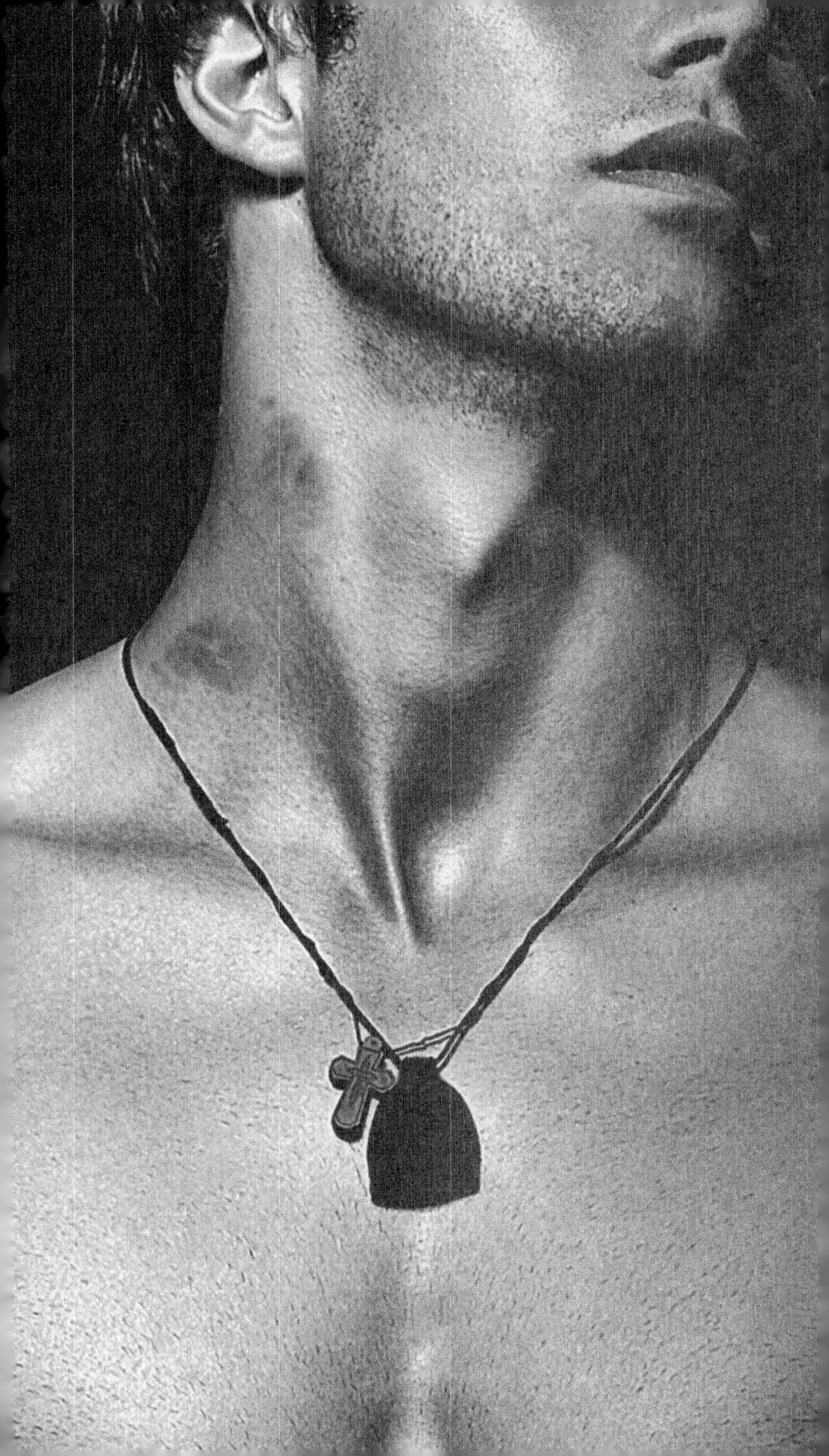

CHAPTER 10
KAI

Holy shit. Now this is a strip club. Walking through Desire is like dipping yourself into liquid gold, expensive, sumptuous, and so fucking sexy. The walls are matte black with mirrors spaced out evenly over the walls. Multicolored lights shine from the ceiling, the seats are a deep red leather, and the tables are a heavy duty black wood. The floors are high gloss black that reflect the array of colors from the lighting. In the middle of the room is a circular stage with a pole in the middle. The bar is long against the far wall and is not too dissimilar to what you would see in a high-end bar in Manhattan.

Lev and Jules walk further into the club where the song Bad Girl—by Avril Lavigne and Marilyn Manson—pounds through the room where a hot as fuck busty redhead slides up and down the pole on stage. This is nothing like the dive bars back home, that's for sure. Everything is so shiny and clean, absolutely no expense spared in the club. A high membership fee, no doubt, to enter this joint.

"Like what you see?" Lev purrs into my ear, causing me to flinch away from the show. His intense eyes glitter with amusement at my reaction. Lev is scary as fuck, and his smile is sadistic. I imagine he likes to cut his lovers up for pleasure. Just a vibe I get from him, so I don't really want to piss him off.

"Yeah," is all I can say, my throat feels dry as fuck as I try to make sure not to come across like a prudish dick. Which I'm not. But I feel on edge around the brothers. A warm body comes up behind me and I know it's Jules. He radiates a protective warmth, like a sleeping bag that insulates me from the unpredictable elements. Shit. This is gonna be exhausting, trying not to piss off the brothers while also holding down my dirty attraction to Jules.

"Be careful, the girls love new meat. Make sure you fuck and leave, and none of that falling-in-love shit. Don't want that mess in my club," Lev says, slapping me hard on the shoulder with his big hand and nodding his head towards the bar.

"He's trying to get a rise out of you. Just ignore him," Jules says into my ear as he holds me tightly on the shoulder where Lev just slapped me. He uses it to guide me over to where Lev is now speaking to a woman at the bar. She's pretty hot, actually. All the girls are hot, but having Jules around me and touching me in an almost possessive manner has me solely focused on him.

"Bonnie, this is our newbie guard, Kai. Jules's nephew," Lev says, smirking at Jules, who quickly removes his hand.

"*Step*-nephew. We're not blood-related," I bluster out. Why do I feel the need to constantly correct people on our biological relationship? I may as well tattoo it on my damn forehead.

Bonnie tosses her brown hair over her shoulder and gives me a warm smile, leaning in to kiss me on the cheek.

"Aren't you a handsome one?" she says, and I grin in return. I'm really trying to act like this behavior is all normal to me and that I'm cool. It's so much pressure, especially as I can feel Lev and Jules staring at me from either side. Is this a test?

"Shy, too. I like it. I'm always here hon, if you want some company," Bonnie says in a purring voice, a seductive spell she has crafted from experience. I'm stuck for words.

"He won't. Kai is here to work. He doesn't need the distraction," Jules says. I nearly sprain my neck with how fast I turn to face him, both annoyed and thrilled by what he said. I'm not a child, I can fuck whoever I want, and I don't need him guarding me. But, his words also have a tinge of jealousy to them, which makes me slightly giddy with joy that it may not just be me that feels this attraction.

"Calm down, Jules. It's not like you haven't fucked half the girls in this club," Lev says, now causing me to feel a jealousy that is unwarranted.

"Now, now, boys. I'm sure Kai is old enough to think for himself," Bonnie says, and I'm thankful to her, because this is weird as fuck.

"We'll be in the back, Bonnie. Come on you two, let's get to work," Lev says, and we follow him through the club. Rude Boy, by Rihanna, is now playing as another dancer takes to the stage, and I purposefully don't look, as I can feel the annoyance in Jules's gaze on the back of my neck. Have I pissed him off?

We walk down a small corridor at the back of the club and enter an office, which I assume is Lev's. A huge mahogany desk, paneled walls, and oversized leather chairs fill the space. The room smells of cigars and leather. Lev takes a seat in the large chair behind the desk, and I take a seat on one of the small sofas in the corner, just as Jules sits in a chair directly opposite Lev.

Lev opens the desk drawer and pulls out a wooden box full of cigars. He offers one to Jules, who takes it, then Lev turns the box to me.

"Would you like one?" Lev asks as Jules watches me.

"He doesn't smoke," Jules says, lifting the lighter to his cigar.

"How would you know? You don't know me anymore," I say, irritation taking over the politeness. This babying is pissing me off. He's right, though, I don't smoke.

"You're a feisty thing, aren't you? I like that," Lev smiles and takes a long inhale of the cigar, unblinking eyes never leaving mine, causing me to squirm in my seat.

"I'm not a kid. I can answer for myself."

"You're definitely not a kid. Let's start again. Kai, would you like a cigar?" Lev asks again, but this time he's watching Jules. I refuse to look at Jules as I know I'll lash out and have a full tantrum.

"No thank you. I don't smoke," I say. A deep smokey laugh comes from Lev as he leans back in his chair.

"So I do know you," Jules grumbles, his relentless gaze on me. I clench my fists as they rest on my lap. I want to both equally slap him and kiss him.

"No, it was a good guess. Plus Mom probably mentioned it," I say, crossing my arms and leaning back into the sofa.

"She never said a word. Why is it so hard to believe that I know who you are, Kai?" Jules says. I'm stunned we are having this conversation right now in front of Lev.

"You don't know me. I hardly know you. You don't know I like dick," I say, and god knows why. Jules stills at that, but Lev doesn't let the comment go.

"Now that is good news—no need to feel like you can't ask for dick, Kai. We love some of that around here. Apart from your *Uncle* Jules. He goes through women like it's a sport. Such a waste, as he has a great looking cock."

"What?" I say, not realizing my voice could go that high pitched. How the fuck would Lev know what his dick looks like?

"Don't get jealous, we've had many threesomes. With women of course," Lev says with a gleam in his eyes. The bastard is taunting me, my crush on Jules blindingly obvious.

"Leave him alone, Lev," Jules says, where he leans forward and stubs out his cigar in the large crystal ashtray on the desk.

"Or what?" Lev asks, his whole demeanor shifting from playful to dark. He really looks fucking crazy, but Jules doesn't seem too affected and remains silent, his eyes firmly on Lev, but after a moment of silence, Jules breaks the staredown.

"I thought so. Now, if your family drama is done for the night, let's go through what we do here and how the clubs are run," Lev says, and I focus for the next hour on Lev. I have to remember I've come here to better my life. That means no distractions and no dreaming over all things Jules.

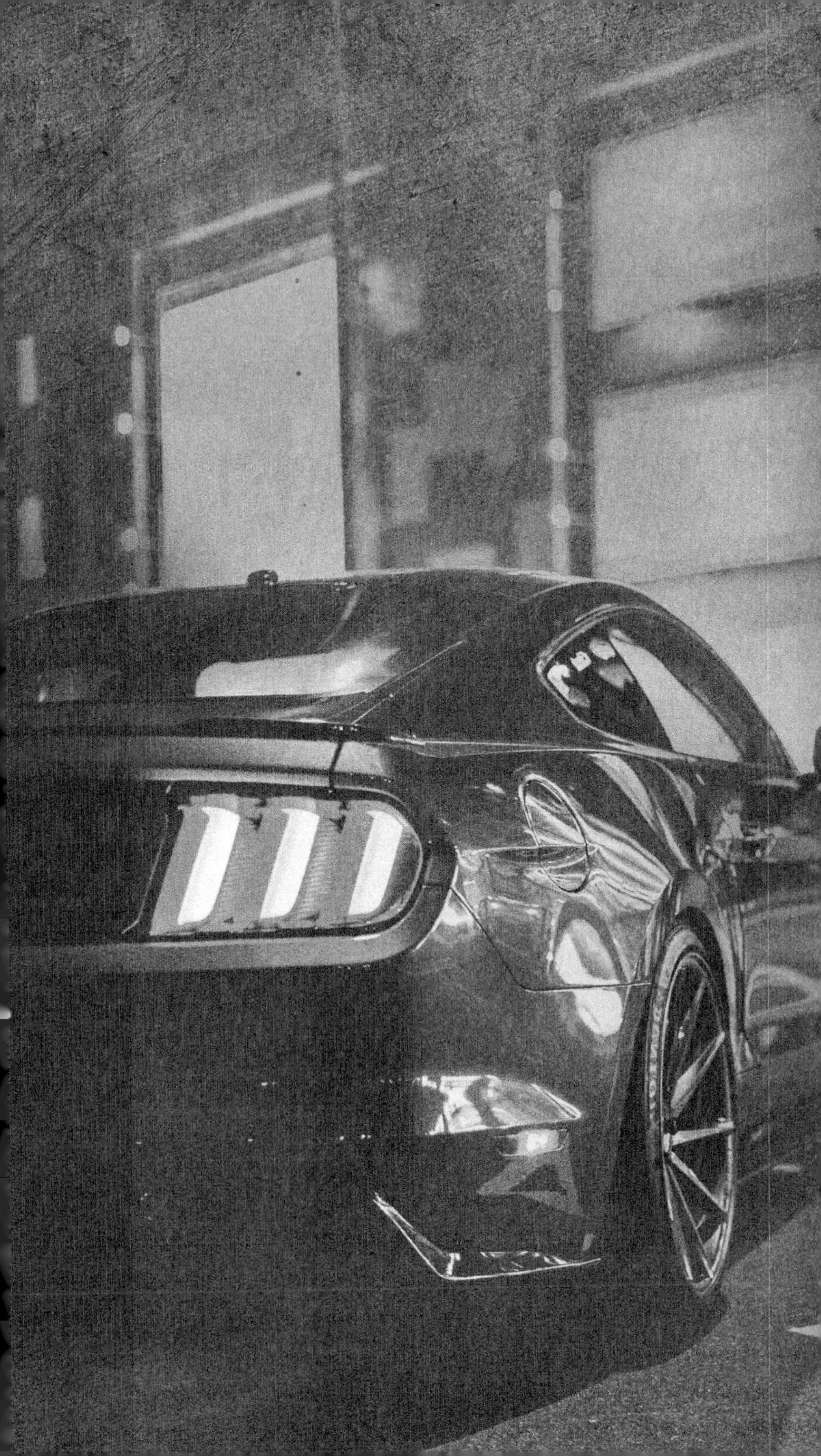

CHAPTER 11
JULES

Fucking Lev. I swear the guy can see into my mind like clear glass. And why the hell did he bring up the threesomes? Was he trying to embarrass me or make me out to be some kind of whore? Even though he wears the title of manwhore like a damn crown. Lev is not only a beast when it comes to his job and family, but he is on another level with the way he treats the women we've taken to bed. Completely feral. God help anyone who manages to get him to settle down, although the chances of that are as likely as unicorns flying out of my ass. I also didn't like the way he eye-fucked Kai. I need to keep him away, because Kai wouldn't be able to handle Lev and his sadistic nature. Kai just needs to focus on his job and to have more focus in his life. But what if Kai likes Lev? I swear to god, I'm gonna punch myself for these stupid thoughts, because why the hell should I care so much? He's an adult. It's just because I'm concerned. He's family. That's all.

"You're too fucking obvious," Lev says as he takes the seat beside me. After the meeting, I brought Kai back into the main club to get him familiar with the layout and for him to get to know the workers here. Kai is currently talking to Simon over at the bar while I sit here festering in my confusion of all this anger and possessiveness my nephew brings out of me. Instead of watching the show on stage, I've been solely focused on every move Kai makes and wanting to smack Simon for standing so close to him. Ridiculous.

"I've no idea what you're talking about."

"Don't play dumb. You wanna fuck your nephew."

"*Step*-nephew. We aren't blood-related, and he's also a guy," I say defensively. I think Lev has the memo, as I've reminded him and everyone else a million times over already.

"Still not hearing that you don't wanna fuck him. If it makes you feel better, he wants you too."

I glare over at Lev, hoping it burns him to the ground. He talks such bullshit, and I want to wipe that arrogant grin off his face. I've never seen him smile as much as he has today, courtesy of all his meddling.

"Shut the hell up, Lev. I think you've done enough shit-stirring tonight."

"So you won't mind me giving his ass a go then? It would be a sin to let a hottie like him pass me by."

Just the idea of that has my blood pressure so high I should be dead. Unable to control the red haze of anger at the thought of Lev touching Kai, I find myself forgetting who I'm talking to and lean across the table.

"Don't you fucking dare! You keep your hands off him."

I'm so lost in the maze of frustration and anger that Kai has managed to bring out of me in the last twenty-four hours, that I leave myself unguarded as Lev's large hand grabs me around the throat and the teasing sparkle in those green eyes morph into pure violence.

"Watch it, Jules. I don't mind removing that disrespectful tongue if it teaches you a lesson in respect. Understand?"

The grip he has on my throat has me clutching the arms of my seat. If I show panic, Lev will think I'm weak, so I try to calm my thoughts and my breathing until I feel his hand slowly loosen before leaving my throat completely.

"I understand. I just want him focused."

"Whatever helps you sleep at night, nephew fucker. Ain't no shame in wanting him, though. Now get him home. I want him out meeting the crews tomorrow and showing him the ropes."

I stand with a nod in acknowledgment and walk over to where Kai is talking to Simon. Kai eyes me with concern, making me think he just saw my interaction with Lev.

"Time to go. You're shadowing me tomorrow so we need to get some rest. You coming, Si?" I say.

"I'll stick around and head back with Lev," Simon says, but his eyes are focused over my shoulder. I turn to see where he is looking and it's no surprise that he's staring down Carlos, who is smirking back at Simon.

"Or are you staying to have another showdown with Carlos?" I say, smiling when Simon looks back at me, brows furrowed that I've called him out. Something is definitely off with those two.

"The fucker deserves to be beat down. I hate him and his arrogant ass. Always looking down his nose at me," Simon says, with a sharp sneer on his lips, like the idea of Carlos has left a bitter taste in his mouth.

"Who's Carlos?" Kai asks.

"He's that smug fucker in the pretentious suit who is staring at us. He's Lev and Dima's distributor. Take my advice and keep away from him. Nothing but trouble," Simon says.

"He's not that bad. I get along with him fine. Ignore him, Kai," I say as I nudge Kai's arm and tilt my head, signaling for us to leave.

"Whatever," Simon grumbles and walks away toward Lev, who is still sitting at his table, smoking his cigar and watching over the club like a King watching his congregation at court.

"That was weird," Kai says as we walk toward the exit.

"Yeah, Si hates Carlos and Carlos loves to push his buttons."

"You mean they want each other?"

"I think Carlos wants Si. But I'm not sure if Si would stab Carlos if he touched him."

"Is there anyone normal that works here?"

That makes me laugh, because he's right. We're all crazy and tainted.

"I think your best option is Seb, for any normal conversation, although that disappears whenever he's near Dima."

"That's something, I suppose."

It is. At least Seb is the closest to a normal human among us. But the longer you spend with this fucked up family, the crazy seems to spread like a disease. Infecting every part of your being until you're living and breathing the brutal life that ironically saved us all in some way.

As we get into my car and head home in silence, I pray to god that Kai doesn't lose himself completely.

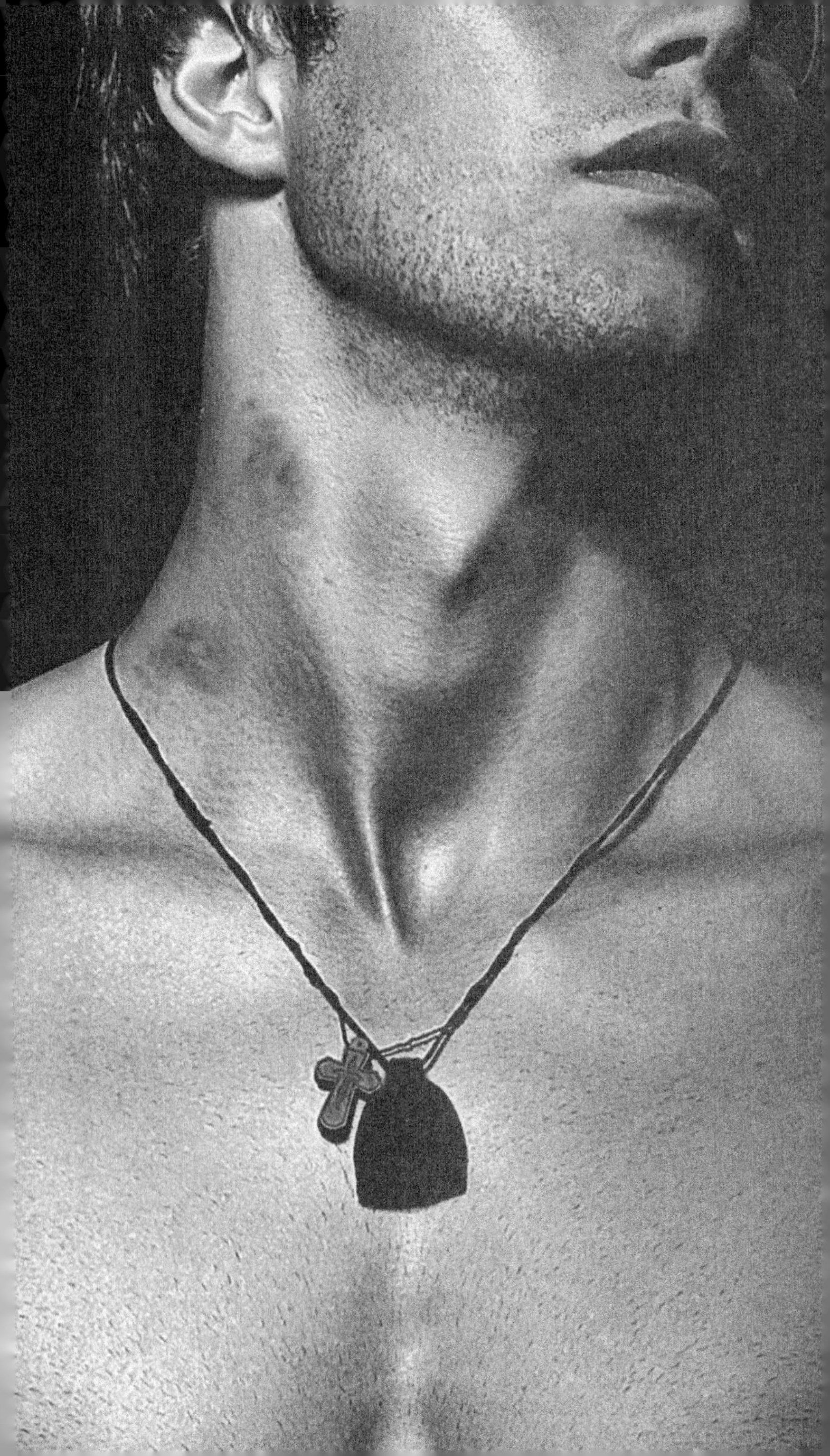

CHAPTER 12
KAI

Tonight was a lot to digest. I think every emotion flooded my system: excitement, fear, anxiety, and confusion. The point of how dangerous these guys are has been driven solidly home in the short amount of time I've spent in Lev's presence. While he scares the fuck out of me, I want to do well for him and Dima so that they'll keep me here. I can see myself adjusting to this life, I just hope my past stays there and that Zac lets things go. Jez has been quiet since his last text, and I would be lying if I said I wasn't nervous about the idea of going home to visit Mom. Zac is small potatoes compared to the Kozlovs, but he's a nasty fucker.

"How do you feel now that you know what we do here?" Jules asks, as we start to drive out of town. The street lights fading into the background as I stare into the side mirror. I catch a glimpse of my face in the reflection and it's the first time I've seen myself not look so tired, so downtrodden with nothing but questions in my eyes, asking myself what the hell I'm going to do with my life.

"Good. Lev's intimidating. Simon was cool. I thought he'd hate me because of how annoyed he was when we met, but he explained a lot about the job and the club. I'm more relaxed about things."

"That's great. It's pretty easy here if you just follow the rules and do what's asked of you."

"I won't let you down."

"I know."

Jules looks over at me with a small smile as we pull onto the driveway. Just as I get out of the car, a motorcycle pulls up next to us. As the rider dismounts the bike, he takes his helmet off and holy fuck, he's smokin'. I've never seen this many hot men in one place before, I'm borderline tempted to change from being bi to just gay, as these guys are sinfully attractive. A beautiful smile stretches across his gorgeous face, and pretty eyes light up as he walks towards us.

"Hey Jules," he says.

"Hey Seb. Great timing. Kai, this is Seb, Dima's husband. He also bartends at Starlight. Seb, this is Kai, our new guard," Jules says, and immediately my thoughts race with how hot Dima and Seb must look together.

"Great to meet you, Kai," Seb says, holding his hand out for me to shake. He grips my hand firmly, and his kind smile reassures me that I will get on with him. Jules is right; he is the most normal here.

"You too. Nice bike," I say.

"Thanks. You ride?" Seb asks.

"No, it's something I'd love to learn, though," I say.

"I can teach you if you want?" Seb offers.

"Err, I don't think Dima will like that, do you?" Jules says, chuckling.

"I don't give a fuck what D says, Jules. Haven't you learned that by now?"

"Hey, it's your funeral, just keep me out of it," Jules says as he guides me to the side entrance.

"Nice meeting you, Kai. If you get bored with the cavemen, pop over to the bar for a drink," Seb shouts as we walk away, and he heads into the main house.

"Thanks. I will," I say as I wave him goodbye.

"He's nice," I say to Jules as we walk towards our house.

"He is, but be careful. Dima is very possessive, and Seb encourages it. You don't wanna be caught in the crossfire."

"He can't be that bad."

"Kai, he murdered Seb's fiancée and her lover. Actually, Seb technically murdered his ex, but that's not the point. So yes, he would hurt anyone he thought was a threat or meant harm. There are no rules here. This is considered the norm. You need to remember that."

"Are you fucking kiddin' me? Seb killed someone? Wait. What really happened to that guard, Zayn?"

"He betrayed the brothers. He had to die."

"Fucking hell, Jules. What have you brought me into?" I say, looking at him head-on as we stand outside the door to our home.

"A new start. A family. Yes, we're bad people, but we protect each other and have a good life. You need to make it work in your head, Kai. Worrying about it only means you'll make mistakes. Just go with it."

"I can do that. Just go with it, it's only murders. No biggie. How dumb of me."

"Kai, watch it."

This is the most surreal moment I've ever experienced. Jules talking so candidly about life here like it's not a big deal. I swear we drove through a portal to a new world when Jules brought me here. But what can I do about it?

I'm now firmly interwoven into this underworld, and I need to get out of my head and accept it. How I accept it I don't know. For now I'll just have to fake it.

"What the hell am I supposed to tell Mom?"

"What your mom doesn't know won't hurt her, Kai. Trust me."

I scoff at that. *Trust me*. Yeah right. This has disaster written all over it.

It's the following week, and much to Jules's annoyance, Dima has me working at Starlight with him tonight. Lev wanted Jules and Simon with him at Desire for a meeting with Carlos about future shipments, and thought it would be good for me to know the layout of this club in case I'm needed here. To be honest, I'm glad of the reprieve, as Jules has not left my side. While my obsession over him is still present, his overbearing attitude towards me stirs the petulant side of me. Plus, it's a nice change of scenery, coming to the bar.

Starlight is what I would describe as decadent. Sultry music from the live band on stage with burlesque dancers, the crowd that fill the tables on the main floor all have the appearance of money and influence. The bar is modern and similar to the one at Desire. While Dima is out back, I head over to grab a soda and say hi to Seb, since the bar is less busy now that the show is on.

"Hey Seb," I say as I lean my elbows on the bartop.

"Kai, great to see you. Want a drink?"

"I'll have a soda, please."

Seb grabs a tall glass, fills it with ice and a slice of lemon, followed by the soda and hands it to me.

"Thanks. Great bar."

"Yeah, it can get a little rough sometimes, but I love working here."

"Does Dima mind you working?"

"Mind? The fucker didn't have a choice. It was a deal-breaker before we got married. If D had his way, I'd be chained to him the entire day."

That makes me laugh, Dima is alarmingly possessive of Seb from what I've witnessed. I can't help but be a touch jealous though. I've never been wanted like that, I mean, I've never even had a boyfriend or girlfriend before.

"You have anyone back home, Kai?"

I take a sip of my drink, trying to stop myself from retreating into my shell. I'm not ashamed that I've had nobody special in my life, but I'm not exactly shouting it out loud for everyone to know, as in my mind it sounds pretty pathetic.

"Nah. Not a lot of choices back home. Had to travel to another town for hookups, and that was rare."

"Well, maybe you'll score some action here."

"Maybe."

"Are you okay, Kai? I know we don't know each other, but you can talk to me. I promise I won't share anything you tell me. Even to D."

"I don't know. I'm just lost. Had a bit of trouble back home before I left. The guys I hung around with have said they'll hurt me if I go back."

"What! Does Jules know?"

"No! No. And please don't say anything. I'm sure it's fine and they're just angry with me. They don't do shit like that. I think I just bruised some egos by leaving without saying a word. Not that I had a choice in leaving."

"You know, you don't have to stay here, Kai. This life isn't for everyone. I mean, fuck, it isn't for me but I've found a way to live beside it and have a life with D. Maybe you need to find a way or start somewhere else. I'm sure Jules would understand."

"Ha! He wouldn't. I haven't seen him since I was sixteen. I barely know him, Seb. But he's barreled in and started to control my life already, you should've seen him in Lev's office on that first night. It was embarrassing, being spoken to like a child."

"I know that feeling well. If anyone knows about controlling, possessive guys, it's me," he says, laughing, which lightens the mood. "But you like him too? Am I right?"

My eyes look straight into Seb's and he isn't mocking me, his gaze is soft and encouraging me to trust him.

"I'm that obvious," I say, taking a final gulp of my water.

"Yep. You both are."

"Both? Nah, Jules doesn't like me like that. Also, he's straight."

"Trust me, Kai. Jules is the same as the brothers. Their love language and foreplay is asshole possessiveness, with a hint of violence if anyone tries to touch you. I guarantee, Jules would fuck up anyone who got near you."

"He's straight."

"So was I, and look at me now."

"But..."

"You need to stop overthinking things, Kai. Take on one thing at a time. Get adjusted here. Jules isn't going anywhere. Maybe it'll fizzle out, but my advice, gain your footing here with the respect of Lev and D. The rest can come later."

"You're right. Thank you."

"Anytime. You want a refill?"

"Please."

Relief. That's all I feel after unloading my fears onto Seb. Safe to say I think Seb is awesome and might now be my top confidante. He's right. I need to situate myself in the fold of the brothers first. Everything else will have to take a backseat. Even though I want to rush into anything Jules would give me with both feet.

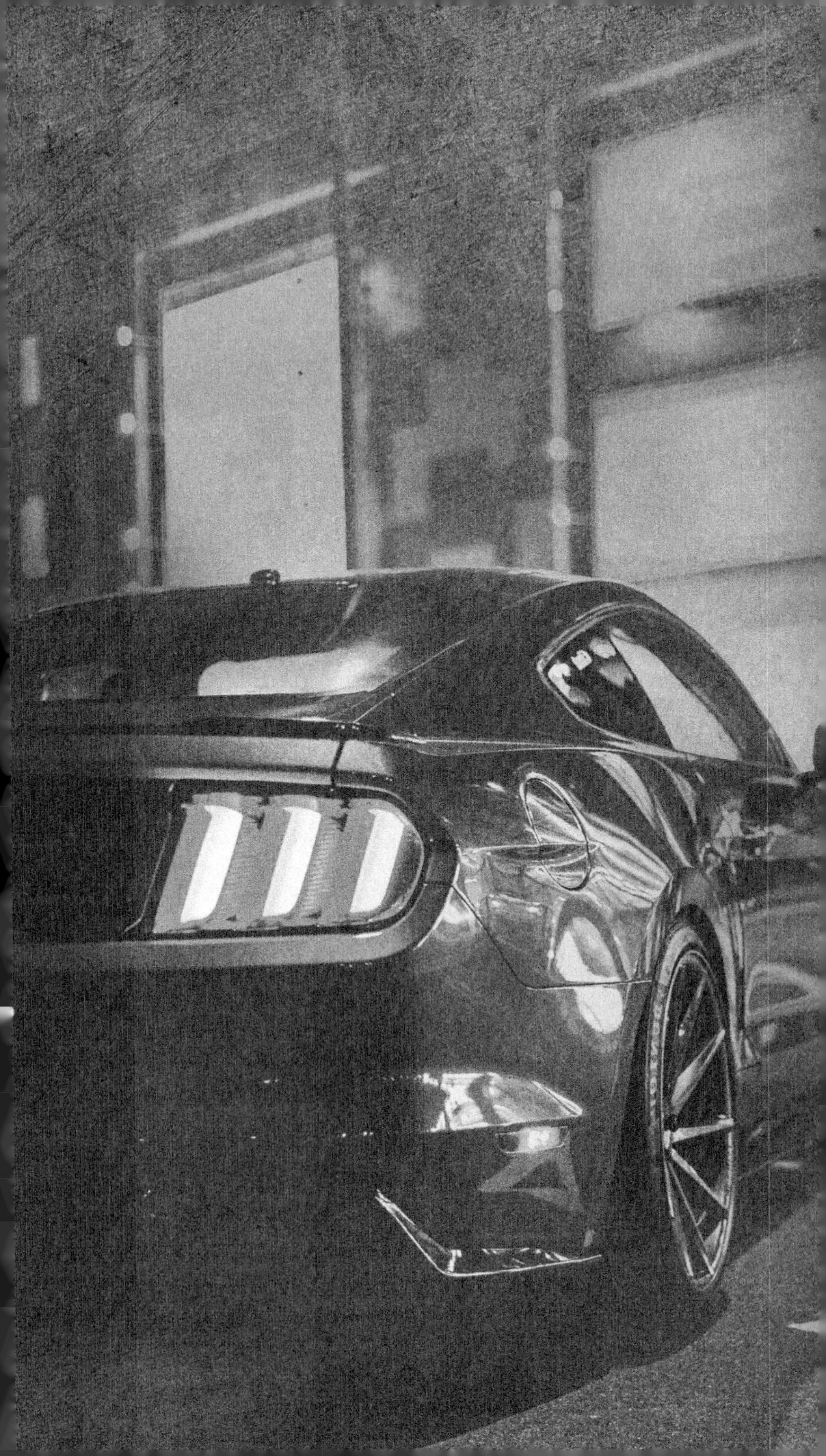

CHAPTER 13
Jules

"Jules, you can head out. Simon will stay," Lev says.

"Okay. Should I go over to Starlight? Will Dima need me?"

"Kai's there. I'm sure he has it covered."

"I never said he didn't have it covered. But he's only just started."

"He isn't technically working, Jules. Dima just wanted him to get familiar with the bar. You know this. So why don't you take your sickening pining ass over to check on him."

"Pining? I'm not pining. I'm looking out for him."

"So you keep saying, but I ain't your therapist. So fuck off and do whatever you need to do."

"Charming. See ya later."

I don't get a response, so I drive over to Starlight. I genuinely am only trying to help, I don't think it's wrong for me to keep an eye out for Kai. I promised to take care of him for Jenny, and keep him under my wing.

Parked, I walk toward the club and head inside. As I walk into the main area, all of the tables are full of happy patrons as usual. The lights are dimmed in a sultry red that casts over the stage where a jazz band plays alongside a beautiful woman who is singing vocals. Her raspy voice carries over the room, blanketing it in all things seductive with arousal intent.

Walking further into the bar, I stop short when I spot Kai at the bar, speaking to a young woman who I don't recognize. She has long, thick black hair and is wearing a backless knee length fitted dress. I can't lie, she's hot as fuck. That's until she throws her head back dramatically, laughing at something that Kai has said into her ear, very closely into her ear. I clench my fists, trying to quell the storm brewing inside me. My stomach tightens when the woman places her hand on Kai's arm, a clear sign of flirting. A tornado of pure jealousy takes over my entire being, and I would quite happily eliminate the bitch to get her sights off Kai. He should be focused on his job, not flirting and trying to get some ass while he's still on trial.

Feeling eyes on me, I turn to the side to see Seb behind the bar watching me, a deep frown mars his face as he purses his lips. He then looks over to Kai, then back to me again and a slow smile spreads across his face, which confuses me more than the judgemental look he just gave me. As I look back to Kai and notice the girl has gotten closer to him and Kai hasn't backed away, I can't hold off any longer and walk over with determined steps—target in sight. As I get closer, a hand grabs my arm, and I look to see that it's Seb. How did he get from behind the bar so fast?

"Calm down, Jules. Let him have some fun before you go all psycho on his ass."

"I don't know what you're talking about."

"You're just like the brothers. A bunch of alpha assholes. Fine, I can't stop you, but take my advice, and don't be hard on him."

"That's awful fucking advice, and I'll go as hard on him as I like."

Seb laughs and turns to leave.

"Like I said, possessive asshole, but who am I to judge?"

Exactly. I mean, Dima kidnapped Seb for fucks sake, so I would love to know what he considers going easy on someone.

With each step closer to Kai, my anger increases as the girl starts whispering into his ear. That's it.

"What are you doing?"

My question stops the conversation between the budding fucking lovebirds. The girl looks at me, confused, and Kai just stands there gawking like he has witnessed the devil spawn from the ground. Damn fucking right I have. Yes I know, I have no right to be a dick, I don't own him, and he doesn't answer to me. But tell my mind and body that. This is all kinds of fucked up, but if he doesn't walk away from this girl right now, I will physically remove him myself.

"What do you mean? I'm just talking. Jules, this is Chloe, Chloe, this is Jules, a work colleague."

"A what, now?" I say.

"Err, should I leave?" Chloe says.

"Yes. You're not needed here. Leave before I escort you out myself."

"Jules! Stop it. What's gotten into you?"

"You should be working, not trying to get your dick wet, Kai," I say, and I'm aware I'm lying. I don't want him near anyone.

"Dima said it was fine to have a drink with Seb at the bar. I'm not doing anything wrong."

"Well Seb is on the other side of the bar, and she isn't him," I say, pointing to Chloe who we both now notice has left. Kai turns to me, and his beautiful face morphs into rage. It gets my blood flowing and my dick interested. Annoyed Kai does things to me, and I'm already one hundred percent addicted. I want to see what other reactions I can get out of him.

"You're a controlling asshole, Jules. Why do you keep thinking the worst of me?"

"I don't see any bad in you, Kai. That's why I'm pushing you."

"No, you're being a cunt, and I would love to punch you in the face right now."

Now we're talking. Foreplay of the best kind. I move closer to Kai, barely an inch between us and I grab his throat with my hand, enjoying the soft skin of his neck. Our chests push together as I pull him close and I fucking love it.

"Give it a try, sweetheart. But I warn you, I will have you pinned on your back in seconds, begging for me to let you go," I say. My voice has turned all caveman and growly, a voice that only Kai can get from me. He seems to have a hidden lock when it comes to my reaction to him as I've never felt like this about someone before. Feral. Hungry. Nasty and so damn horny.

Kai lifts both hands to try and remove my tight hold on him, but I don't want to let go. His eyes darken, his pouty mouth panting against the strain on his throat, his words come out stubborn and raspy.

"I'd love to see you try. You underestimate me."

"I always love an underdog," I say as I squeeze him even tighter. His eyes close, and his cheeks pinken.

"Okay, can you guys leave now? I don't want you fighting or fucking in the bar," Seb says from beside us, removing us from the bubble that surrounds us. Shit, this is getting out of control.

"I second that. Get back to the house," Dima says, who has appeared from thin air. Or maybe I was too taken up with Kai to notice him arrive.

"Don't you need me to stay back?"

"If you two hadn't been in a weird standoff, you'd have noticed Simon arrived. Now get out," Dima orders. Kai quickly composes himself and walks off toward the exit as I follow closely behind him. He gets into my car and doesn't speak.

"Kai..."

"Don't. Can we just get back, please? You're fucking with my head."

"I'm not trying to fuck with your head. I'm trying to guide you, to remove any distractions,"

"I'm allowed to have fun. I wasn't doing anything wrong,"

"Kai I swear to god, stop pushing me. You shouldn't be flirting with anyone, and that's final."

"Are you my fucking dad? You can't tell me who I can flirt with, Jules. You're not the boss of me!"

"Yes, I fucking am. You'll do as you're told, Kai, or so help me you'll regret testing me."

"You wouldn't dare touch me."

I grab his hair at his nape and tug on it hard until he shouts out.

"I wouldn't be so fucking sure about that, Kai. Now, be a good boy and be quiet."

I'm so aroused right now, it's not even pleasant. I want to rut into him and show him who's boss. His attitude will be my undoing, and I've no idea what lengths I'd go to, to keep him in line. Kai slowly nods his head in agreement, so I let go and start the engine.

We drive in silence, walk into the house without a word, and part ways to our own rooms where we don't speak or see each other for the rest of the night. I have to draw a line with this unspoken connection that's building like wildfire between us. Too much chemistry. I'll just stick to being his family, guiding him through life here and hope we can get past it.

But I want him.

But you can't have him.

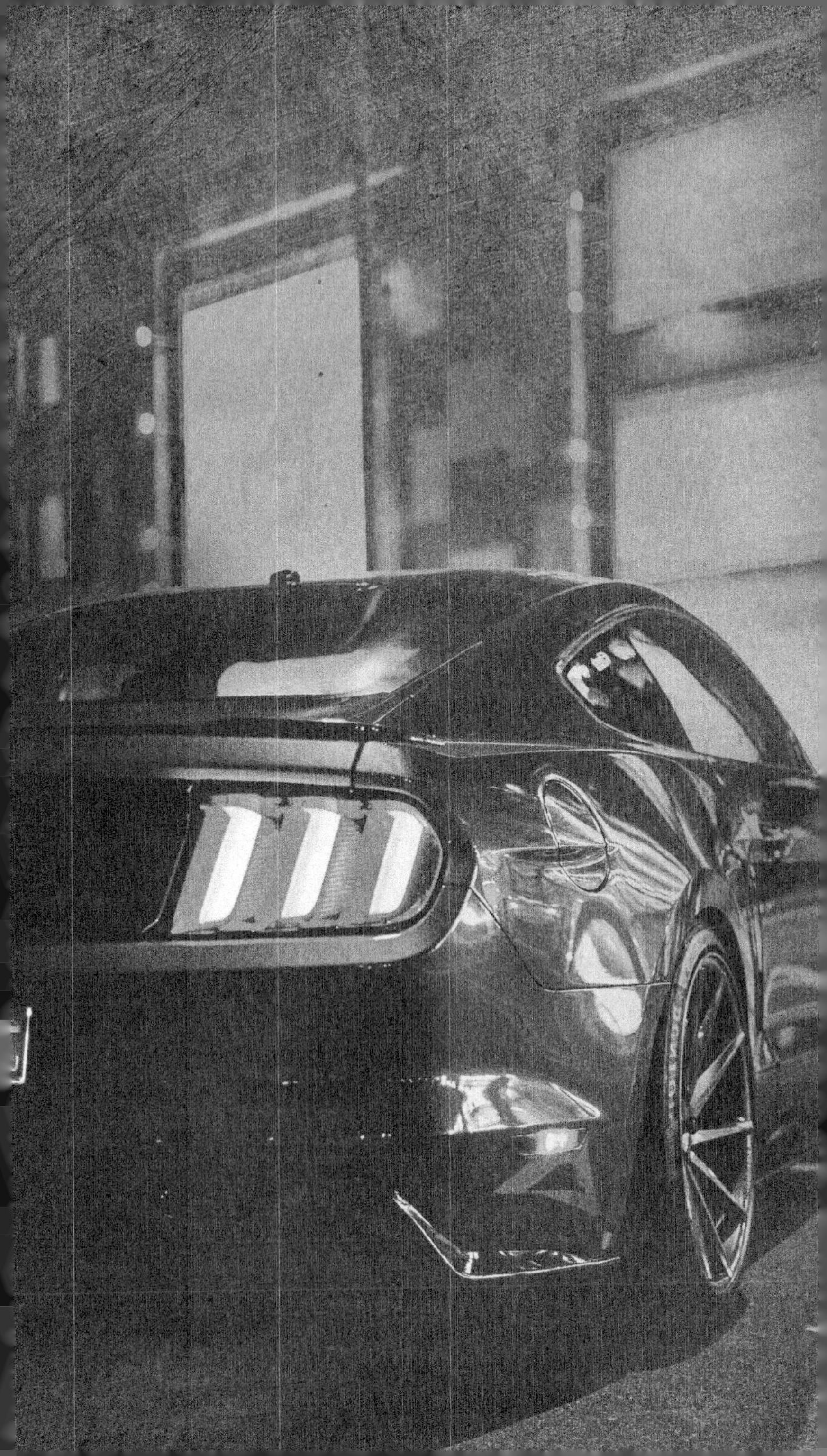

CHAPTER 14
Jules

A month flies by, and I swear I've aged another twenty years. On the positive side, Kai is doing well, he has adapted fast and spends most of his time on jobs with Simon or at Desire. The negative is that the line is slowly becoming blurred between us. I've caught him watching me on more than a few occasions, which I can hardly berate him for as I've been focused on him just as much. I can't help it. My eyes just find him in any room, and I'm transfixed. I should feel revulsion. He's my step-sister's son, but being cocooned here within the Kozlov family, everything outside of it doesn't seem to matter. All these feelings and emotions and the need to claim him have overridden the fact that he's a guy and is Kai. I always thought I was straight. Maybe being straight for me is subjective. I'm not gonna freak out about it as I'm surrounded by gay men; it's just a little surprising because it's an attraction I've never felt before. But it's more than surface-level attraction. There's no denying Kai *is* gorgeous. But his combination of bratty and sweet nature nearly brings me to my knees. I would love nothing more than to spar with him and then rock him to sleep with my cock in his mouth. That's just a dream. Kai is the most off-limits person to exist as a potential lover, and I need to get my body's reaction to him to fall in line with the rational thoughts in my head.

That's the drama in my personal life, but what's aged me is the fucking mess we have going on in one of our crews, which has resulted in one of them becoming Lev's fuck buddy? Partner? Who the hell knows at this point. We know Lev is fucking Aaron, who, by the way, is the most bizarre person I've ever met. But his brother, Jake, who heads up the crew in question, is planning to try and ruin Lev and Dima's business and take over. We know they were working with some of Carlos's men without Carlos's knowledge, and we're now biding our time to swoop in and take Jake down. The fucker has a perverted obsession with Aaron, and his downfall will be a welcome result.

Standing in the kitchen of the main house, I pour myself a coffee as I wait for Dima and Lev. This is the new norm since both of them have partners that have taken up their lives, me waiting around like a chump. You'd think now that Dima is married to Seb, and Lev is having regular sex with Aaron, that they would be nicer. They're not. They're worse. More impatient, more fucking crazy. The only thing that's changed is that they take their sweet ass time in the mornings.

"Hey Jules," Aaron says as he walks further into the kitchen, heading over to the coffee machine. His black hair is all disheveled, and with his black ripped jeans and tee, he looks like he just rolled out of bed.

"Hey."

Aaron turns to look at me with a large smile on his face that I still can't tell if it's real or not. It looks more demented. I can see why he and Lev fit so well together. I've warned Aaron multiple times about what he's letting himself in for with Lev, but the more I get to know him, the more convinced I am that it's Lev who needs warning off Aaron.

"Where's Kai?" he asks.

"He's gone with Simon to see Carlos. Why?"

"No reason. Just wanted to say sorry to him for last night."

"What happened last night?" I ask, my voice tightening as scenario after scenario races through my head of why he'd need to apologize. I just know that whatever Aaron is about to tell me, I won't like it. The fucker's big brown eyes shine with fake innocence, aware that what he says will piss me off. Aaron may be off living in cuckoo land half the time, but he knows how to push everyone's buttons.

"I came onto him to make Lev jealous. Didn't he tell you?"

"You did *what*?"

"I mean, he's sexy as fuck, but nobody can beat Lev."

"That was stupid, Aaron. Lev could've hurt him."

Aaron rolls his eyes and rinses his mug in the sink just as Lev enters the kitchen.

"Don't be dramatic, he hurt my ass instead," Aaron says, laughing, before stopping abruptly when he turns to see Lev standing there watching him, with a less-than-amused expression. It's an expression I've seen over the years that he normally wears before he fucks someone up, but I get the impression this is meant more as a warning, or foreplay.

"That was nothing compared to what I'll do if I see you flirting with him again, doe," Lev warns before walking up to Aaron and grabbing his neck, stealing a brutal kiss that looks borderline painful. It's the only way to shut Aaron up, apparently.

I continue to stand here like a fucking ornament as I wait for the horny duo to finish. I don't mind them kissing, but I mind the intrusive thoughts of what it would be like to have Kai's lips attached to my own.

"Jules, let's go. We can drop Aaron off on the way to the club."

I nod and walk ahead of them to Lev's car, getting in to wait for them to follow. As I wait, I send a quick text to Kai.

> Why didn't you tell me Aaron came on to you last night?

The reply is almost immediate.

Kai

> Because it wasn't a big deal. It was only to make Lev jealous. No harm done.

> That's not the point. He could've put you in Lev's firing line.

Kai

> You need to chill. Nothing bad happened.

> Don't tell me to chill, Kai. This is serious.

Kai

> Whatever.

Whatever?! What the fuck kind of response is that? I'm fired up now. Texting 'whatever' is a written eye-roll intended to annoy its recipient to explosive levels. Mission accomplished. I swear I will give him a lesson in taming his belligerent ways. Kai has become more snarky with me over the past few weeks. How I can enjoy that trait and hate it just as much is beyond my understanding.

As Lev and Aaron get into the car, I drive on autopilot, all sounds drifting off into the distance while my thoughts are firmly filtering all things Kai, no different from every other day that has passed since I brought him here. As I look in the rearview mirror and watch Aaron in the backseat, I notice how good-looking he is when he's not grinning like the Joker. Christ. What if Kai wanted Aaron? What if Lev had hurt him? How the fuck would I explain all this to Jenny?

I try to convince myself that I'm more concerned about Lev hurting Kai than being jealous that Kai would actually want Aaron. It's so stupid. Kai is an adult, and he can fuck who he wants. I know that. But just the vision in my head of that happening with anyone makes me want to smash the window screen with my fists. Screw it, I won't allow him to fuck anyone.

He's not yours, Jules. He's family. But not in blood. Shut the fuck up, Jules.

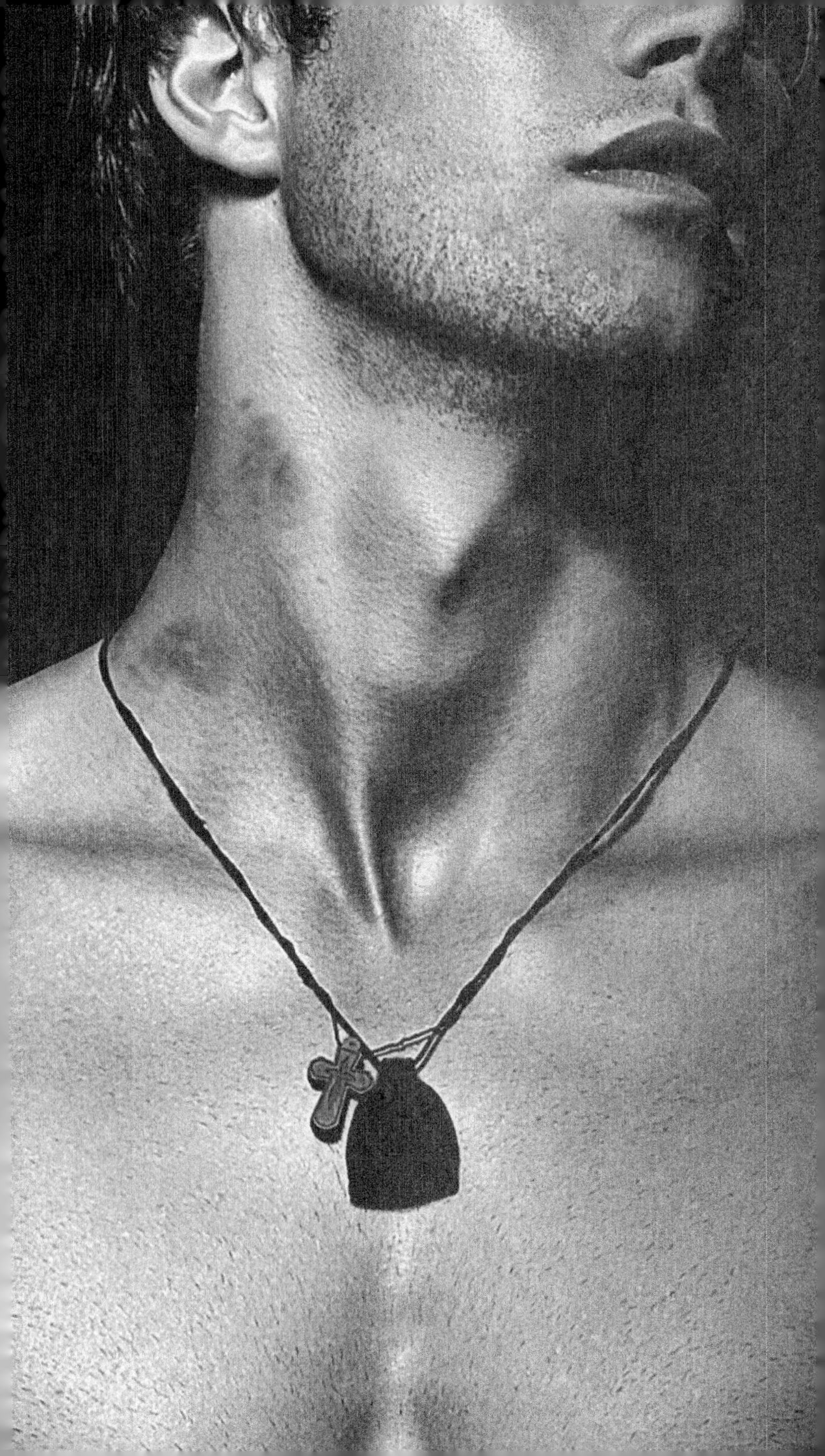

CHAPTER 15
KAI

Jules is becoming suffocating, and not in a good way. I'd prefer to be suffocated by him with his weight on top of me as he fucks me senseless. Unfortunately, this suffocation is like having an overbearing parent. Why can't he see me as an adult? I've been here for weeks now, I've followed the rules, the brothers are giving me more responsibility, and I don't question anything, and still, he gives me shit like those text messages. I would think he was jealous if it wasn't for the patronizing undertone that I could've put myself in harm's way. I can handle myself. I'm tired of him micromanaging me like he doesn't trust me. I was beyond relieved to find out I was working with Si today, as I needed the space before I let out all my frustrations onto Jules. How can someone who drives you completely mad be the one person you want so badly?

"Can you stop bouncing your knee like that? It's annoying as fuck," Simon says from the seat next to me. I immediately stop the movement, unaware I was doing it in the first place. It's Jules's fault.

"Sorry," I mutter, and I have to physically restrain myself from starting to bounce my leg again. This place is depressing. We're sitting in a small office at the docks, waiting for Carlos to arrive to make payment, and I have to say I'm disappointed. Carlos is so suave that I expected meetings like this would be in a mansion adorned with chandeliers and the finest furniture. I suppose that's what you get when you compare this life to a movie. Not as glamorous as you'd think.

"The fucker is late," Si says as he checks his phone.

"Is he always late?"

"No, only when it's me. I swear the dick does it to piss me off."

"Of course I do, it's the only highlight of my day," Carlos says, and I jump in my seat, not expecting his voice. How the hell did he creep in here so quietly? I turn to look at him over my shoulder as he gracefully glides into this shithole of an office, immediately making it look regal. He's incredibly attractive in an elegant way, with the manner he dresses in. His shirt and pants look like they have been pressed to within an inch of their life and wouldn't dare crease. He's tall and lithe with a beautiful olive tone to his skin that plays peek-a-boo through his shirt that's unbuttoned down to his pecs. He doesn't seem to notice me though, because those intense pools of brown eyes are firmly on Simon.

As Carlos takes his seat behind the desk, a guard I don't know stands behind us near the door, and my heart starts to beat a little faster at the unknown. This is the first time I've been here, and the tension is so oppressive you would think we were being buried alive.

"Let's just get this over with. We have shit to do," Simon says.

"And who is this?" Carlos asks, nudging his head toward me.

"Kai. A new guard," Si says.

"Hmm, very nice. Are you enjoying your new job, handsome?" Carlos says, and I stiffen at the sexual tone. With the way he's watching Simon, I would say it's intentional. It can't be too obvious to Simon, as he easily takes the bait.

"You keep your fucking hands off. Now, let's get down to business."

"Can we not have a polite conversation, little lion?"

"Don't fucking call me that, and no. We can't. Just sign the paperwork so we can go. The money has already been checked by your men when we got here."

"I know. Always so serious."

Carlos watches Simon like he is about to leap over the desk and run away with him, while Simon stares back at him as if he is imagining all the ways he can tear him apart. Simon hates Carlos, and Carlos wants to claim Simon. It would be pretty hot to watch if I wasn't worried that Simon was about to put a bullet in Carlos's skull. I can all but feel him shaking next to me in anger. I'm not sure how long the stare-off lasts, and I briefly wonder if I should say anything or keep my mouth fucking shut. But I opt for the latter.

Carlos slowly smiles, showing his perfect white teeth. Fuck, he really is sexy. He slowly lifts his pen from the desktop and signs the papers confirming the transaction with the Kozlovs. Carlos picks up the piece of paper and holds it out to Simon. Simon studies it, I guess weighing up the option of whether Carlos will grab him if he takes it.

"Give it to Kai. It was nice doing business with you, Mr Silva," Simon says as he stands and goes to leave.

"I love it when you call me that," Carlos says. Simon hesitates for a moment but doesn't turn to acknowledge him. He's taking the high road, and with the tightness in his shoulders, it's taking everything he has not to respond.

I take the papers from Carlos and thank him as I follow Simon out like a little dog. Shit, that was intense. As we get into Simon's car, he lets out a long breath before revving the car to life.

"That was heated in there. Is he always like that with you?" I ask as Simon drives us out of the docks.

"If you're asking if he is always a fucking dick, then yes. I hate him. Keep away from him, Kai. You can't trust him," he says.

"Okay," I say in response, but not feeling the hate toward Carlos like Simon. I think he's quite a nice guy. But then again, what would I know?

The ride back to the house is silent, but not weird. I'm up in my head about Jules, and I assume Simon is up in his head about Carlos. I need to speak to Jules about his behavior, otherwise, things are gonna turn sour fast. I want him to respect me as his equal, not as the little boy he once knew. As we pull to a stop on the driveway, everyone appears to be home, from the amount of cars that are parked, along with Seb's bike, and without a word, Simon goes into the main house and I walk back to the guard's home. It's lunchtime now and I'm starving, but I just know Jules is there waiting for me. I open the front door and take off my jacket and shoes. I hear movement in the kitchen, but I scuttle towards my bedroom and enter my bathroom where I douse my face with cold water, hoping it will realign my thoughts so I don't blurt out nonsensical bullshit while I stand my ground.

With my head held high and back straight, desperately trying to give off confidence on a kick-ass level, I walk into the kitchen, where Jules stands facing me, his back resting against the counter and a look of pure annoyance on his face. His nostrils flare as I approach and he squints at me with those ice-cold blues that make my steps falter. All the fake confidence is draining as fast as a sink of water, and I can't stop the fidgeting of my hands. But like a lightbulb going off in my head, another feeling takes over. A wave of searing anger as I remember the years of his lack of presence, the absolute audacity of this guy to think he can act like my dad, like his morals are so high that he forgets what the fuck he does here. It makes me shudder with suppressed rage, and my mouth then spews out everything that I want to say to him.

"What?" I snap.

"Excuse me?" he says, uncrossing his arms so that they relax beside his body. He stands to his full height, and his brows raise in utter shock and simmering irritation at my evolving attitude. I've always been respectful to him, and I don't think he appreciates this side of me. Well, tough shit. It's his fault that he brings it out of me with such ease.

"Well, I'm waiting for you to have another go at me. What did I do now? Did I not kiss the brothers' shoes? Did I forget to say thank you after dinner last night? Will I not get a bedtime story, *Uncle* Jules?" I say, thoroughly proud of my snark.

"Who the hell do you think you're talking to, Kai?"

"I'm not sure, my dad? My daycare teacher?"

"Reel in the sass, Kai, before I teach you some manners."

"Oooh like what? Do I get a naughty seat?"

"What the fuck is wrong with you?"

"YOU! I can't fucking breathe without you criticizing or questioning me, talking to me like a kid. I've done everything asked of me here. The guys respect me, why can't you?"

"I'm trying to protect you. Keep you in line. Like last night, you should've been on your guard more. You don't know Lev like I do."

"Oh shut the fuck up, Jules. Lev knew what Aaron was doing."

During this argument where my mouth has loosened to such epic proportions that I can no longer control what I say, I've become so relaxed with the verbal vomit flooding out of my mouth that I've actually forgotten who I'm talking to and where I am. The silence in the kitchen right now is so deafening, I have to fight not to cover my ears with my hands. I told him to shut the fuck up. Those four words have pulled a trigger on Jules's restraint as in the very next second he slams into me, pushing me into the wall, grabbing my throat with one hand, and gripping my wrist like a vice with his other. Cold blues bore into mine, the full weight of his body pressing me further into the wall, so hard that I worry for a second we might have splintered the plaster.

"The next time you speak to me like that, I will rip you apart, Kai."

The way he says those words has me fighting a groan. I've reached new heights of freakiness as this is turning me the fuck on. Jules's heavy pants hover over my own mouth, and his unblinking stare holds me captive. There is hardly any blue left with how much his pupils have dilated. I need to apologize and calm the situation, but I don't. Instead, I want to push him, because I think he wants me as much as I want him. That's what this is all about. He's jealous of what Aaron did. It makes sense now, as that's the only issue he brought up in this little dalliance of insults.

"Do it, you fucker," I say, hissing it into his face, taking the challenge. His eyes widen at my response, so I take the opportunity to knee him in the groin, which has him falling back, releasing me from his hold as he curls over. I'm both terrified and thrilled at what I've just done, but I make the mistake of not moving.

Why am I not moving? Jules tilts his head up and a large vein on his forehead bulges which I've never seen before. It's so prominent, I'm concerned it may burst. The longer I stare at it, I swear it moves, waving at me, warning me to back the fuck off its owner before he unleashes hell on me.

But that just makes my pulse spike. Jules has never looked this demonic before, the air is potent with his desire to hurt me. Yet, I still don't move. Having gathered himself from the assault, he stands and composes himself.

Then my vision alters to fuzzy lines when I feel the full force of his body tackling me to the ground. Pain radiates across my shoulders from the hard impact onto the floor, but my dick has never been happier.

Yep, fucking freaky.

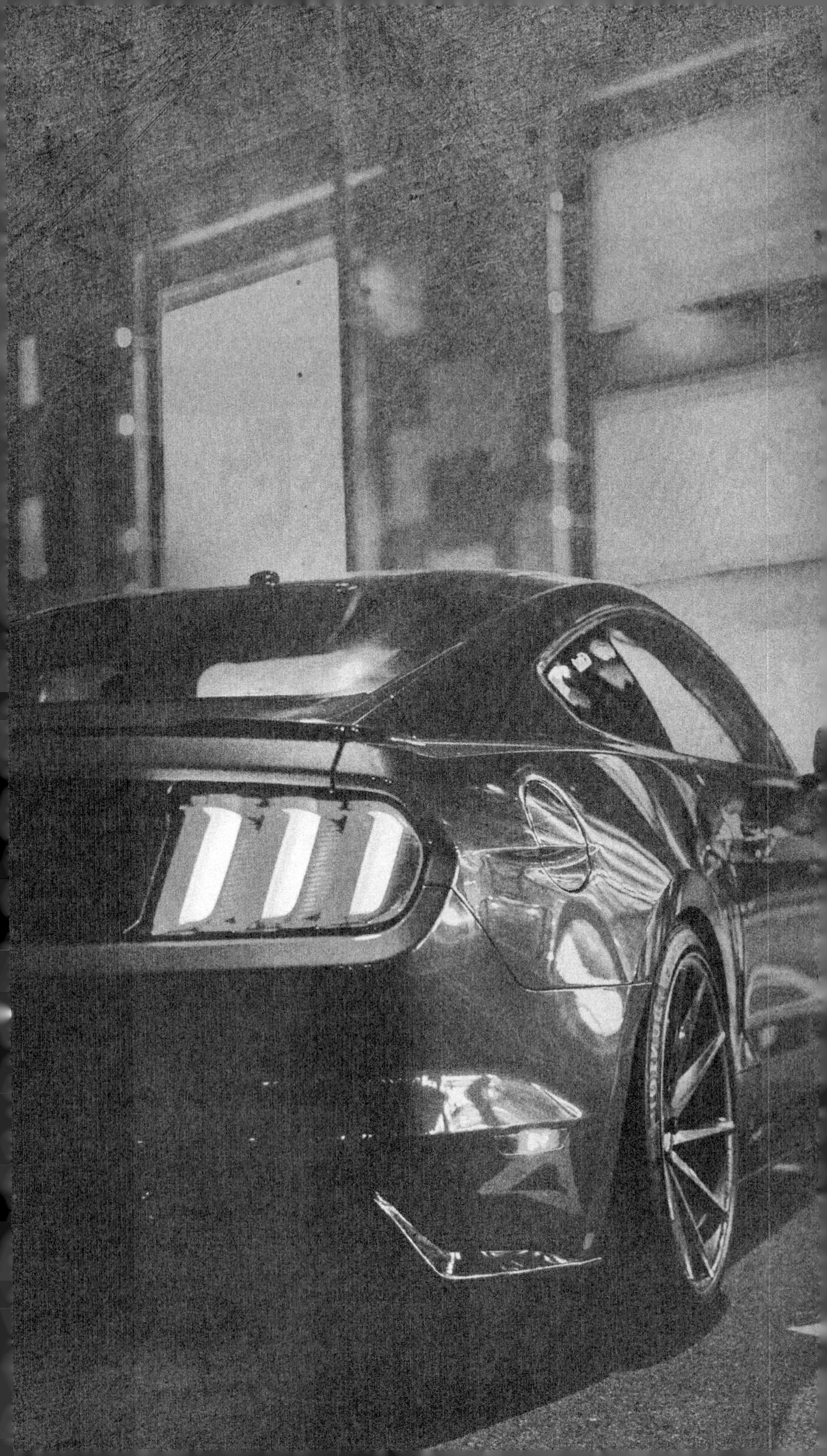

CHAPTER 16
Jules

The little shit. Nobody talks to me like that, and certainly not Kai. He's never raised his voice to me or challenged me, and it pisses me the fuck off. But it also makes my dick swell in my pants at how he stands up to me, challenging me head on. This is all new to me as I've never thought about exploring some roughness in regards to sex. But with Kai, I want to equally wrestle him and dine out on that beautiful body of his until he purrs in my ear for more. Kai is such a paradox. His feisty attitude mixed with a soft innocence. Even with what he has done in the past, and what he has to do here, it fails to taint him. In my eyes, at least. This is all so dangerous. Another side to me has awoken, and I can't seem to shut that part of myself down. A need to have him. To care for him and protect him. The yearning to actually have another person in my life. The more I think about it, the more appealing it sounds to have him rely on me. Although, the picture we make right now as we wrestle on the ground hardly evokes a perception of romance.

"Get off me, Jules."

I rest my forearm across his upper chest and straddle his thighs. Kai is completely at my mercy, unable to remove himself from my grip.

"Should've thought of that when you started spouting shit to me."

"I meant every word. You're nothing but a jealous pussy."

"Is that right?"

"Don't play me a fool, *Uncle*. You want me, and it pisses you off that someone else may want me too."

"You need to shut the hell up."

"Why? You want it. The hard dick in your pants tells me all I need to know. So why don't you be the big bad man and take it?"

"You're family, Kai. I can't take anything, even if I wanted to."

"Stop with that. You aren't my uncle, by blood or otherwise. You've been gone so long you're more like an old family friend. Now take it. I want you to take it."

More and more of my resolve is slipping as Kai manages to roll his hips under me, our hard dicks rubbing together. It feels so fucking good that I don't hold back the growl from the contact. A smug smile lights up his face. The little shit is proud to have broken that last piece of resolve I had holding me together, cutting the thread that had kept me sane, keeping him at arm's length.

"You don't know what you're asking."

Kai rolls his hips again and my body automatically responds as I lean in closer to his mouth. The sweet scent of his breath plays on my lips. So fucking close. I could just do it, take what I want and then we can move on. Scratch that itch. But I know that wouldn't happen. As soon as I claimed those lips it would seal his fate. He would become mine in all ways. A bond that would never break unless death broke us apart.

"Kiss me, Jules. *Please*."

The capacity to make rational choices exits my brain, and I slam my lips to his. Those beautiful, soft, plump lips that open so eagerly for me to enter with my tongue. I can't hold back. I ravish that mouth with everything I have, my tongue exploring his with a determination to lap up every flavor he can give over to me. His little mewls and moans have a direct link to my groin as it grinds into his, creating the perfect friction. Our mouths open wider, convinced we can swallow each other up—drink all that frustration, attraction, and all the wrongs of what this means—with each deep caress of our mouths. This is pure fucking heaven. I don't want to leave or remove my body from his for a second. On one hand, this is a colossal mistake, but on the other, it makes everything inside me click into place, that this is right, meant to be.

A throat clears in the open living area, which has the desired effect of ending the moment. I watch Kai, his lips are wet and pink from the intensity of the kiss, his breathing is erratic, and with those glossy eyes staring into mine, I'm unsure if he heard the disruption.

I sit up and remove myself from the straddling position I had over Kai, and sit my ass on the ground as I look up at Simon, who has the biggest fucking grin on his face, a rare sight, as Simon is as serious as you can get.

"Well, well, well. Did I interrupt family time?"

"Shut the fuck up Si, you're not funny."

"I guess this explains your brooding over the past few weeks," Simon says, looking directly at me. I stand and Kai follows, but remains behind me.

"I haven't been brooding."

"If you say so. But don't worry, your secret's safe with me. I don't care who you fuck."

"I'm not worried."

Simon looks over my shoulder toward Kai, then back to me.

"Just make sure it doesn't interfere with our work."

"Fine. Can you fuck off now?" I say, wanting Simon to leave so I can talk to Kai.

"I will, but you're coming with me, Dima wants us to collect payments from the crews. Lev wants Kai covering the house."

"On his own?" I ask, incredulous at the suggestion. It's too soon for Kai to be taking on such responsibility. In my opinion.

"I think Kai can handle himself, Jules. Besides, it's not your choice," Simon says, and I want to punch him.

"It's okay, Si. Jules thinks I should be in a nursery or going on playdates with other kids," Kai chirps up behind me, sarcasm in full effect.

"Watch it," I say in warning. He just rolls his eyes at me and storms past me, heading for the door, while Simon continues to watch like this is some kind of amusing TV show.

"Where are you going?" I ask.

"Unless you're deaf, *Uncle Jules*, you should know that I'm going to do my job and what my boss has requested me to do. You know, like most responsible working adults," Kai sasses at me and slams the door behind him, leaving me in a limbo of wanting to slap his ass raw or swaddle him up to keep him with me at all times.

"You got your hands full there," Simon says, chuckling. I think he's too smug right now, so I decide to get a jab in and humble the bastard.

"Could be worse, I imagine Carlos is more than a handful."

The look Si shoots me is full of warning that I may be grappling him on the floor next. Everyone has that button to press that sends them into a crazed spiral, Simon's is the mysterious Carlos.

"Don't mention him again unless you want a broken jaw. Your point is noted."

"Fine by me, but the warning goes both ways. Stay out of mine and Kai's business."

"Yeah, yeah. Come on, we got work to do."

Shelving my conversation I need to have with Kai for later, I zone in on the task at hand with Simon and leave everything else behind as we drive off.

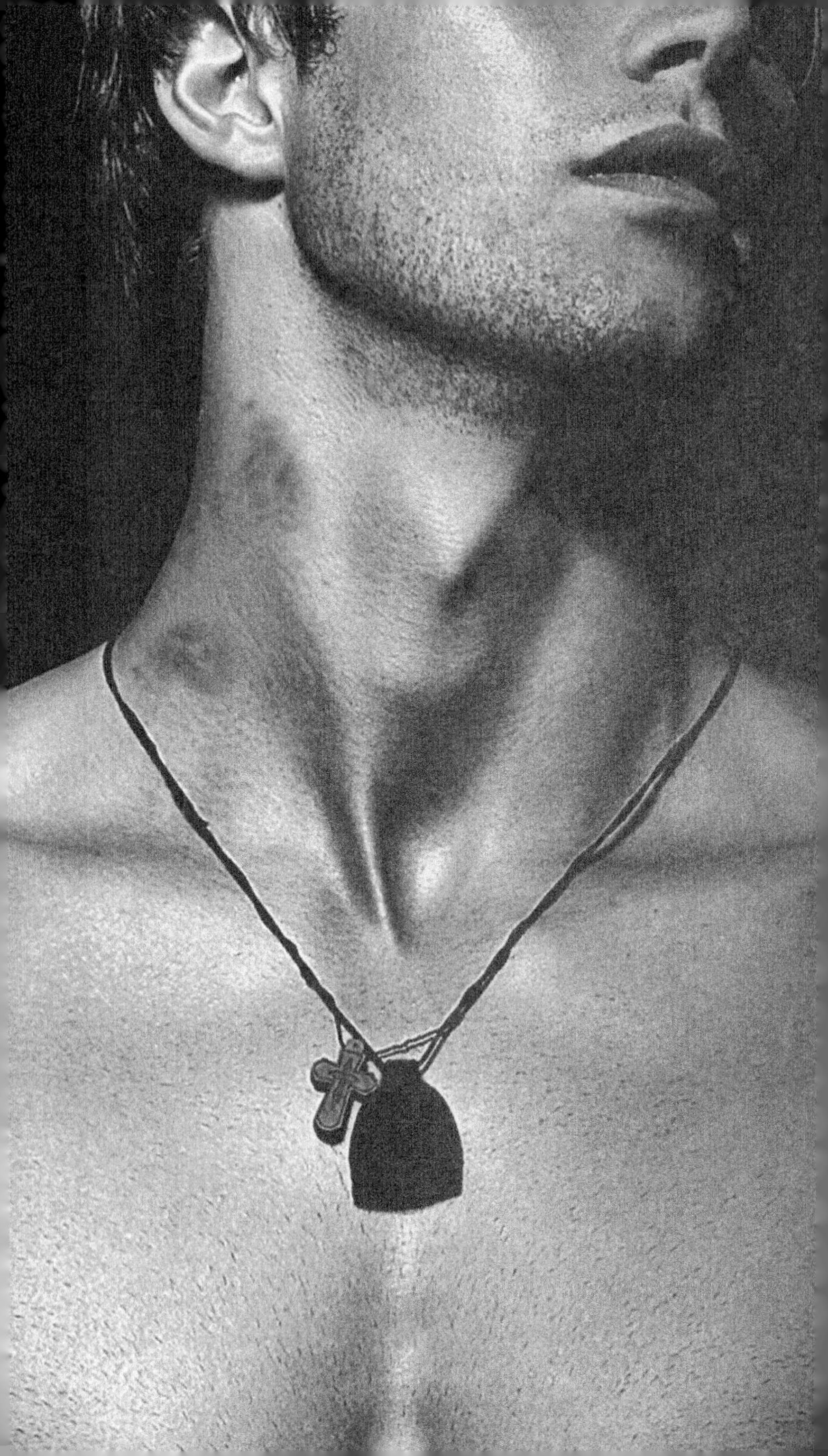

CHAPTER 17
KAI

The quiet in this big ass mansion is driving me insane. Pacing around the entrance hall in the main house leaves me with nothing to do but repeat my encounter with Jules over and over in my head. Trying to dissect every word and act, and piece it back together like a puzzle, hoping it will make sense. But nothing. All my thoughts are frantic, in a thrilling way, but also with a hint of fear. Fear that we have taken it too far with that kiss, and what the fuck it would mean for my mom if this went further and she found out. But the swelling ache in my chest blocks it all out when my mind drifts to those lips on mine, the claiming intention behind it. It makes me live in hope, a dangerous hope, as I'm already putting too much weight into that moment. That Jules will be my shield in life, my protector. That he is some kind of superhero that will make everything else in my life right, while I stand in the background basking in his love and attention. Love. That's another thing that should have me halting the breaks on this car crash waiting to happen. I've wanted Jules since I was a teenager. Over those years I really thought that it was love, even though his contact with us was rare, it made me feel things I'd never felt before. But I was an inexperienced teengager with a crush. It couldn't have been love. But now, after spending all this time with him, it's morphed into more. This searing blade that cuts deep into my soul whenever he is around me is another level of love that will destroy me. I know it will, because how could this ever possibly work? Internally, I shake my head at myself over the whirling thoughts that won't quit, as to why am I even contemplating any of this. I don't even know if Jules regrets that kiss, or if he just did it to shut me up.

I rest my head against the wall and zone out, focusing on the chandelier that sparkles like diamonds hanging from the ceiling. I encourage the swirls of light to take me into a trance to clear my mind into some kind of zen state, so I can just rest my overworked, Jules obsessed brain. I'm not sure how long I stand there before I hear quickened footsteps from down the hall where Dima's office is. As I turn my head, I can't help but smile when I see Aaron come into view. He's a freaky fuck, but I like him.

"Hey Kai, can you take me to my apartment, please? I need to collect a couple of things. Lev said it was cool."

That sounds perfect to me, because I need to get out of this house.

"Sure, let's go."

It doesn't take long to get to Aaron's apartment where I pull up to a stop on the street outside of the complex.

"Don't be long, Aaron. I don't want Lev pissed at me."

"Kai, don't say shit like that to me. Getting Lev pissed at you is more of an incentive as it would be hot as fuck to watch him get all angry," Aaron says, leaning his head back onto the headrest, his eyes closed and a demonic grin on his face. This is fucking awkward, as the guy has zero social awareness and boundaries, but I'm not about to get myself fucked up in the pen, even if it does make Aaron happy.

"Go get your shit, Aaron."

"Okay, okay. Just kidding. I won't be long."

Aaron gets out and slams the car door shut. I run my hands over the steering wheel, admiring the gorgeous interior. It's a dream to be driving an expensive sports car like this, and Dima said I had access if needed. It's a sweet ride. I tap my hands on the wheel to a beat that I make up in my head and immediately feel a little more relaxed. Which Jules must sense, because my phone pings with a text from the controlling dick.

Jules

> **All good?**

> Yep. I'm just out with Aaron.

I've already pressed send by the time I reread the text and realize how it sounds.

Jules

> **What do you mean, out? Does Lev know? Why aren't you at the house?**

> Chill out. Lev knows. I've brought Aaron to his place to get his things.

Jules

> **You armed? Be careful, Jake's crew are a risk.**

I'm torn between hitting my head against the window or screaming until I lose my voice. The need to be sarcastic wants to win this tug of war, but I take the high road.

> All safe. Talk later.

As soon as the message reads 'read' my phone rings, Jules's name written across the screen. I can't do this right now, so I decline the call. The guy is taking up too much of my life as it is. Plus, I know it'll piss him off to be ignored.

A chime alerts me of another text and I look down and can't help the laugh that bubbles up out of my mouth. He is so damn easy to piss off.

Jules

> Answer the phone, Kai!

> I'm working and this conversation is unprofessional. I'll talk to you back at the house.

This is such a mic drop moment that I want to high five myself. Thinking that somewhere nearby, Jules is losing his ever-loving shit not knowing how to deal with me. Such a gratifying moment.

Jules

> I'll show you unprofessional.

I really hope he does, because this anger flirting is turning me on so much I'm questioning if my morals require medical intervention.

My phone starts to ring again and as I look down at the screen I'm jarred to see Lev's name. I answer straight away, only to hear his booming voice on the other end.

"Where the fuck are you?" Lev says.

"What do you mean? You told me to take him home," I say, confused by this conversation.

"Yes, an hour ago. It shouldn't take this long for him to get his shit."

"Sorry, Lev. He hasn't come back down yet. Do you want me to go check?"

"What a fucking good idea. Keep me on the phone."

Shit. Sounds like I'm in trouble. Time has flown by and I hadn't even noticed. I get out of the car where I'm hit by the cold air of winter. Muttering to myself about how fucking cold it is, I head upstairs towards Aaron's apartment. I stand outside the closed apartment door and shout through.

"Aaron, you ready to go?" No answer.

Lev again shouts orders down the phone at me to just go in, which I do while yelling Aaron's name.

Checking all the rooms, I get to a bedroom and notice blood on the floor. All of my insides shrivel up at the sight.

Not only for wondering what the hell has happened to Aaron, but that it happened on my watch.

"Oh shit, Lev, there's blood on the floor in what I think is his room, it looks like his bag of stuff has been left."

Loud cursing ensues before he orders me to come back to the house. I'm dreading the response I'm going to get. Nerves overtake my entire body, nausea hits the pit of my stomach. How did I not notice that Aaron had been taken? This is all my fault. Again, a failure, letting everybody down. I deserve everything I get. Arriving back to the main house thirty minutes later, I open the door to find the brothers and Seb congregated in the entrance hall. Before I get a chance to say anything, a hard punch to the face by Lev has me collapsing backward into the wall.

"Do your job properly next time, Kai, or you won't be alive to tell the story, I don't give a shit if you're Jules's nephew. Do we understand each other?"

The burning ache in my jaw is overwhelming. I want to cry but I'm also numb. What if something bad has happened to Aaron? I'll never forgive myself.

"Sorry, Lev. I'm so sorry."

"Stay here with Seb. We found him, so we're going in," Lev says, still holding eye contact with me, letting me know that he will end me if I fuck up like this again. I'm actually shocked he hasn't already. I nod my head in acknowledgement as Dima and Lev gather up to leave, leaving Seb behind with me. As the door closes, Seb gently pats me on the shoulder, his beautiful brown eyes full of sympathy.

"He's like that with everybody, Kai."

I have nothing to say in response. Jules was right, I wasn't ready and I may never be.

"Don't worry, he'll be okay. It wasn't your fault."

"But it was my fault, if I wasn't focusing on fucking Jules, I could've done something or, I don't know, just stopped it."

"He been giving you shit?"

"Yeah, something like that."

"Come on, let's go get a drink while we wait for news."

I follow Seb into the kitchen, but his words do nothing to comfort me. If I could swap places with Aaron right now, I would. Yet again I'm the cause of somebody else's hurt and upset. Maybe I'm cursed, as I'm struggling right now to remember a time my actions caused anyone happiness or pride in who I am as a person.

This is Jules's fault. He brought me here. I never wanted to come here, but I followed, believing that he knew best. That Mom knew best.

Well, fuck them. If anything happens to Aaron tonight, it's not just his blood on my hands.

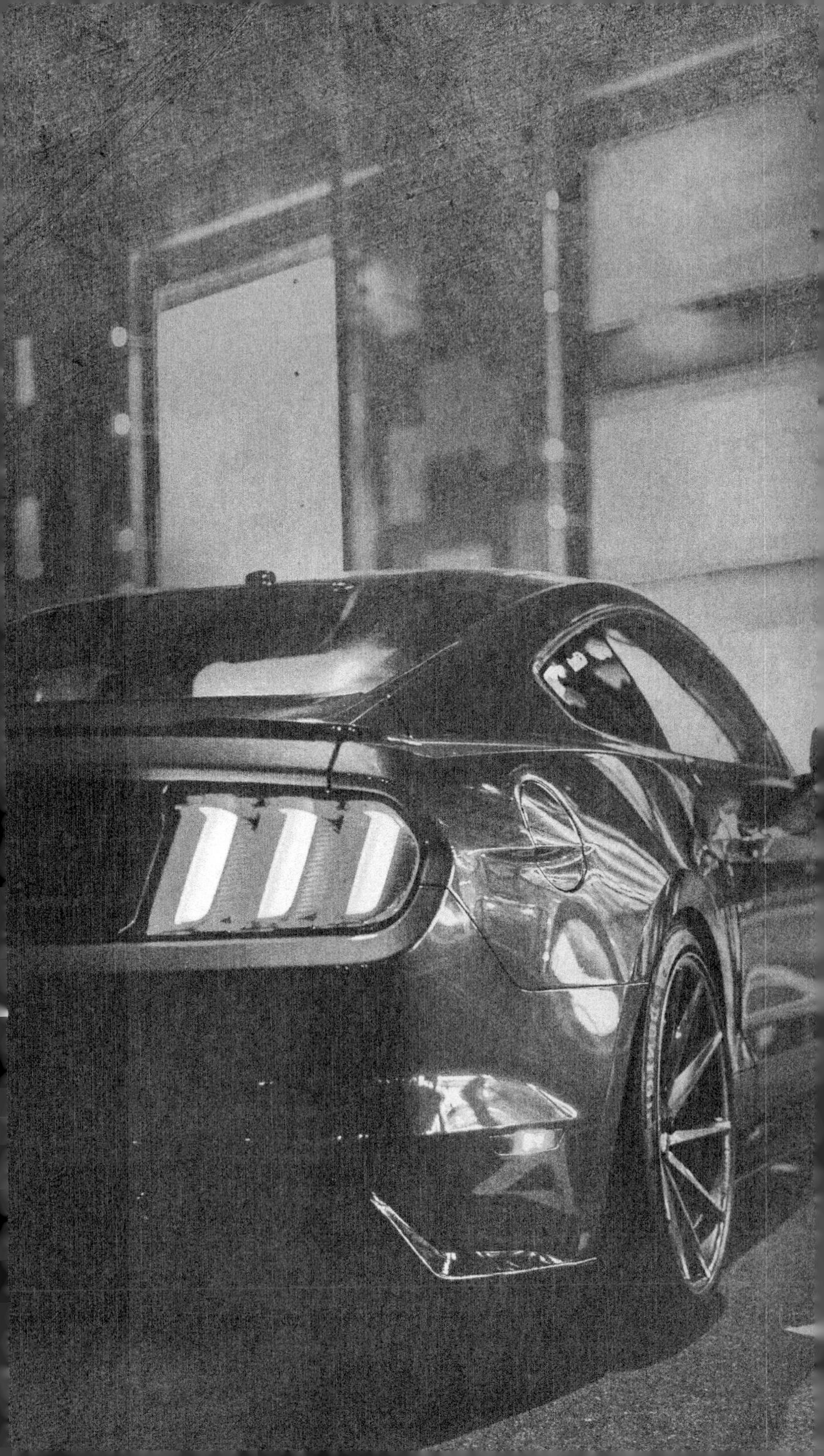

CHAPTER 18
Jules

I'm anxious to get back home to Kai. To make sure he's okay. Well, I know he's okay, otherwise I'd have been told, but I need my eyes on him. Today quickly shifted to total chaos after Aaron was taken. Luckily we got to him in time before his brother Jake did the unthinkable to him, but that doesn't diminish what Aaron has gone through. I know I call him weird, but he's a cool guy, and to see him bundled up in Lev's arms in such a vulnerable way, it made me think of Kai and how he's dealing with this, especially as he was on Aaron's watch.

Everyone is back at the house, but since Simon and I are keeping watch over Jake and his accomplice Tommy in the holding pen, I haven't had the chance to go see Kai, who I hope is sleeping. I shouldn't worry so much, I know he's made of strong stuff. But today was a lot, and I know the brothers will want him in on the action tomorrow, and I'm concerned how he'll handle it. Lev and Dima take things pretty far in most interrogations, but considering this is Aaron, I'm positive Lev will go into supreme psycho mode, because whether he wants to shout it out to the world or not, Aaron is his man. A man he'd kill the world for. Which would be romantic if it wasn't so screwed up. But who am I to talk? I'd do the same for Kai. I don't know how I got here with these enormous emotions that he stirs in me, but I can't hold back. I subconsciously claimed him the day I collected him from the police station. My inner beast decided he was ours. I sound as crazy as Lev.

"Fuck, this is boring. Why didn't they just kill the fuckers when we got back?" Simon says, leaning against the wall beside the locked door that leads down to the holding pen.

"You know why. Lev wants Aaron to decide what to do, and he wasn't in the right state of mind when they got back."

"Yeah, I know. I'm just bitching. Tired as fuck."

"Same. We can rest after it's done."

"You seen Kai?"

"No. Dima wanted me here when we got back. Seb said he went back to the house to get some sleep."

"Well, nothing like being thrown in at the deep end. I hope he ain't squeamish, because you know Lev is going to go to town with them."

"He'll be fine," I say, hoping the confidence of that declaration will be true.

Hours pass as sunlight rises. Simon and I traded off having one-hour catnaps during the night, which I'm sure has me feeling more shitty than if I'd just stayed up the entire night. My mind hasn't switched off from Kai. It's been torture having to remain here while he's only out back. I would feel better if there were cameras in the house so I could at least have eyes on him. And a tracker. It would help me relax a little. Did I mention I'm turning into a controlling and possessive asshole?

I'm mid stretching to get the kinks out of my back, when Seb comes into sight, as he walks down the corridor carrying what looks like two cups of coffee, exactly what I need right now. I nudge Simon as Seb approaches and hands the cups to us.

"Thought you boys would need this," Seb says.

"You read my mind. Thanks," I say, grabbing my cup with both hands, nearly burning my tongue with how fast I gulp down the sweet caffeine.

"You know when they're coming down?" Simon says, before gulping his own drink down.

"Yeah, Lev and Aaron are on their way with D."

"You not staying?" I ask Seb, which earns me a flat expression. I knew he wouldn't, but it's fun to rile him up.

"No thanks. I've got shit to do while you all play. Have fun," Seb says as he turns and leaves.

Half an hour later, most of us are gathered in the holding pen where Jake and Tommy are tied up, awaiting their grizzly fate. I've seen Lev at his most crazy, but it's nothing on this. With Aaron by his side, Lev is unrecognizable. The hunger for pain and blood emanating off him so strongly, I swear I can taste the metallic flavor on my tongue.

As things are about to get started, I wonder where Kai is, only for him to walk through the heavy door into the pen as if summoned by my thoughts. My eyes immediately fly to the bruise on his jaw, my body moving before I can do anything to stop it, as if tethered to him by a thread. I hold his face in my palms. Kai refuses to look at me. The meek boy ever present on the surface, flitty and unsure. I thought he didn't get hurt.

"What the fuck happened?" I ask Kai. Instead, Lev responds.

"I did it. He was supposed to watch Aaron and didn't notice he'd been taken by these pricks," he says, eyebrows raised, daring me to question him. I know it's written all over my face. *How dare he touch Kai, how much I want to punch Lev for touching what's mine.* Lev has always been able to read me like a book.

"Careful Jules, remember you recommended him, and if you have a problem with how I deal with my men, you're more than welcome to sit down between these two," he says, pointing between Jake and Tommy.

Not wanting to add any more fuel to the fire that's already at explosive levels in this room, I mutter a half assed 'sorry' before averting my attention back to Kai.

"What are you doing down here?" I say to Kai, not convinced he should be a part of this.

But you made him a part of it when you dragged him here.

"I fucking told him to come down here, now if you've both finished your daily catch up and questioning your boss, it's time to move this shit along," Lev says, and I know this isn't over.

"Kai, you get over here now," Lev orders.

"You stand here and observe, when I ask you to do something, you do it. Understand?"

"Yes, I understand," Kai says, his voice dull and monotone, so unknown to me. Have we broken him? Will Kai want to leave and never look back?

The morning drags on, blood is spilled and secrets shed. I also learned today that Aaron has a violence kink, which in a way doesn't surprise me. Lev and Aaron are in their own little world when Lev orders us all to leave so he and Aaron can deal with Jake together. Fuck knows what they're gonna do to him, but I wouldn't want to be him right now.

I stand outside the holding pen door with Kai, trying to gauge where his head is at. He still refuses to look at me.

"Kai, talk to me."

"There's nothing to say. I fucked up and Aaron nearly died."

"It was a mistake. It wasn't your fault."

"It doesn't matter what you think, Lev blames me and I blame me, too."

"Bullshit. Lev should never have given you that responsibility, it was too soon."

Finally, Kai looks at me but not in the way I crave. I want those eyes to be full of adoration and the need to be with me, not the venom that is fully aimed my way.

"Save it. I don't need the 'I told you so' speech. We all know you are right and everyone else is wrong. Perfect Jules. The fucking saint who kills and tortures."

"I never claimed to be a saint, and I certainly am not going to mother you through this. It happened and you need to stop projecting that shit onto me."

"Whatever."

Kai rolls his eyes like a grumpy teenager, forcing the controlling asshole inside me to break free. I grab him by the shirt collar and pull him close to me.

"I'm losing patience, Kai. Maybe you need to be toughened up."

"Let me guess, you'll be the one to do it?"

"I sure as shit ain't letting anyone else touch you. I think a little sparring session will sort your attitude out."

"What? You wanna spar me?"

"Yep. Tonight when things have calmed down, we're heading to the gym and you will sweat this out."

During this little chat, I fail to notice that our lips are almost touching. Kai's body is vibrating under my touch and it thrills me to the core. He loves the authority, the push and pull, and fuck do I love it too. My dick gets hard even thinking about grappling with him later.

"You gonna hurt me, Jules?" he whispers, so faintly that I nearly miss it. His eyes are heavy, his breathing deep and rapid. That delicious pink tongue pokes out to moisten his lower lip.

"Yeah. I think I am. And you'll fucking love it. The pain. The blood."

"I think you mean our pain, our blood. I won't go easy on you, either."

"You better not."

I'm so fucking tempted to take those lips with mine right now, but the moment is disturbed by a loud bang of the door behind us where Lev appears with Aaron. They look like they've taken a bath in blood. Great. Clean up will be a blast.

"You can start clean up, we're done for the day. But Jules, tomorrow we're going to talk about your little outburst earlier," Lev says, which I expected.

"I figured," I say, just as they both walk away, an air of contentment emitting off them both, which resets the previously filled tension in the house to a more peaceful state.

"You go get yourself something to eat. Me and Simon need to get started on clean up."

Without responding, Kai just nods, and I watch him slowly walk away down the hall, admiring his perfect bubble butt, hoping I get a chance to squeeze the life out of it later.

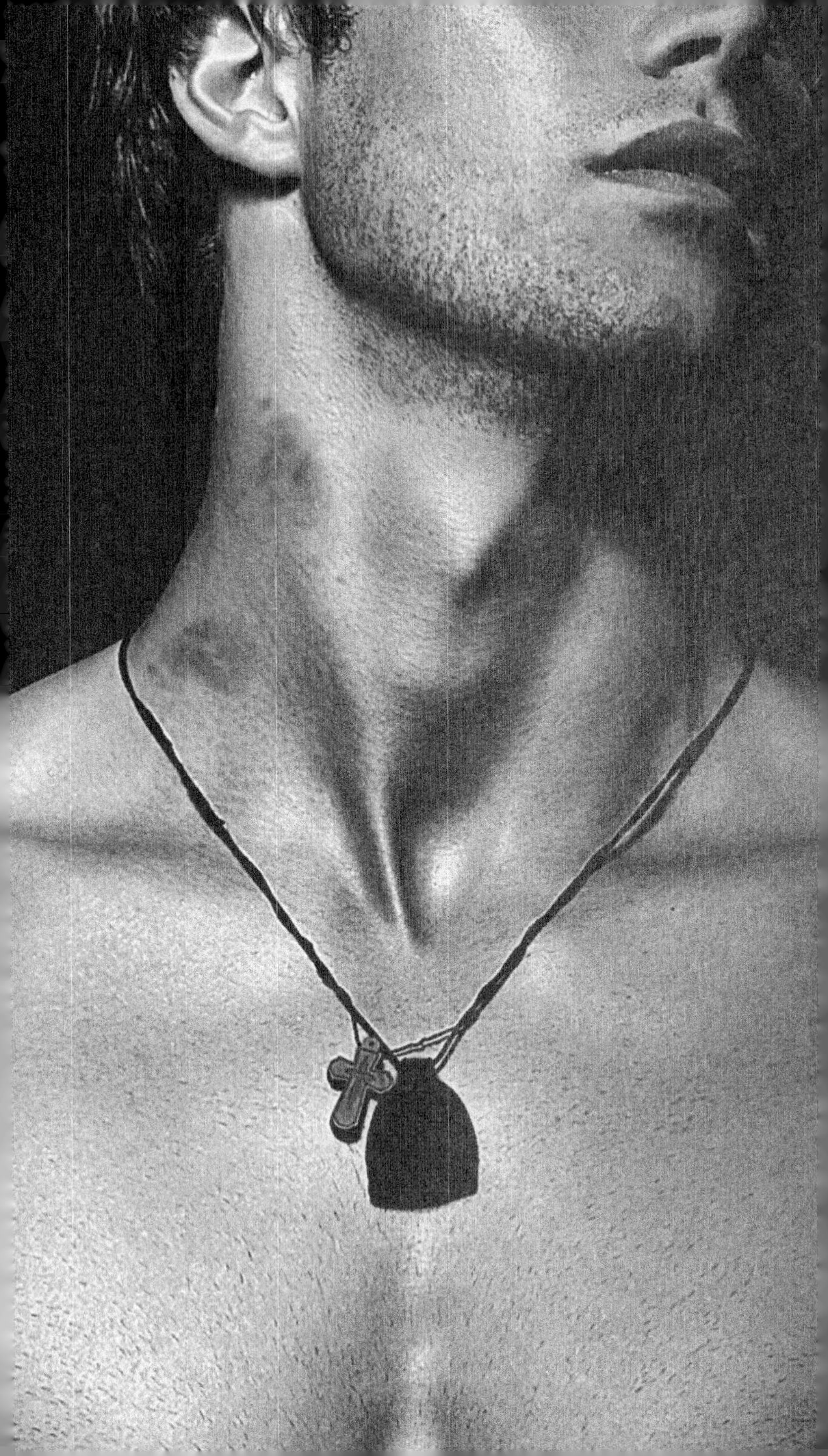

CHAPTER 19
KAI

I'm on the verge of a breakdown. The past twenty-four hours have been a whirlwind of emotions, stuck between running away where no one can find me, drowning in a never-ending sea of guilt, wondering about all the 'what ifs' had they not found Aaron in time. Being in the holding pen earlier today was not at all like I expected. I was numb. Maybe from shock, or maybe I was too afraid not to follow through, but it didn't upset me or even disgust me. The problem is that I don't know who I am anymore. Leaving home, I had hopes that my life would become clear, and I would have direction. But the opposite has happened. The years of pretending to be someone I'm not, the mask I wore in my everyday life has been shredded here, and it scares me. Do I even have a choice now? If I wanted to pack my bags and leave, would the brothers allow it? That's not even including the mindfuck that is Jules. His harshness is my undoing and yet another thing

I didn't know about myself. I like his edge, his threatening controlling manner. At least I feel something real when I'm around him. But whether that's a healthy emotion or not, I think I need to revisit that on a day where the rest of the shit in my head is sorted out.

Grabbing my gym gear, I undress out of my pants and shirt, and put on my basketball shorts and a tank top. Nerves and excitement war with each other over this little sparring session Jules has planned for me. Maybe it will help. Just as I begin to tie my laces, a knock on my door has me looking up to see Jules entering the room. Fuck me. Why didn't I think about this more? He's wearing the same clothing as me, and Christ does he look sexy. I know I'm staring. I have no idea if he's spoken or not as I can't stop fixating on that massive solid chest. Since when did Jules have tattoos? Across his pecs he has some kind of tribal pattern that pokes out from behind his tank top. I want to rip it off so I can see the full thing. Trace it with my tongue.

"Kai, did you hear me?"

I really have to try hard to force my eyes higher to his face, but I manage it.

"What?"

"I said, are you ready to go?"

"Yeah. Can't wait to kick your ass."

A deep rumble leaves Jule's throat. All dirty and full of innuendo. I would blush if I wasn't so damn eager.

"It's me that does the ass kicking. As you're about to find out."

My cock is thrilled by the idea, but I tame him best as I can since the material on these shorts hide fuck all.

"I think you're all mouth."

"And I think you're stalling. Come on."

I follow Jules out of the room as we head toward the main house. He's certainly taking my mind off all that's happened and I'm grateful for the reprieve. Even if it's just for an hour.

Lev and Dima's gym is pretty sweet. They have the standard set up with weights in one section of the open-plan area, then on the other side of the room are two punch bags that hang from the ceiling in the corner. In the center of the room, a dim glow from the lights casts a warm hue over the mats that cover the floor.

Since I've been here, I've used these facilities many times. But never when I've been in here has it felt so oppressive. And I mean so oppressive that you could take a bite out of the thick tension in the air. The fact that we're not speaking adds to that tension. Call me crazy, but things are about to change. I can feel the seismic shift between us. For days it's been building and I don't think either of us can hold back any longer. I know without a shadow of doubt, if Jules touches me, I won't be able to pull away.

Jules removes his tank top, sneakers, and socks, and stands in the middle of the mats. Obviously I have to take a moment to peruse that fucking masterpiece of a body. I don't question the lack of clothing and I remove the same things. Jules's eyes scan my chest and abs, he licks his lips like I'm a main course he wants to dine on, and fuck do I want that. Slowly I approach him until we are a foot apart. Jules's chest rises and falls with the same anticipation that is rushing through my own body. He takes a step back, his muscular frame flexing, ready to start.

"Ready?" he says, voice low, a mix of primal and arrogance.

"Bring it," I say, unable to hold back the smirk on my face.

We tussle for what feels like hours. Grabbing, pushing, grappling until one of us lands on the ground. We don't speak. We don't keep score. This unspoken conversation between us is the most erotic foreplay I've ever been part of. My limbs are sore, I'm hot all over from the exertion, sweat drips from every pore of our bodies. But I know we're reaching the peak of this fight. I like the hurt his touch gives me, the tenderness of the bruises that I know will develop by morning. I want his hands to hurt me, his inflicted pain on my body followed by the sweetest touches as he makes me fall apart. I want him to adore me. To love me. To ruin me.

"One more round?" he says, wiping his forehead with the back of his hand as he stands in an attack position. I can't put into words how excited I am.

"I'm ready to knock you on your ass."

We lunge at each other, our bodies collide with a thud. Grunting and panting. I grip Jules's shoulders, my muscles straining as I try to push him back. But it's no use, Jules is a powerhouse, and with one swift, practiced move, he twists me into a bear hug, forcing our torsos to press tightly together. I can feel the heat radiating off his body, our breaths mingling as we both struggle for dominance. The friction between our bodies is intoxicating, each movement sending a jolt of electricity through my veins. Jules's hand slips lower, fingers digging into my lower back, pulling me closer, the proximity now igniting a fire that has spread from my very core.

With a sudden burst of strength, I twist free, spinning myself behind Jules and locking my arms around his waist. I rejoice in the feel of his solid muscles of his abdomen as they contract under my hands, the scent of sweat pungent in the air, as the raw, animalistic intensity of our sparring has us both vibrating with need.

Jules bucks, trying to dislodge himself, our bodies move in a heated dance of power and resistance. He arches his back, pressing against me, creating the most unbearable but delicious pressure against my rock hard cock. Our breaths turn into gasps as the potency of the struggle escalates with each second that passes.

In a sudden rapid move, Jules spins around, our faces nearly touching, his eyes dilated with desire. My pulse races at the tantalizing closeness of his lips with mine. He clutches my hips, pulling me flush against him, sliding together in the most sensual way. I hold onto his shoulders, my fingers digging into the firm muscle as I lean in. Lips so close. The air is charged around us, every inch of my skin is tingling with anticipation of finally breaking the tension that has crackled like a live wire between us.

Then, Jules charges forward, pushing me down onto the mats, his large body pinning me in place. My breath catches in my throat as his weight settles over me, our eyes locked, communicating that this moment holds a promise of more. Something beyond just the physical.

I gently move my hands over his chest, feeling the steady thump of his heart under those solid contours of his body. The climate in the room becomes scorching, searing me like a brand, knowing I will remember this moment for the rest of my life. Jules's face comes closer to mine as my fingers tighten on his skin in a silent plea for more, for the inevitable culmination of the fire that has been building between us.

Jules's lips curve into a knowing smile, reading every thought as clear as day on my face.

"You're mine now," he murmurs, in a low timbre that sends a shiver down my spine.

With a breathless whisper, I surrender to him.

"Prove it."

In a blink of an eye, Jules claims my lips in a kiss that is as fierce as our sparring, a cocktail of all the emotions that have been simmering beneath the surface for weeks. Our bodies meld together, a tangle of limbs and sweat, both lost in the devastating sexual connection that has been ignited between us. The intensity of our kiss builds as the world around us fades away, leaving only the heat of our bodies, the sound of our breaths, and the alluring pull of our desire. Nothing else matters right now, only the undeniable, drunken passion that has overtaken us.

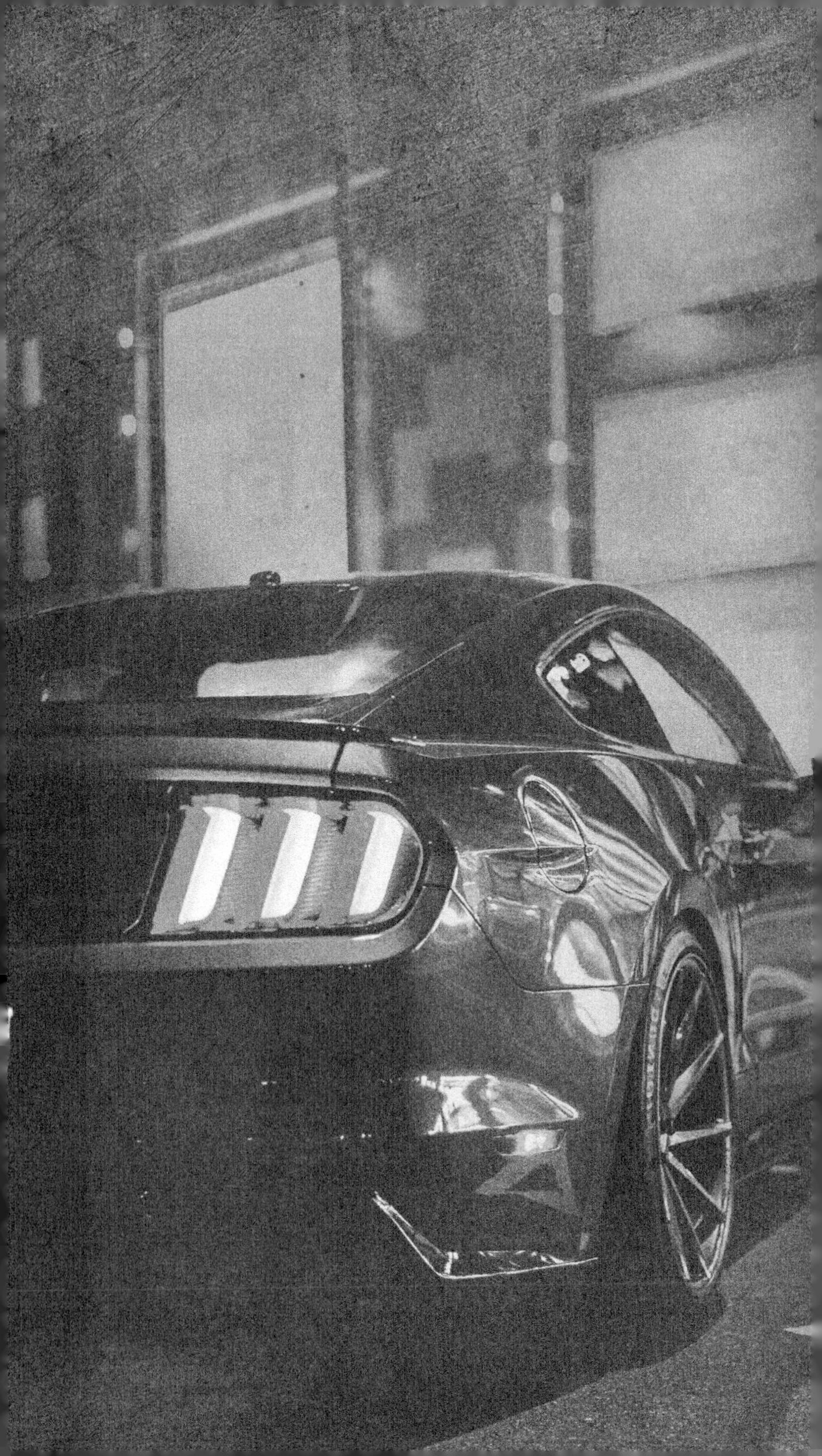

CHAPTER 20
Jules

This is where I belong, wrapped up in all things Kai. His body beneath mine has solidified his place in my soul. I want to binge on his flesh, destroy him so he feels my absence for days. Have him craving for me to return and give him what he needs. As our tongues duel in this dance of pure erotica, my insides become soothed. It doesn't matter who is against us, even Jenny. I will not allow him to be anywhere else but with me, I don't give a fuck. They'll just have to get on board that Kai is mine, or fuck off into the sunset. He is the unsolved mystery that for years I've been trying to fix, without fully knowing what it was that I needed to repair.

Kai whines as I thrust my dick against his, our sweaty torsos making this whole sensory experience push me over the edge. I slow down the kiss as I don't want to do anything more in here, I want full privacy for what I want to do to him. I suck his lower lip like a candy, reveling in its juiciness.

"Fuck, Jules."

"I know. We gotta stop, we need to go back to the house before I explode."

"Don't stop now, it's starting to get good," a voice says behind us. Aaron. But not just Aaron, Seb is standing next to him with his mouth open, looking like he's not sure whether to look away or keep watching. Aaron, on the other hand, has no shame.

"How long have you been standing there?" I ask. Kai quickly pushes me off him and jumps to his feet, his face turning red from embarrassment.

"Long enough to become invested," Aaron says, grinning while roaming his eyes over my chest.

"Lev will fuck you up, talking like that," Seb says.

"You say that like it's a bad thing. I live to get the asshole wound up. More fun for me," Aaron says.

"Seb! What the hell is going on?" Dima demands as he storms into the gym, taking in the scene in front of him. Great. Seb rolls his eyes, but just before he goes to answer, Dima gets in first.

"Were you two fucking in my gym?" Dima asks, his handsome face screws up as if this is the most offensive thing possible.

"No…no, er, Jules was just sparring with me. Training me," Kai says. His eyes pleading, worried this may get him into trouble.

"They were about to," Aaron mutters.

"And you were watching? You looking for some attention, beautiful?" Dima says to Seb, grabbing his jaw with his hand.

"No I wasn't, D. Aaron brought me in here to show me something, but failed to say what."

"Yeah 'cos I know how dick whipped you are and you wouldn't have come in if I'd have told you they were fucking."

"We weren't fucking," I say, annoyed that this is becoming a thing. Worried Kai will withdraw. All I want to do is get him to my room.

"You were foreplay sparring, getting ready to fuck. I'm not blind," Aaron says, a sulky tone lacing his words like I've intentionally ruined his fantasy. Considering what he went through yesterday, I'm happy to see him up and about.

"Shut up, Aaron. Why don't you go find my brother and bother him. You two, go fuck somewhere else. I don't give a shit what you do, but don't do it in my house, and especially not in front of my man," Dima says, pulling Seb to his side like he's worried the poor guy will run away.

"D, you're overreacting," Seb says, trying to keep a hold on his patience as he visibly grinds his teeth.

"I'll show you overreacting, don't think you're getting away with this, beautiful," Dima says and pushes Seb toward the door.

"So nobody is fucking, then?" Aaron says, whining like a child.

"Doe, if you don't get out here in the next ten seconds…" Lev's voice shouts through the open door where Dima stands smirking.

"Oh fuck yeah," Aaron says, trotting off for the psycho orgasms I'm sure Lev will give him.

I turn and look at Kai, who I'm happy to see is smiling at me. The light sheen of sweat glistening across his skin that reflects from the lights has me wanting to lick it off him.

"They're the most crazy assed couples I've ever met."

I walk over to him and hold him by the neck, stealing a quick kiss from those plump lips.

"Couldn't have said it better myself. Come on, Kai. I'm far from finished with you."

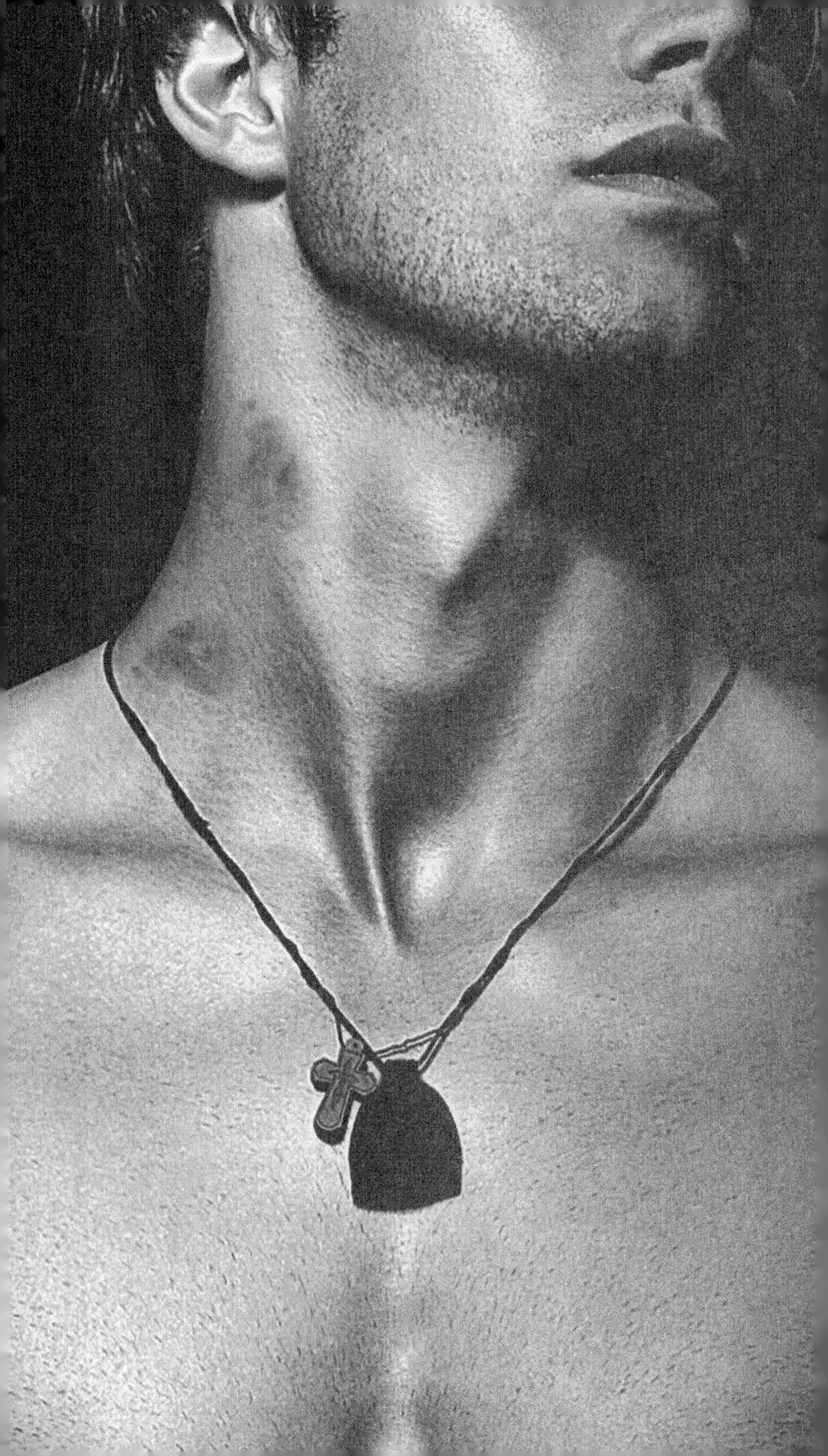

CHAPTER 21
Kai

As soon as we arrive back at our house, Jules manhandles me into his bedroom, before locking his door and throwing my overstimulated body onto his bed. When I land on the sheets, I'm completely enveloped by his scent—all masculine and sex. For a second, my mood dips when I think back to yesterday and what happened, but seeing Aaron tonight, he seemed in good spirits. However, with Aaron, you can never tell. I need to speak to him and apologize for what happened.

"Where did that mind of yours go, Kai?" Jules asks as he covers my body with his. I love the pressure of him on top of me, I want to suffocate in his presence.

"Sorry, I was just thinking I should talk to Aaron. Say sorry for what happened."

"It wasn't your fault. But I get it, if it helps you."

"Do you really want me, Jules? Because I'm scared. Scared that you'll leave me after you're done."

"Hey, I wouldn't be here if I didn't want you. You're so damn sexy, Kai. I've never had anyone affect me like you do."

"But I thought you were straight? Have you ever been with a man before?"

"No, but it's not something that bothers me. I want you, and that's all I need to know. Don't worry, I've fucked asses before, if that's what you're worried about."

"And why the hell do you assume I would be the one to bottom?"

I do love to bottom, but fuck him for assuming. He smiles at me knowingly and my ass clenches, eager to be filled.

"It's written all over that pretty face."

"Don't call me pretty. Just because I bottom doesn't make me your little bitch. It makes me your king."

Jules grabs my hands in a tight grip and forces them above my head. I could fight back, but I don't want to. I want to be roughly handled, adored, and pretty much just lay here while he does all the work.

"Wrong. I'm the fucking king, and you're my little whore who will do what I say on command."

Oh god. Why does that make my dick jerk behind my shorts? His whore. Fuck yeah, I love that idea.

"Well, what are you waiting for? I want my king to show me who's in charge."

"Your wish is my command. Oh, and by the way. I saw your test results. I'm negative too, and I'm fucking you bare."

Wait..what?

"How...did you snoop through my stuff?"

"Not snoop. You left them in my car. Must've fallen out of your pocket. Or you were giving me a come on."

"Shut up, Jules, and kiss me."

Sinking further into the mattress, I wrap my legs around his waist and grind into him, locking my arms around his neck, pulling us so close together that no space remains between us. We kiss and kiss, tongues, teeth, sucking on lips. The kiss builds until I don't know whose mouth belongs to whom. I moan at the sensation, the tingles that flutter across my skin at this passion-filled tongue fucking. Jules groans into my mouth when he thrusts his dick against mine, making me turn into jelly. I need to be naked. I need him to be naked.

"Naked," I say, panting, unable to pull away from his mouth long enough to get more than one word out.

Jules breaks the kiss and gets off the bed. I lean back onto my elbows, legs parted with my feet on the ground. He stands in between my open thighs and removes his tank top. Clutching the sheets to stop myself from touching him, I focus on every groove and dip of those hot as fuck muscles. His abs are so well defined you could make ice molds in the ridges of his eight-pack. He pushes his shorts down in a quick motion, his lack of underwear revealing the most gorgeous cock I've ever seen. It stands proud against his belly, his smooth large balls look like they're ready to burst. Apart from the small section of trimmed blond pubic hair, he is totally smooth. I'm salivating, wanting his dick in my mouth and ass. If only we could do both at the same time.

Jules leans forward and grabs the hem of my tank top, and rips it over my head. I fall back onto the bed as he stares down every inch of exposed skin on my chest. My nipples tighten, communicating on my behalf how badly they want to be sucked. Then, finally, he pushes his hands into the elastic of my shorts and glides them down in a painfully slow move that nearly tips me over the edge.

I'm going commando too, and my cock slaps against my abdomen as he removes the material. Jules licks his lips, but then his eyes stop on what he sees on my upper right thigh. Ah. I'd forgotten about the tattoo there. Wrapped around my thigh is a thorny rose vine with large black roses adorning it. I got it after I turned nineteen. I was struggling with life and needed an escape. The pain as the artist worked helped redirect my thoughts and emotions. It felt good, too good. So much so, I've avoided going back before it became an addiction.

Jules gently rubs his fingers over the rose pattern, tracing the lines with a whisper of a touch. It feels so strange to be touched like this, with care and tenderness. I swallow hard, trying to keep the river of emotions at bay. I've longed to be wanted for so long, and having it finally happen is so huge that I'm terrified to get a taste, for fear of it being taken away from me. I continue to watch Jules stare at my tattoo, he is so captivated by it that I think he may have forgotten what we were about to do.

"Do you like it?"

"I fucking love it. So sexy. Fuck Kai, you're gorgeous. All this smooth skin, those ripe brown nipples, your muscular chest, and these long, toned legs. I want my mouth on every inch of you. Gonna eat you up until you can't take anymore. Gonna show my pretty whore who he belongs to."

"Fuck, yes, please Jules, please," I beg, on the verge of whimpering into an uncontrollable sob.

"Turn over and lay flat on your stomach, I wanna see the ass that now belongs to me."

I flop over onto my belly. The sheet rubbing against my cock has me thrusting into the bed. Jules groans behind me. His large hands land on each ass cheek, he squeezes them so tightly I nearly go numb. Then he spreads my ass, and the cold air from the room makes my hole clench. I'm a mumbling mess now, at the sensation. Being on display for Jules like this has me floating away into another dimension. I could come from his attention alone.

"A perfect little bud. Who does this hole belong to now?"

"You."

"You're damn right it does. I'm the only cock it will ever know from now on. And you'll let me have it when I want, whenever I want it, won't you, my pretty whore?"

"Fucking hell Jules, you can live in my ass. Now please, fuck me."

"So feisty and so needy. I want a taste first, sample the goods," he says, his voice set in a deep baritone that makes me shudder. That voice belongs on the smuttiest audiobook out there. Something wet swipes over my hole, and I realize it's his tongue. Holy shit, he's rimming me. I've never had this done to me before, and it's now my new favorite thing.

"Ahhh fuck, that feels so good, don't stop."

And he doesn't. Before long, I start pushing back on that thick tongue, bouncing on it until it slips inside me. Jules slurps and sucks around the edges before plunging his tongue inside me over and over until I'm a sweaty, writhing mess. I want to come.

"Jules, I'm close, fuck, you need to stop," I say, moaning face-first into the bed, trying to control my body from exploding.

Jules, thank god, lets my ass go and harshly slaps my right ass cheek, causing me to yelp in surprise.

"Turn over, Kai."

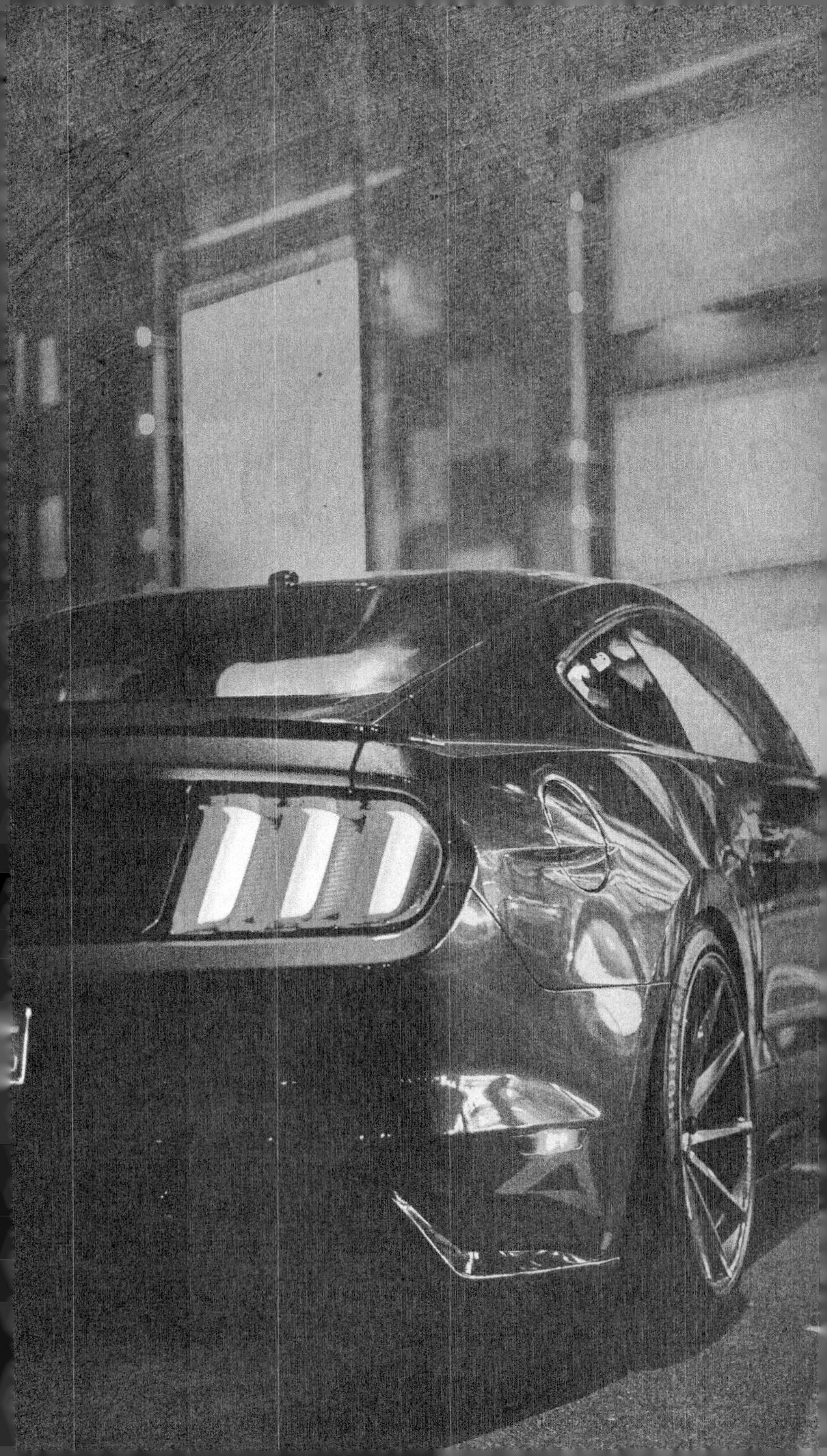

CHAPTER 22
Jules

My dick is so hard I'm scared that it'll snap in two when I enter his hot body. I have never, and I mean *never*, been this aroused and attracted to anyone else in my life. I didn't think in a million years a man would be the one to shred my soul to pieces, let alone Kai. Laying on his back naked, he's a masterpiece. That tattoo was a pleasant treat for the eyes, and I didn't think he could look any more perfect. I guarantee anytime I see that beautiful piece of art, I will be bending him over the nearest surface. Who knew tattoos could be an aphrodisiac? And don't even get me started on that juicy bubble butt of his.

My eyes scan him from head to toe, and I don't know where to start on this gluttonous feast that's spread out in front of me. Looking at his slightly flushed face and the cute little pants leaving his partially open mouth, I decide to work my way down.

"Move up into the center of the bed."

He quickly shuffles backward as I ask, and I follow him, resting my whole body onto his, the contact of bare skin sets my blood on fire. His long hard cock rubbing against mine is pure heaven. I take his mouth in another kiss, filled with dirty promises, as I plan for my mouth to touch every part of him. I slowly lick down his neck and suck hard around his Adam's apple. His body jerks upward, moaning and babbling, pushing his body closer to mine, silently pleading for more. After I'm happy with the small bruise on his neck, I move down to his sternum, kissing and licking before changing direction toward those hard nipples that are screaming at me for attention. I latch on and suck hard, nibbling and swirling my tongue around the bud before repeating the sucking action again. I repeat this between both nipples until he becomes a sobbing mess under me, begging me for more.

"Holy fuck, I need more, fuck, hmmm just like that."

I continue my torture on his nipples until they're swollen and tender before I move lower to his perfectly chiseled abdomen. I suck hard again on the skin around his belly button, his hips thrust up where his hard cock pushes against my chin. I can smell his arousal and feel the wetness where his pre-cum makes a mess against my skin.

The musky scent causes a haze in my mind where nothing matters more than Kai and what pleasure we give to one another. Dick is new to me, but when it comes to Kai, I'm obviously happy to just jump into the whole experience without any doubt. I'm dying to see what he feels like in my mouth, what his cum tastes like. Unable to ignore his cock any longer, I dive in for a taste, sucking on the tip until my mouth bursts to life with his flavor dancing on my tongue. Hands grab my head as he tries to force my mouth to take him deeper, but I'm not gonna do that. I need to be inside him, so it's time to get back to the main course and open him up.

"Why'd you stop?" he says in a huff of annoyance—little shit.

"Who's in charge here?"

"You, but I want you to suck my dick."

I rise up, straddling his waist, and grab him around the throat. I appear to have a bratty Kai when it comes to the bedroom. And that just won't do. I make the rules. I squeeze a little harder around his throat until his face starts to redden. Remembering the last time I did this and how hard he got, I'm pretty sure he enjoys it.

"I will suck, fuck and kiss you when I say you're ready. I think you need to be taught your place. This body of yours is mine to play with now, and you'll enjoy it."

Kai's cock flinches against my ass, enjoying this display of dominance.

"You like my hands around your throat? You wanna come while you fight for breath?"

"Yes," he says, croaking from the pressure.

"Good. Now let me get back to my meal. I'm fucking starving."

He nods as I release him, large red marks covering his neck, and all I can think about is how hot he'd look tied to my bed with my hands around his throat. I resume my previous position, scooting down his body until I'm in between his beautiful thighs. That damn tattoo grabs my attention again, so I start to lick and kiss it until I've covered every part of it. Then just at the base of the rose, I bite into his skin until I leave my teeth marks behind. Kai yells out, his legs trembling around my head as I look up at him. His chest rapidly moves, his head thrown back in utter bliss.

"You like that?"

"Fuck yes, I do," he pants.

"My pretty whore enjoys a little pain and bite with his pleasure. I'm a fan."

"Only for you."

That makes me smile. My sweet Kai has so easily handed himself over to me, and it makes me delirious with joy.

"Knees to your chest."

He hesitates for a second, then grabs the back of his knees and pulls them back to his chest, exposing the most perfect pink hole. I've fucked a few women's asses before, so this isn't new to me. But this knocks all those times out of the park, as nobody is as sexy as Kai. I still can't believe looking at another man's cock has me so turned on I could just cum from watching him. But here we are, and I've no intention of stopping.

Burying my face in his ass, I waste no time in prodding his tight as fuck hole with my tongue. He cries out, which only spurs me on. Fuck, he's loud, and I love it. Who doesn't enjoy hearing their partner's enjoyment? I push my tongue in further with each thrust, his channel is so warm and tight, clenching hard around my tongue, causing me to swirl it as much as I can inside his ass. His flavor makes me dizzy, like I'm high on drugs and need more to keep this feeling alive. Kai starts to push back, fucking himself on my tongue. I've no idea how long I've been rimming him, but as saliva pools onto the sheets and jaw ache takes over as his hole becomes pliable, I move away and wipe the back of my hand over my mouth. Kai looks destroyed, debauched, and ready for more.

"Fuck, Kai. I want you so damn much."

Unable to stop myself from stroking my painfully hard dick, I give myself a couple of tugs. I'd love for his mouth to be on my cock instead, but I'll blow as soon as he touches me and I need to claim him properly first.

"I've wanted you for years, Jules. You're the first man I ever wanted, and it felt so wrong, but I couldn't help it. This is my biggest fantasy come true."

He's wanted me that long? Holy shit. Thinking back, the Kai I knew then is not the Kai in front of me. Years apart. Strangers in the night. God help me, but he's mine, and looking into those ocean eyes, I know I'm fucking his, too.

I stand up and cross the room to my bathroom and grab the lube that I keep stashed away in the vanity. Kai is still limply laying on my bed. He really is a spoiled little prince, expecting me to do all the work, and I wouldn't want it any other way. He can let go with me when we are like this, let me use him how I want. I climb back onto the bed and rest in between his legs on my knees, coating my dick with lube, before rubbing the remnants over and inside his ass. His hole is so open and ready. I can't hold back any longer.

"Legs on my shoulders." Kai complies, and I rub his calves gently before guiding my dick to his hole and slowly pushing in, fighting any resistance until I'm seated inside him up to my balls. Fuck me. I groan loudly at the sensation of his clenching walls constricting the blood supply in my dick.

"Oh god, you're fucking huge," he says, sweat dripping from his forehead. I sweep down and give him a quick kiss before returning back to my knees.

"Every inch is yours. Time to come on my cock," I say, and I start to pound into him. The room is filled with our loud grunts and moans. There is no way anyone who is in the house can't hear us, but I don't care. I never want to silence this.

"Fuuuck, Jules! Harder, fuck me harder. Choke me," he cries out, and I grab his throat with both hands and set a brutal pace.

"Tap on my wrists twice if you need me to stop, sweetheart. Don't want you unconscious or dying on me."

"Tap twice, got it. Now choke me," he begs, and I squeeze his neck hard with both hands as I destroy his body, while keeping my eyes trained on his stunning face, making sure I don't take this too far.

His ass will be sore as fuck tomorrow, but that only makes me want to fuck him harder, if that's even possible. The headboard bangs loudly against the wall. Sweat drips down my spine, it stings my eyes as droplets fall from my forehead. Kai's abs clench on each thrust, highlighting that sexy as hell six-pack.

"Your ass is amazing. Fuck, it feels so good around my cock. You gonna milk me? Fill you up with my cum?"

"Yes!"

I growl at the sight of Kai in orgasm heaven, he's fucking stunning. His cock is leaking like a faucet. I'd love nothing more than to swallow him down right now, but his ass is clinging to me so tightly I can't move.

"You ready? I'm gonna cum in this hot little ass, Kai."

"Do it. Fill me."

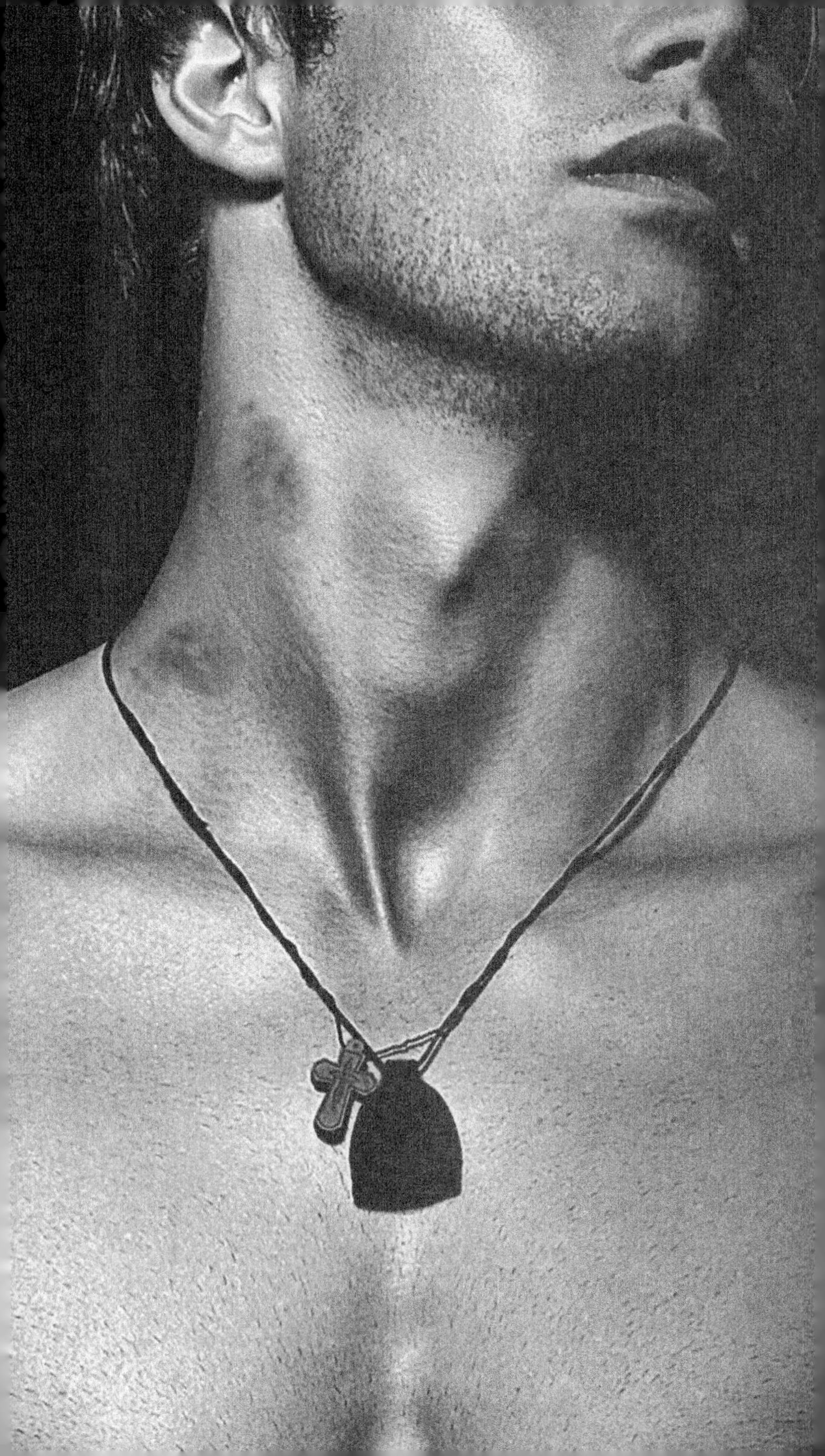

CHAPTER 23
KAI

My body aches all over, my nerves awakened in the most magical way. This is what it feels like to be owned by someone. By Jules. Magical. He has wrung me out, leaving me completely limp as I lay under him while he fucks my ass with such determination my body is on the verge of splitting open. My voice is hoarse from the never-ending sounds he's pulling from me, and he's no better. Growling and groaning like a beast. A predator that's taking pleasure in his prey, and I bask in it. I'm so close to coming without even touching my cock as his hands tighten around my neck like a heavy band, making it difficult to breathe. The discomfort is a dull pain that radiates around my throat but feels so damn good. My vision blurs, my head feels light and erased of all thoughts but him. He removes one hand to stroke my cock as he keeps the other in a tight lock on my neck. My throat burns as the sensation of elevating above myself takes over as I cum, and fuck do I come hard. As soon as the first spurt leaves the tip of my cock, Jules removes his grip from my throat and pounds into me harder, digging his fingers into my thighs, and I quake in overwhelming pleasure. Air slowly fills my lungs as a lingering soreness throbs in my throat and my ass. And I fucking love it.

"Fuck...cumming, I'm cumming," Jules grunts above me as warm liquid fills my ass, making me clench, wanting to keep him inside me where he belongs. Like a dead weight, he collapses on top of me. Our sticky, overheated bodies lock together, and I can't find the strength to move or think. My whole body has shut down, and I'm drifting off into a mind space of nothingness. Just peace. Contentment.

"Kai? Can you hear me?"

Hmm, I love the sound of his voice. I'm so sleepy. Why the fuck is he shaking me?

"What?" I whine, not even opening my eyes.

"I think you blacked out for a second. Are you alright?"

"I'm fantastic. Now, leave me alone. I'm tired."

Jules chuckles. I'm aware he has removed himself from my body, but my eyes are so heavy I can't open them to see what's happening. A wet cloth wipes at my abdomen, and my heart skips a beat at him taking care of me. A hint of panic again attacks me as I'm afraid of already becoming too clingy for his attention. What if he tires of me? What if I'm too much hassle? Gentle fingers pull me from the edge of despair over my failings, as they stroke my throat. I wince at the tenderness on my skin.

"Did I go too far? I think you'll bruise."

Forcing my eyes open, which is a struggle, I stare up at Jules, who is looking down at me with concern in his eyes, his brows scrunched together, and a look of regret.

"Jules. I loved it. I would've stopped you if it went too far. I needed it, so please get that look off your face. I'm an adult."

"I know you are," he says.

"Good."

"Are you feeling better about everything else? You know you can talk to me."

I push Jules onto his back and snuggle into his side.

"A little. It's not just Aaron. Jules, nothing I've done in the past seven years has been good. Mom has had enough of me. *I've* had enough of me. I thought coming here would help, but I just fucked up more. Something is wrong with me. Everything I do hurts someone, and I don't know what to do. It's like I'm defective."

Jules grabs the back of my hair to pull my head back up to face him.

"You stop that shit right now. We've all made mistakes when we were younger, and that includes your mom. Nobody is perfect, but you want to make life better for yourself, and you're doing that. Here with me. What happened with Aaron was bad, but it could've happened to any of us. I think you're fucking perfect, and I'll tell you that every day until you believe me."

A tear escapes my eye, and I move in closer to Jules's protective arms around me, allowing myself to let him overrule the self-loathing thoughts that fill me daily.

"Don't ever leave me."

"Not a fucking chance. You're my pretty little whore. All mine, and you better remember that."

"Please don't call me that in front of the guys."

"I won't. It's just for us. Now sleep."

"Mm-kay," I say on a tired sigh. The beat of Jules's steady heart under my head lulls me to sleep, and for the first time, I start to feel like I belong somewhere.

It's the following morning, and I'm awoken by small bites of pressure on my abdomen. It's painful enough for me to wake from the deepest sleep to attack whatever is causing the discomfort. Just as I'm about to sit up, my heavy eyes open to find Jules is the assailant who is currently sucking and biting all over my chest and stomach, leaving behind a large pattern of hickeys. I swallow hard at the sight, noting the soreness on my neck and in my throat, transporting me back to last night when Jules choked me into the most mind-blowing orgasm of my life.

"Morning," he says, voice all raspy from sleep. Fuck he's so damn hot. He moves his head lower and continues to place bruises all over my inner thigh and around my tattoo.

"What are you doing?"

"I'm marking you. Staking my claim."

"You're insane."

Jules pulls away and climbs up my body, resting his forearms on either side of my head. He then looks down into my eyes.

"You're right. And you're in trouble if you've only just worked that out."

"I kinda like it. But how do I stake my claim on you?"

Jules tilts his head to the side, baring his neck to me, and I need no further instruction or invitation. I pull his neck down to my mouth and suck hard into his skin until purple and red blooms on his tanned, smooth skin.

"Hmm, that feels so fucking good," he growls as I pull away, admiring my brand of ownership.

"Everyone will know what we've done. Do you think they'll be okay with us?"

"Kai, I don't give a fuck who knows. And if they have a problem, that's their issue. I've already told you, you're mine, and I plan to keep it that way."

"I love how possessive you get over me," I say as I push my dick up into his. It turns me on so much to see him lose his shit over me. I still can't believe he wants me. I'm still nervous. The back of my mind is constantly at war with the rational side of my brain, telling me he will leave me. Get sick of me. I always screw up, so is it inevitable that I screw this up? Would he fight for me?

Christ, I'm a needy fucker.

"Always. Now stop grinding against my dick. We don't have time to fool around. Remember you're with Simon today, to collect earnings from the crews."

"Fine."

I push him away in what can only be described as a tantrum. Jules just laughs at me as I jump to my feet to grab my clothes before heading back to my room. As I start to stand, a hard slap hits my ass cheek, and fuck does it burn.

"What the fuck was that for?" I snap, turning around to face Jules.

"Your attitude."

"Fuck you."

Jules stands and pulls me up against his hard, naked body. Both our dicks are dueling on their own, hard and ready for battle.

"I think I'll stick to fucking you. Now go get ready."

"Bossy asshole," I say, grumbling as I quickly throw my shorts on and stomp out of the room. My ass hurts with every stride until I reach my room and go to take a shower. I turn the faucet on, waiting for the water to heat up, I assess myself in the mirror. Holy shit, my body is covered in hickeys. My neck is starting to bruise from his strong hands, and I'm transfixed with how I look. I can't resist running my fingers over each mark he has left, excited at the soreness of the evidence he's left on my body for anyone to see.

It's perfect. He owns me. And I crave more.

As I get into the shower, I allow myself to enjoy the steaming warmth of the water that soothes my aching muscles, and alleviates the pain of Jules's marks. I'm truly awake for the first time, to who I am and who I want to be. How did I not see it before? The years of sticking around with those assholes back home, restricted me much more from life than just achieving a better living situation. It robbed me of being who I am, a man that wants to be free to love and fuck whoever I want. To have something for myself. In this case, to have the man who has just ruined me for any other to own me completely and for us to show it to the world. But is that reality? While it may or may not bother Jules, my mom is a huge problem in this. Will she accept it? She will most likely look at it differently than others. She sees Jules as her brother and my uncle, and I don't think we will be able to convince her otherwise. Whether it hurts her or not, Jules wasn't in my life, he didn't play that role, and the reality is that we aren't related. But I doubt she'll see it that way.

The question is, am I willing to give up the only family I have, the woman who raised me, for the opportunity to chase after love? An all consuming, life altering, possessively obsessed, can't-live-without love?

And as much as it breaks my heart...I think the answer would be *yes*.

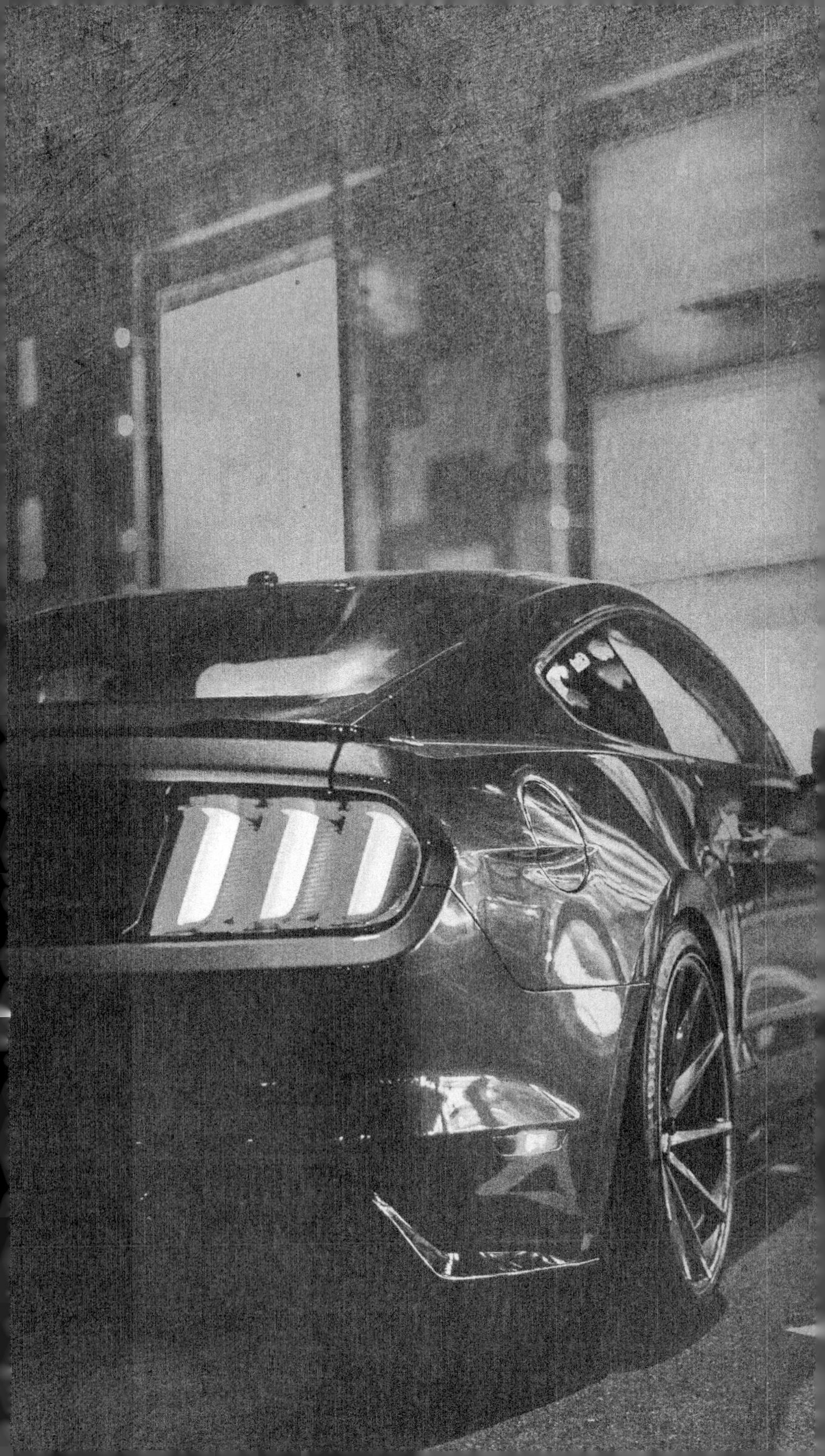

CHAPTER 24
JULES

Kai left with Simon before I was out of the shower, and now I'm walking over to the main house for a meeting with Lev and Dima. I know I'm gonna get called out on questioning Lev in front of everyone in the holding pen. To be honest, with the high I'm riding today after the amazing night with Kai, I don't think anything can touch the good feelings buzzing in my body. I just need to make sure I don't show it on my face. If Kai and I are going to do this together, we'll have to separate our relationship and work, otherwise it will spill into the group, and it won't be a pretty conclusion if it affects any business for the brothers.

The house is quiet when I enter the kitchen, so I walk through the downstairs corridors until I reach the office that is mainly Dima's, but they share when needed. I give a quick knock before I open the door and walk in to see Dima and Lev sitting across from one another at the large wooden desk that fills half the space. Dima is sitting on the business side in his ridiculously opulent leather chair, and Lev is on the other side in a similar seat.

"Hey Jules," Dima says in greeting. I close the door behind me as Lev stands from his chair, silent, as he strolls towards me and punches me in the stomach with as much power as he can summon. I crunch over, holding my stomach as I try to gasp for air, fuck that hurt. He doesn't give me much chance to get my bearings before he pulls me upright and grabs my face with both hands until the bones in my lower jaw ache from the pressure.

"I should end Kai for letting Aaron be taken by that sick fuck," he seethes in my face.

That comment has me wanting to fight back. If Lev was so concerned, he should've taken Aaron himself.

"You should've never given him the responsibility, he wasn't ready."

"I think he proved that point, smartass. He's a liability, if he can't handle a little babysitting then what can he handle? It's his last chance, Jules."

"I understand."

"Oh, and one more thing, you question me or Dima like that ever again and I will put a bullet in your head,

Jules. We're in charge. Loyalty and respect first. Are we clear?" Lev snarls at me, spittle flying from his mouth. He's a caged lion that's been allowed to challenge his subordinate. I fucked up because I allowed my distraction with Kai to take over.

"It won't happen again. You have my word."

Lev stands back and adjusts his shirt, watching me for any hint of a lie before nodding.

"Good. Now sit, we need to run over some stuff."

I'm still dazed by the assault, but I try to brush it off and sit in the chair next to Lev that faces Dima, who looks contemplative. He watches me with those sharp blue eyes, scanning me for information.

"What's going on between you and Kai?" Dima says.

"We're working shit out. He's a little shaken about Aaron, still."

"And so he should be," Lev says.

I don't argue with Lev after everything that's just happened in this office. I don't want to inflame the situation anymore than it already is.

"So, you're fucking, then?" Lev asks, giving me his standard conversation whiplash.

"No, we're…" I start to say before Dima cuts me off.

"You must be fucking as you didn't have that hickey yesterday."

"It's not just fucking. He's mine."

"Ha! Welcome to the asshole club. Aaron's mine and Seb belongs to Dima. As long as that's clear it'll all be good. Nephew fucker," Lev quips.

"Step…"

"Step-nephew. Not blood. *Yes we know*," Dima says, rolling his eyes at me.

"Anyway, D and I have decided to take on a new guard. After everything that's happened, we're more open to snakes than before so we need extra security. Our cousin, Ivan, will be joining us this weekend when he gets back from Europe," Lev says.

"Ivan? Fuck I haven't seen him in, what, it must be ten years since he was last here?"

"Yeah. We speak every now and then and he wants to put down some roots, so we said we needed extra guards, and his contract with the security team he works with has ended, so he's coming home," Dima says.

"What's gonna happen with rooms? We're full out back, unless you want me to move out?"

"Nah, Ivan can stay in one of the spare rooms here for now. We've also contacted an architect in New York. It's time we expanded, so we're planning to build on the land at the side of the house. There's enough acreage for you all to have a single story home each," Lev says.

"You kidding me? Wow. That'd be amazing."

"Its gonna be a fucking nightmare. Can't deal with shit like this, so we're letting Ivan oversee the actual work after we've had the designs drawn up," Lev says.

"You're such a caveman, Lev. You'd be happy with just a shed," Dima says.

"Yeah, I would. I don't give a shit about the spoils like you. Such a materialistic princess."

"Shut the fuck up, brother. Does any princess you know look and act like me?"

"I only know you. And you and Seb are princesses who like nice things from nice places. Fucking snobs."

"I ain't no snob! Nothing wrong in wanting a nice home."

"If you say so, princess."

"I'm gonna fuck you up," Dima says, rising to his feet.

"You're such a drama queen. You know I'd beat your ass."

"You're really pushing it, Lev."

Just as I think war is about to break out, the door opens and in walks Seb.

"D, I need you if you're done here?" Seb asks.

"Aww has it been longer than an hour since D bred you, Seb? Missing him already?" Lev jokes and I can't help but chuckle. Dima however, doesn't find it funny, judging by the downright murderous scowl he turns towards Lev.

"Fuck off, Lev. Aaron's looking for you and he doesn't look too great," Seb says.

"Where is he?"

"Gone back to your room. I told him to go lie down. I think he had a flashback or something, I found him in the gym with his headphones on."

"Fuck," Lev says before stomping off in a hurry. After Aaron was taken, we found out from Lev that he uses his headphones and music to help him when he goes through an episode of flashbacks or when his mind gets too full. While he seems perky, I suspect these attacks will happen from time to time, no matter what Lev does.

"D, my bike won't start and I need a ride to work. Can you take me?"

"I've got a meeting with Carlos, but Jules will take you," Dima says to Seb.

"Jules, can you stay at the bar with Seb until I get there? Should only be a couple of hours."

"No problem. You ready, Seb?"

"Yep. Let's go."

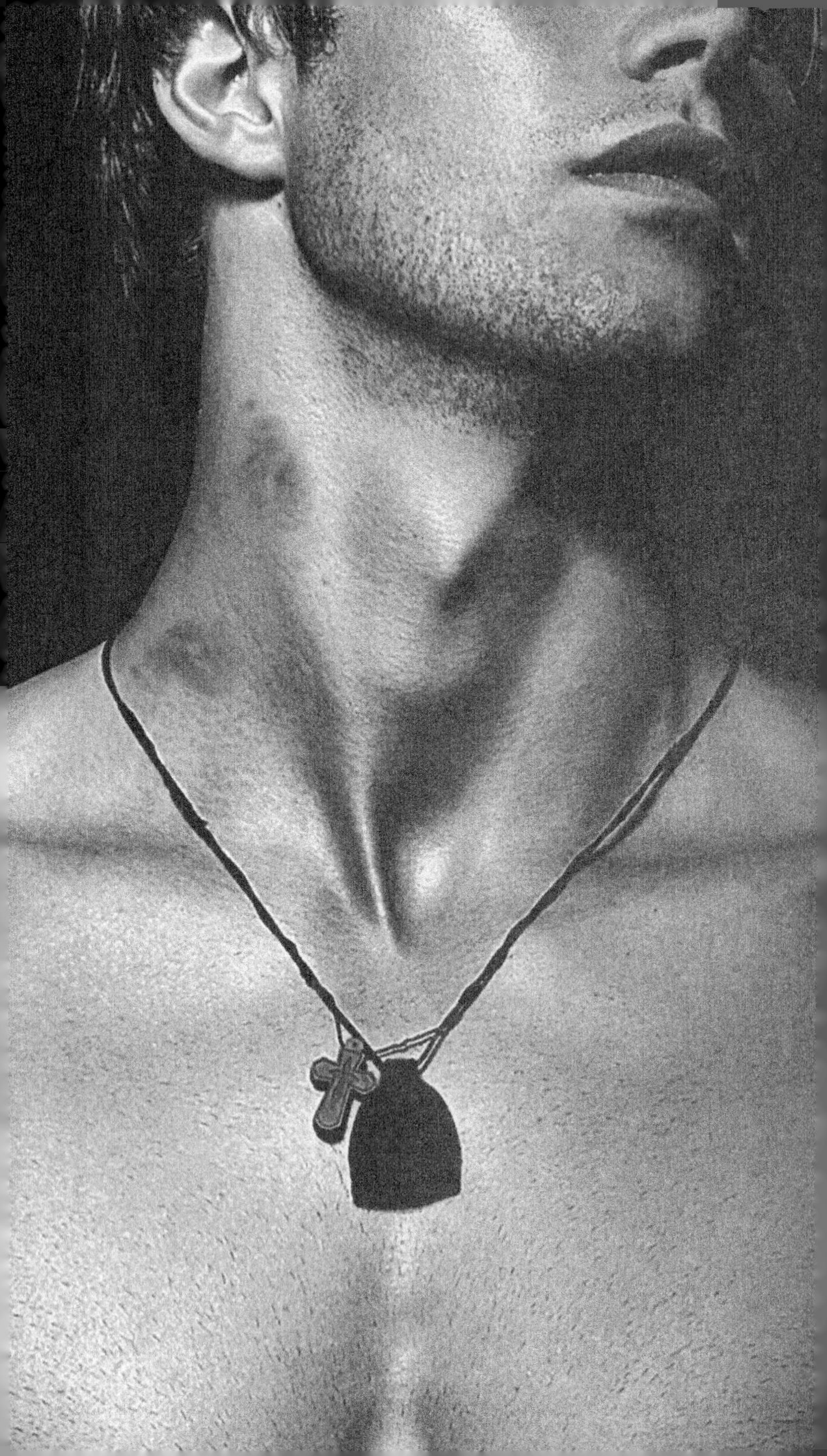

CHAPTER 25
KAI

"Jesus, Kai. Did Jules fuck you or beat you last night?" Simon says, as he eyes my neck when I meet him out the front of the house to go over to Desire with him this morning.

"No comment," I say, not wanting to discuss what happened between Jules and me. I'm happy for people to know about us, but I don't like discussing my sex life, and given how forward everyone here is, I think that will be something I'll have to get on board with.

"I'd say it was both with the noises coming from his room last night. You fuckers are loud. Do I need to buy earplugs?" Si teases.

"Just drive."

"Oooh someone is coy, are you blushing, Kai? Oh this is fucking awesome. If the sex banter is too much, I suggest you tell Jules to leave your neck alone as you're going to get a hammering from the brothers when they see you. And the girls at the club."

Ugh. Great.

"Good to know. But I'm not discussing it," I say as we drive off to the club. Hoping to put an end to this grilling, I focus my eyes out on the streets through the passenger window. It's so fucking cold this time of year, I hate to leave the house. Everyone walking the streets are layered up to their noses, fighting off the cold air that threatens to give you frostbite. I'm being overdramatic, but it feels that way. Why people insist on going shopping in the winter is beyond my comprehension. Just order online.

"You will. That's how they are in this family. Dima and Lev make you share everything. They might be tough bastards, but are not dissimilar to a gossip group."

I don't know why, but this conversation is irking me. I want to keep what happened last night between me and Jules. It was our time, and personal to me. I've never allowed myself to let go like that and talking about it is like I'm cheapening what it meant. Or maybe I'm overthinking this and need to stop being such a whiny brat. I turn to look at Simon and decide to test his theory that we all have to 'share.'

"What about you and Carlos? Have you fucked?" The words are out before I can regret it. But fuck him. If I have to share, then so does he. Simon's grip on the wheel tightens, his jaw pulses from grinding his teeth. A response is building, and from the tension vibrating off him, it will be a snappy response. As that's Simon. Very serious and always so defensive when it comes to Carlos.

"Why the hell would you think that? There is no me and Carlos, and I would rather be flayed than fuck that asshole."

"There's just a lot of sexual tension between you both." *God, shut the fuck up, Kai.*

Simon slams the brakes on in the middle of the road and moves his body to face me. Murder is written in those brown eyes. I do wonder for a second if he might actually kill me. Horns blare around us as we remain stationary on the road, but Si is so focused on me he doesn't notice.

"You need to shut the fuck up. There is *no* sexual anything between me and Carlos and I'll rip your tongue out if you mention it again. The only tension there is hate. Pure, consuming, fucking hate."

I'm torn between feeling threatened and smug as he protests too much. There's definitely a sexual vibe, and I can't wait to see it bubble over between them. The vitriol Simon holds against Carlos is so toxic I think they would kill each other during sex.

"Let's make a deal. You quit the questions about Jules, and I'll not mention Carlos again?"

"You're such a smartass," is all I get in response as we start back on our journey. I decipher from him calling me a smartass that he's agreed to the rules.

A few minutes later, we park outside Desire, and enter the building through the side door. Even with the club empty, it's still fucking gorgeous. I follow Simon through the club to the bar, where Bonnie is going through some paperwork.

"Hey, Bon," Simon says in greeting.

"Hi hon. Kai, nice to see you again. I see the vampires paid a visit last night. Or did someone try to strangle you in your sleep?"

My hand flies to my neck and words lodge in my throat. I look at Simon but he just smirks at me. His eyes dance with the 'I told you so,' look and that he's leaving this to me to deal with.

"Something like that," is all I can manage to say.

"Well send them my way, I love a little choking with my lovin'."

Thoughts flick to images of Jules fucking Bonnie. Shit, has he fucked her before? Jealousy rises in my chest as the green-eyed monster wants to show himself. I've never felt territorial before, but now I'm looking at Bonnie like competition I need to take down.

"He won't be interested."

Bonnie's eyebrows raise in humor at my response. Simon chuckles next to me, and I feel like a kid who's been caught in a lie. My eyes are looking everywhere else, avoiding eye contact.

"Steady on, hon. I'm only teasing you. Although I would love to meet the mystery man, or is it someone we already know?"

She's really starting to piss me off, and Simon is about to get his face punched if he doesn't stop chuckling next to me like a damn high schooler.

"Can we just get started on what we're here to do? Looking over the books, I believe?" I say, proud of myself for taking charge. This is foreign, but I like the power shift when I notice Bonnie withdraw slightly.

"So shy boy has some teeth. That's good, you'll need them around here."

She bends down behind the bar and retrieves a large stack of files that she passes over to me.

"You boys want a drink?"

"We'll take two orange juices, Bon. Can you bring them over?" Simon says.

"Of course."

Bonnie winks at me before turning to make our drinks and Simon nudges me to follow him. We walk over to one of the tables at the back of the club.

"You did good back there. Snarky Kai is a blast."

"The brothers won't be mad I was rude to her?"

"Nah, you stood your ground, and that wasn't rude. Now, down to business. Every week we check the cash flow that Bonnie records with receipts every night, and then we check the girls' rosters to see who turned up and if anyone is slacking and not making any money. Slackers get the boot, then we'd need to recruit."

"Okay."

Bonnie walks over and silently leaves our drinks as we immerse ourselves in the endless paperwork. It's cool, and it's something I don't think I'll have any trouble doing on my own in the future.

Things are starting to look up a little, giving me a burst of hope that things are finally coming together.

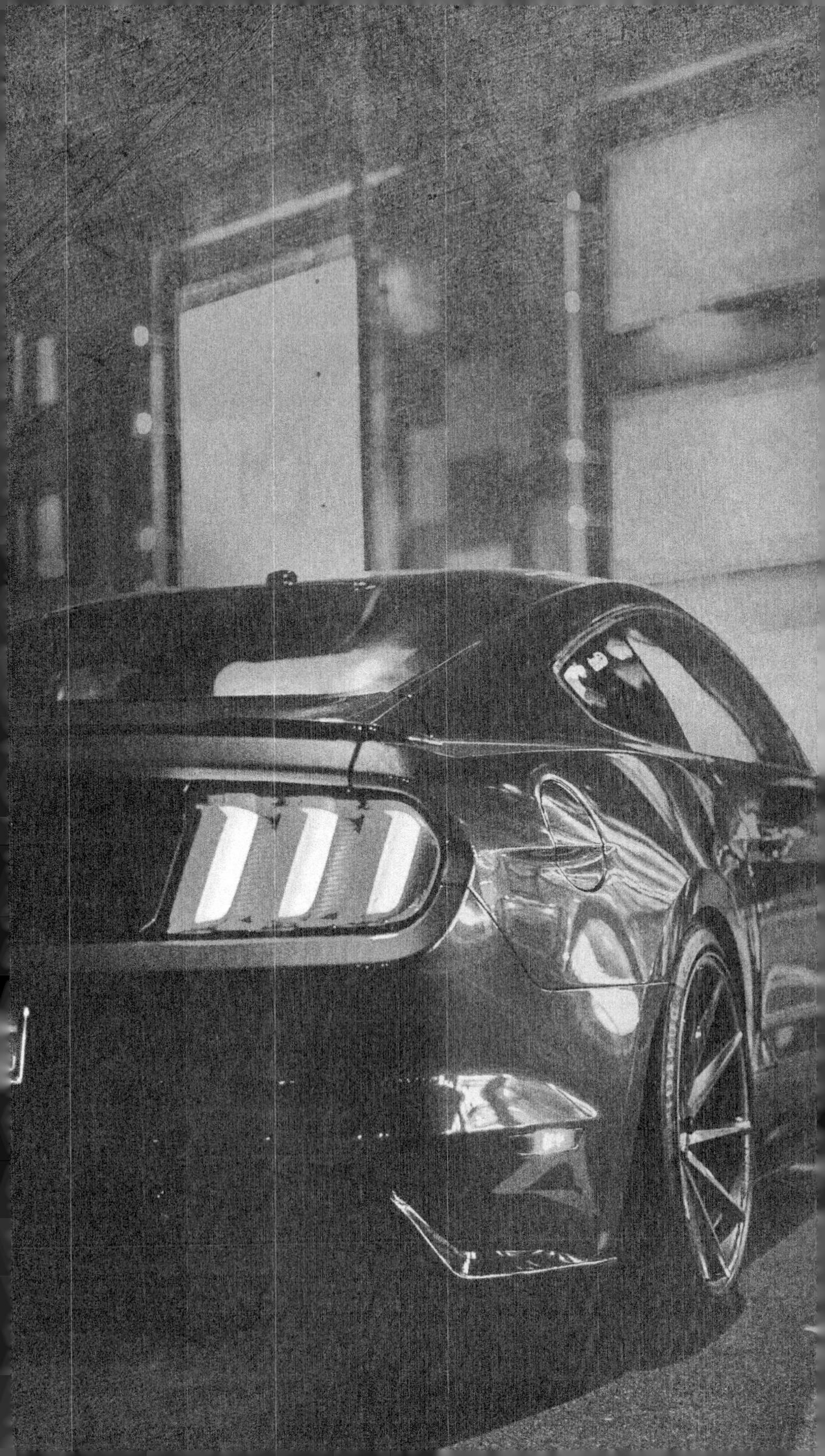

CHAPTER 26
JULES

"How's Kai today?" Seb asks as we walk into Starlight. It's a good question, one I've asked myself, as I don't know. We only had a brief conversation before he left, but I'm worried now that he's had time to process what happened last night, that he may have had second thoughts. I'm in the other camp and feel fantastic after last night. It was the most phenomenal sex I've ever had. Earth shattering. Life changing. So much so I want more. If we didn't have to work I'd still be inside him, trying to find what other noises I can get him to make.

"Jules?"

"Yeah?"

"You're off in your own world there. I said, how is Kai? But I assume from your blissed out demeanor that you're daydreaming about him, and he's probably on a high too?"

"You're as bad as D. Do you guys do anything other than gossip?"

"Sure we do. We talk and fuck. But I'm not meaning to be nosy, it's just, I know Kai has been struggling and I've been a little worried about him."

My ears perk up at that little nugget of information.

"Struggling with what?" I ask, as Seb's eyes widen as if he has said too much.

"You know, moving from home. Settling in here," he says, and I know him well enough to know when he's being sketchy.

"What aren't you telling me?"

"Nothing!"

"Not buying it, but I can hardly force you when you're the boss's hubby can I?"

Seb laughs. I'm partly joking but my mind is trying to read between the lines. I know he's found the adjustments tough, and also what happened with Aaron, but not enough that I would think it would cause Seb any concern. Actually, Seb is a bleeding heart so he could be reading way too much into it.

"I'll talk to him tonight."

"I think that's a good idea. You want anything before I do inventory?"

"Nah I'm good, thanks. I'll just hang around and wait for Dima to show up."

"Cool."

With that, I whip out my phone from my pocket and take a seat at one of the tables near the bar. Before I know it, I'm texting Kai.

> You good?

It takes a few minutes for a response, which in fairness, I expect, as he's working. But it pisses me off nonetheless. I don't like being left hanging, especially by him. When I message him, I want an immediate response. Arrogant prick that I am, I assume he's glued to his phone, waiting to hear from me.

Kai

> I'm good. Just going through the books with Simon.

> Anyone else there?

Kai

> Bonnie is here and one of the other girls. Why?

Be on your guard and don't let them distract you. They'll be trying to get a taste of your dick.

Kai

> After seeing the mess you've made of my neck, they know not to bother. Trust me. Your claiming marks have been noticed by everyone. Including fucking Si.

Good. Then they know you're off limits.

Kai

> You sound deranged.

Only for you.

Kai

> Stop flirting. Si is looking at me weird and I'm getting hard.

Does my whore need attention? I'll bind you to my bed and spend hours giving you all the attention you want.

Kai

> I'm going now.

And I'm not done.

Kai

> Byeeeee!

Such a little shit. But fuck does it get my blood pumping.

You'll pay for that. A little discipline will be dished out later.

Three dots appear on my screen, then disappear, then reappear, but no message comes through. He's nervous. And so he should be.

A text alert comes through, and I'm hoping it's from Kai, but disappointment sets in when I see it's from Jenny. Not that I don't want to talk to her, but it's a little awkward when I'm hard as fuck from verbally sparring with her son.

Jenny

> Hi Jules. How's Kai doing? I miss him.

Has Kai not been in touch with his mom? Instead of texting, I press the call button where she answers straight away.

"Jules, hey I didn't mean for you to call. I thought you'd be busy."

"I'm just waiting on my boss, so I'm free right now. Has Kai not called you?"

"No. I had a text a couple of weeks back but nothing since. How is he?"

'He's really good. Settled in with the guys and is working hard. It's been full on, so that's probably why he hasn't called."

"That's fine. He's a grown man. I know you'd call me if things weren't working out."

"I would. Don't worry. How are things with you?"

"I've been okay. Missing having Kai at home as it's been quiet. But Tim has been visiting a lot, so it's been nice to have company."

"Officer Tim?"

"Yes, and I'm not talking about it."

I laugh, as I can feel the heat coming through the phone from her blushing.

"I won't ask again."

"Good," she says, but it's followed by a long silence. Something is wrong.

"What's wrong, Jenny?"

"Why do you think anything's wrong?"

"I can sense it. You're a little quiet. Has something happened?"

"Fuck, you're perceptive. It's probably nothing, but you know that gang Kai hung around with?"

"What about them?"

"Well, they've been hanging around since Kai left. I never really used to see them when he was home, as he spent most of his time out with them. But for a few weeks they've been passing by the house when I get home from work. Or I've seen them in their car outside of my work during the day. I might be imagining things, as it's not everyday, but….I don't know. It feels off."

It feels off to me, too. I briefly wonder if Kai has told me everything about the guys he hung out with.

"You told Tim about it?"

"No, it'll only worry him and I don't want to be a burden."

"Jenny, tell him. It may be nothing, but if it's out of the ordinary, I'd feel better knowing you were being looked after."

"You're right. He's coming over tonight, so I'll bring it up then."

"Good. I'll have a word with Kai."

"Don't you dare! I want him focused there, not worrying about me. I'm sure it's fine."

I'm not convinced of that, but I can subtly try to find out more from Kai.

Hearing footsteps, I look up to see Dima walk into the bar, nodding his head for me to follow him into the back office.

"Listen Jenny, my boss has just got back, But I'll tell Kai to call when I see him later."

"Thanks Jules. Bye."

I get up to follow Dima into the office and sit opposite him.

"What's wrong with your face?" Dima says.

"My face?"

"You look…emotional or something."

I roll my eyes, it amazes me how he and Lev could get partners. The pair of them together don't even amount to one full emotion. Yet he notices it on me.

"Just thinking. I've just spoken to Jenny and she mentioned that the gang Kai hung around with have been appearing at her house and workplace."

"They been threatening her?"

"No. She said it's not every day, but its never happened before. I just feel…unsettled."

"Gangs are known to be reactive if a member just leaves. Did Kai leave on good terms?"

"I don't know."

"You didn't ask?"

"Why would I ask? I was too busy dealing with the fallout with his mom and moving him here."

"You were too busy eye fucking him, you mean."

"D, I mean this with the utmost respect, but fuck you."

That gets me a large smile from the demon himself. Dima is a lot easier to have banter with, unlike Lev, who has zero ability to take a joke.

"Just ask Kai."

"Jenny doesn't want me saying anything."

"Fucking hell. This is why I don't do families."

"What are you talking about? You have a brother and a husband. Plus me and Si. That is a family."

"Yes, but we're normal. Not all emotional and shit."

"You mean human."

"Whatever. Just sort this shit out, I want you focused. Carlos is having more trouble in his crew. Money has gone missing from our last import. I've offered our services."

"What kind of services?"

"Customer services. You know, ask a few questions."

"Ahh, that kind of service. I'm down. Been a while since I got my hands dirty."

"That's what I want to hear. Now call Si and tell him to meet us with Kai back at the house within the hour."

A little bit of violence mixed with some Kai should make a great evening.

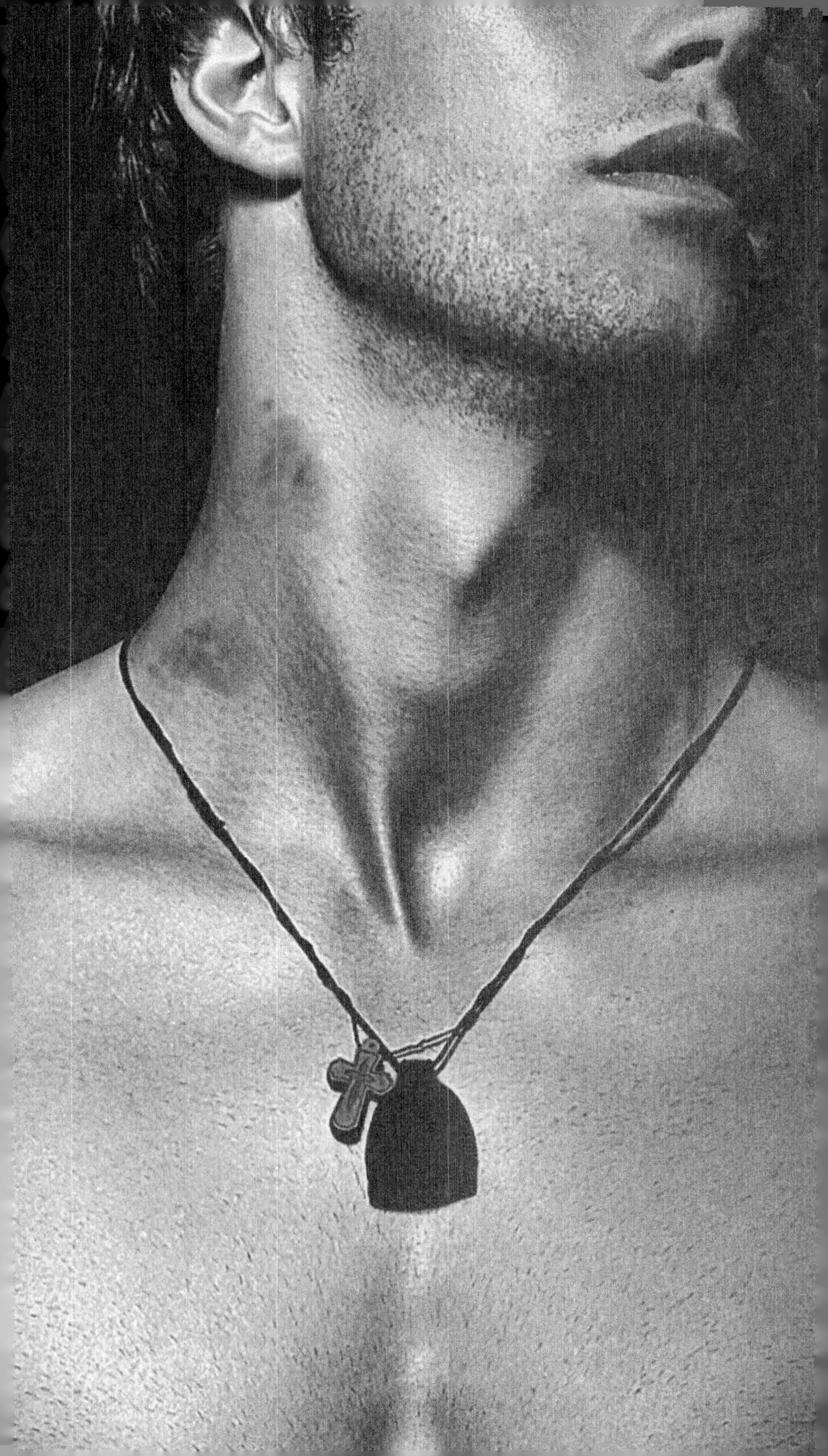

CHAPTER 27
KAI

"Kai, we gotta get back, Dima wants a meeting with all of us," Simon says, as I finish the last page of financials for the club.

"Did he say what it's about?"

"Nope. Come on. Don't want to keep him waiting."

As we gather up our things, and pass the books back over to Bonnie, we quickly head out and make our way back to the house. I'll admit I'm a little nervous to know what Dima wants to talk to us about. I would press Simon for more, but he's so changeable in his moods, I daren't poke the bear. I haven't heard from Jules again since our last texting session where he threatened to punish me. Damn, that sounds more thrilling than it should. I love being his ragdoll. My ass is still sensitive from the fucking last night, but I'm more than willing to take more. As much as he'll give me. Even after my shower this morning, I've felt small dribbles of his cum leak out of my ass. The idea that a part of him is with me at all times is so fucking hot. I wouldn't be embarrassed if people could smell him on me. I want them to. I want them to know I'm his and he is mine and to back the fuck off.

We arrive back at the mansion, and I walk with Simon into the main house and into the kitchen. Everyone is present, apart from Aaron and Seb. Seb must still be at work, and I have no idea where Aaron is. As soon as I enter the room, my eyes find Jules. My heart races at the sight of him, he's so big and such an alpha. I want to run over to him so he can lift me up in his arms. Like he can read my mind, a small knowing smile lights up his handsome face, those blue eyes piercing a hole into my soul. Fuck, I need him so bad. I want my punishment so bad. Curiosity of what he'll do is at the forefront of my mind, erasing the room of anyone else but him.

"So, heads up. Carlos has some stealing fuckers in his crew. They've stolen some of the money that we paid Carlos for imports, so we have been asked to help with his investigations. He'll be bringing the boys over tonight. I need you all down in the holding pen at seven o'clock." Dima says. My stomach drops at the thought of being back down in that room again. I'm not quite sure I have the stomach for that side of things, but I need to push through after all the shit that happened with Aaron, because I have a lot to prove. I just hope I don't throw up or pass out.

"Will Carlos be down there with us?" Simon asks, as everyone turns to face him.

"Yeah. Why? That gonna be a problem?" Lev says.

"As long as he keeps away from me, then it's fine."

"This is business Si. Any shit you have with Carlos you leave at the door. We don't have time for your childish fights," Dima says.

"Fine. Sorry," Simon says.

"Everyone go rest up and eat. Or whatever it is you wanna do. If it turns out to be fun down there, it could be an all-nighter," Lev says, grinning like a lunatic. So excited that he gets to play.

"Can I join too?" Aaron says from behind us, standing by the open kitchen door. He must've been standing there for the whole meeting.

"No, doe. You'll be distracting," Lev says. He eyes Aaron with such intensity that the temperature in the room rises to stifling levels, affecting all of us. Those two radiate chemistry, and mostly in a toxic way.

"*Please*? I want to watch you use Steve for the first time."

"Who the fuck is Steve?" Jules asks.

"It's what he's called his new switchblade. Fucking stupid if you ask me," Lev grumbles.

"Why Steve?" I ask, genuinely curious.

"The guy from Blues Clues. I used to love it when I was younger."

"Are you shitting us? You named your blade after a kids TV show presenter?" Dima asks, his eyebrows so far into his hairline with disbelief that we all feel. But this is Aaron. He's a little bit out there from time to time.

"Yes. Now can I please watch?" Aaron says as he slowly approaches Lev. I still can't get a read on Lev, so I'm unable to predict what his answer will be.

"We'll talk about it back in our room, doe. Come on."

Lev grabs the back of Aaron's neck and guides him out of the kitchen while I stand there dumbfounded at the conversation that's just happened. These guys are fucking crazy.

"Let's go, Kai," Jules says, gesturing for me to follow him out of the kitchen patio doors.

"You coming, Si?" Jules asks.

"Nah. Gonna go out for a while, besides, I don't want to listen to you two fucking."

Before I can say anything, Si walks out along with Dima, leaving just me and Jules to head out to the back house.

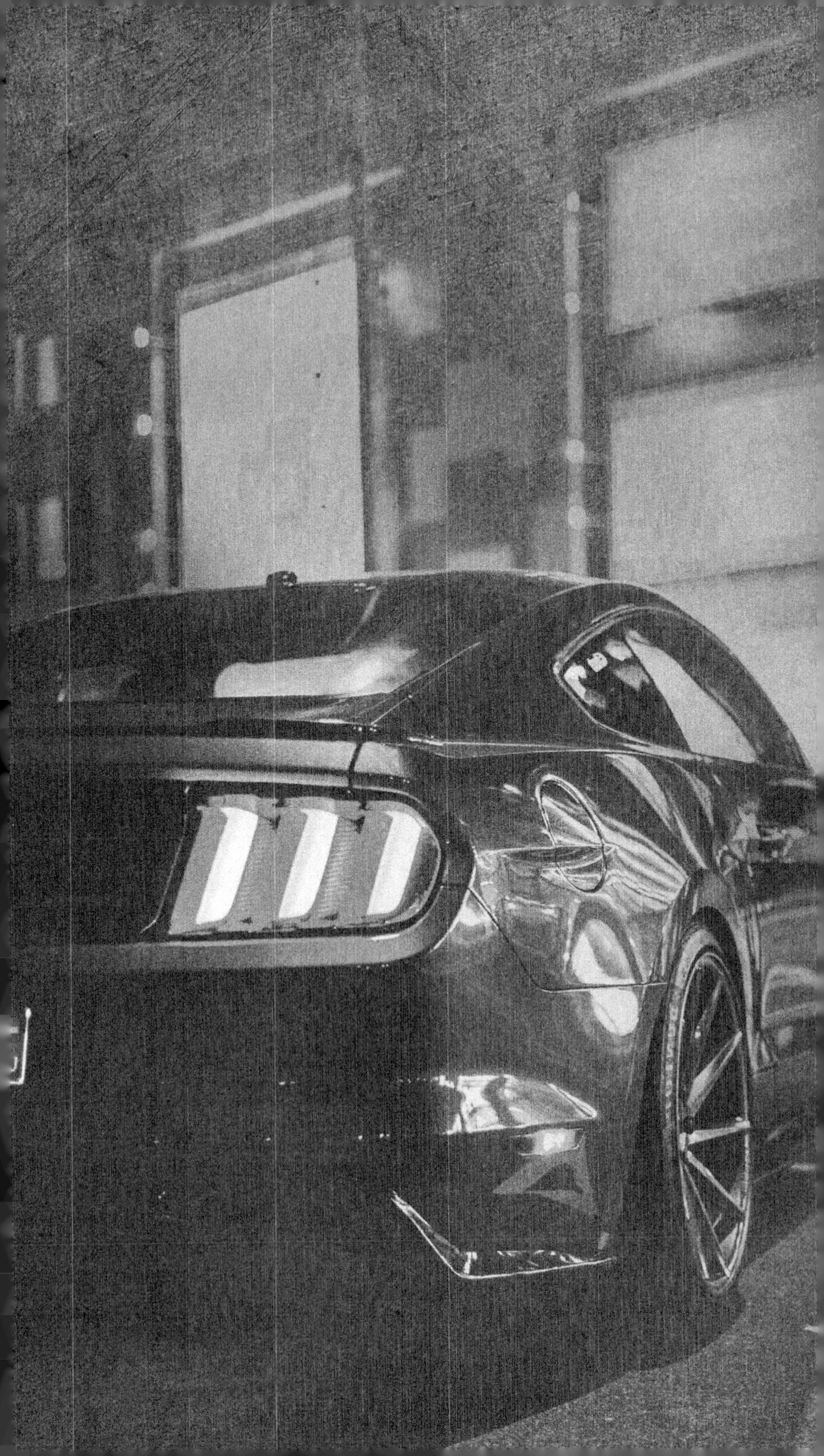

CHAPTER 28
JULES

As soon as the door closes behind us, I have Kai pinned against the wall, devouring his perfect mouth. Today has been torture not to have my eyes on him or be able to touch him. All sense and logic dissipate into the air when I'm holding him. I have to get my fix.

"Don't ever ignore my texts or cut me off again, Kai," I whisper harshly against his lips. Tugging hard at his hair to tilt his head back, giving me room to lick and suckle over the bruises my own hands left last night on his smooth neck.

"Or what?"

"Or I'll tie you up and beat your ass so hard you can't sit down. If that doesn't work, I'll lock your dick in a cage. And I won't allow you to cum. I'll finger fuck your hole and suck on those nipples all night long, but you won't be allowed any release."

Kai groans, rubbing his hard dick against mine. I pull away and hold his hand, dragging him to my room. I push him into the bedroom door as it closes and gently grip his sore neck.

"Stay there until I say you can move." He nods in reply but doesn't speak. The air is charged with nothing but sex and arousal, making me feel drunk.

I walk over to the bed and sit on the edge, facing him. I undo the buttons on my shirt until my chest is exposed. Kai watches every move, trying so hard to hold himself back. I then unzip my pants and pull out my dick and stroke it a couple of times, spreading the wetness from my tip down my shaft.

"Get naked."

Kai begins to move toward me, but I stop him.

"No. I want you to stay over there and undress."

Slowly, I tease myself with long firm strokes of my achingly hard dick. Kai first removes his shirt, exposing that hot as sin chest, looking as delectable as ever. He then removes his pants, and I nearly lose my shit when that sexy tattoo comes into view. The bite mark I left last night is still visible. I want to bite it again. He then removes his underwear, that allows his fat juicy cock to slap against his belly, and what a sight he makes. I need his mouth on me.

"Crawl to me."

"What?" he asks, a hint of shyness in his timid voice. That just makes me harder.

"You heard me. I want you to crawl to my dick on your hands and knees. *Slowly.*"

Lowering himself to the floor, he starts to crawl. That perfect ass is arched, and the view is mouthwatering.

"Eyes on me."

Those ocean eyes meet mine, full of heat and want. His lips are parted, small pants escape them, and I can't wait to thrust my cock into the warmth of his pouty mouth. I part my thighs, still dressed with only my cock out as he gets closer and closer, until his sweet breath ghosts the head of my dick.

"Now suck."

I expected maybe a little hesitance or nervousness, but Kai shocks the shit out of me when he swallows my cock whole until his nose is flush against my pubes. Fucking hell, it feels amazing. His throat constricts around my cock, and spit flows freely down my shaft as he moans at the feel of me inside him, he starts gagging before he pulls off and catches his breath. His eyes are wet, but it doesn't deter him. He holds onto my dick with one hand and grabs my balls with the other. He lowers his mouth and sucks on my balls with all the affection he can give. I'm lightheaded from the most epic blowjob of my life. A niggle of jealousy at the thought of how many guys he has practiced with flits through my mind, but that soon disappears when he starts to suck the head of my dick. The suction is unbelievable, like a powerful vacuum, he destroys my cock with his mouth. I see his hand move out of sight, and I realize what he's doing.

"No. You can't touch yourself. Hands on my thighs."

Following my orders without question, he places his hands on my thighs and proceeds to take my dick on a wild ride. Fast-paced sucking up and down, swirling his tongue around the tip before repeating the motion again. I hold onto his head and force him down until he has swallowed me to the max, and I keep him there. The cries and gagging along with my moans are the most sensual thing I've heard. I'm soaked. My dick is so wet from his spit, and the tears running down his cheeks as he struggles to breathe dampen my groin. He looks so fucking beautiful. I hold him for as long as he can manage before he slaps my thigh, and I let him go. He falls back onto the floor, struggling for air while his hard cock screams for attention.

"On your knees, my little whore."

Wiping the back of his hand over his mouth, he moves into the kneeling position, awaiting my next command.

"Open. Time for your reward."

Kai stares at me, unblinking, with his mouth open wide. I slap my dick hard against his tongue a few times before I shove it back into his mouth and fuck his face like a wild beast. It doesn't take long for the familiar sensation of my impending orgasm to hit. My back is sweaty under my shirt from the exertion. My balls ache and tingle when I'm just on the edge. Kai holds my balls and tugs on them hard, moaning loudly around my dick, causing me to erupt on a howl as I cum down his throat. My thighs shake as spurt after spurt is released. A neverending feeling of complete satisfaction rolls over my body.

When the room finally stops spinning, I look down at Kai, who is watching me and waiting for whatever I have planned next.

"Get on the bed. Lay on your back."

He rushes onto the bed and lays flat in the middle. A slight sheen covers his skin, so damn lickable. I lower my face to his thigh where that damn tattoo taunts me and suck and nibble around the bite mark I left there yesterday. He opens his thighs more for me as I start to lick at his taint, then I gently tongue fuck his balls.

"Jules, please make me cum. I'm so fucking hard," he begs. He can't keep his body still with how much he needs to cum. But he isn't getting it. Not now. This is his punishment. And because I'm a tease, I slowly drag my tongue on his cock from root to tip, losing myself for a second in his alluring scent, but then pull away. Much to his annoyance.

"Where are you going?" he says as I move away from the bed.

"This is your punishment for ignoring me. You made me cum as an apology, and you don't get to cum as a punishment. You can wait until later."

"You fucking asshole!" he shouts, standing from the bed. He then walks over to me and pushes me in the chest, but I grab his wrist.

"I can always make it a week?"

"You're fucking cruel," he sneers at me, and I'm overjoyed. The feisty and confident Kai is starting to make an appearance.

"If you think that's cruel, then you're naive. Unless you want me to show you cruel?"

"Fucker."

"Keep going with the insults. It makes me so hot seeing you lose your shit."

"You're fucking crazy. You're no different than the psycho brothers."

That makes me laugh. I wouldn't say I'm a psycho, but I get what I want, and I don't mind who I have to take down to get it.

"Give me a kiss," I ask, lowering my voice.

"No," he says, crossing his arms in defiance.

"Last chance. Give me a kiss, or you won't come for a week."

"Then I'll just jerk off."

"You won't be able to when I put you in a cock cage."

"You wouldn't dare."

"Oh I would. Even if I have to get the brothers to hold you down while I do it. I told you before, you're mine, and I'll do what I want. And I want a kiss."

It's so amusing, watching the conflicting expressions pass over Kai's face. He wants to fight back, he wants to submit, he wants to punch me in the face, and he also loves this and wants to kiss me.

"You're still an asshole," he says before surging forward to kiss me. Tongues dancing in a sultry dance. I can feel my dick start to stir again. Even with his resistance, Kai melts into me, losing himself in the kiss, his cute mewls have me wanting to fuck him so hard, but we have shit to do. Regretfully, I end the kiss and take him in my arms.

"You need to shower, then eat. We have a long night ahead of us."

"Yeah. I guess," he says, sighing out the words.

"What's wrong?"

"I'm nervous. Last time, it was too much, and I'm not sure I can stomach it down in that room again."

"It'll get easier."

"But what if it doesn't? Will the brothers be mad?"

"You can't help it, Kai. We'll just have to ask them not to include you on that side of things, or you could just watch. Ivan is starting this week, so it might not be a problem, he loves that shit."

"Ivan?"

"Dima and Lev's cousin. He's moving here this weekend to work with us."

"Oh. That might be good. Is he nice?"

"Do you think Dima and Lev are nice?"

"No...not nice."

"Then there's your answer. He's more talkative than the brothers, so don't worry."

"You keep saying that, yet all I do is worry."

I smile as I keep my arms wrapped around him. It'll all work out.

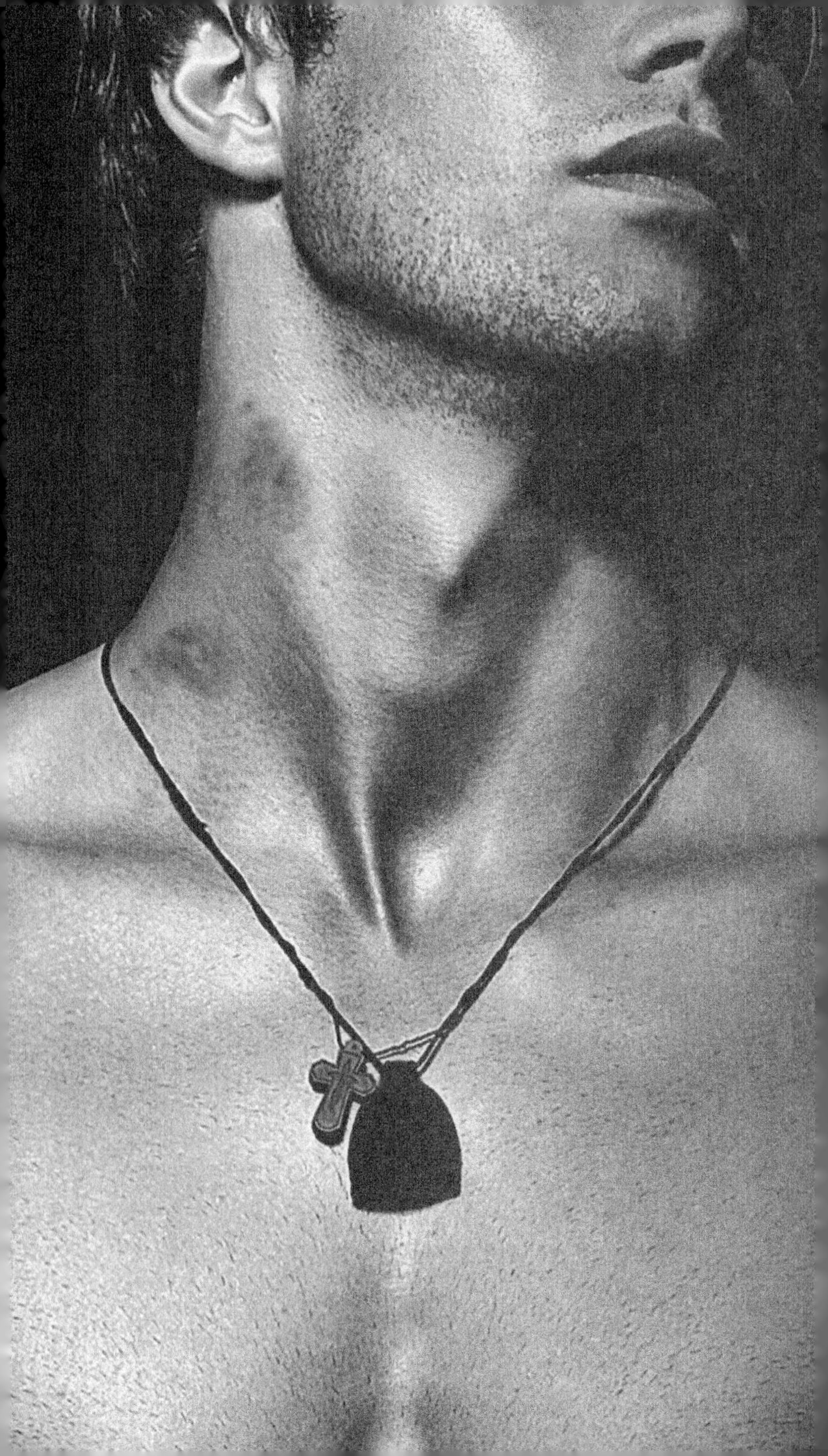

CHAPTER 29
KAI

After getting washed up and fed, Jules told me to head over to the main house to be ready for Carlos and his men to arrive. I would be lying if I said I wasn't nervous, the food from earlier churning in my stomach just even thinking about what is gonna happen in the pen. It was easier to deal with last time, as I was in shock from Aaron being taken, along with the fear instilled in me by Lev that it was my fault. Can you desensitize yourself to this kind of shit? Beating up a few guys in a bar is one thing, but this sadistic torture is a level I'm unsure I can get with.

Walking into the house, I freeze as I watch Aaron sitting at the kitchen table, scrolling through his phone. I haven't really spoken to him since what happened, and for my peace of mind, I need to apologize.

"Hey Aaron," I say, tilting my chin up as he looks up at me. A warm smile spreads across his face, and it's the first genuine smile I've seen on him.

"Hey, Kai. You okay? You look weird."

"Weird?"

"You know, nervous. Like you wanna get away or something."

"You may be right on that last part."

Aaron tilts his head to the side and watches me. I can see why Lev calls him doe. Those large Bambi eyes are so captivating, especially when the manic grin is nowhere to be seen. I walk over and sit across from him, building myself up to try and say the right thing.

"I'm sorry, Aaron."

"For what?"

"For you being taken, for not protecting you. I should've gone up to the apartment with you or checked on you sooner. If I had, then you wouldn't have been..."

"Shut the hell up, Kai," Aaron says, spitting my name out in annoyance. I look him in the eyes, all the softness from a second ago replaced with vacant look. A look that always takes over his face whenever Jake is mentioned.

"Sorry."

"Stop apologizing, it's irritating. Listen to me, it's not your fault. None of it had anything to do with you. Jake did this. He's the one I blame, not you. *Ever*. You got it?"

For a moment, I'm breathless. How can he not blame me?

"Seriously, Kai. You need to stop the self-pitying shit, believe me, it gets you nowhere. This isn't your guilt to feel. So shut that shit down, as I'll be more pissed at you thinking you did wrong. Now, can we stop the moody sadness vibes and go play?"

"Play?"

"Yeah, in the pen. Remember, I want to try Steve out," Aaron says, smirking as he holds out the new switchblade that Lev bought him. He shows off the untouched sharp steel blade, the handle made of smooth solid black wood, embossed in some kind of pattern similar to tree branches that are intricately engraved into it in silver or steel. It's beautiful and also terrifying.

"You're so damn crazy, Aaron."

He shrugs, unbothered. I know what happened affected him, but in a weird fucked up way, Lev's psycho nature is what grounds him and keeps him in the present. As I watch him gently run his fingers over the blade with a sappy far away look in his eyes, I decide to let the guilt go. I have to for my own sanity.

"I am. Now let's go, I'm dying to see my man in action."

"Oh god, you're both sick."

He waggles his brows at me.

"And from the bruises on your neck, I'd say you're just as sick, too, Kai. Does your uncle Jules get you off by choking you?"

"Touché. And don't call him my uncle. He's just Jules."

"I'll take that as a yes."

We both laugh as we head down to the holding pen. I'm glad I cleared things up with Aaron. I still feel responsible, but the guilt starts to feel less and less with each step we take. That was the first hurdle. Now, I need to see if my stomach can take what's behind those doors.

We enter the pen to see Dima, Lev and Simon hanging around, chatting.

"Aaron, sit in that chair in the corner. Do not speak or move," Lev says.

I wait for Aaron to come back with a retort to Lev, but he doesn't, he just leisurely strolls over to a chair that is in the far corner that faces the center of the room, and sits down. Resting his hand on one thigh and rubbing his switchblade with the other, he looks so relaxed. Too relaxed. Holy shit, he isn't relaxed, he's turned on. Aaron's face is all dopey and focused on Lev. Lev stares back at him, nostrils flaring. It's borderline fucking indecent. Jules had mentioned that Aaron has a violence kink, but this is not what I expected, as I've never heard of such a thing.

The door to the room opens, and I spin around to see Jules walk in with Carlos, two of his men that I've never met, and a guy with his hands bound.

"Carlos," Dima says in greeting.

"Dima. Lev. Thank you for accommodating us," Carlos says. He walks further into the room and moves closer to Simon, who takes a step back, a threatening glare aimed at Carlos not to get any closer.

"Not happy to see me, little lion?" Carlos says, mockingly.

"Call me that name again, and I'll smash your face in."

"Shut up, Si. I've warned you before," Lev says with a warning etched in his words.

Simon moves to the other side of the room to stand next to a quietly seated Aaron.

"I thought you were bringing two guys?" Dima asks, pointing to the one guy with bound hands.

"The other one ran away before we could get to him, but my brother is on it," Carlos says.

"Ahh yes, how is Enrico?" D asks.

"Trouble. Nothing new. Shall we begin?"

"Thought you'd never ask. Kai, would you make our guest comfortable?"

I swallow hard at the command, I can feel the blood drain from my face, but I push through and guide our 'victim' over to the chair that's in the middle of the room. He's very quiet, although that won't last long.

"I don't want him dead. Just disfigured enough to keep him around as a warning," Carlos says, his voice cold and detached. Goosebumps trail along my arms at his words. I look over at Jules and the burning look of desire and wickedness that has taken over his face has me frozen in place. His eyes are black from how dilated his pupils are, his nostrils flare and I swear I can see his pulse flicker in his neck. He really does enjoy this shit.

Me however...I don't think I can do this.

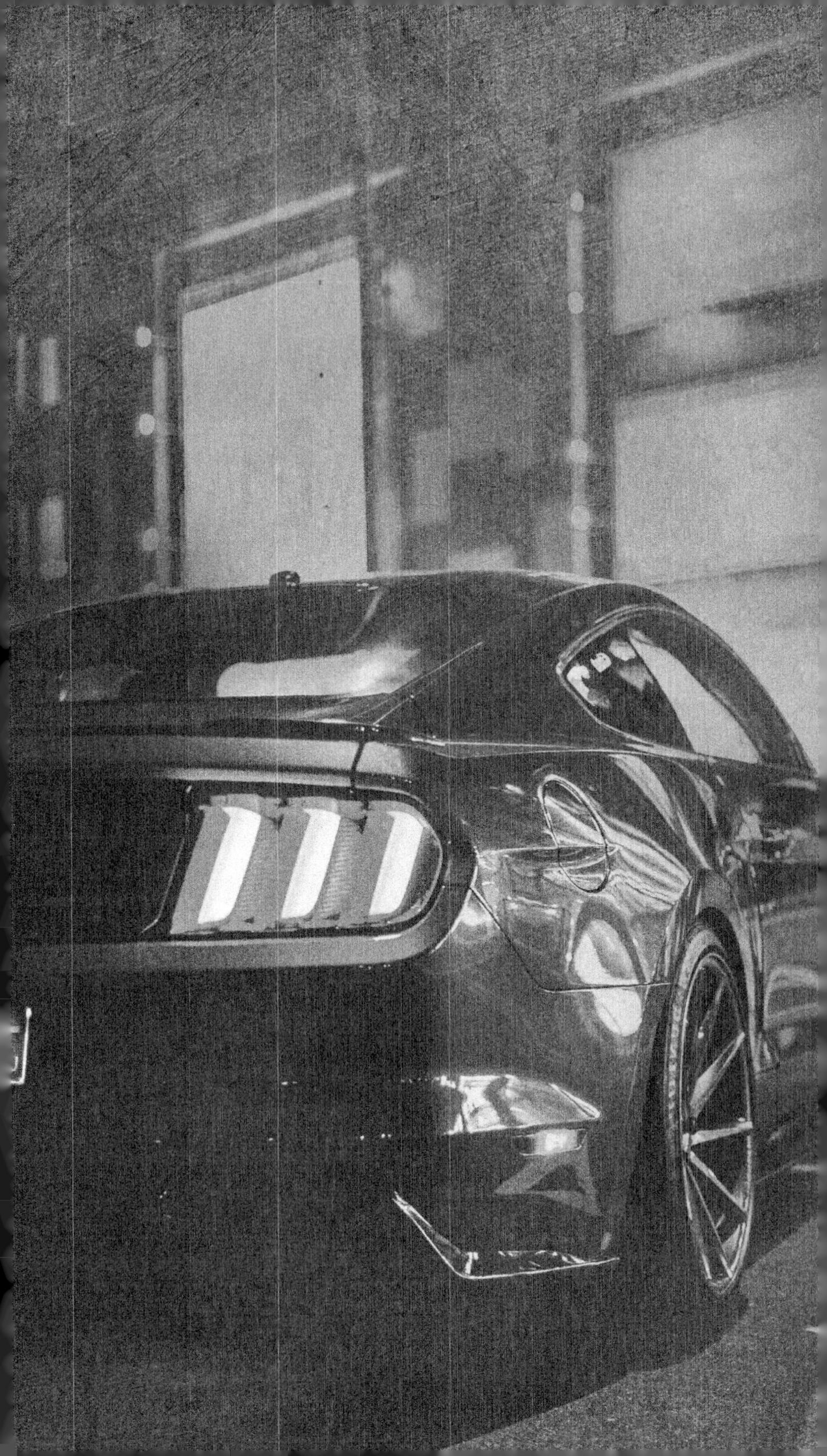

CHAPTER 30
JULES

I'm all amped up to get this show on the road, until I look at Kai who looks like he's about to pass out. His face is ashen and his skin looks clammy. I look over at Simon who is watching Kai with the same concern before he looks at me with a questioning look. I go over to Kai, and help him situate whoever the guy is we're questioning, and secure him in the seat.

"I don't need your help. I'm fine," Kai quietly hisses at me.

"You look like death. You shouldn't be in here if it's too much," I whisper back.

"Is there a problem?" Dima asks as he approaches us. He assesses Kai closely and I know he can see it across Kai's face.

"Kai, why don't you keep an eye out front, make sure we're secure," Dima says. Kai flinches but knows not to question. He looks at me with such hate, as if this is my fault. And maybe it is, but he can't be down here like this as it puts us all at risk.

"Kai…" I start but he pulls away and cuts me off.

"Don't fucking touch me."

Boy, do those words piss me off. This impulsive behavior is getting out of hand and I'm fucking furious.

Without another word, he storms off, barging past one of Carlos's men who laughs as he pushes Kai in the shoulder.

"Fucking pussy," the unnamed and now dead man says.

"Fuck you," Kai snarls, pushing the guy in the chest.

"That's enough. On second thought, go back to the house, Kai," Dima orders and Kai is out of there as fast as the speed of light.

Who does this fucker think he is? I rush over to the guard and slam him into the wall before punching him in the face. He was unprepared for the assault, so I use his slowness in response to get as many hits in as I can. His nose makes a crunching sound when my knuckles connect with the bone, but it's not enough. I grab him by the shirt and slam him again hard against the wall.

"You have a death wish, talking to my man like that?"

The ugly fucker spits in my face, which enrages me more, stoking a fire in me that's already burning brightly. So I react. I pull him forward and knee him in the ribs, forcing him to collapse onto the ground. The so-called hard guy is groaning, clutching at his side, but I can't hold in the beast. The rage. He touched Kai and insulted him. I won't be able to let it go unless I hurt him.

"Boss, you not gonna stop this?" the second guard says to Carlos.

"No. We're here as guests and he insulted one of their men's partners. I would do the same. It's all about consequences," Carlos says while looking at Simon, who scowls back at him. I kneel on the floor, pulling the man's hair, forcing him to face me.

"Are you ready to say sorry?"

"I'm sorry your man is a pussy, you dumb bitch," the guy barks at me and I can't help but smile. This pent up energy for a fight, to dispel the lingering anger I have from the whole Kai situation to this point is so damn satisfying.

"Jules!" Aaron shouts out from the corner and throws his switchblade toward me, which I manage to catch with one hand.

"What the fuck, Aaron?" Lev shouts.

"Steve was bored."

I grip the man's hand and face it palm down on the floor, and with nothing but adrenaline coursing through my veins and Kai's face in my mind, I lift the beautiful blade and stab it down into the guy's hand. Screams of pain echo in the room as the sharp steel penetrates the flesh.

"I can't deal with the noise," Dima moans. Always complaining about the crying and screaming from anyone we have in the pen as he's susceptible to a migraine. But he loves the blood too much to not be involved. Still, it doesn't stop him from complaining every single time.

"That was so fucking hot," Aaron says, his gaze entranced on his blade that's now lodged in the hand of this fucker.

"Doe...." Lev warns.

"Shut up. At least Jules has done something. Dying of boredom over here. Can I have Steve back now?"

"Back up now, Jules. We need to get started on pisspants over here," Lev says and I turn to see the guy secured to the chair has pissed himself. Gross. I bend down and pull the blade from the moaning asshole who touched Kai, and toss it back to Aaron, who looks like I've just given him the best Christmas present. My heart thuds like a racehorse, the adrenaline rush now subsiding, but not being replaced by the quiet I'm used to. Kai's the reason. I'm so fucking pissed that I want to cut this guy in front of me to pieces so I can get control over these feelings that only Kai prompts in me.

"Simon, move this crying asshole over to the side," Dima says.

Simon grabs Carlos's injured guard under the arms and drags him over to the other side of the room.

"You wanna fix your man up, there are medical supplies in the fridge and cabinets on the back wall," Dima says to Carlos. Carlos then orders his uninjured guard to go clean up the whimpering idiot. And he had the nerve to call Kai a pussy.

Lev goes to the back wall where their array of torture tools are neatly displayed, and ponders for a few moments on what to use. He finally chooses the reliable blow torch and a jagged knife. Carlos wants the guy fucked up, those will certainly do the trick.

Crouching in front of the piss stained quiet man, Lev dangles the knife in his face. This guy may have an impassive expression on his face, but the fact that he pissed himself tells me he's already under immense stress. I doubt this will take long.

"Now. I've heard that you may know about or may be involved in taking money that didn't belong to you. Care to share with the group what you know? The more you tell us, the less drawn out this will be," Lev says. The nameless man keeps his eyes down, his breathing is off the charts, practically hyperventilating.

"Not gonna talk? Let me help with that."

Lev stands and yanks the guy's hair so hard he cries out, unable to fight Lev tilting his head back. Lev wastes no time in taking the knife and slicing his face from his upper cheek to the corner of his mouth. The skin peels open, revealing the fat and muscle underneath. Blood begins to ooze down his face, which only gets worse as his mouth widens in screams of terror. Lev lets go and steps back, smirking as he admires his handiwork. I daren't look over at Aaron. I just know from how quiet he is that this is affecting him. It wouldn't be out of character for him to be jerking off to the show. You couldn't make this shit up of how fucked up this house is. I've lived here with the brothers so long, that I believe they're normal and the outside world is screwed up. This situation just highlights how dumb that is. Then again, I'm part of this family, so that makes me just as bad. Fuck. No wonder Kai can't deal with it. I just assumed most people could adapt. But still, the little fucker shouldn't have lost his shit with me like that.

"Can we tape his mouth shut? This is unbearable, especially with the other whining asshole," Dima moans at Lev.

"Not in the mood, D. Deal with it or fuck off."

"Is it always like this?" Carlos asks. I hadn't noticed he was standing beside me.

"Yes, and worse," I say, as Carlos smiles at me, amused by the whole thing. Fucking hell, another unhinged bastard. Just when you think there's no more of us, another pops up.

Lev lights the blow torch and adjusts the flame, directing it at the nameless guy's chest.

"Ever heard of a burn necklace?" Lev asks the guy. He's shaking uncontrollably in the chair, fighting against the binds to move as far away from Lev as he can. The gaping wound on his cheek will leave a monster of a scar.

"I asked you a fucking question."

"No!" the guy shouts, panting, on the verge of fainting.

"It's like a pearl necklace, but not as fun. I'm gonna ask you a question. If I think you're lying, I'll give you a demonstration of the perfect burn necklace. Or you could tell us the truth, and maybe I'll stop."

The guy nods as tears stream down his face and sweat gathers at his brow.

"Do you know who stole the money?"

"Yes."

"Good. See how easy that was? Next question. Give me a name."

"I-I can't! He'll kill me."

"Such a shame," Lev says, his tone mocking in sympathy, shaking his head slowly from side to side. He aims the blowtorch at the guy's neck, adorning it with the perfect necklace shaped burn. The skin singes and bubbles as it congeals under the heat. The screams are piercing, but rapidly morphs into a chant. A chant of a name.

"Stop!! Enrico, Enrico, Enrico..." he babbles. Lev turns off the torch and looks up at Carlos. The guy's babbles then turn into nonsense as his eyes roll back, seconds away from becoming unconscious.

"Enrico? Carlos's brother?" Dima asks. But he gets no reply from the semi conscious guy. D slaps him across the untouched cheek.

"Hey...wakey wakey. Are you telling us Enrico, Carlos's brother, is the one that stole?" Dima asks.

"Yes...yes," he gasps before passing out.

Everyone turns to Carlos, who seems unmoved by the situation. He runs his fingers over his bottom lip, contemplation written all over his face as he watches the now unconscious man.

"Thanks for your help. If it's not too much trouble, I would appreciate your men helping me get them back into the car. I will take it from there," Carlos says.

Neither Lev or Dima ask questions, though I wish they would so we'd know what the fuck has been going on.

"Simon and Jules, untie him and take him out front," Dima orders us, and like a well oiled machine, we get to work on getting these guys out of here and cleaning this fucking mess up. Lev disappears with a very clingy and horny Aaron, and after myself and Simon are finished in the holding pen, we walk back through the quiet house. Simon offers to stay in the mansion to keep a watch after everything that's happened. And I take my tired and agitated ass back to the house to confront Kai. Let's hope he's ready for what I have planned, because I need a release. And I need to put my man in his place.

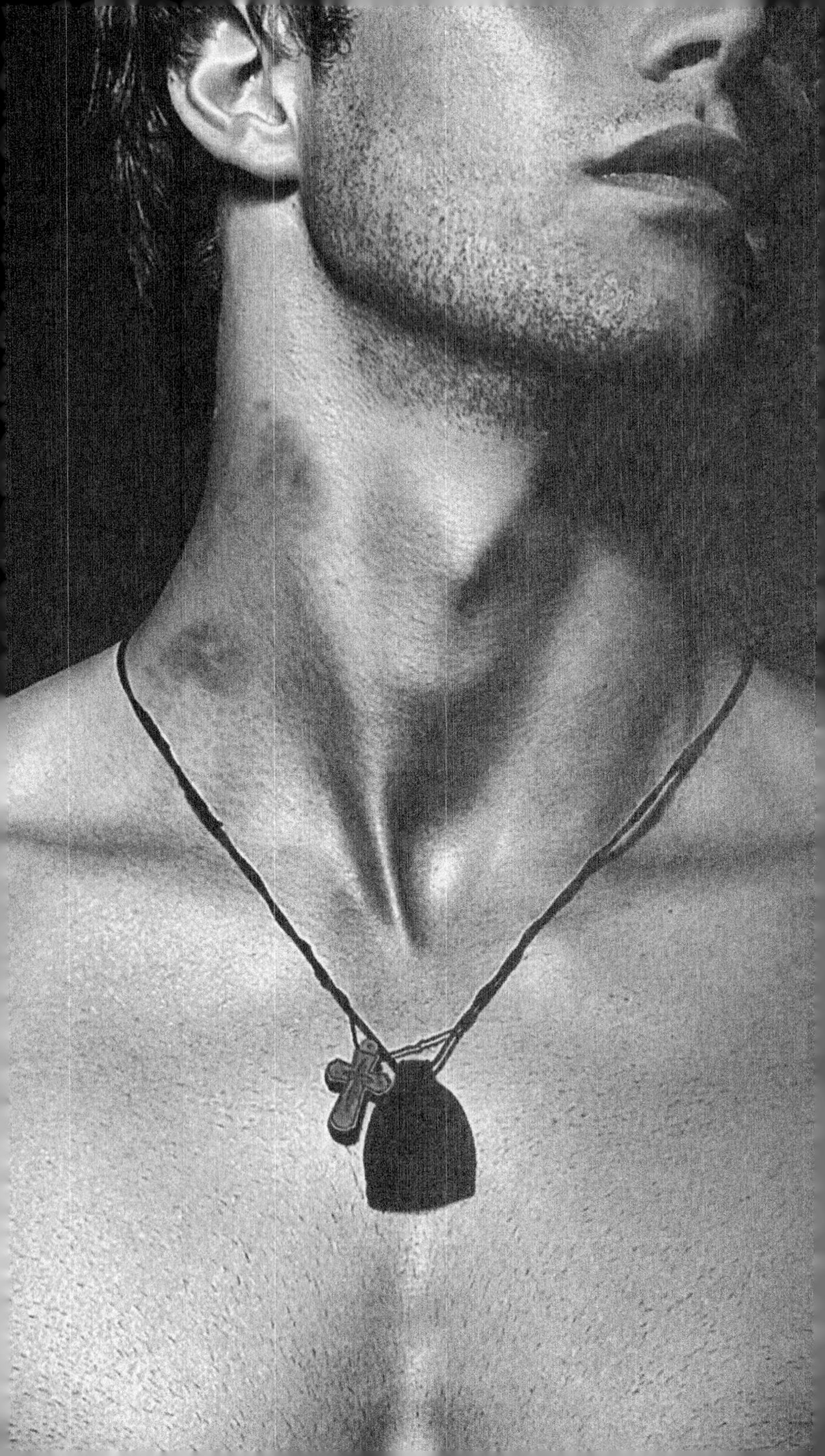

CHAPTER 31
KAI

Weak, weak, weak.

That word repeats on a loop as I stare back at myself in the bathroom mirror, wearing nothing but a towel. I thought a hot shower would help calm my temper, but it's done nothing other than make it worse, the quiet only making my internal thoughts louder. It was so embarrassing, what happened in the pen, that I don't think I can show my face again. Jules didn't help, trying to control the situation as usual, making things worse.

Water droplets drip over my torso, the bruises on my body have changed color, the tenderness hardly present. I look defeated and tired, the shine in my eyes now dull and unmoving, my mouth droops with sadness, the muscle refusing to turn it into a smile. I don't look twenty-two. I look old and haggard. What the hell have I let happen to my life? I should be at college or working, partying with friends, being free in the world to explore and have fun. To treat everyday as if it's my last. But instead, I can't help but consider that I've come to the end of the road. If I've proven anything over the last few years, it's that I'm pointless, an unnecessary shell of a human that offers nothing to no one. After spending the night with Jules, I really felt things had changed for me, that I had hope and a future. That I had a man who could love me and fill those empty parts of me deep inside that yearned to be wanted. Was it all a lie? A dream? Am I that fucking naive to have put all these expectations onto one person?

Maybe I should pack a bag and set off into the night. Cut off from everything and everyone. Even my mom. I've been such a shit son. I've ignored the countless texts and calls, because I don't know what to say to her. I can't tell her what we do here. I can't tell her why I can never come home, because of the threats from Zac. I certainly can't tell her about Jules. So what can I say to her? Every word out of my mouth would be a lie, and she would know it was a lie. Moms are like bloodhounds when it comes to sniffing out the truth from their kids, in my experience anyway.

A loud bang repeatedly thumps against my bedroom door. I locked it when I came back as I knew Jules would hunt me down. He was just as pissed at me as I was him, maybe more so.

"Kai! Open the door!" he shouts, repeatedly banging on my bedroom door. I don't answer as I walk back into my bedroom. I just stare at the door, hoping telepathy is a real thing, that he gets the message to go away.

"Kai!"

Remaining quiet, I walk over to the small window that looks back onto the woodlands surrounding the Kozlov property. The moon is bright tonight, shining over the trees and house with a soft glow. The branches sway in the mild wind that feels like shards of ice on the skin because its so fucking cold.

"Kai, I swear, if you don't open the door, I will kick it in."

I'm sure you will, I think to myself. I don't care. I mean, what can he possibly do to me that will make me feel worse than I already do? As I continue to watch the trees, Jules goes silent and I think he may have given up. That is quickly proven wrong when the sound of shattered wood fills the room, and I turn around to see Jules burst through my destroyed door. At least he's a man of his word. I don't move as he approaches me, getting in my face like he can demand things from me. But from the dark look honed in on him, I know I've pushed him too far. I can't be mad about it though, he's warned me. I just don't care anymore. He can do what he wants.

I don't resist when he seizes my wrists.

"I warned you. This is for your own good. You're not a failure, Kai. But you will not defy me."

His grip tightens like an iron vice, the pain triggering a hint of emotion in me. Excitement with a small hint of fear. Pulling me closer, the heat of his breath washes over my skin, his smell fills my nostrils, his cologne, and if possible, the scent of danger radiates off him. It fills my head with the comfort of home, but I fight it. Unwilling to allow him to put me under his spell, refusing to enjoy any part of this.

"Look at me," he commands, and I'm unable to resist, too tempted to watch him as his dark eyes bore into mine. In a move not too different from his sparring tactics, he spins me around and presses me face first against the wall next to the window. The cold surface bites into my bare skin in contrast to the warmth of his body at my back. He raises my hands above my head and locks them together at the wrist, his large hand holding them in a hard hold. With his free hand, he aggressively pulls away my towel, leaving me completely bare and open to him. But still I don't fight him.

With the same hand, he traces a path down my spine, slow and deliberate, building up the anticipation, reminding me of his control. I'm unable to withhold the shiver it elicits from me, my need to be defiant is warring with wanting to just submit to the feeling of how good this truly feels.

Then out of nowhere, a sharp stinging slap ricochets off my left ass cheek. I cry out at the sudden move, unable to control my reaction. But he's a step ahead of me and sets a relentless pace, delivering one slap after another, each strike a punctuation lesson I'm being taught. That I'm his and I don't disrespect or defy him. I feel a wetness against my face, realizing they're tears. The sting has turned to a burning sensation that hurts so bad, but feels so good. I don't know if I love or hate it, the line blurring between pleasure and pain.

"Are you going to defy me again?"

"No," I gasp when another slap lands.

"Does it hurt?"

"Yes," I hiss.

"Does it feel good?"

"Yes, no. God, yes," I pant, my voice hitching as I try to latch onto one feeling, but I can't.

"I love seeing you like this, Kai. So conflicted. A sobbing, needy mess."

When he finally stops, his panting breath closes over my ear.

"Now, tell me. Who do you belong to?"

I want to say 'you', but the stubborn part of me that's trying to keep some control so he doesn't win this takes over.

"Myself."

A harder slap across my now destroyed ass has me screaming out as I rise onto my tiptoes. Holy shit, I can't keep this up.

"Again, who do you belong to?"

"You! You sadistic, controlling bastard!"

I hate him in that moment, hate how he makes me feel, but beneath the hate is a dark desire, an undeniable connection that left me wanting more. Always wanting more.

"Good. Now don't move. Keep your hands above your head."

I hear shuffling behind me, a belt hitting the hard floor and the sounds of clothes being removed. My heart starts to beat out of control. My dick that's been hard the entire time, which I ignored, is rubbing against the wall and I'm dying to touch myself. It's like being prevented from scratching an itch, making you crazy and a trembling mess.

"Suck," Jules says as he pushes two fingers into my mouth. His naked body is pushed up behind mine, his cock rests against my crack where I automatically grind against it. Jules moans as I suck his fingers like a starved whore while gyrating on his cock like an experienced stripper. Spit drips down my chin and over his hand as he removes it and moves them to my ass, where he slides his fingers between my cheeks and pushes his slick fingers against my hole. I push back, but he doesn't tease, he surges his thick finger forward, breaching the muscle until it's knuckle deep inside me. The mild burn on my cheeks along with the internal burn of him stretching me is so overwhelming. It doesn't take long for him to locate my prostate, his dick pounded it the other night like a dream, but his finger rubs it with such precision, I nearly jump in the air.

"Feel good?"

"Yes, more," I groan as he torments my g-spot like an expert in prostate milking. His other finger quickly joins in on the action which turns me into a complete mess. The stretch, the pressure and prostate massage is so good, I'm already on the verge of coming.

"Turn around."

Unsteadily on my feet, I lower my hands and turn to face him. Fuck he looks feral. The want in his frantic eyes for me pulls me up sharp. The intensity of it makes my stomach swoop. To have a powerful man like this want me so badly has all the negative thoughts shutting down.

"Hands back up over your head. Put this leg over my shoulder," he says as he kneels on the floor in front of me. Oh my god. This is the hottest thing I've ever witnessed. I throw my right leg over his shoulder, my dick in his face and my ass wide open. Then, as only Jules can do, he has me howling in seconds, turning my brain into mush.

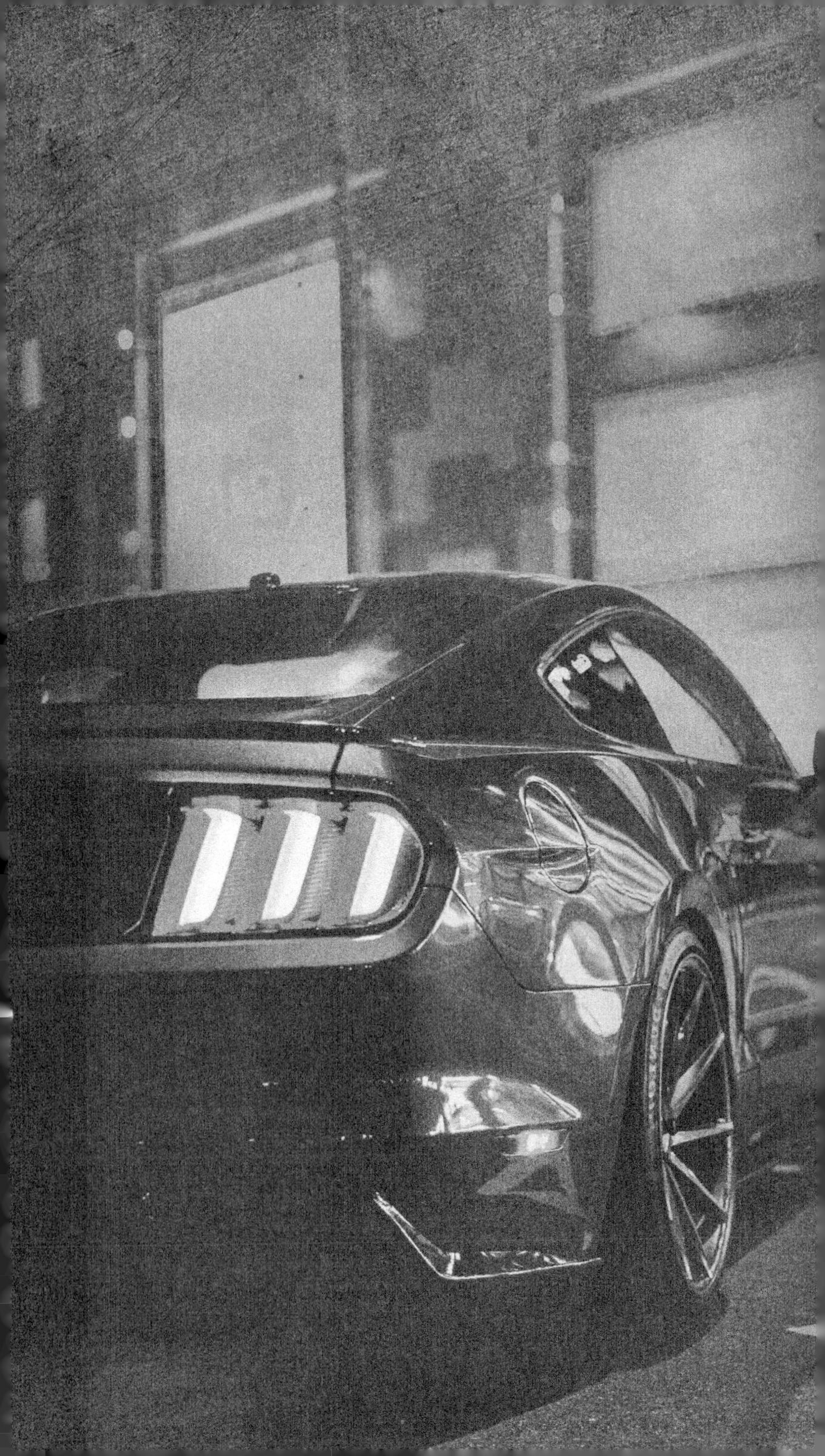

CHAPTER 32
JULES

He's finally given in. No more pretending to not want this, to not want me. Kai can't hide anything from me, I can read him like a book, and I can sense what he needs. A bond ties us together, linking our psyches. The snarky brat is his reaction to fear, the fear that he's a let down and that everyone around him will just give up. Well he's in for a surprise, as I have no intention of giving him up or letting him walk away. These emotional meltdowns have to be dealt with, and luckily for him I know this is the way. The aggression, adoration and dominance pushes him into a lighter place mentally. He needs to hand over some control in order to be clear headed, and as a control freak, I'll happily be his guide.

On my knees with his leg over my shoulder, Kai is something else to look at. Beyond breathtaking. All these years of fucking around, never giving a fuck if someone got off, as long as I had a release, have come to an end. Tonight is about him and I plan to make him cum like he never has before, with my fingers in his ass, my handprints on his cheeks and his dick in my mouth.

I stroke his thigh that is over my shoulder while I lubricate my fingers with my mouth, making sure they are drenched enough to fuck his ass into oblivion. He grinds his balls into my face, panting, and eager to be touched. As soon as my fingers are wet enough, I move them behind his balls and rub them along his taint, following the path to his hole. Both fingers slip in easily, and I locate the button of destruction, pressing hard on the swollen gland. As I massage inside his tight channel, I remove my hand from his thigh to grab his cock and guide it to my mouth. I've been dying for my first taste of him. My first blowjob. I can't wait.

When the head of his dick hits the back of my throat, Kai arches his back off the wall, moaning at how good it feels. My two fingers set a steady rhythm of plowing his hole, stroking his prostate on each entry. His cock feels so good in my mouth, heavy and warm, his flavor a blend of shower gel, bitterness and salt. I could eat this daily, especially if he reacts like the slut he is right now. I suck him at the same pace as I finger him, the sounds of saliva and suction similar to a porn show. I swallow him down until my nose meets his hairless groin, and I moan around his cock, eliciting another loud groan from the gorgeous man himself.

"Jesus, Jules, I can't hold back."

I pull off his dick for a second, to respond.

"Then don't. Show me how you taste. I want to see if my pretty whore tastes as sweet and salty as I think he will."

I go straight back to work and suck him as if my life depends on it. His hands suddenly grab the back of my head before large spurts of cum land on the back of my tongue and down my throat. Fuck, he tastes amazing. His thigh on my shoulder shakes and grips harder onto me as he cums and cums. I continue to milk his prostate for every last drop.

After he finishes, his leg slides off my shoulder, slumping against the wall. I feel really fucking proud of myself with that BJ. I stand up with a hard as fuck dick, as Kai catches his breath.

"On your knees."

Those wide eyes look up at me before zooming in on my hard dick. He quickly kneels in front of me, ready to suck me, but I have other ideas.

"No. I'm gonna cum on that pretty face."

"Don't call me pretty."

I laugh before humming as I stroke myself with a tight hold of my shaft.

"Spit on my cock."

I watch Kai as he hovers over my dick that I have aimed at his mouth, and he coats it in saliva. I get back to stroking myself, and the wet slide feels amazing. My hand is moving so fast I'm concerned I may chafe myself. My ass clenches as the force of my orgasm builds, my balls tingle and I swear my cock gets bigger.

"Shit, gonna cum. Open your mouth."

Obediently, Kai opens his mouth, staring at me in awe, like I'm some kind of apparition. A low growl escapes me as I spurt all over his face, in his mouth and on his neck. He closes his eyes, relishing the moment. When my orgasm fades, I rub the tip of my dick over his mouth, pushing it in for him to clean me up. I hiss as he licks me clean, sensitive from the eruption he tore out of me.

"Do you like tasting me? Hmm? Want to eat my cum as a treat, my pretty whore?"

"Yes. You taste so good, my favorite treat."

"That's what I like to hear."

Kai looks so sleepy right now, his eyes droopy and his body nearly collapsed into a heap on the floor. I bend down and lift him into my arms.

"What are you doing?" Kai yelps, holding onto me for dear life.

"Carrying you to bed."

Considering we're similar heights and not too far off in build, he's fucking heavy. But I like treating him like this. I know he does too as he snuggles his face into my neck.

I place him on his bed then grab some tissues off the nightstand to clean his face, before covering him with the sheets.

"You're not leaving me are you?" he says quietly into the pillow. I slip into the bed behind him, as the big spoon.

"Never. Besides, we need to talk."

"Noooo, can it wait? I'm tired."

"No, Kai. It can't."

He turns over so we're facing each other and waits for me to continue.

"First of all, this is the second time I've warned you not to sass me in front of the guys. You crossed a line tonight, in front of business acquaintances. That little tantrum could've caused problems in the interrogation. Don't do it again, otherwise it'll be the brothers punishing you rather than me."

"I made such an ass out of myself."

"Yeah, you did."

"Wow, you really are the meaning behind tough love."

"I don't sugar coat shit. You're an adult. You have to deal with it. Now, the second thing, why is your mom messaging me to say she hasn't heard from you?"

"Oh fuck, really?"

"Yes. Have you been lying to me, Kai? Did something happen back home?"

Kai turns rigid at the question, telling me everything I need to know. He hasn't told me the full truth, and will most likely lie to me again and say it's all fine.

"I haven't lied about anything. Why are you asking? Is Mom alright?"

"If you called her, you'd know."

"Point taken. You know you can be a mean fucker, don't you?"

"If that's how you want to see it. I just answer truthfully. Truth is important in relationships and in our line of work."

He ponders the statement like I hoped he would. I'm inwardly willing him to tell me what actually happened back home. But predictably, he shuts down.

"I agree. I'll call her tomorrow. Is that all? I'm exhausted."

"You better call her tomorrow, otherwise I'll use the belt on your ass next time."

"Yeah right. Funny."

"Do I look like I'm joking?" I ask as I grab his neck to get the point across, using physical language that he understands. That I'm in charge.

"I promise," he rasps, before I let him go and briefly kiss him on those plump pink lips. He turns over and I cover his back with my own body. Protecting him from anything that may come near him.

My Kai. All fucking mine.

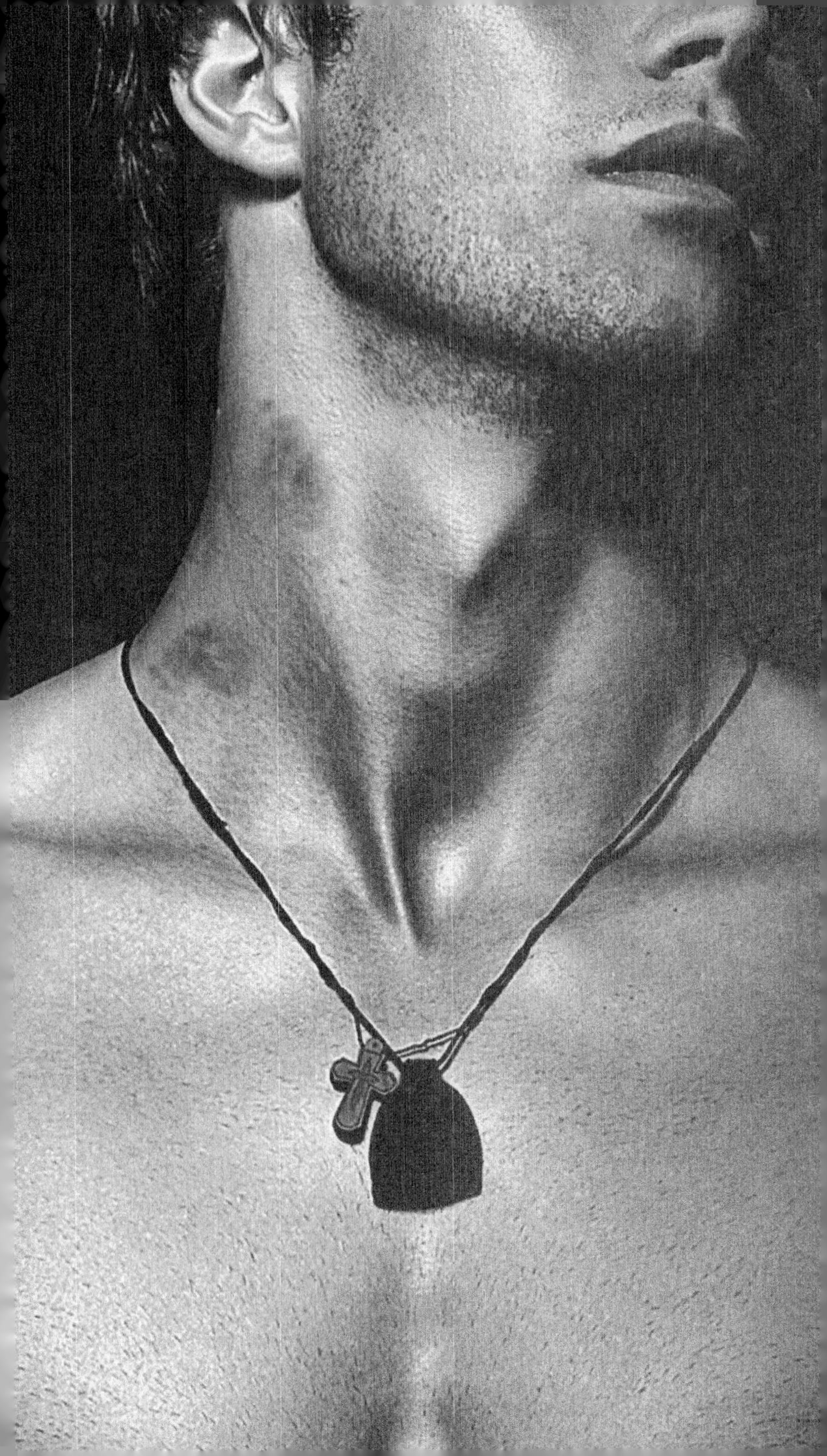

CHAPTER 33
KAI

My alarm on my phone wakes me before I'm ready to leave the deep slumber of sleep. I bury my head into my pillow, refusing to acknowledge it's a new day. I don't want to face anyone today, not after what happened yesterday. What Dima and Lev must think of me is a question I'm not too keen on exploring.

I turn my head to the side to see Jules still asleep, looking more angelic than he really is. I decide to let him sleep a little longer, and get up to go take a piss before my bladder bursts all over the bed. After relieving myself, I wash my hands and brush my teeth so I don't kill Jules with morning breath. I look at myself in the mirror and see the hickeys on my body are fading fast, the bruising around my neck is more subtle. I don't like the idea of his marks on my skin disappearing. I hate that it erases his touch. I enjoyed the soreness and the bold statement they represented, of ownership. I'm so lost in thoughts as I rub each mark while

I stare at my reflection, I fail to notice Jules walking up behind me until he grabs me around the waist.

"Admiring yourself?" he teases as he kisses my shoulders.

"They're fading."

He looks up into the mirror and scans my body, he strokes his fingertips over each fading mark, like he's committing them to memory.

"I'll just have to give you more. Can't have you walking around unmarked, can we?"

Jules catches my eyes in the mirror and smirks at me with a look so sultry, I almost feel shy.

"Want me to put my stamp back on you? Hmm?"

Again, I get swept up in the bubble that's all Jules. Nodding my head frantically in agreement, as I can't find my voice to speak. Too needy for him to get started.

"Turn around," he whisper growls, that deep voice causing my eyes to roll back with how sexy he sounds.

I turn and Jules buries his face in my neck, and starts to suck. I grab onto his shoulders so tightly, my fingers digging into his flesh to help with the pain. It hurts so fucking good. After he is done with the first, he proceeds to do the same on the front of my throat and the other side of my neck. His lips hold on to my skin so tightly, the uncomfortable pressure has me squirming, and I start pushing his head harder into my skin, needing more. I begin to mewl as he moves down to my torso and repeats this hickey ritual.

"Oh god, Jules. Suck my nipples, mark them too."

I'm frantic with need, my nipples are so hard, dying to be treated the same way with that talented mouth. Jules doesn't question and moves down to my left nipple first, but he doesn't suck, he bites. Hard.

"Fuck!"

That fucking hurts, but as he licks the bite, the sting travels over my body to every erogenous zone. Goosebumps cover every inch of me as he sucks around the buds, it's borderline too much. He moves over to my other nipple and treats it the exact same, I look down and see a speckle of blood on one of my nipples from the bite and it turns me on even more.

"I'm bleeding," I rasp. Jules looks up at me from under those thick lashes.

"Only a little. Your blood on my tongue tastes so fucking good."

My head falls back on a moan at his words, his mouth assaults me further, down to my stomach, the suction is so hard all the tenderness I've missed returns, filling me with happiness.

"Now you look perfect again," he says as he stands in front of me, inspecting his work. I spin around and look back in the mirror and my eyes widen. These hickeys are larger and angrier than the last ones. I love them. My new favorite outfit. My nipples are red raw and swollen, when I touch them I wince. Having material rub against them today is going to hurt, but it'll be a reminder of Jules. How he owns me.

"Get that sexy ass of yours ready. We're late as it is."

"Do I have to leave the house? I'm gonna die of shame when I see the guys."

"Yes you do have to leave the house. Deal with it."

"Whatever."

Jules grabs my balls and yanks on them hard.

"Ow, what the hell?"

"Attitude, sweetheart. I've already warned you twice now."

"Okay, but can you let go?"

Jules grins and walks out of the bathroom, leaving me sore, horny, and a total bitch in heat for him.

Half an hour later, Jules and I are walking into the main house, where we're greeted by Aaron. He leaps out of his seat, excitement sparkles in those big brown eyes, and I've no idea why he is so happy to see us.

"Oh man, Jules, that was fucking epic yesterday. I haven't even washed the blood off Steve yet as it looks so pretty."

"Happy to entertain," Jules says, his voice level as he shrugs his shoulders.

"Why? What happened yesterday?" I ask, totally confused.

Aaron is behaving like an excitable puppy, and its freakin' me the fuck out.

"You didn't tell him, Jules?"

"Wasn't important," Jules says with another shrug, before heading over to the counter to make a coffee.

"Can someone fill me in?" I ask.

"So your man, he fucked up that dude who called you a pussy. It was so awesome, and pretty hot. My Steve is no longer a virgin."

"Wait! He what now? Jules? What did you do?" I ask, nervous of the response, but weirdly excited if the butterflies in my stomach are anything to go by. Now that's odd.

"He's not dead, if that's what you're asking. Even if he deserved it. I just taught him a lesson."

"With Aaron's switchblade?"

"He's called Steve," Aaron says.

"Let's just say he won't be able to use his left hand for a long time," Lev says as he fills two cups of coffee, while I stand here dumbfounded. He hurt the guy for me. I'm annoyed as my ego takes a hit that he had to do this in my honor, but the flutter in my heart at how romantic the gesture was overtakes the bad. What the hell is wrong with me? Have I been here too long?

I walk over to Jules and hold his face in my hands.

"You did that for me?" I whisper, too emotional to talk loudly.

"I'd do more than that. I look after what's mine. I'd cover the streets in blood for you, Kai."

"That's the most romantic thing I've ever heard," I say, as I lean in to kiss him softly.

"Lev has said more romantic things than that, but I get it. It's hot when they hurt others for you," Aaron says as I laugh at his skewed view of the world.

"For fucks sake, what did I say about making out in my house? Quit it," Dima says as he walks into the kitchen with Seb.

"Stop moaning, D. You're like that with me all the time," Seb says.

"Yes, but it's my house."

Seb rolls his eyes, sighing in defeat at Dima's broody nature.

"Roll those eyes again, beautiful and see what happens," Dima says, but Seb just smiles and pecks Dima on the lips before sitting at the kitchen table, unaffected by the threat.

Still lost in the land of fairies that Jules did that for me, harmed another in my name, I forget that I may be in trouble for yesterday. Before Dima brings my ass back to planet Earth.

"Kai. Stop staring at Jules like that and tell me what the fuck happened yesterday?" Dima says.

"D, don't go hard on him," Seb says.

"Seb, stay out of it. This is business. So, Kai, explain," Dima says, as he crosses his arms. He's so fucking intimidating, it would be easy to curl up and hide away. His piercing eyes don't blink as they sear into my soul. There's no mercy or empathy in his tone. Not that I expected there to be.

"I don't know. I thought I could handle that side of things, but I started to feel off and I just couldn't cope with it."

"You should've said something beforehand. You completely derailed the whole interrogation. Fortunately it was Carlos, but it would've been very difficult if we'd had someone else in there. You're gonna have to find a way to deal with it or you'll be no use to us."

"I can't go back home," I say, pleading that they don't get rid of me.

"Who said you would be going back home?"

"Dima..." Jules growls.

"Do you not listen, Jules? You're employed by us. I couldn't give a fuck if you're screwing each other. You're treated all the same. You were hardly any better down there, reacting like a possessive boyfriend."

"That's fucking rich coming from you. You seem to forget what your husband got us all involved in," Jules says, and I'm horrified. What the hell is he doing?

Dima walks towards Jules and gets in his face, his hands grab onto Jules's shirt, making sure he can't move.

"I would watch that fucking mouth of yours. I've allowed you enough leeway when it comes to Kai. But no more," Dima says before shoving Jules in the chest. I rush to Jules's side, and hold his hand in mine.

"Leave it, Jules. It's not worth it."

"See? Listen to your boyfriend. I wanna see you in my office in an hour, Jules. We have shit to discuss," Dima says before turning on his heel and leaving the room. Seb quietly gets up to go and follow him, and Aaron sits watching, while filling his mouth with cereal, enjoying the show being put on for him.

"Jules, don't risk anything for me."

"Shut up, Kai. It's too late for all that, I'd risk everything for you, so get used to it."

"Can I do anything? Maybe talk to Dima?"

"No. Leave it to me. But you can go and call your mom."

I nod quietly and kiss his cheek, before quietly walking out of the kitchen to our house. I'm so emotional right now, everything I feel for Jules is bubbling to the surface and I can't control it. I don't want to call my mom as she'll know something is wrong. But I promised Jules I would.

I'm awful at lying, but it's not the right time to tell her about the Kozlovs or what's transpired between me and Jules. Let's just hope I can sidestep any questions that may give me away.

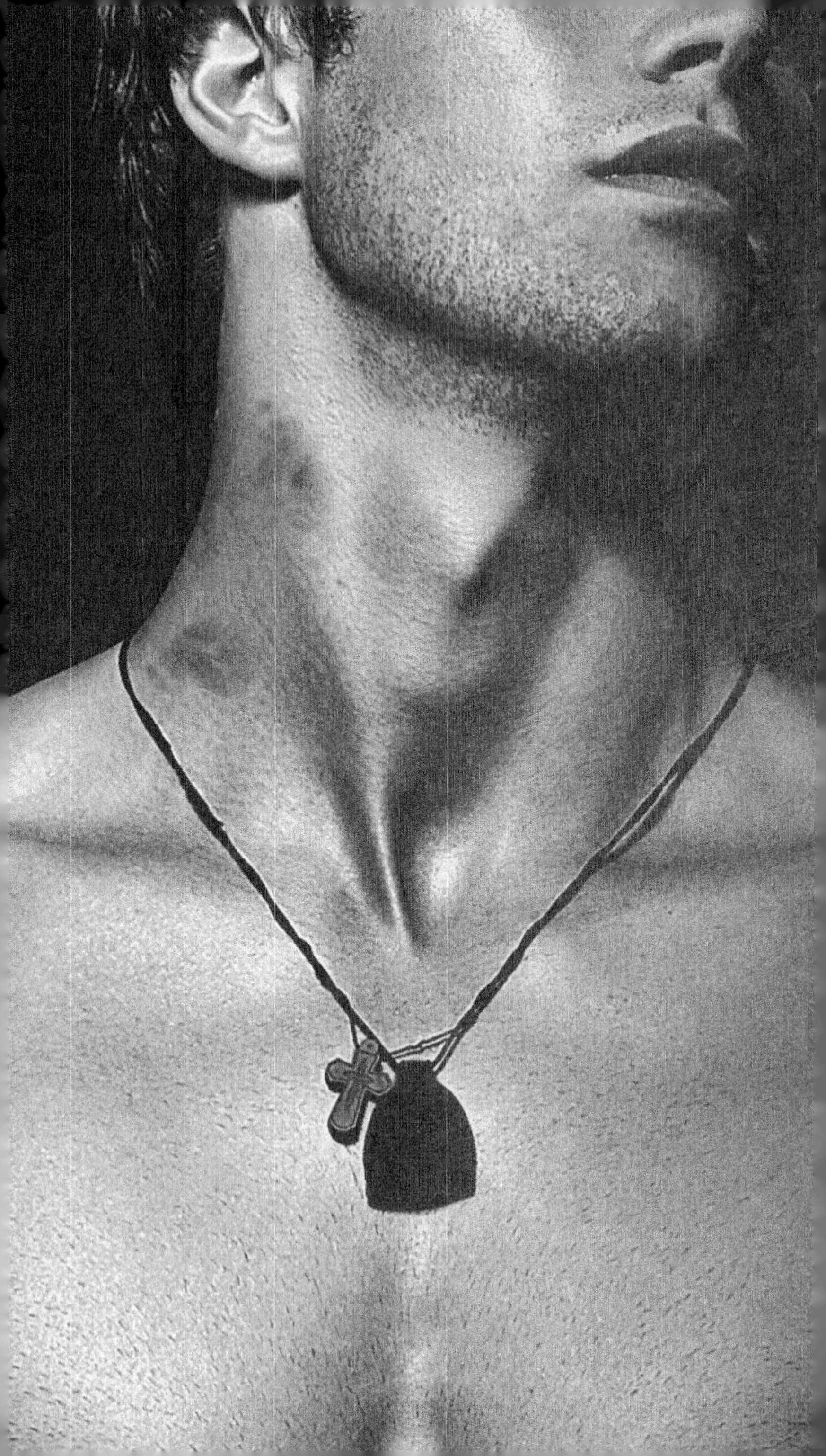

CHAPTER 34
KAI

Sitting on the edge of my bed, I stare at my phone, my mom's contact details taunting me, daring me to just call her. I can do this. I press the call button and hold the phone to my ear, waiting for her to answer. As the rings continue, I can hear my heartbeat that's thumping in my ear. Slow breaths, Kai.

"Kai?" she answers. Her voice lilts to a higher tone of happiness. I'm such a piece of shit for not calling.

"Hey Mom. Sorry I haven't called. It's just been hectic here," I say, forcing a chirpiness to my voice to hide the worry that plagues me of how she'll react to everything that's happened.

"That's okay. Jules mentioned that you've been working hard. So, tell me everything? How's the job? Are you happy?"

I smile at her eagerness to know that I'm doing better, that I'm on the straight and narrow. If only she knew my bosses ran a drug cartel and have a holding pen that they love to torture and kill in. Not to mention her step brother is fucking me. Fuck, I feel sick.

"Not a lot to tell. I do some security work and have been helping with the business, you know, doing the books and learning more about how they run. I'm enjoying it," I say. Liar, liar, pants on fucking fire.

"That's amazing, Kai. I'm so relieved, honey. Doing honest work and standing on your own feet is the best thing for you. I'm so proud of you."

Okay, not enjoying the guilt. I want to slap myself. Hard. But as Jules said, what she doesn't know, won't hurt her. Only, it will fucking hurt when she find out the truth, which she will. It's not like we can keep this a secret for years on end. She's bound to want to visit. Oh shit...what if she wants to visit? The pressure's too much. We need to tell her, even if it's just about us. If there is an us.

"Kai, are you still there?"

"Yeah, sorry, bad signal. Enough about me, how is it back home? You good?"

"I can't complain. Working and breathing as usual. Tim has been spending a lot of time here too, it's been quiet without you."

"Good. I'm glad you're not lonely, Mom. He's a decent guy."

"He's a friend."

"Uh-huh."

"Cheeky. Anyway, when are you paying your mom a visit? This is the longest I've gone without seeing my boy."

And there we have it. Problem number three. I'm not sure I can go home after the threat from Zac. I'm still of two minds about whether they meant it or not, as I haven't heard anything more from them. Can I risk it?

"I'll try and see what time off I can get from the bosses, and I'll let you know."

"Listen to you all grown up and a working man. I understand if you're busy, honey, you've just started there, but it would be great to see you, even for a few hours."

"I promise to sort something out. Look, I've gotta go now but I'll text you next week."

"Okay, love you Kai."

"You too, Mom," I say before ending the call.

I did it. Somehow I managed to lie well enough that it didn't raise any suspicion. Guess I am learning here.

I continue to hang around the house, washing my clothes and tidying up. I try to repair the broken lock on my bedroom door to no avail. Jules should really repair it, considering he broke it. Speaking of Jules, it's been a couple of hours and he hasn't come back to the house yet. I decide to head over to the main house to see what the plan is for the rest of the day.

The kitchen is quiet as I walk in, so I walk further into the house as there is normally someone milling around. As I turn the corner out of the kitchen, I walk into something similar to a brick wall, or should I say someone?

"Sorry, didn't see you there. Which one are you?" the mysterious hot man says to me.

"Who the hell are you and what are you doing in this house?" I demand as I move back from the beast standing in front of me. Am I in a dream? He's fucking beautiful. He's so tall, and I'm six foot one. His muscles appear to be made from rock, because it had hurt bumping into him. He has beautiful golden skin, deep and warm brown eyes, a closely shaved beard like Dima's and hair as black as the night, currently tied up in a man bun. He grins at me and pokes his tongue out to lick his upper lip. God, is that a tongue piercing?

"You finished checking me out?"

"What! I wasn't checking you out. I was trying to remember if we've met before, as you still haven't explained who you are."

He chuckles and does an unashamed once over of my body.

"I'm Ivan, Dima and Lev's cousin. Didn't they mention me?"

Ahhh now that makes sense. I can see the similarities, especially with Dima. He's definitely the largest of the three.

"They did, but I thought you were arriving on the weekend," I say, relaxing a little more into the casual conversation now that I know he's not an intruder.

"Managed to get a flight a few days early, wanted to get here and settled. So, which one are you?"

"I'm Kai."

"Nice to meet you, Kai."

"He's also Jules's man, so I'd keep away," Lev says as he strides into the hallway.

"Really. That's a shame."

Heat blooms on my face and neck, this guy is off the charts sexy and intense. But he has nothing on my Jules. My Jules? Christ, I'm becoming a sappy bastard.

"Come on Ivan, I'll take you over to the club to get you up to speed."

"I'm down. Catch you later, cutie," Ivan says, and winks at me as he leaves with Lev. I've regressed to a teenager who blushes at any form of flirting. This is just great.

"I'd shut down the blushing, Kai. Jules won't like it with another guy. Trust me," Lev says as he follows Ivan out of the house.

Jules has no worries as it's not Ivan or anyone else I want. I'm just not used to this openly obscene flirting that goes on here. What's another guy to add to the group of crazy? If anyone has to worry it's Lev, as Aaron will love to wind Lev up by showing Ivan attention.

I turn and start walking towards Dima's office to see if that's where Jules is. I know Dima will go hard on him because of me and I wish there was something I could say or do to make the situation better. Maybe some desensitizing therapy would work? Force myself to watch lots of torture and graphic movies to help with whatever it is that causes me to be on the verge of throwing up. Or to find a way to put myself into shock like the first time, as I don't even remember much of that interrogation.

As I approach Dima's closed office door, I can hear a raised voice that I'm sure is Dima. I should leave and just wait for Jules to finish. But because I'm too damn curious for my own good, I put my ear closer to the door and instantly regret it.

"He's too soft, Jules. He ain't made for this life."

"He just needs some time."

"Stop fucking lying to yourself and to me. He's not in the room. He's a liability waiting to happen and you know it."

"Seb isn't made for it either and I don't see anyone complaining."

"True. But Seb stepped up when he needed to and doesn't pass out at the sight of blood."

"What do you want me to do?"

"I want you to admit you fucked up bringing him here, and that he needs to leave, and you need to open your eyes that you and him will never work."

"You're right, I do question if I should've brought him here, and yes, he is too sweet in nature for this. It's not like I knew this beforehand. I was trying to help him."

"And you have, but if he can't do the hard stuff, what use is he to us? You need to let him go. Jenny will never approve of you both, you know this."

"Yeah, I know."

Not able to hear anymore, I stumble back and stare at the door as if I can see through it. Devastation momentarily pins me to the spot. He doesn't want me here, he just said it so clearly that he doesn't want me here, he thinks me coming here was a mistake. What the fuck am I doing? My eyes begin to fill with tears. I really thought he wanted this as much as I did. And to hear him talk so carelessly about me...it fucking hurts. Spinning on my heel, I dash out of the corridor and bump into Aaron in the hallway, who hands me a set of keys. Jules's keys. Aaron is like a sleuth in the house, he knows everything that's going on, as he's so quiet when he moves from room to room.

"Take these and go clear your head," Aaron says, before giving me a small smile as I jog outside to get into Jules's car. As I approach the car, movement behind me has me quickly turn to see Jules running out towards me, shouting my name. Concern is written all over his face. Aaron tries to block his way as I get into the car, but his attempt proves pointless as Jules manages to dodge him, but he isn't quick enough to catch me. The engine comes to life, and I put my foot down and speed out of the driveway with no fucking idea of where I'm going. As soon as I pass the gates, I allow the tidal wave of tears to drench my face, letting myself drown in my broken heart, the weakness he sees in me open for everyone to see. At home I was too much trouble, an annoyance, and here it's no different, only I'm seen in a different light. I'm too soft, weak. Still a fucking failure.

As I whiz down the back roads, Na Na Na by Chemical Romance plays on the music station, drowning out all reality. The only thing I know right now is that I need to escape him.

However, that plan goes out of the window, as in typical Kai luck, I spot headlights in my rear view mirror, gaining on me. Fuck this. I speed up, silently praying there may be a cliff at the end of this road so it'll all just end. Then the loneliness and struggle for life will be gone.

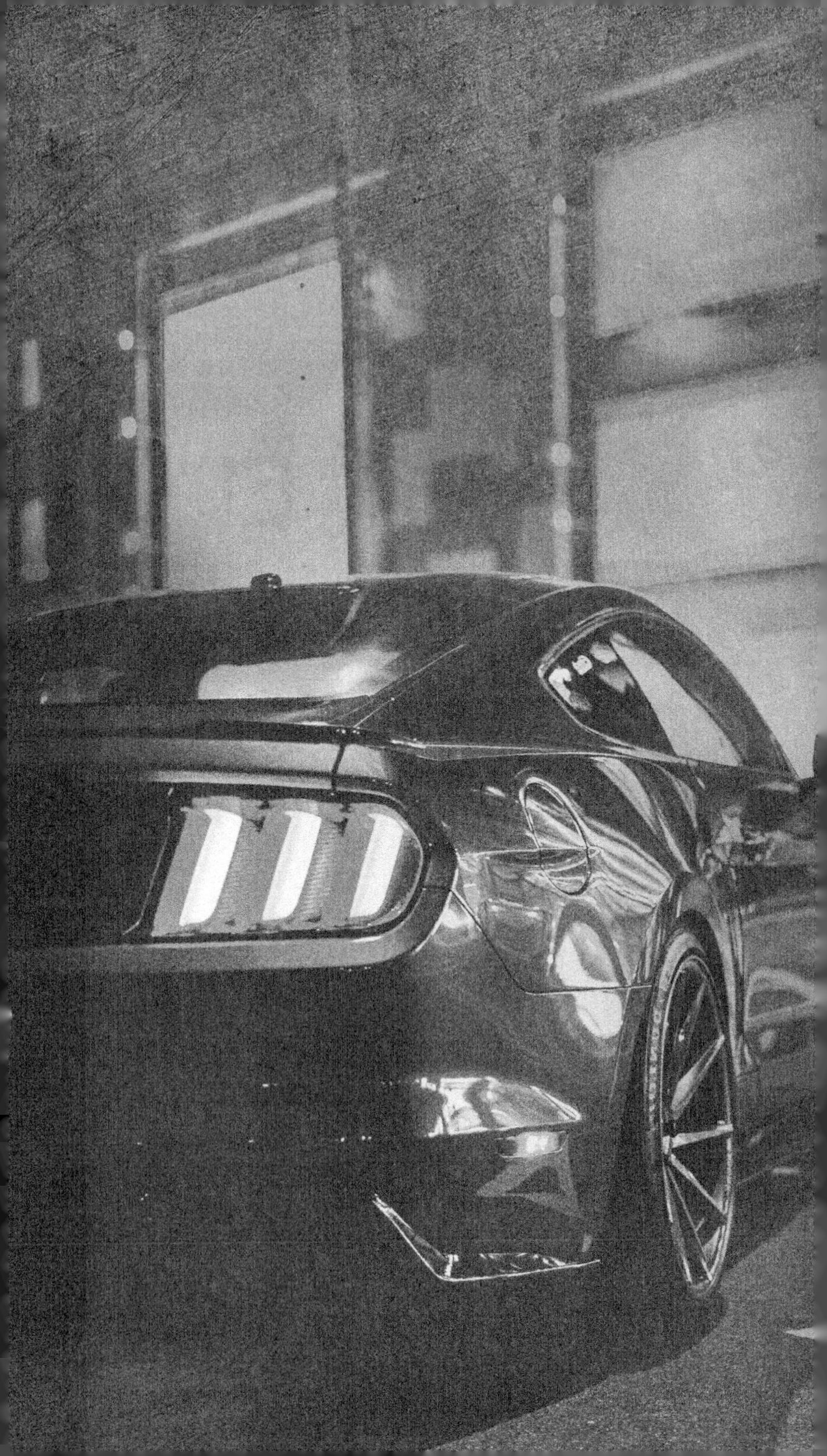

CHAPTER 35
JULES

With trepidation, I go to Dima's office to get this meeting over with. I have no idea what he's gonna say, but I'm just gonna have to take whatever it is and move on. The one good thing about the brothers is that after they've said their piece, they move on and don't hold it over you. Unless you fuck up again, but I get that.

I knock on the door twice before turning the handle and entering the office, noticing Dima isn't alone. Holy shit, is that Ivan?

"Ivan? Fuck man, it's good to see you. I thought you were getting in this weekend?" I say to Dima and Lev's cousin, who stands and greets me with a brief hug. If I had to describe Ivan, it would be to say that he's insane. Well he was, it's been ten years since I last spoke to him, and I don't know what he's been doing during that time, but weights is clearly one thing, because the guy is a tank.

"Jules. Long time no see. Couldn't wait to get started, so I thought I'd surprise the dickhead brothers."

"It was hardly a surprise, you texted me with your flight details," Dima says, rolling his eyes. They've always had a competitive banter, glad to see it hasn't died.

"Yes but you were surprised by that text, so it still counts."

"Why don't you go and annoy Lev. I need to talk to fuckface," Dima says.

"What a great idea. See ya both later," Ivan says grinning, strolling out of the room like a beast.

"Sit," Dima says, not wasting any time to get into it. I walk over and sit in the seat Ivan just vacated, and await my fate. Will this be aggressive Dima? Moody Dima or psycho Dima?

"What the fuck is going on with Kai? You vouched for him, Jules, and I gotta say, I ain't impressed." Aggressive Dima it is.

"I think we need to calm down. He knows he screwed up..." I say, but Dima interrupts me before I get to finish my sentence.

"And which fuck up are we talking about? The Aaron one? Or when he made a fool of himself and us with Carlos?"

"Give him a break, D. He's new to all this. We said it'd take time."

"You're too emotionally involved with him. If you can't separate you both fucking and what happens with work, then you can't be together. I've never seen you this unfocused, Jules. Decisions need to be made."

"What the hell is that supposed to mean?"

"Kai has to go."

"What?"

"He's too soft, Jules. He ain't made for this life."

"He just needs some time."

"Stop fucking lying to yourself and to me. He's not in the room. He's a liability waiting to happen and you know it."

"Seb isn't made for it either and I don't see anyone complaining."

"True. But Seb stepped up when he needed to and doesn't pass out at the sight of blood."

"What do you want me to do?"

"I want you to admit you fucked up bringing him here, and that he needs to leave, and you need to open your eyes that you and him will never work."

"You're right, I do question if I should've brought him here, and yes, he's too sweet in nature for this. It's not like I knew this beforehand. I was trying to help him."

"And you have, but if he can't do the hard stuff, what use is he to us? You need to let him go. Jenny will never approve of you both, you know this."

"Yeah, I know." I hate admitting it out loud, but I know she'll never accept us. It doesn't change things, I'll be more than willing to carry that burden for Kai. He's worth it.

"But I'm not letting him go. For you or anyone."

A thud outside and running footsteps interrupt our conversation as I get up and open the door to see the back of Kai running away. Oh shit, he was listening. I turn to D, who is now standing beside me.

"I'll leave with him. He's non-negotiable, D. Fuck you and Lev," I say, before hightailing out of his office, chasing after Kai. I catch up to him just as he is about to run out the front door.

"Fuck, Kai, wait!"

I can't believe he was spying. I know what it must have sounded like, but it's not what he thinks. Yes, I do think he is too kind-hearted for this job, but I didn't say I wanted to send him away on his own. I have every intention of going wherever he goes. Doesn't he know by now that I will never let him go? What a mess. I may have ruined any hope of happiness I had with Kai. He may be tough on the outside, but Kai just wants to be loved and cherished, especially by me. I know I've ripped his heart out. I just fucking hope he believes me.

Running outside, I see Kai get into my damn car. A smirking Aaron tries to block me, making it obvious where he got my keys from. Just as Kai leaves the driveway, Seb pulls in on his bike, and without thought, I dash over to him, pushing him off the contraption.

"Hey, what the fuck do you think you're doing, Jules? I've just had it repaired!" Seb says as he pulls off his helmet.

"I need to get to Kai before he does something stupid. I promise I won't hurt your precious bike," I say.

"Be careful with him, Jules. He's been going through some shit, some self-doubt. Don't go barrelling in there, worsening it. He needs to feel wanted."

What the hell is he talking about? Since when did they become best buddies?

"How the fuck do you know all this?"

"Because he talks to me. Look, you just need to listen to him, let him explain."

What the hell is he not telling me? I haven't got time to wait around listening to riddles, I need to get to Kai. I rev the engine and speed off after him with Seb's words in the back of my mind.

Luckily, Kai is not too far ahead of me as I catch up with him, trying to wave him down. I've got no idea where he's going, as we travel further down a country road that leads to nothing in particular. Surrounded by trees and barren land, I race up beside him on the driver's side, desperate to get his attention, but he just ignores me. It's a challenge trying to balance the bike and look at Kai at the same time without falling off it, but I can tell instantly he's been crying, and it makes me want to hit something. But I'm also frustrated that he didn't wait long enough for me to explain. So fucking stubborn and reactive.

"Kai, pull over the fucking car!" I yell, slamming my fist on the driver's window. All I get in response is his middle finger, which only enrages me more.

I wobble slightly on the bike as I try to keep up with him, as the terrain becomes rougher the further we travel. The road up ahead is a dead end, much to my relief, and forces me to pull back so that I'm behind the car. Kai will have nowhere to go.

Kai obviously hasn't noticed the sign when he slams the brakes on hard, drifting my car to the side as he tries to gain control. Everyone knows how much I adore my car, but at this moment in time, I couldn't give a shit if he wrecks it. I just wanna make sure he's okay. He doesn't move as I block off his exit with Seb's bike. I slowly dismount it before walking over to him and the driver's door, nearly yanking it off its hinges.

"Get out of the fucking car. Now Kai," I growl at him before a rumble of thunder in the distance drowns out the silence. Rain starts to patter down slowly around us as the sky becomes darker. You would think my mood and the weather were connected, with how it represents what I feel right now. I want to yell at him, I want to comfort him, I want to fuck him. Jesus Christ, I want to own him fully.

"You don't tell me what to do, Jules. Do us both a favor and go back to the house and leave me alone."

I slam my hand down on the roof of the car.

"I'm not going anywhere. You need to listen to me, Kai, what you heard back there wasn't what you thought. Now get out of the fucking car before I drag you out."

If looks could kill, the glare that he's throwing my way would do it right now. His eyes that are normally the innocent soft blue have been swollen up by his black pupils, and glower with fury like I've never seen before. I must say, it's pretty hot.

"Go fuck yourself, *Uncle* Jules."

With both hands, I grab him by the top of his shirt and pull him out of the car. I drag him around to the hood while keeping a firm grip on him.

"Don't call me that, you little shit. I'm the farthest thing from your uncle."

"That's not what you said back there. From what I heard, I'm nothing to you, nothing but a weak annoying nephew, an embarrassment," he says harshly into my face. Our noses brush against each other, but not in a loving way, more in the way of who is fighting for dominance. A wrestler before a fight. The rain ramps up into a heavy shower, both of us wet beyond the point of caring, only focused on the primal showdown.

"I never once called you an embarrassment. You know how I feel about you, Kai. I wasn't arguing with Dima because I want you gone, he was angry because I wouldn't back down. If you'd stayed longer you would've heard me say I'd go with you. I've never thought you were weak, but this life isn't for everyone and it's my fault you're in this position. I'm sorry if it hurt you, but you need to hear what I'm saying."

"You've gutted me, Jules. How am I supposed to believe you? How do I know if it's me that's the one that's being lied to? To talk about me like that behind my back, again treating me like a kid. I thought we'd gotten somewhere."

"I'm not lying, Kai. You're all I think about. You're all I want."

"And what is it you want? Keeping all this a secret from Mom? For me to be a hassle to you? Always protecting me because I'm such a fuck up?"

"That's bullshit. You know I've wanted to tell your mom. You're the one who wanted to wait. If I could brand you and claim you in front of the world, I would. You have to believe me, Kai, you were made for me and me alone."

Kai pushes into me and places his mouth next to my ear, breaking me with what he says next.

"I don't believe you."

Like an ignition, a key turns on in my heart, my body rumbling like a V-8 engine surging to life, full of need to show Kai who truly owns him and how much I need him. I grab his throat with my hand and squeeze as hard as I can. The rain makes it more difficult to get a full grasp on him, but I manage it.

"You better believe in the devil because he's about to claim you over the hood of this car, and no praying to God will save you."

Before Kai gets a chance to respond, I latch my lips to his, brutally taking his mouth with mine, showing him the only way I know how, that I will never let him leave me without a fight.

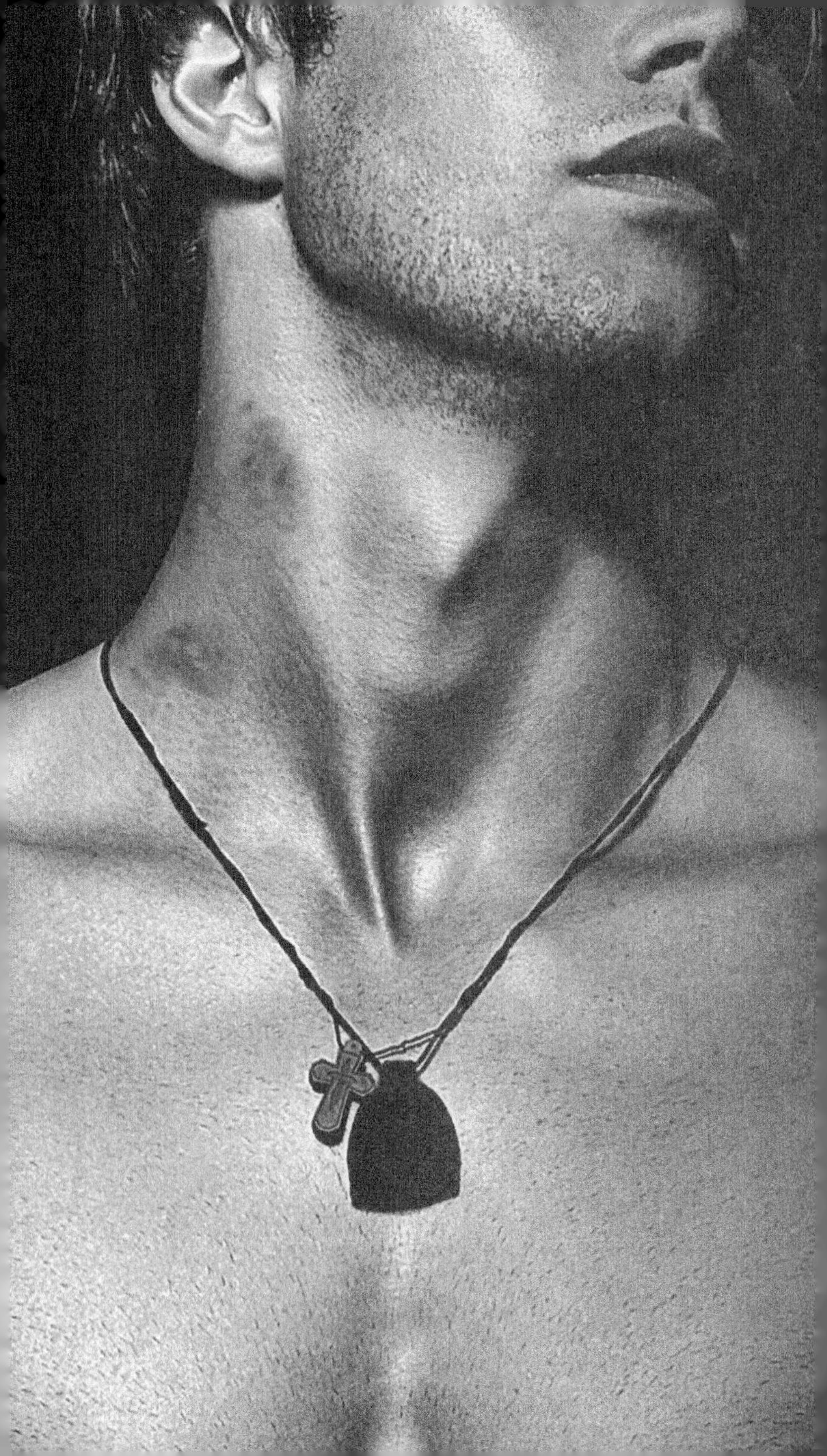

CHAPTER 36
KAI

This mother fucking asshole. Thinks he can just kiss me and manipulate me with words he thinks I want to hear. Maybe he is telling the truth, but hearing him agree I was too soft was like a punch in the chest. I was expecting him to fight more for me. Maybe he did after I bolted, but I can't keep up this charade. The lies and hiding and pretending to be someone I'm not is slowly destroying me. Jules was the only thing keeping me up, but now I only feel like he's pulling me down. I want him so much that I'm scared I'll stop breathing if I leave.

I push away from the kiss, my spine straightens, ready to fight my corner. It's about time Kai became the aggressor in this story. Forming a fist, I curl my fingers tightly into my palm, focusing on that sexy face, he looks seconds away from lurching at me, but I'm quicker. I rotate my hips and shoulders as I extend my arm and land an almighty punch across his face. His head snaps to the side and he stumbles awkwardly, correcting his balance before peering at me with a mixture of shock and delight. I exhale sharply, getting ready for him to attack back. The last thing I expect is the large grin that forms. All teeth, with a sharp edge. I think I'm in trouble. Blood drips from his mouth that he rubs away with his thumb, the rain quickly washes it away before he approaches me again.

"You want a little rough play?" he growls, which is then followed by a loud crack of thunder. His eyes have lost all color and kindness. I wouldn't be surprised if he morphed into a wolf right now.

"Fuck. You," I snarl, pushing him in the chest, but he doesn't move.

"Never gonna happen. Now, hit me again."

He doesn't have to ask me twice. Before I know it, my fist is curled again and I land another blow to his face, this time on his jaw. I shake my hand as it fucking hurts, punching iron. We're so drenched right now, it's not even funny. The adrenaline coursing through me stops any feeling of the cold winter air.

Jules was ready for my attack this time, because he quickly responds by slapping me hard across the face before pinning me against the car by the neck. The sting in my cheek hurts so bad. I'm a little taken aback that he hit me, but why not? I hit him. And I enjoyed it.

"What? Didn't you say our blood, our pain? I think we both should suffer, don't you?"

"I'm the only one suffering here. Don't pretend you give a shit."

With ease, Jules manhandles me by using his hold on my neck to walk me over to the hood of his car, and swings me around until I'm bent over it. The sick thing is? I want it. I want him to take me, to make it hurt. The physical hurt is the only thing that will override the pain in my heart.

Warm wet lips suck hard onto the back of my neck. I shout out into the rain when I feel his teeth dig into my skin.

"Gonna fuck you real good, Kai. I'm gonna claim you for good. All the animals out tonight will hear you as I take you apart."

Fuck, his words have me shuddering beneath his weight as he pins me harder into the hood. I reach out my hands above my head trying to gain purchase onto something as he starts to yank down my pants and underwear. The cold air has my balls shrivelling up, but my hard dick loves the wet slide against the metal. I'm too disoriented to know what he's doing, or how fast he is doing it. The rain, the car, the cold night and Jules going fully unhinged has my senses in disarray.

Rough hands part my ass cheeks, and a thick, slicked finger finds my hole, prepared with travel lube, the arrogant bastard. And without any warning or build up, he forces his way in as I rise to my tiptoes at the burning intrusion. I moan at the relief of having him back inside me, he massages my bundle of nerves so perfectly, my body responds to the pleasure by riding his fingers that have now turned into two inside me.

"You're so hot inside. Look at my pretty whore, completely submitting to me as a perfect whore should. So shameless, Kai. So damn slutty," he groans into my ear as a third finger joins in on the party. I'm a blubbering mess. I just want him to fuck me. To make me feel before I go back to hating him and leave this fucking place. Just like they all want.

"Jules, fuck me, please, fuck me hard. Fuck me until you leave an imprint of your dick inside me," I ramble, nonsense leaves me from the overwhelming finger fuck he's performing on me.

"Hell yeah."

His fingers leave my body and a hard, wet cockhead is replaced at my entrance. I clench just as he pushes forward, wanting it so bad that my ass is excited. Steadily, his cock glides into me, returning to where it belongs, and the fullness just fills me with elation. A euphoric feeling of ownership. *The ownership that's a lie. He doesn't want me here.*

Jules shows no mercy on me, and fucks me like I asked. Hard, unforgiving and fast. The hard, thick flesh no doubt will leave an imprint on me, and I welcome it. The car creaks beneath us as the rain starts to lighten, turning into drizzle as the sounds of our fucking are the new soundtrack on this back road.

"Harder, do it harder!" I shout. Long groans are the only noise I can make as he somehow manages to ramp up the speed. My ass is gonna be sore but I don't care. Jules can fuck me to death for all I care, if it's him doing it, I'll allow it.

"Fuck, Kai, shit, you're so tight around me. I'm gonna fill you up," Jules moans as a warmth fills me on the inside. His cum doesn't stop as it spurts from him in long streams. As he comes, toward the end of his orgasm, he reaches around and grabs my dick, jerking it with great speed and determination. I've been on the edge so long it only takes a handful of strokes before I erupt on a shout, all over the hood of his car. The love of his life.

Jules keeps his body covering mine, making it hard to breathe beneath him.

"You need to believe me, Kai. We'll leave here together, or stay here together. There is no separating. We're joined together forever. Believe me or not, it still doesn't change that you're mine for eternity."

I'm on the verge of crying again and it pisses me off. These words this morning would've had me smiling at Jules like he hung the moon. Now it just makes me feel as pitiful as Dima described. I am too emotional. I'm too human. I don't think I possess whatever it is you need to be in the Kozlov family, or even with Jules. I have to look out for myself. But for now, I do the one thing that I have been taught well. I lie.

"You're right. Can we get back to the house now? I'm freezing and dying to get clean and warm," I say, hoping he's convinced by my acting.

"Yeah. Come on. You take my car and I'll meet you back at the house."

Jules pulls away from me and we straighten ourselves out in silence. After I've made myself look decent, I turn to see Jules watching me. Searching my face, for what I don't know.

"Don't ever lie to me, Kai."

Fucking hell. Let's try this again.

"I'm not lying, Jules. I'm cold and tired. Plus I'm allowed to still be upset."

"Fair enough. Let's get out of here."

Jules walks over to Seb's bike and waits for me to drive ahead of him. I watch him in the rearview mirror and say my goodbyes. It's better this way.

When we arrive back at the Kozlov's, Simon is the first to greet us as we both pull up, stomping out of the house like he's on a mission.

"Where the hell have you two been? And what the fuck happened to your face?"

I look at Jules, refusing to answer. I want no part of this. Tired of being on the receiving end of a verbal bashing.

"Out. Had a fight. Now we're back. What's got your panties in a twist?" Jules says, not helping Simon's mood in a positive way at all.

"I've had Lev calling me, breathing down my neck wanting us to head over to the club."

"Where's D?"

"In a meeting. Can we go? Lev won't be getting any happier."

"Alright, you need to chill. Kai, will you be okay here?" Jules asks. After everything that's happened today, he has the nerve to ask me that?

"You tell me."

"Stop brooding, I'm only asking. I know you'll be fine. Come on Si, before you piss yourself."

Jules takes his car keys from my hand and clutches my jaw so tightly, the ache radiates to my ears.

"Don't doubt me, Kai. I meant what I said earlier." He then leans in and sucks my lower lip into his mouth. I can't control the groan when he bites down hard before sweeping his tongue over the area. What's wrong with me? Every hurt he has marked on my body rejuvenates my soul. It's not normal.

Just like that, he walks away with Simon, leaving me stranded in a dark place of concussion and fear. Confused with how I feel and with the wants he brings out in me, and fearful of how I'll keep living without him.

"Oh good. He hasn't totalled my bike," Seb says as he struts over to his bike, giving it a once over.

"He didn't go far."

"Come and have a drink with me, Kai. You look like you could use it."

I'm about to decline, but decide against it. Maybe Seb can help clear things up for me. The guy has been pretty great to me since I arrived. I follow him into the house, and veer off to the kitchen, the hub of this home. I love this space, I could see myself quite happily preparing many meals in here.

"You want a beer? Water? Coffee?"

"I best stick to water, thanks."

Seb grabs two waters from the fridge and we sit at the table, both quiet as we take a couple of sips.

"What's going on, Kai? Why'd you run off like that?"

"I was listening in on a conversation between Jules and Dima. They think I'm weak. Well, Dima was telling Jules how weak I was and how he should end things with me, and Jules didn't disagree. Said that he shouldn't have brought me here."

"I can see why that would hurt. Ignore Dima though. He's a bastard."

I laugh at that. Seb and Dima's relationship is less co-dependent than Aaron and Lev's. Dima is the only crazy one in his relationship and Seb has no issue standing up to him. They're certainly entertaining.

"Yeah, it hurt. But now I feel misplaced again. He said I only picked up on some of the conversation, that he told Dima he would leave with me."

"But you don't believe him."

"Honestly, I don't know."

"Jules is a straight shooter, Kai. He wouldn't say anything just to appease you."

"It's not just that. I can't stay here knowing what people truly think about me. It's embarrassing. Nobody wants to be known as the weak link."

"Not everybody thinks that."

"Dima does, which means everyone else probably does too."

"Ha! You'd be wise to notice that nobody here agrees with a lot of what D says."

"Maybe."

"What are you gonna do?"

I shrug, avoiding the question as I'm sure I know the answer. I just don't want him running to tell Jules.

"Be careful, Kai. Don't do anything rash."

Seb is such a good guy. I'll miss our little chats.

"I won't. I promise."

Lie, lie, lie.

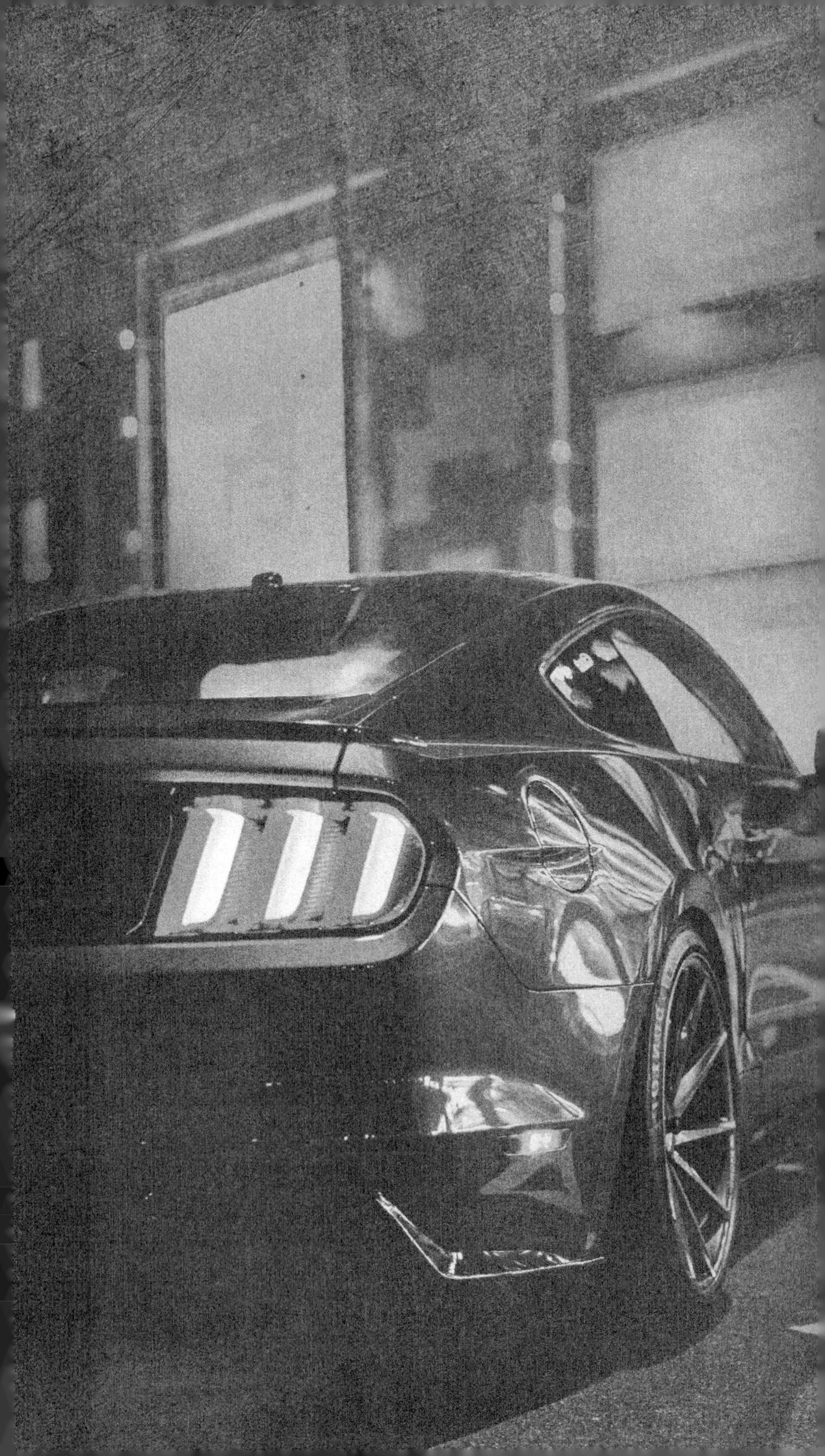

CHAPTER 37
JULES

"So, who punched you in the face?" Simon asks me as I drive us to the club.

"Why do you wanna know?"

"Because I wanna shake their hand for getting a hit on you. Miserable fucker."

"I think you must be talking about yourself, because nobody is more miserable than you."

"That's a fucking lie."

"I've never seen you laugh. Once. You have a constant scowl like someone has shit on your breakfast. I still can't believe you get laid as often as you do."

"I have smiled and I only scowl because everyone pisses me off, which isn't my fault. And you know I'm hot. I don't need to do anything other than just be myself for the ladies to flock."

"I missed that smile, unless you're talking about the one you do when you're fucking someone up. But that doesn't count. Also, how the hell would I know you're hot?"

"Dude, you're fucking a guy. I'd say that means you know."

"Kai is the only guy I've wanted to fuck."

"Really?"

"Yeah."

"Anyway, you're avoiding the question, who hit you?"

"Kai."

"You're shitting me? You let Kai hit you?"

"The first one he landed on me without warning, but I encouraged the second."

"Why?"

"Because it's fucking sexy. Rough foreplay is the way to go."

"You're sick. Should've guessed, though, with the bruises the guy has on him daily. You're a monster, Jules."

"He enjoys it, so that doesn't make me a monster."

"Sure it doesn't."

We arrive at Desire and jog inside, as it's cold as fuck this evening. It's already dark, and I'm dying to get back to Kai to warm up with him in my bed. Something was off about him when I left. He's so damn stubborn, not listening to what I'm saying, too quick to give into the fear and negativity that he's a failure.

Walking inside, the familiar smells and music instantly relax me. This is what I know, what I live. I haven't seen Dima since I ran after Kai, and I have to admit, I'm curious about what he thinks. I respect the brothers and what they've given me. They became the family I lost over time and never let me down. But things change.

"Hey boys, Lev's over at his table with that sexy as fuck hulk guy. Want me to bring over a drink?"

"Hulk?"

"She means Ivan. He arrived early."

"Good, now we can have someone else share the load. We'll just have our usual sodas. Thanks, Bonnie."

We maneuver around the tables of pussy horny men, and set our sights on Lev and Ivan.

"I've been waiting for over an hour for you to show up."

"Don't look at me. Jules was getting the shit beaten out of him."

"Shut the hell up. I told you I wanted it."

"Wait, are you saying Kai did this?" Lev asks, his brows nearly reaching his hairline.

"Yep."

"Wow, hot and feisty. Your guy is smokin, Jules," Ivan says. Before I know it I've grabbed his shirt, pulling him out of his seat, which is impressive given the size of him.

"I dare you to touch him, or even look at him."

"Calm down, my man, just saying."

I push him back down into his seat while he smiles like an arrogant prick that he got a rise out of me. I bet the fucker knew Kai was mine.

"Simon, this dickhead is Ivan, Ivan this miserable fuck is Simon. And he's straight."

"Thanks for the introduction," Si mumbles and gives Ivan a chin-up in greeting. I don't miss how Simon scans the room. No doubt looking for the name we shall not mention. Luckily he doesn't appear to be here this evening, which is a relief as I can only handle so much drama.

"This looks cozy, room for one more?" a voice asks, and we all turn our heads to see Aaron standing with his arms crossed, watching Lev as if he's working out where to skin him first. That clues me in that Aaron has yet to meet the elusive Ivan.

"Doe, what are you doing here?"

"I was bored at home. You said you'd be an hour. It's been two."

"That's 'cos these fuckers were late," Lev says, pointing between me and Simon.

Aaron strolls around the table until he is behind Lev, and leans over his shoulder until his mouth is at his ear, and is that his switchblade pointed at Lev's dick? Typical Aaron.

"Who the fuck is this guy, Lev?" Aaron sneers.

"Ivan. My cousin. I already told you about him."

"Oh," Aaron says and stands up straight and walks around to Ivan.

"Nice to meet you. You look like Dima but bigger."

"You too, Aaron. Nice blade."

"Thanks. You go near Lev, and you'll find him buried in your throat," Aaron says, and it's fucking chilling to witness. Not many people creep me the fuck out, but Aaron, when he smiles like that, sends a shiver even down my spine. Worse is, I believe his threats.

"I don't fuck family," Ivan replies, amusement twinkling in his eyes at the storm that is Aaron.

"Jules is fucking his nephew."

"Step-nephew. You know we aren't blood-related, Aaron. Stop stirring."

"I can pretend you are, though. Lev, I wanna go home."

"I'm in a meeting, doe. You'll have to wait. Come here."

Aaron bounces over to Lev and straddles his thighs. Zero shyness between these two has Lev brutally kissing Aaron like they are on their own. Lev pulls away and grabs Aaron's hair with his fist.

"Now be quiet, then we'll go home and I'll fuck you to sleep," Lev croons at Aaron.

"Mmmm, sounds good."

"I'm gonna love it here," Ivan says as he winks at a dancer who passes our table, giving him the fuck me eyes.

"Let's get down to business so we can all go home. Dima has arranged for an architect to visit the property next month. We need to expand, and we think it's time you all had your own space. Ivan will be overseeing the project to make sure the architect and builders stick to plan. He's also pretty talented in interrogations and intimidating fuckers, which is a huge bonus. Jules, we're gonna put you on Starlight and have you assist in any meetings with Carlos or other associates. Simon, you and Kai will take on more here. You did a good job with the books, which I hate doing. Me and Dima want to start expanding, but that's in the future. All good?"

"I think you'll wanna speak to Dima before you settle on those plans. I doubt he'll want me at the bar with him. Besides, I may not be here."

"What the fuck do you mean you won't be here?"

"Ask D. It's best you hear it from him."

"I'm getting too old for all this shit. Get home. Ivan, go with the guys. I'll drive back with Aaron."

None of us respond, and we get up to leave. Leaving Aaron clinging onto Lev like a life raft. It makes me crave to be close to Kai. My Kai.

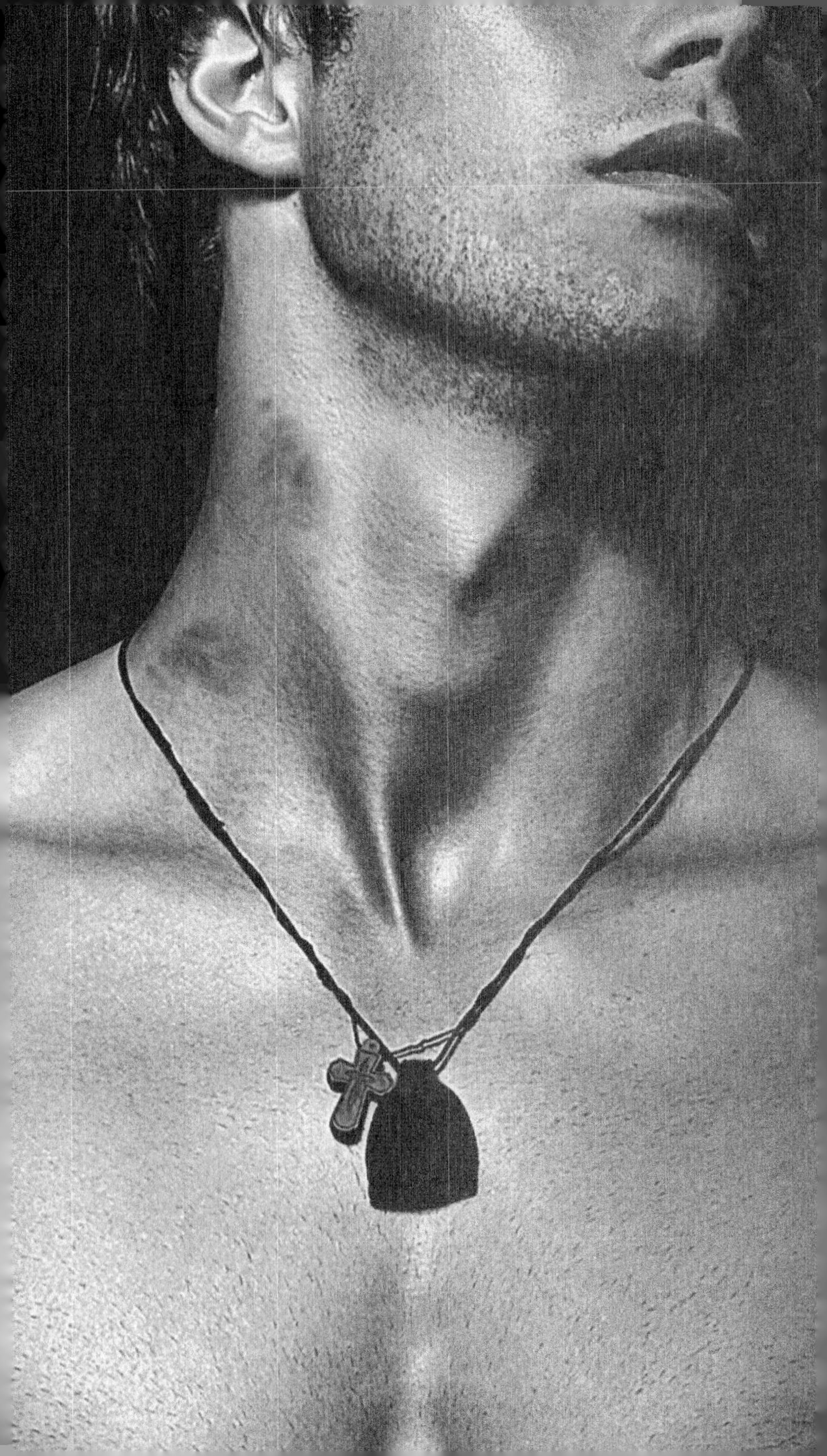

CHAPTER 38

KAI

It's getting late and neither Simon or Jules are back, which I'm thankful for. I needed the quiet to think. Since I arrived here it's been a rollercoaster, always something happening or someone around. I haven't heard from Dima either, surprising, considering he wants me gone. He won't have to worry as I'm gonna leave. It's better to jump than be pushed. Jules and I are a fantasy, Dima was right, we could never work and Mom would never accept us, no matter what we said to try and convince her. Let's say me and Jules did leave on our own to start again, what would happen to me if he changed his mind and decided I wasn't worth the time? I'd be left with nothing and no one.

As I snuggle further into my pillows with the comforter covering me up to my nose, hoping I get some sleep, the sound of the front door echoes around the house. I can hear muted conversation, Simon and Jules, no doubt. Their voices get closer, and I recognize Simon's door across the hall from mine shut and the light in my room brightens as the door slowly opens. I keep my eyes closed, pretending to be asleep. Jules doesn't talk or check if I'm awake. As usual, he does what he wants, which from the sound of the shuffling of his clothes, is to undress and join me in bed. This is a first.

He climbs in behind me and pulls my body tightly into his, trapped between his arms and legs. It's the most intimate act we've done and I can't allow myself to enjoy it like I want to. It's a natural instinct in me to want to be close to him. He falls asleep pretty quickly, while I have no such luck. I'm wide awake and my brain is in hyperdrive, overthinking everything.

I check my phone and I see that an hour and a half has passed since Jules fell asleep. I untangle myself from his arms, and look over my shoulder to make sure he's still asleep. He looks so peaceful, like a man that sleeps with a clear conscience, which is hilarious when you look at who he is and what he does. Very gently, I pull my legs away and swing them over the edge of the bed, placing my pillow in the spot I laid in. Jules is dead to the world, and now I know this is my chance to leave.

I tiptoe into my bathroom, using my cell phone light to find the bag I packed earlier, and quickly scoop up my toiletries and pack them up with my clothes. I grab the pants and hoodie I left laying out on the side of the bathtub and quickly dress. When I have everything, I walk back into the room where Jules still sleeps and take my last fill of the man I'm completely in love with. This is it. I'm actually walking away.

With small careful steps, I walk down the hallway to the front door, put on my shoes, and grab my coat off the rack. As I hoped, Jules's car keys are in the bowl on the hallway table. He'll go mad, but I don't have access to another car. The front door opens and closes quietly, no sign of anyone moving in the house, so after locking the door behind me, I make a run for the car. All of the lights are off in the main house, and the only noise is the wind in the trees and the nocturnal animals starting their day. The moon again is bright tonight, lighting my way to the front of the property.

Before I know it, I'm in the car, engine on and ready to go. My stomach twists, making me hesitate for a brief second. It's like I'm leaving a part of myself behind, the magnetic energy between us already trying to pull me back into that warm bed with him.

No, this is for the best.

I watch the mansion fade into the night as I drive further away. I had no plans on where to go, but I know where I *want* to go. Home. I need to see my mom, and surround myself with familiar things that I took for granted. Am I a little concerned about the whole Zac situation? Yes. But not enough to stay away. I'm sure as long as I stay out of their way, things will be good. It's not as if they would know I'm home, the road I live on doesn't lead to anywhere they hang out. I connect my music to the wireless and settle in for the three hour drive.

Things will feel better once I get some distance.

Liar, liar, liar.

Just over three hours later, it's the early hours of the morning and I pull up onto my mom's driveway. It's actually really good to be back home, I didn't realize how much I missed it until now.

Using my key, I quietly let myself in, and straight away I'm swallowed up in the comforting house smells that's everything Mom. I remove my shoes at the entrance hall and creep down to my bedroom, closing the door gently behind me. Everything is as I left it, like time has stood still. Being back now feels like I never left, the only difference is that the issues I had here are now new problems I've brought home. Issues I won't be able to discuss with my mom. It sucks.

Without undressing, I collapse onto the bed and cover myself with the comforter. The long drive has exhausted my brain enough that I have no problem drifting off.

I have no idea how long I sleep, but a gentle shake of my arm has me waking up to see my mom sitting on the edge of my bed. A frown is etched on her face, probably wondering what the hell I'm doing here.

"Kai, are you okay? Why didn't you call to let me know you were coming home?"

"It was a last minute decision. Good to be back though," I say as I sit up and give her a hug, and fuck do I need it. I want to cry, but manage to hold it in as all I seem to do lately is cry.

That's because you're weak.

"I'm happy you're home, but are you sure everything is okay? You seem…I don't know…sad," she says when I pull back, and she lovingly watches me. Always looking out for her son.

"Things have just been stressful, I needed a break. I'll only be here a couple of days," I say. She'll assume I'll be going back to Grinston, but in truth I have no idea where to go.

"Why don't you get cleaned up and I'll make us some breakfast before I have to go to work."

"Sure."

Mom leaves the room, and before I head to the shower, I tentatively check my phone, waiting to see dozens of messages from Jules. Nothing. Not surprising, I suppose. It's six-thirty in the morning, so he won't be up yet. Dragging my tired ass out of the bed, I cross the narrow hallway and start my morning routine. Shower, brush my teeth, shave, piss and talk to myself in the mirror. I look so damn tired, my eyes have dark circles and there is sadness in them that's difficult to ignore. I try to keep my eyes focused on my face, because I don't want to look lower, knowing my marks have faded. The hickey is still visible on my neck, but as I give in and stare at my torso, a wave of sadness and loss drowns me at the barely there bruises. I feel naked without them. Lonely without the tenderness and proof of ownership. This is it. Jules doesn't own me anymore and it fucking kills me. This is so stupid and unhealthy. Who the hell wants to be covered in hickeys and handprints so that they can feel whole? I rub my face hard with both hands, shaking myself out of this low mood, and turn my back on the mirror.

Returning to my room, I quickly dress in my jeans and a sweater, then walk out into the kitchen, which is open-plan with the living and dining area, and start to make a pot of coffee. Mom enters the kitchen about five minutes later, dressed for work. She works as a receptionist at a local car dealership, which she really enjoys.

"What do you fancy? Pancakes? Sausage?"

"I'm not hungry, thanks. Coffee will be fine."

Mom pins me with that look, she's about to dig as she knows something is wrong and her patience has come to an end.

"Okay, what's wrong?"

"Nothing. I told you, I'm just tired and needed a break."

"Don't bullshit me, Kai. I don't have time this morning. What's happened? Have you fallen out with Jules? Do you hate the job?"

"I haven't fallen out with him, but he's…a lot. Controlling. I don't know, he and some of the others treat me like a kid and it's tiring trying to convince them I can do the work."

"Oh, honey. It's always hard when you first start a job, it's not unusual to hate it at first while you try to find your feet. I'm sure Jules is just trying to help. They always say you should never work with family."

I want to correct that statement as he isn't family. He's the love of my fucking life who I hate. Maybe not hate, but really dislike right now. Why hasn't he called yet? Fucking hell, now I'm upset that he hasn't called when I up and left in the middle of the night. I'm a mess.

"You're right. I'll be fine after a couple of days away."

"Are you sure? I can have a word with Jules, I don't mind."

"No! No, I'm an adult, I can handle it."

"I know you can. Well, now that you're home, I'm gonna try and get the afternoon off so we can spend some time together, they owe me after all the extra hours I've worked. Then you can tell me about the girl or boy who gave you that nice hickey."

My hand flies to my neck and I flush like a teenager caught hooking up by their parents.

"Nice try, Mom," I say as I move over to her and give her a hug. This is exactly what I needed. "An afternoon together sounds perfect."

This is what it must be like being a sloth. I don't think I've ever just laid around the house doing nothing. I'm bored and I'm hungry, but I want to wait until Mom gets back so we can have lunch together. She texted me earlier to say they were letting her off at lunch for the rest of the day, which will be great for us both to reconnect. Just as

I'm about to lay down on my bed, my phone rings and a coldness runs over my flesh. Don't tell me how, but I know it's Jules. My hand clenches, desperate to reach out and talk to him, but I'm too stuck in self doubt and fear. It's better to lose him now than later down the line when he realizes he wasted his time on me. Just as the ringing stops, it starts all over again. The annoying sound grates on my nerves, so I do the most mature thing and rather than facing my problems, I silence them. I silence the call and set my phone into 'do not disturb' mode. Ignorance is bliss. Pocketing my phone in my jeans, I leave my room to go grab a drink from the fridge. I need something to do so I don't call him back. As I'm at the fridge grabbing some orange juice, the front door sounds and I look around the corner, relieved that Mom may have been let go earlier than I thought. As I walk into the living room, I nearly drop the cold glass of juice onto the floor, because standing right in front of me is Jez and Zac, and it doesn't look like this is a welcome home party. Zac looks like he normally does, unwashed and gunning for a fight. His dull, doped up eyes stare at me with nothing but hatred. Jez looks unfamiliar to me now, he always was friendly and happy to see me, but now his hazel eyes hold just as much resentment as his brother's. They warned me not to come back, but I honestly didn't think they'd know, considering I'm driving Jules's car and I haven't gone into town.

"Why are you both here?" I ask, trying to keep my voice as level as possible to hide the rising nerves in my gut.

"I was about to ask you the same thing. Didn't we warn you not to come back?" Zac says as he walks around the room, running his dirty fingers over the back of my mom's sofa. The whole move makes me uneasy, especially with Jez just standing there, glaring at me and not saying a word. I place my glass down on the table and shove my hands into my pockets, hoping to come across as non threatening.

"I'm only here for a couple of days, and I just thought you were angry. I'm not sure why you're upset. You don't need me."

"You were part of the gang, Kai. Brothers. You can't just leave with no word. You abandoned your position, which puts us in a bad spot. One man down, one man less bringing in the cash. You're a deserter," Zac says as he walks back to the middle of the room to stand next to Jez.

"Deserter? It was hardly a cartel. We were just friends who hung out and did shit," I say.

"You really are a dumb fuck if you think I'd believe that. I fucking hate guys like you. You always looked down your nose at us, thinking you were better. Complaining when asked to do anything, too weak to follow through on the hard stuff."

"So why does it matter that I left?" I say, giving that sentence more sass than I should given that it's two on one.

"It matters because you broke code, and also because I hate you. Look at you in your nice new clothes and expensive car, not giving a shit about the boys who've been there for you and giving you everything you needed to survive."

"I was gonna end up in prison if I continued hanging around you. Hardly providing me with a good life."

"It was better than nothing. I mean, you were born to a loser teenage mom and a dad who didn't stick around to meet you. You had to bring in the cash somehow so your mom had a reason to keep you around. I mean, since you left the poor bitch is still struggling to get by. But don't worry, we've been keeping an eye on her."

"What do you mean you've been keeping an eye on her?"

"Just making sure she's safe at work and that she gets home okay. She seems a little lonely though. I might have to join her one night, help keep her bed nice and warm."

"Don't you fucking touch her!"

"Why not? Nobody else wants her. I'd say she's free game."

"Get out you sick fuck. I'll call the police, you can't just break in here and threaten us," I say, taking a step back toward the front door.

"The door was unlocked. And I'm not threatening you, that implies I'll change my mind. Jez."

Too distracted by having my full focus on Zac, I didn't notice Jez move before he clocked me in the face, knocking me off balance enough for him to stand behind me, and lock my arms behind my back. Zac walks forward until he is a breath away from me, his stink makes me want to throw up, but I'm stuck, unable to move anywhere.

"Weaklings always get what they deserve, fucker," Zac says as my breath hitches and my eyes widen, shock taking control over my body. A searing pain pierces my stomach and my eyes look down at the knife now sticking out of my body. It's agony, like a bolt of lightning, sharp and intense, radiating around the knife lodged in my gut. Zac pulls the knife out and I grab hold of the wound, trying to stop the bleeding. As I look up at Jez, betrayal floods my heart as he stares at me with no remorse or care for what's just happened.

"Why?" I rasp at him.

"You deserved it. I hope it fucking hurts, you piece of shit, and don't worry, we'll look after your dear mom," he says, then they both bolt out of the door.

I land onto my front, unable to hold myself up. A sudden overwhelming heat spreads through my body before morphing into a coldness, as if the life is starting to drain from me. I manage to grab my phone from my pocket and with bloodied shaking fingers, press the return call button to Jules. Tears stream down my face, I've fucked up so much in my life, maybe this is for the best. Jules's phone calls out until it reaches his voicemail. Just my luck I won't get to talk to him. My breathing becomes labored and my phone that's now rested on the floor, I pull myself closer so my mouth reaches the mouthpiece.

"Jules...I–I-I've been s-s-stabbed. L-l-l-love you, i-it h-hurts," I say, my words slurring.

The initial shock of what's happened turns into a throbbing ache. Every heartbeat sends a wave of hurt through the knife wound, fluctuating between sharp and dull. Each breath becomes a struggle, I'm losing so much blood. Time stretches as I fight to stay conscious. I'm aware of a voice talking to me and I'm not sure if it's someone in the room or I've died. Hands grab me and I'm vaguely aware of being turned over. Fortunately, the stab wound doesn't hurt as much as it did. I just want to sleep.

"Kai! Kai! Keep awake, buddy, I got you. Help is nearly here," the voice says. It sounds like Officer Tim, but that can't be right. It's a dream. It's all a dream.

"Kai! Can you hear me?" another voice says, unfamiliar to me, repeats on a loop. Why can't everyone be quiet? I just want to sleep, so I do as my body wants and fall away into the welcoming warmth of unconsciousness.

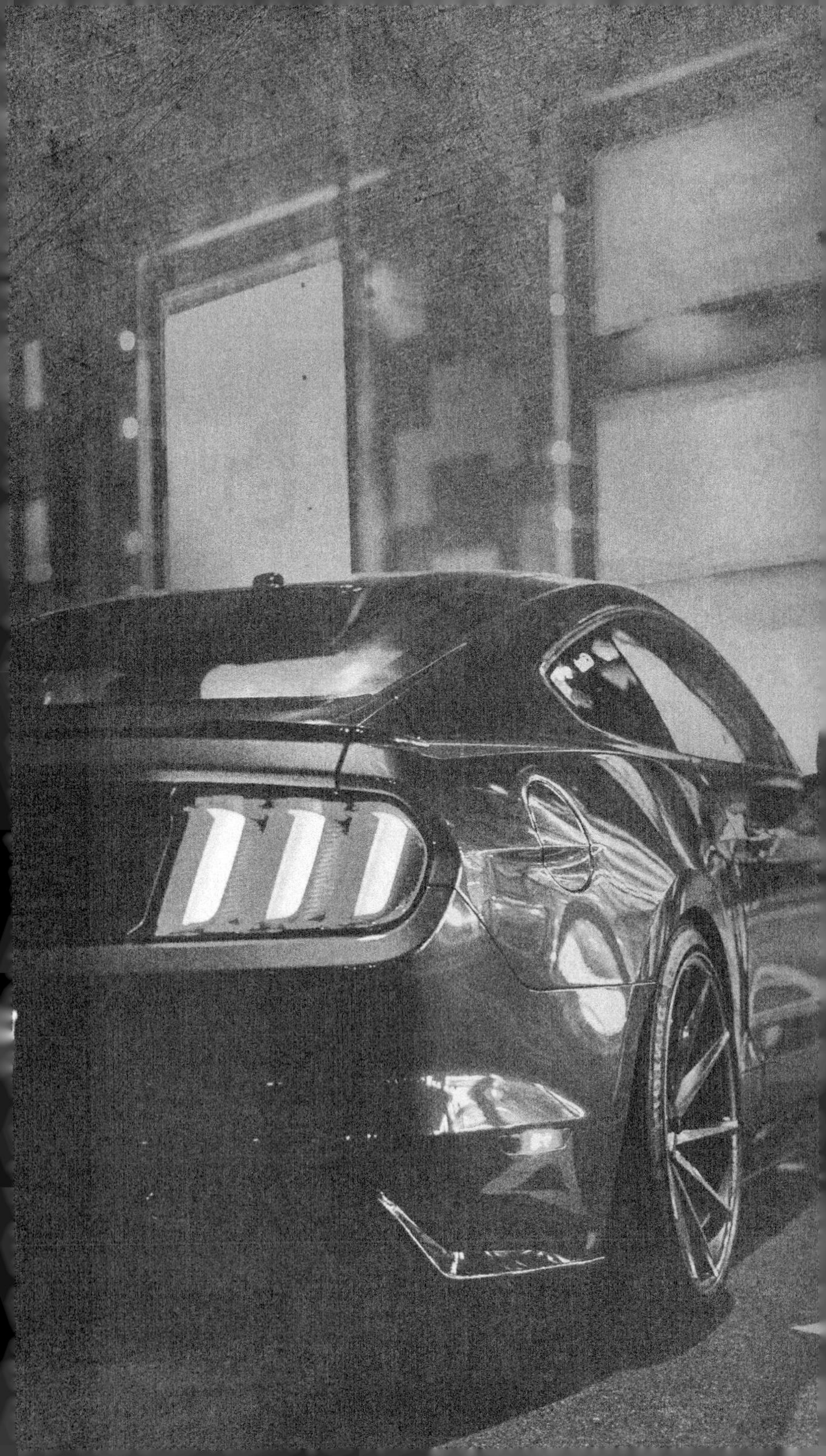

CHAPTER 39
JULES

Before I even open my eyes, I know Kai isn't in the bed with me. The smell of his hair and the heat of that body is missing, immediately putting me in a bad mood. I stretch my arms above my head, and eye the closed bathroom door. He can make it up to me in the shower. This needs to be a new rule, he can't leave the bed before I wake.

I saunter over to the bathroom naked, and frown when I open the door. The lights are off and no sign of Kai. Alarm bells start ringing, and I switch on the light to see all his toiletries have gone off his vanity. The little fucker. I stomp over to his closet, only to open it up to a bare space, leaving no sign he was ever here. The fucker lied to me. If he thinks he can just walk away over a misunderstanding, then he doesn't know me at all.

I pull on my pants, grab my phone off the bedside table, and call Kai. No answer. I try again. No answer. I'm fuming, I'm fucking unstable with rage. How dare he ignore me? How dare he leave me? I've tried calling him at least fifteen times now, and the frustration of not being able to force him to answer takes over and I throw my phone on the bed and storm out into the hallway. Don't ask me why I checked, but because he stole my car before, I'm pretty sure the shithead did it again. I look down at the bowl on the hallway table.

"Fuck!" I yell. He stole my car.

"Hey, what the hell is with all the noise?" Simon says, looking half asleep as he approaches me.

"Kai has left and stole my fucking car."

"Left? But why?"

"He heard me and Dima talking yesterday and it was just a big misunderstanding that he thinks I'm lying about."

"Have you called him?"

I give Simon a droll look.

"What a fucking genius idea...of course I called him."

"Don't take it out on me, fuckhead."

"Can I use your car?"

"Sure. Do you know where he went?"

"I bet he went home to his mom."

"Make sure to tell Lev or D before you leave. I don't want them breathing down my neck again because of you disappearing."

I grunt in response and go back to my room to get dressed. I don't have time to do anything else. I need to see Kai and make him see sense. Before I go to leave, I go back to Kai's room to fetch my phone and see a missed call from him and a voice message. Just as I'm about to play the message, my phone blares in my hand and I see Jenny's name on the screen. Almost tempted to ignore it so I can listen to Kai's message, I answer, not at all prepared for how she sounds on the other end of the phone.

"Hey Jenny,"

"Jules! Oh thank god, Jules…he's been stabbed, my baby, Jules…" she sobs uncontrollably into the phone and I stiffen.

"Hello, is this Jules?" a man says on the phone, while I can hear Jenny crying in the background and the sound of sirens.

"Who's this?" I ask.

"Sorry, it's Tim. Jenny's friend. Look, we are at the ER. I found Kai today at home; he'd been stabbed. Jules, he's in a pretty bad way, he's lost a lot of blood, and they've just rushed him to surgery. Jenny needs you here."

Time freezes, where I'm standing in an open field of nothingness. Like a cool breeze that drifts over me, I become numb. Kai's been stabbed. Kai. My Kai. I swallow hard and try to focus on moving my body, to answer Tim, but it won't cooperate.

"Jules? Did you hear me?" Tim says.

"Yes. What's the name of the hospital?"

"Lang Grove Hospital. We're on the third floor waiting area of the ICU."

"On my way."

I turn to see Simon standing at the doorway of Kai's room.

"Kai's been stabbed. Gotta get to the hospital."

"What? Is he okay?"

"No. I need to get there."

"You can't drive. Let me call D and I'll come with you."

"No."

"Yes, now get your shit together and meet me out front," Simon says as he calls Dima on his cell.

As Simon explains to Dima what's happening, I stare at my phone, pondering whether to listen to Kai's voicemail. Later. I need to get to him.

"Lev and Ivan are gonna go with you. They're waiting out front."

"Why do they both need to come? I thought you were coming?"

"Dima needs me here. Besides, I think D is worried you'll spiral. Thinks you need extra protection from starting shit."

"Whatever, I just want to get to Kai."

As I briskly walk to the front door, I hold onto the handle, trying to compose myself. I'm a thread away from snapping. I need to hurt someone, I need to find the fuckers who did this. And most of all, I need Kai alive. Otherwise, I'll lose myself. I know it.

Walking to the front of the main house, I see Lev, Dima, and Ivan waiting for me, gathered around Lev's jeep.

"Call me if you need help. Don't go too crazy; you're not protected over there like you are here," Dima says to me, and I appreciate the gesture. He isn't an emotional guy, but this is his way of showing support.

"Crazy? You haven't seen crazy when I find the fuckers."

"Like I said, call if you need assistance," he says, before patting me on the back and walking back into the house. Seb is standing at the doorway with Aaron. While Seb looks sad, and conveys it with the small smile he sends my way, Aaron is on the verge of losing his shit. The guy oozes violence when he is like this, cold eyes, tight lips, and his focus one hundred percent on Lev. I bet they had an argument about whether he could come before they came outside. But this is my vengeance. I'll paint the fucking town red, spread the cunts' innards across town, all to show you never touch my man and if you do, you will pay in blood and pain of the worst kind.

Just before I get into the car, Seb comes over to me. He doesn't speak at first, and from the way he rocks on his feet from foot to foot and stairs down at the ground, he's giving off major nervous vibes.

"What is it, Seb? I don't have time to hang around."

"I promised I wouldn't say anything, but with what's happened I regret it."

"Regret what?" I ask, keen to move this conversation along.

"Kai told me a while ago that he had issues with that gang he hung around with. They were angry when he left.

Well, more than angry. They said if he went back home they'd hurt him."

I stiffen. The pure rage that courses through my body has my back stiffen like a shard of ice. He knew.

"And you're just telling me this now?"

I push Seb in the chest and he stumbles backward as Dima flies over to us, ready to kill.

"Get your fucking hands off him!" Dima yells.

"D, it's fine."

"Like hell is it fine," Dima says.

"No it ain't fucking fine! You knew the danger he was in and you never told me?" I shout in frustration.

"Jules, last warning," Dima says, getting in my face.

"Fuck you. Fuck all of you. Such fucking hypocrites. The way you all went off at Kai for Aaron, but Seb does something and suddenly it doesn't matter."

Dima grabs me by my coat and pushes me into the side of the car.

"Dima, leave him," Lev says.

"You're walking a fine line, Jules. Remember who we are," Dima snarls at me and with all my strength I push him away from me.

"And you forget who I fucking am. I may not be a psycho like you, but I have no problem killing any fucker in my way when it comes to Kai. I'd gladly slaughter you and everyone else here to keep him safe. So do your fucking worst."

Dima watches me for a second before Lev grabs my shoulder.

"Get in the damn car, Jules."

"I'm so sorry, Jules. I care about Kai too. I'd never want to see him hurt. Never," Seb says as a tear escapes his left eye and Dima pulls him close.

I can't do this. I'm so close to losing all control right now, so I turn and get into the car. After a few moments Lev gets in, followed by Ivan.

"What's this?" I ask as Ivan puts a large leather case next to me before getting into the front passenger seat.

"Just something that will help. You'll see," Ivan says cryptically. I don't have time to think about it. Now I just have to sit here and twiddle my thumbs until I get to my Kai.

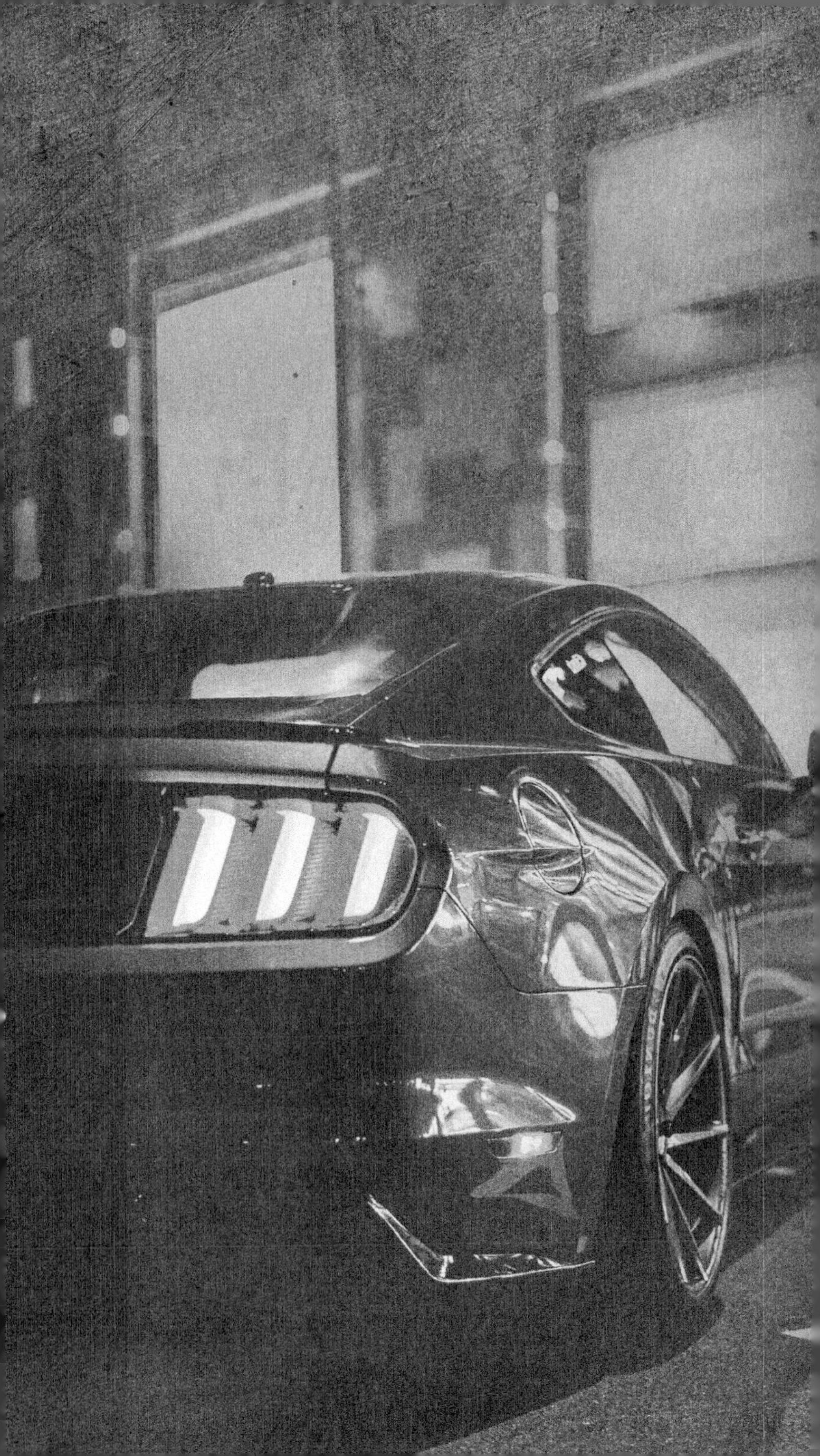

CHAPTER 40
JULES

This car journey feels like we've been travelling forever. We've all remained silent, which I'm thankful for. Even though Lev has been keeping a regular eye on me in the rear view mirror. I'm ready to explode, to do some serious damage. I look down at my phone in my hands and stare at the flashing message from Kai. Whatever is on that message will send me into a spiral, but while I'm contained in the car, it may be the perfect time to listen.

Putting my phone on speaker, I press play on the voicemail, completely unsure what to expect.

"Jules…I–I–I've been s-s-stabbed. L-l-l-love you, i-it h-hurts."

"Fuck! Fuck, fuck, fuck!" I yell as I punch the back of Lev's seat.

"Hey! Calm the fuck down. You can't do nothing right now, and fucking up my car isn't gonna change shit. Wait until we get there, then after you've seen him, we go find the fuckers," Lev shouts at me. I rest my head on the back of the seat and close my eyes, gripping onto my phone so tightly, Kai's soft, crying voice playing on repeat. And he still managed to tell me he loves me. Little shit. My head starts to hurt, trying to process this shit, I need blood. I need Kai.

"We'll get whoever did this, Jules, and when we do, we'll make it as painful as possible," Ivan says as he turns to face me. His big brown eyes lock on me, conveying his loyalty. He hasn't altered. That look in his eyes is the same as the sadistic fucker from when we were young. Ivan is as deranged as the brothers, the difference is, he hides it with a welcoming smile and a fake softness. He's the definition of predator. I'm actually glad he's here.

"Good," I say, and I replay the message from Kai. Over and over and over until it's ingrained into my soul.

"Shut that shit off, Jules. It won't help. We're about five minutes away from the hospital. You need to focus and be calm for Jenny," Lev says. He's right. I forgot about Jenny. This is her boy and she needs me, but I need Kai. I guess she's about to find out the truth as any pretending, hiding who I am, is over. The real Jules is out to play and he wants to start some shit.

We arrive at the hospital and park. Lev and Ivan follow me out of the car toward the hospital entrance. Everyone stares as we pass by, which I suppose isn't unusual. Three intimidating stacked dudes with tattoos who are dressed like the fucking mafia are bound to have you flinch away.

Fortunately the nurse at reception is helpful, and directs us to where we need to go. This hospital is a fucking maze, another obstacle keeping me away from Kai. We take the stairs to the third floor as I don't have the patience for the elevator, and walk into the waiting area where Jenny's eyes find mine as soon as I walk in, and she throws herself into my arms.

"Thank god you're here. My baby," she cries into my neck and sobs uncontrollably. I don't feel anything. I hold onto her, but my focus is only on one thing and one person. Emotion doesn't come into this now. Answers and consequences do.

I peel Jenny away from me, impatient to know what the hell is going on.

"Where is he?" I demand.

"He's in surgery. They had to start a blood transfusion because he's lost so much blood. We're just waiting for more news, but they said it could be hours, depending on what they find," she says. A tall broad man stands behind her and rests his hands on her shoulders. Quite an average guy, I'd say he was mid forties. His brown hair graying, deep smile lines around kind hazel eyes.

"Hey, I'm Tim, Jenny's friend," he says, extending his hand over her shoulder toward me.

"Hey, she's mentioned you. You found Kai?"

"Yeah, I dropped by just on my break to return Jenny's jacket, the door was ajar and then I walked in and saw Kai bleeding out on the floor."

"Did he say anything?"

"No, he was drifting in and out of consciousness until the paramedics arrived. Then he was out of it."

I nod, but all I can see in my mind is images of Kai on the floor of his home. Scared, bleeding. Dying.

"Any leads?" I ask. Tim raises a brow at me.

"Not yet. We haven't been able to talk to Kai. Officers have been checking over the scene. Don't worry, we'll get who did this," Tim assures, and I don't believe him.

"Jules, who are they?" Jenny asks, looking over my shoulder at Lev and Ivan who look like they're standing guard.

"The one with the man bun is Ivan, a work associate. The scowling one is Lev, my boss."

Jenny looks back at Tim and then back to the guys before settling her eyes on me.

"They're not the kind of men I expected you to work with," she whispers.

"What were you expecting?" Lev says from behind me. The guy has the hearing of an owl.

"I didn't mean any offense, it's just you look, you know…" she stutters.

"Hot?" Ivan says, not helping. I turn to stare him down.

"Not the time. Why don't you both go get some coffee or something," I say.

"Good idea. Call me if you have any news," Lev says as they turn to leave.

"They're quite scary, Jules," Jenny says.

"Yeah," is all I can say before I collapse into one of the chairs.

"Who do you work for?" Tim asks, and I don't like his tone. It's a formal cop tone.

"Security."

"Oh yeah? What kind?" I turn to look up at him and want to punch him.

"The none of your fucking business kind."

"Jules! Don't talk to him like that," Jenny scolds.

"I'll talk to him how I want."

"Look, I didn't mean any offense. I was just making conversation."

"Sure you were. Why don't we talk about who could've done this. Jenny? Any ideas?"

"I don't think it's fair to question her like this. We'll begin formal questioning when Kai comes around."

"Is your name Jenny?"

"Jules, please stop. Same for you too, Tim," she says on a sigh and sits next to me.

"I do wonder if it was those friends of his."

The fucking gang. Of course.

"The gang? The ones you've been seeing hanging around?"

"Yeah."

"Wait, what? Have they been following you? Why didn't you say anything?" Tim asks, totally blindsided that Jenny has hidden this from him.

"I didn't want you worrying."

As they start to squabble, luckily my phone rings. Dima's name flashes across the screen, and I stand to walk away from them so I can hear him.

"Hey," I say.

"How is he?"

"In surgery. Don't know much yet."

"You know who did it?"

"I think it was the gang he hung around with. They'd been low key stalking Jenny. When he gets out of surgery I'll go hunt them down."

"You need to be careful. I can't protect you from the cops over there. However, I've spoken to Carlos and he has some men in that area who can give you access to one of their warehouses. They've also offered to dispose of any mess."

"Really? Why would Carlos offer that?"

"Payment for us helping him with the interrogation. Carlos comes from a wealthy family with power. Call him when you're ready to move and he'll have some men waiting for you there. He'll give you the address."

"Thanks."

"Always. When this is over, bring Kai back here with you."

What the hell? I'm too high on the taste of revenge to question him right now.

"I will."

Dima grunts on the other end of the line before hanging up. That's the closest you'll get to affection from the brooding man, but I'm so fucking grateful to him and to Carlos. I walk back over to Jenny and Tim who are both silent as I sit down.

"Everything okay?" Jenny asks.

"Yeah, that was my other boss, Dima. Just checking in to see how Kai is doing."

"That was nice of him. They must be some great guys you work with, being here with you and so supportive," Jenny says.

"They're alright."

"I need to go to the restroom. I won't be long," Jenny says as she gets out of the chair and heads off out of sight.

"You live in Grinston, right?" Tim asks.

"Yeah."

"Lev and Dima. Unusual but memorable names. I had a buddy at the station talk about these Russian guys who run a drug business in that area. Apparently they own the cops too."

"Is that so?"

"Jenny would lose her mind if she knew where you'd taken her son. I assume given your background you plan on revenge? Because if you are, I'd advise against it. I'll bring you in."

Fuck this arrogant prick. Standing from my seat, I grab him by the collar and force him back into the opposite wall. His breathing heavy, his eyes wide with panic.

"Pretty brave of you running your mouth, making threats."

"You're just a thug that'll bring nothing but danger to that boy's life," he hisses at me.

"What's going on?" Lev says, approaching from behind me with Ivan.

"This cocksucker was telling me he knows all about you and D. Apparently we're a danger," I say as I laugh in his ugly face with no humor.

"Dangerous? Well that's fucking boring. You threatening my men, Timmy?"

"It's Officer Lovell," he sneers as I push him harder into the wall.

"Whatever, Timmy. I think your little pea brain is tired, and you may need to rethink things. You could get hurt when you say the wrong thing to strangers," Lev warns, moving closer to Tim.

"Threatening me now?"

"Nope. Don't do those. Now why don't you be a good boy, Timmy, and sit and wait for your girl to come back, otherwise you'll be in the ER on your own."

"I just don't want you starting shit here. Let the police do their job," Tim says.

"Because they're so good at it. We're fine with the police doing their job, Timmy."

I push away from the asshole and walk over to Ivan to create some space.

"You're a bunch of animals."

"Really? That's a compliment to me, dude. Fuck like them too," Ivan says, grinning like a fun, likeable guy. It isn't real. We're all in a stand-off, which Tim is losing.

Jenny comes back and stops in her tracks, watching us in concern.

"You better not be fighting, Tim?"

"No. We're just talking."

I scoff at that and take a seat with the guys, a small distance away from Jenny and Tim. Tim's a possible issue for another day, he just needs to keep away from me. There's only one person on my mind.

Come on, Kai. I need to see you.

Hours pass, my ass and back hurt from the uncomfortable seats. I'm going mad. If we hear nothing in the next ten minutes, I swear I'll barge into that operating room.

"Are you Kai's family?" a female voice says, and we all jump up like our asses are on fire.

"Yes, I'm his mom. How is he?"

"Kai's lost a lot of blood. We had to run a blood transfusion which is now working well. He had some internal bleeding from a ruptured spleen which thankfully we managed to fix. We need to keep a close eye on him for any post-surgery infections or complications, so we'll be keeping him in the ICU. We're keeping him under sedation for now and giving him plenty of fluids."

"So he'll be okay?" I ask.

"We're optimistic. He was very lucky that the knife wasn't bigger."

"Can we see him?" Jenny asks.

"Yes, but only two at a time. The nurses will take you down shortly."

"Thank you so much, Doctor," I say, and let out the breath that I feel like I've been holding onto this entire day.

The doctor smiles and walks away. Relief washes over my sister's face as she comes to hug me. A nurse approaches and asks us to follow.

"Will you be okay, Tim?" Jenny asks.

"He'll be fine. We'll look after him," Ivan says, grinning as he guides Tim back to the seating area. Even Lev smirks at the move. Ivan is certainly gonna bring some life into the house.

As we enter Kai's room, I bristle at the sight of him. Machines beep all around him, an IV drips, along with the blood bag that's giving him what he needs to survive.

His normally golden skin is pale, his upper body is bare, and my eyes don't move from the large bandage where the stab wound is. My jaw clenches and I twist my fists. Those assholes won't know what's hit them. I allow myself to move closer to the bed and look at his beautiful face. There's a faint bruise on his jaw that's new. The marks I left on him are nowhere to be seen, apart from the tiny hickey on his neck. The urge to climb into the bed with him and demand he wakes up and tell me what happened overwhelms me. But I resist. Jenny rushes over to the chair at the side of the bed and clasps his hand with both of her tiny ones and talks to him about everything and nothing. I can do nothing but stand at the end of the bed looking at my man, who was nearly taken from me. The longer I watch him, the more my walls build up around me, protecting me, making me stronger for what I need to do next.

"Jenny, what were the names of the guys he hung around with?"

"I don't know all of them, only Jez who was his best friend, and his brother Zac. Why?"

"No reason," I say as Jenny goes back to talking quietly to Kai, stroking his hair. This whole situation is like an out of body experience. I briefly wonder if it's a nightmare that I'm yet to wake from. This is the first time anyone I truly cared for has been hurt, and it's so unsettling and foreign to me that it dents my armor that has served me well over the years.

The nurse comes in and checks Kai's vitals.

"How long will he be under for?" I ask.

"The doctor will keep him sedated until tomorrow. If you need to rest, now is the time to do it, while he sleeps."

Rest is the last thing on my mind. But while Kai sleeps, I think I'll make a visit to his so called 'friends'.

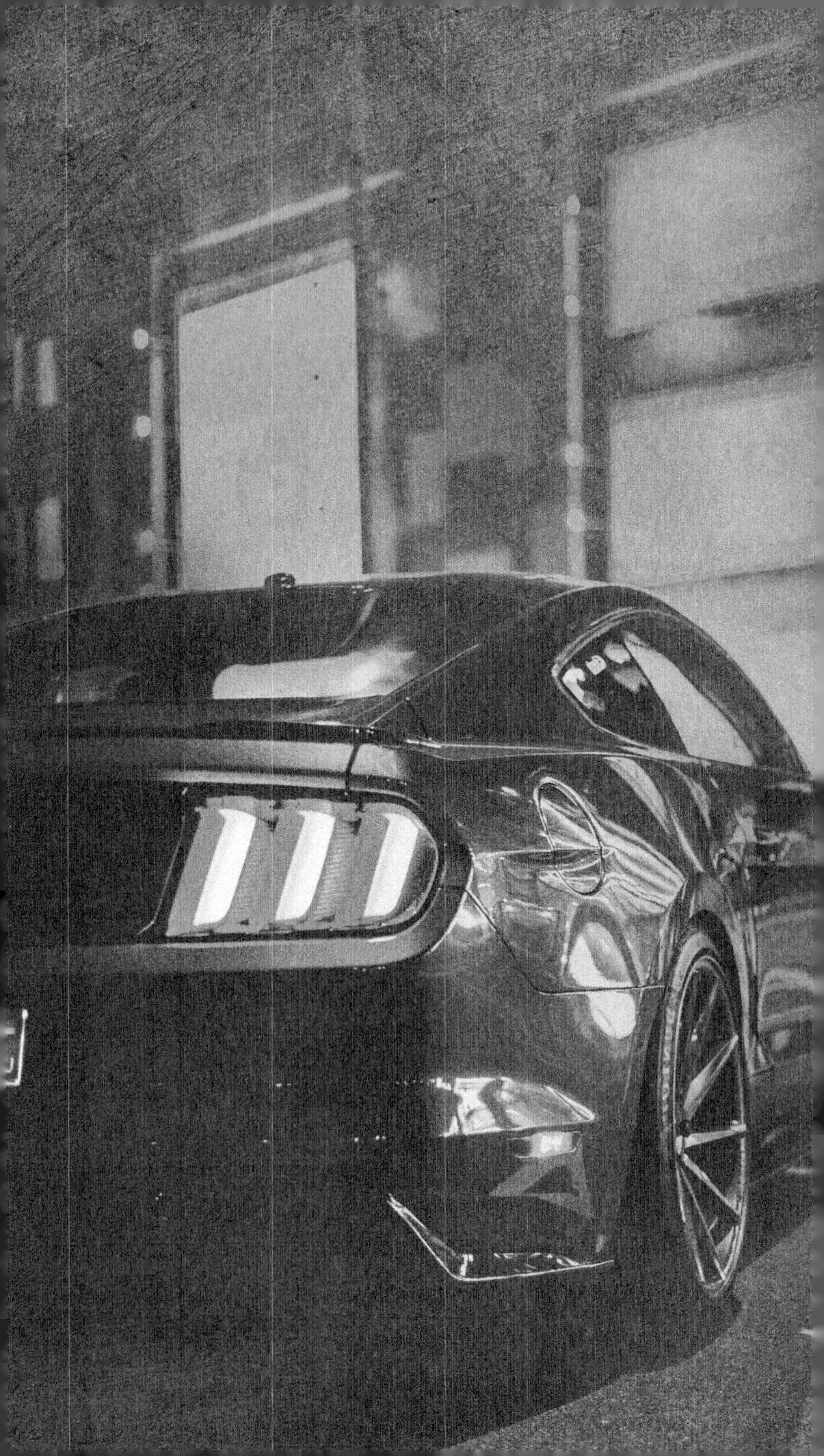

CHAPTER 41
JULES

Jenny didn't notice me leaving Kai's room, and I'm glad. She doesn't want the answers to the questions I'm not in the mood to hear. It's a strange feeling, leaving Kai. My brain has neatly packaged up the emotional part of me that wants to stay with him and watch over him and tucked it into the back of my mind. All I can think about is vengeance for Kai. I won't be able to rest, knowing they're out there, unaware of the shitstorm they've created. The thirst for blood is rampant, I'm nearly trembling with excitement to get this shit going. Only then will I be able to come back and be what Kai needs, and he can rest assured that payment for his hurt has been paid in full. I intend to get that payment tonight with a little added interest.

Walking further down the corridor, Ivan, Lev and Tim all stand, awaiting news of different kinds.

"Tim, you can go in and keep Jenny company. Call me if there are any changes, but the nurse said they won't be waking him up until tomorrow," I say.

"Hang on, where are you going?" he asks. Look, I don't actually think he's a bad guy. But he's a cop and cops ask too many fucking questions.

"Nowhere that concerns you," I say before moving closer to Ivan and Lev. Tim huffs out a long breath and the sound of his boots squeaking against the floor disappears further into the distance behind me.

"Today. It has to be today we end them. I can't sit on this, Lev."

"Didn't think you would. I already contacted D while you were with Kai. Carlos has men at the location. I have the address."

"Dima still wants to help after what I said?"

"Shut up, Jules. Don't play dumb. If anyone knows what it's like to get bloodthirsty, it's us." Lev says, and I suppose that's fair.

"What about this little gang? Do we know where they are?" I ask.

"Yep. Wasn't too hard to narrow down with it being a small town. They call themselves 'The Skins', hardly a name that blends in. Fucking stupid ass name. Two of them were arrested yesterday morning, Dean and Tex, for disorderly conduct," Lev mutters.

"Can't have been them who did it, so that leaves the brothers Jez and Zac," I say.

"Do we have a gang name?" Ivan asks Lev, derailing our conversation.

"What do you mean a gang name? We ain't a gang," Lev snaps, insulted at the very idea.

"Well, we kinda are," Ivan says.

"No we fucking ain't, Ivan. Can we go? I'm excited to play," Lev says grinning, rubbing his hands together.

"I want control of this," I say.

"We can manage that, but you finish when I say, we can't linger for too long," Lev says as we start to make our way out of the hospital.

I'll be back soon, Kai.

After a ten minute drive, we arrive at an apartment complex in a shitty ass part of town. It's late evening now and too fucking cold for anyone to be out on the streets. We park on the side of the road and get out of the car, and walk up to the entrance of the depressingly gray building.

"What's the apartment number?" I ask Lev.

"1D."

As we head inside, a musty damp smell floods my nostrils as I take in the worn out entrance. Paint peels off every wall and along the wooden bannister that leads upstairs. We climb up to the first floor, the apartment we want is the second door on the left of the narrow and dark corridor. Not a window in sight.

Lev and Ivan stand on either side of the door, out of the peephole line of sight, and I knock on the old brown door twice. Footsteps approach, and the door opens. A guy with a bald head answers, keeping the door chain on its bolt as he peers through the gap.

"Can I help you?" the guy says with an attitude I can't wait to beat out of him. Is this Zac or Jez?

"Are you Jez?"

"No. He ain't here right now."

This guy is so high, he's struggling to keep his eyes focused on me.

"That's too bad. I have some weed for him. A new batch."

"Really?"

"Yeah, but I can come back."

"No...no you can come in. I can help you instead."

Bingo. That was way easier than I thought. Just as he unlatches the door, I step through into his hallway while Lev and Ivan barge their way in, slamming the door behind them before Lev gets this piece of shit in a headlock. He clutches at Lev's forearms, but Lev isn't going anywhere.

"What's your name?" I ask as I move further into the living area. What a shithole. The place reeks of weed and sweat, the furniture is all falling apart. I don't think this place has ever been cleaned. I turn to face the idiot who is still clinging to Lev.

"Zac," he rasps.

"Just the man I'm looking for."

Lev pulls Zac upright, and Ivan joins him as they take an arm each, holding Zac up in a standing position. Open to anything I give him.

"This may come as a shock, but Kai was stabbed earlier today at his home. I heard you were friends, so thought it would be a nice thing to let you know."

Zac watches me, he doesn't respond, unless sweating profusely is a response.

"Nothing to say? That's okay, I'll keep talking and you correct me if I'm wrong with what I think happened."

Still no response.

"I think your brother did it. I heard Jez was his good friend and I think you're covering for him."

"No. Jez would never do that, he was with me today."

"Oh, so you were there too?"

"No."

"Hmmm, you see, I think you're a dirty little liar. I know you've been watching his mom for weeks. But what I want to know is why you were watching her? Luckily for you, I know ways to make someone talk."

His breathing hitches, anticipation of the unknown must be tearing him apart inside.

"Ivan, hold his hand out."

Ivan stretches his arm out and firmly grips his wrist.

"What! I don't know anything man, please," he whines, trying to pull away.

"Did Kai beg you to stop?"

"Don't do this," he says, trying to portray a softness I know fuckers like this don't possess.

I move over to his outstretched hand and grab his little finger, pulling it backwards as slow as I can. Zac starts to yell, trying to move his hand.

"I'll stop if you tell me, or I will break each and every finger."

"Stop."

"No. Where's your brother?"

"Don't hurt him. We can sort this out between us," he says, begging.

I pull back hard on his finger. Just a little more pressure, if I put my weight into it, it should break.

"Ahhh! Stop! Fuck! It was me, okay, it was me and nothing to do with Jez."

"Do you know how embarrassing it is that you gave in so fast? You really are pathetic."

"Who cares about Kai! He's dead and nobody will miss him," he shouts, the pain overtaking sense.

I grab him by his dirty, ugly face.

"I care. You put your hands on my man, and I won't let you get away with that. Also, when you plan to kill someone, always check that they're dead first before you run. Kai is very much alive."

"What?"

"Do you still have the knife?"

"Fuck you! You don't have shit on me to prove it."

Suddenly I can hear Kai's voice, the message he left me replaying in my mind.

"Jules...I–I–I've been s-s-stabbed. L-l-l-love you, i-it h-hurts,"

All I can see is him bleeding out alone on his mom's floor. That this fucker nearly killed him. The message replays over and over and I want to yell out to stop it. I need to keep focus, but I'm lost in the wave of emotion and what's happened. Anger. Hate. Fury. Blood. Before I know it, I have both hands wrapped around Zac's throat, like the jaws of a dog, they lock in place. The wheezing sounds coming from this asshole thrill me. I love the feeling of his neck in my hands, that he's so vulnerable, I could snap his neck like a twig.

"Jules! Let him go. Not here. Fuck!"

The door flies open and a surfer looking dude with long brown hair storms in, which pulls me out of the place I was just locked in.

"Jez?" Ivan asks.

Jez looks at his brother, who is now unconscious but still breathing on the floor, then moves his beady eyes over to the three of us.

"Who's asking?" he says.

Ivan smiles and walks over to him.

"Your worst nightmare," Ivan says as he punches him in the face, which knocks him out cold, landing on the floor next to his stinky ass brother.

"That was fucking close. What did I tell you earlier? We can't be doing any of that killing shit here. Use your fucking brain, Jules, or I'll take over the show if you can't control yourself.

"I couldn't help it."

"Well try. Ivan, grab the smelly ass one. I'll take the long haired rat. Jules...go get in the damn car and focus your shit."

"Like you wouldn't have done the same or worse."

"No. I would've drugged them and brought them back to our home where I could savor them. Now go."

They get the boys down into the car as quickly as possible. Lev tosses Zac into the trunk, while me and Ivan sit in the back with Jez, taking a seat on either side of him, and head off to Carlos's secured location. The roads are so quiet, you'd think an apocalypse had hit. Not surprising for such a small town, I'd imagine everyone is bundled up in the warmth with their loved ones. While my loved one is in hospital, fighting for his life. One thing I can guarantee, is that these two bastards won't need a hospital, because nobody is coming to save them.

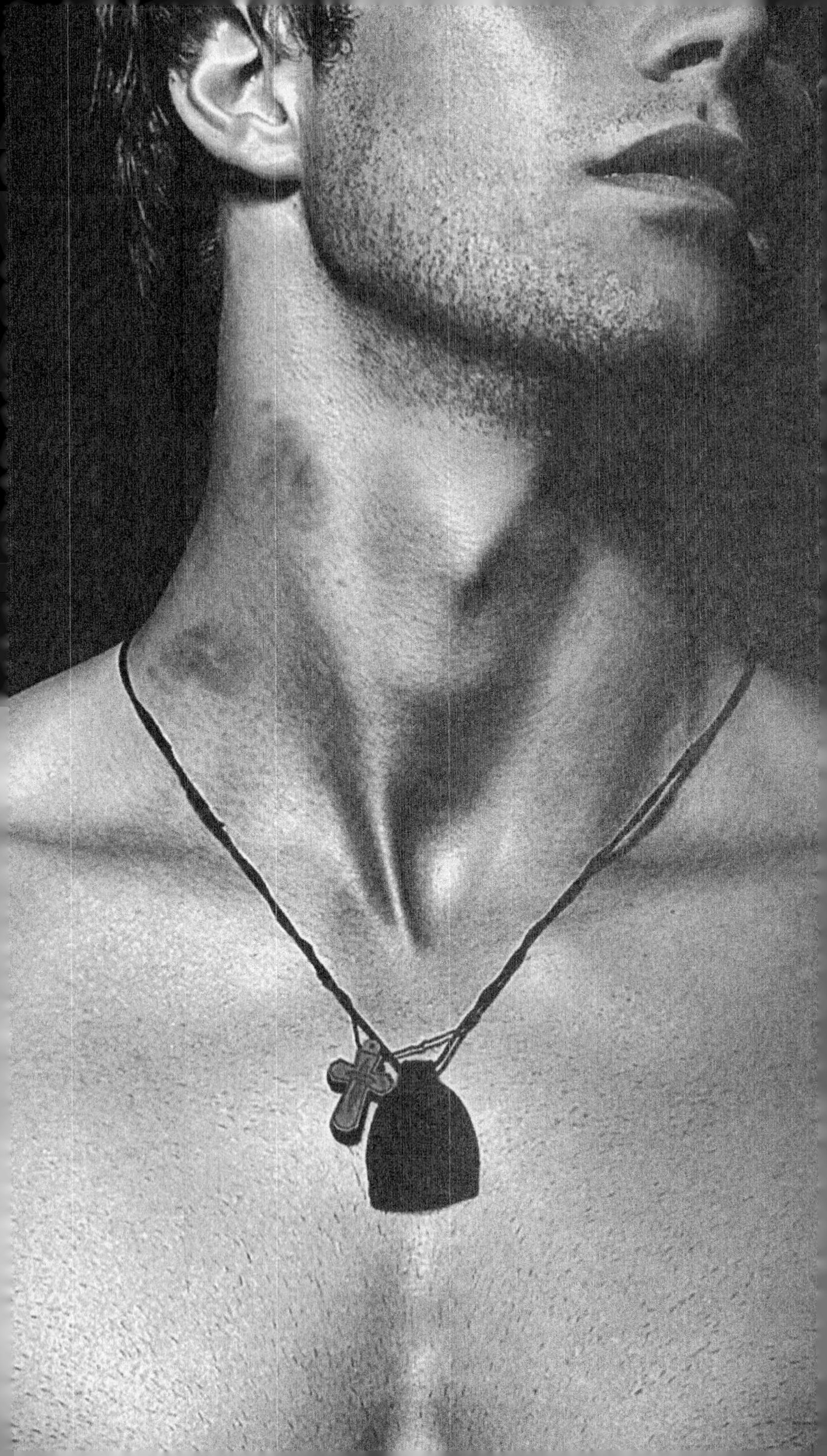

CHAPTER 42
KAI

Am I dead? Or am I dreaming? It's so peaceful here, my body is weightless like it's floating in the clouds. A warm fuzzy sensation spreads from my head all the way to my toes. I'm so tired. I can't open my eyes, the weight keeping them closed is frustrating, because I want to open them. Distant noises echo around me. Voices, I think, and a beeping noise. Why can't I open my eyes? I feel like I'm on the outside of life looking in. I want to come back. My body starts to tingle as the warmth increases, nerve endings twitch as if I'm being recharged back to life.

"I'm so scared, Tim. What if he gets worse?" an angelic voice sings, and a spark of recognition hits me. That's my mom. Open your eyes, Kai. Fuck.

"He'll make it through, I promise."

Is that Tim? Why are they talking like that? Where am I and what is that beeping noise? A searing pain in my stomach hits me, and I want to cry out.

Pain. Stabbed. Zac. Jules.

I was stabbed. The beeping sounds in the room intensify and hands cover my arms. I'm shaking, I can't stop it. Panic ensues as memories of what happened flood back. The blood. The horrific pain and fear.

"Kai, can you hear me?" a voice I don't recognize says, over and over. I know I'm making noises, but why won't my eyes open?

"I need you to calm down before you hurt yourself, Kai."

Jules. Where is Jules's voice? Ah, he's not here is he? I left him.

Jules, Jules, Jules.

I want Jules. Only he can make me better, only he can make me feel safe. But I left him.

"Kai, we're going to increase your sedative, as you need to rest," another voice says. Something cold trails through the veins in my arm, instantly calming my mind. I start to float again, sailing off to a world of peace, with Jules's face the last thing to cross my mind as I black out.

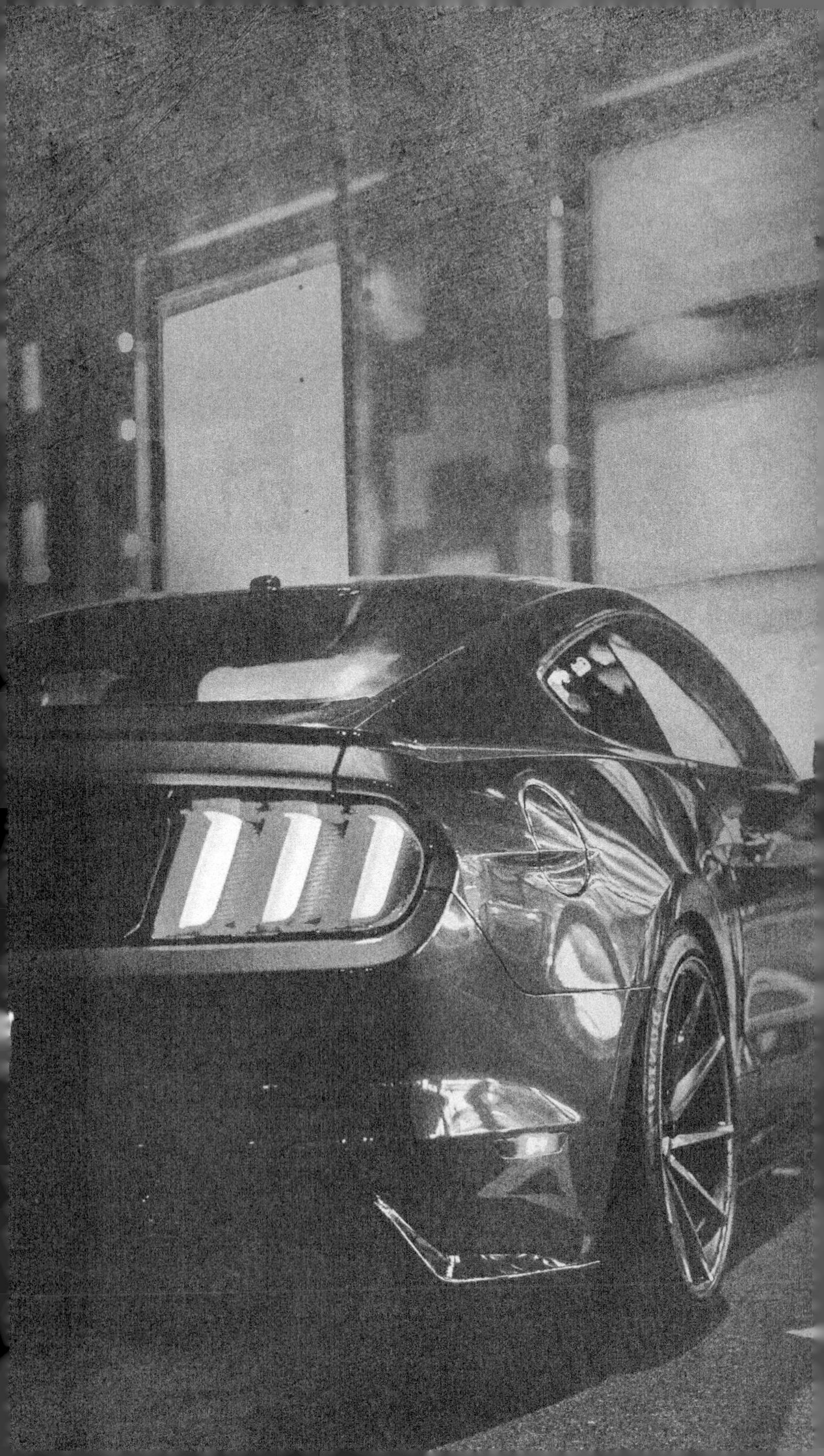

CHAPTER 43
Jules

Wow. This warehouse is impressive. We arrive at the location that's on the outskirts of town, the entire facility is like a security compound. High fencing with barbed wire runs around the perimeter, cameras installed in every corner of the yard where the large warehouse is situated. Lev slows the car down as we approach the secure gate where one of the guards lets us in, and we drive towards the building to be greeted by two more of Carlos's men.

The three of us get out of the car first, leaving Zac and Jez inside the vehicle.

"I'm Stephan. We'll be right outside the main doors until you're done. Leave the bodies inside when finished, we can dispose of them."

I look over at Lev, who looks as dumbfounded as me. Who the hell is Carlos, really? Because a set up like this is not from no small time importer. The guard's appearance and demeanor are entirely different from the guys he has working for him back home. These guys look like the real deal. Dressed sharp, focused, and professional. I'm impressed.

"Sounds good. Come on you two, lets get the fuckers inside," Lev says, and we go to grab them from the car. Lev handles Zac from the trunk, while I take hold of Jez. Ivan reaches into the car and grabs that black case, and I'm dying to know what's in it.

"Where are we?" Jez asks, and I ignore him.

"What are we doing here? People will miss us, you know? The cops have probably already been told," Zac shouts as Lev literally drags him into the warehouse, while we follow behind.

"No they won't. You have no family or friends apart from each other. The other two morons are in jail, so I doubt anyone will miss you. Especially your smell," Lev says, sneering in disgust.

The warehouse is like I thought, one large open space, a few containers lay around randomly on the floor and a small office that's empty is situated in the far left corner of the warehouse. As I scan the room, with a firm grip on Jez, I find what I'm looking for. Heavy metal chains hang from the ceiling at the other side of the warehouse, and I push Jez along in front of me.

"Ivan, give me a hand, hold his arms up for me."

Ivan tugs on Jez's arms, locking his complaining ass into position as I guide the chains over to his wrists and lock them into place until he is secure, dangling like a piece of meat from a hook.

"You can't do this! I didn't do anything!" Jez screams, and so the begging begins.

"What do you want me to do with this dickhead?" Lev asks.

"Secure him to that chair. I want him to watch," I say as I remove my coat, and roll up the sleeves of my shirt. It's freezing in here, but it doesn't get to me. Hot blood of determination and anger courses through my body, heating me up enough for me to function.

"Secure him with what? I haven't got anything," Lev moans.

"I have. Here," Ivan says as we both turn to see him open his large black case and remove a long piece of rope. What kind of Mary Poppins shit is this? Wait…is that a tattoo gun in his bag?

"What else you got in there?" I ask, genuinely intrigued.

"Tattoo gun, knives, more rope, cable ties, clamps, pliers, scalpel," he says but I cut him off by holding up my hand to stop him.

"Why?"

"He loves to play as much as I do, but he carries his stuff around, just in case an opportunity arises," Lev says, chuckling. I remember when we were younger, Ivan had an unhealthy obsession with what the body could tolerate in terms of torture. It appears he has perfected his craft, because this is some crazy shit.

Ivan drags the random chair over to us, and Lev secures Zac with the rope.

"Let Jez go. Take me, but leave him out of it."

"Why should I? You both hurt Kai, and you need to be punished," I say.

"It was me! I stabbed the fucker. You'd do the same if one of yours betrayed you," he shouts, the real Zac joining us, finally.

"How did he betray you, exactly?" I ask, while moving around Jez, inhaling his terrified pants, the stench of fear so strong I can taste it.

"He left! You don't just leave. The fucker always thought he was special. But he was weak," Zac says. I watch him for a moment, looking at his ugly face, thinking that was the last thing Kai saw before he got hurt. I'm gonna slice the fucker open.

"How old are you? Ten?" Ivan asks. He actually looks like he pities the idiots and their idea of betrayal. They've no idea.

"Who is Kai to you, anyway?" Jez says, and I move my focus back to him.

"I'm his uncle."

"Jules?" Jez rasps.

"Yeah. You fucked with the wrong guy. You see, I believe in consequences, and because I'm a nice guy, I want to rid you of the guilt. Cleanse your soul, so to speak," I say, and I move closer to Jez.

"You're gonna kill us, aren't you?" he asks.

"Yes, but not yet. We'll take a while to get there first."

Before he can respond, I form my hand into a fist and pull back my arm. My muscles coil, then release like a spring, smashing him in his face. The pain, like a sharp shock from contact with his stiff jaw, travels down my forearm. But it'll be worth breaking every damn finger.

Zac yells out for me to stop, and Jez swings his face back to face me and grins. The fucker actually grins. In the years I've been doing this, I've learned you have three different kinds of reactions. One is begging and offering to do anything or to sell a family member to save their life. Two is remaining calm, accepting your fate, and not fighting it, then the third is like what Jez is displaying. Anger and annoyance, becoming a mouthy shit, thinking if they spout enough hatred to you, you'll suddenly get feelings and let them go because they hurt your sensitive soul. I actually prefer those as it makes it more fun to break them down into nothing. Which I will, with my very own fists.

"I should've had a turn too, finished the pathetic loser off. It was fun to watch him cry like a baby," Jez says, and that's all the green light I need to get this party started.

"Ivan, take his top off."

With a huge smile, Ivan grabs one of his knives from his bag and strolls over to Jez and uses the knife to slice through the material of his sweatshirt, ripping it off into pieces, revealing Jez's naked chest. I want to see the damage caused, for his skin to turn from pale to purple. Jez shivers from the freezing air, but he does a good job in schooling his face like this doesn't bother him.

I begin the onslaught of beating his body until my muscles ache with overuse. I start with his ribs, my fists connect with the hard flesh, dull thuds mix with the occasional sound of crunching bones. His yells of pain ring out in the large open space like a symphony. I use him as a punchbag, alternating sides until his skin reddens. My hands hurt like a bitch, but I power through. I grunt with every hit, my fists now smashing his face, my goal is to keep going until his face is left in a pulp of mushed flesh and blood.

"Ahhh!" he shouts, when I connect with his mouth. Blood flows like a tap from his nose. The sounds are spectacular. Crunching, wet squelches with every punch, destroying his face.

My arms scream in protest at the exertion. I'm covered in sweat and puffing air like I've run a marathon. I remove my shirt in hopes of cooling down, and fall into a steady rhythm.

One-two, one-two, one-two.

I mix the hits between face and body. The shouts of pain have become low whimpers, his body becoming more lax as he slumps, suspended by his arms. Every time my fist connects with his flesh, an image of Kai's broken body blurs my vision. The hate builds and builds with every blow. I'm angry, I'm pissed. Angry that Kai left, pissed that he lied, seething that he got hurt and I wasn't there to protect him. Vengeful enough to spill blood in his name.

My arms turn to jelly, exhausted physically, but mentally I've barely begun. I've no idea how long I've been at this, but Jez is unrecognizable. Still alive, though. Barely.

I flex my fingers and wince at the pain in my hands. I don't think they're broken, but they'll definitely be swollen. Turning to look at Zac, I'm almost tempted to challenge him to a fight. The anger and devastation written over his face is almost too much to resist. He has nothing to lose and would probably be a good opponent.

"You're a fucking monster! I should've stabbed that bastard in the neck, bled him like a pig!" Zac yells.

"But you didn't. You hurt my man, and I'll hurt you. Nobody touches him but me."

I wipe the sweat off my brow and look over at Ivan.

"Want to give us a demonstration with your bag of fun?" I say to Ivan.

"Thought you'd never ask," he says and all but skips over to his case of goodies.

"Now, let me show you my new toy. I had it custom-made in Europe and have been dying to use it," Ivan says as he removes the tattoo gun from his bag. He even has his own extension cable to run from the socket. I watch him set the gun up and wonder for a moment what's so special about it as, so far, it just looks like an average tattoo machine.

"What are you gonna do? Tattoo pretty flowers over his body?" Lev says snarkily.

"I could, but I'd prefer to use this," Ivan says and holds up the needle that you normally attach to the gun. However, this needle is different; it's shaped similarly to a razor but a lot smaller, and it looks like it could cut through leather with ease. Ivan is one crazy sick fucker to think of this, but I'm down to watch.

"What are you gonna do with it?" I ask.

"So many options, man. We could flay him, cut out sections of his skin, or give him a circumcision."

"A what?" I ask.

"Circumcision. You know, when they cut off your foreskin."

"I know what it is, but why?" I say.

"Because it fucking hurts, and it's fun. Trust me, anything to do with the dick has them screaming, unlike anything you've ever heard."

"That's an awesome idea. What if he's already cut?" Lev says.

"Then we'll do something else. Just watch and enjoy, boys."

"I should've filmed this shit, Aaron would've loved it," Lev mutters to himself.

"Don't you fucking touch me!" Zac wails. Like we'd listen to him.

"Why not? Dicks that are cut are pretty hot," Ivan says as he finishes assembling his kit.

"You're not looking so hot, Zac," I say.

"Fuck you!"

"No thanks, I'm happy fucking Kai."

"You're disgusting, fucking your own family. Maybe that's where I went wrong, should have fucked him so bad you would never get to again. Always thought he was soft," Zac says, his lip curled in disgust. He gets what he wants from me, a reaction I'm only too happy to show him. I swing my arm to the side and with sharp force, I backhand him across the face. It lacks the depth and impact of a punch, but I like the demeaning nature of it. It's almost a dismissive act. My knuckles sting, already sore from beating Jez, but watching Zac's face jolt to the side, his nostrils flaring in resolve, trying not to show how much it hurt, makes it worth every bit of pain.

"We need to move this along. Ivan, get started," Lev says, and Ivan happily obliges. He kneels at Zac's feet, still tied to the chair, and opens his jeans and pulls out his sad flaccid dick.

"Yes! He isn't cut," Ivan says, on the verge of becoming overly excited. Lev stands to the side and watches with complete focus. He loves this kind of shit, and he and Ivan together will be a nightmare.

"Get off! No!" Zac screams as Ivan turns on the gun.

"Don't be ungrateful, trust me, you'll love the look of it when I'm done," Ivan says, as he then lowers the vibrating blade around the tip of Zac's cock. With precision, he pulls the foreskin over the head and moves the blade down his shaft until the flesh rips apart. Wow. The screams. I want to close my eyes and absorb the pain, its so alluring to hear this fucker hysterical. He's shaking so hard that Lev has to hold the chair still so he doesn't fall over. Lev is completely enraptured by the process. Ivan is completely unbothered by the yelling, his tongue touching his upper lip with concentration, and all I can do is sigh with relief.

We've got them. Kai will never have to think about them again.

Kai's face again appears in my vision. That cute dimple, his ravenous and innocent eyes, so contrasting in their wants and desires. The tattoo gun stops whirring and Ivan sits back with the blood covered piece of skin. Zac is bleeding profusely from his dick, where Ivan went a little too deep, but who the fuck cares.

"Still want to talk shit?" I ask. He doesn't answer. His pale skin is drenched in sweat, his eyes have glossed over, his mind not in the room with us.

"Finish it, Jules. We need to leave," Lev says, and I nod in agreement.

I walk over to Ivan's case and retrieve a long sharp blade. Feeling at peace, I stride over to Jez, who is barely conscious. I hold his head back and slice the blade across his throat. His throat gapes open as loud wet gurgles leave his mouth before he stops breathing. One down, one left to go.

Spinning around, I look at Zac, and what a fucking sight. Lev is still holding onto the chair as Zac's weight falls to the side. Without any words, I walk over to him. His eyes open, staring at me as though he's looking through me.

"You never should've touched what's mine. Now you pay the price," I say, my face contorting into a bitter smile as Lev yanks his head back for me, and I slowly slit his throat, watching and listening to every gasp and gulp, and admiring the fountain of blood that now spills down his body.

As soon as he takes his last breath, the cold from the night sends icy chills across my bare chest. I'm covered in blood, my body hurts like hell, but all I want to do now is go to Kai.

"Here, put your shirt and jacket on. We got a suite at the local hotel, and the concierge sent some new clothes to our room. Then you can go to your boy," Lev says.

"Thanks for this," I say to him. He stares at me, blank of any emotion I could read on his face, and he nods.

"No thanks needed. Now let's go. Ivan, pack away your shit, we need to head out," Lev says, and Ivan gets to work.

"What do you think they'll do with the bodies?" I say.

"No idea, but D said we can trust them. Don't worry about it."

That's good enough for me. I dress back into my shirt and coat, which will both need replacing, and we walk out of the warehouse with a quick exchange of goodbyes with Carlos's men. Lev warms up the car as we leave the compound and head to wherever this hotel is. I need to get cleaned up as I'm now itching to get back to my man. My Kai. And when he's better, he has some explaining to do, along with a punishment for ever thinking of leaving me.

Fortunately, my coat covers the evidence of the carnage we left behind at the warehouse, enabling me to go to the hotel and clean up. After a shower and a change of clothes, compliments of the concierge service, I take an Uber to the hospital, leaving Lev and Ivan behind.

When I get to the hospital, I walk as fast as I can to Kai's room. As I arrive at his door, I notice that Tim is not here, only Jenny, who is fast asleep in the chair next to Kai's bed. I quietly walk over to the other side of Kai, so as not to wake Jenny, and gently stroke my bruised fingers down his pale cheek. His chest steadily rises and falls, no other sound in the room, apart from the beeping monitors.

"Hey, you're back," Jenny says, yawning as she stretches in the uncomfortable stiff chair.

"Any news?"

"He started to wake earlier, the sedation had worn off. He was quite agitated, so they gave him something to put him back to sleep again."

"Why didn't you message me?"

"Because it happened so fast, and it didn't take long for the doctors to settle him."

"You should've told me. Anything that happens with Kai, even a sneeze, I want to be informed."

Jenny goes silent and looks at me, wide eyed in disbelief.

"Okay, you need to back the hell up. I didn't see the point in worrying you."

"Not your call to make."

"And what the hell is that supposed to mean? He's my son, Jules. Of course it's my call."

"Kai's an adult and he'd want me here."

Jenny goes quiet again, her face now in contemplation. Her eyes narrow on me, questions buried under that curious gaze.

"He called out for you."

"What?"

"When he was panicking. He muttered your name several times before he went under again. I didn't realize you'd gotten so close."

"He's everything to me."

She nods slowly. "Yeah I know. He's family. I'm sorry, I'm just tired."

I'm seconds away from telling her Kai is not family. He's my soul. My life eternal. My beginning with no end. But of course, idiot Tim enters the room to ruin the chance for me to come clean.

"Jules. You're back."

"Anyone tell you what a perceptive cop you are?"

"Jules!" Jenny hisses at me.

"It's fine. Why don't we go get some rest. Jules is here to take over."

"I don't know. What if he wakes again?"

"Then I will call you," I say, not taking my eyes off Kai's face. Her presence is starting to annoy me as I want Kai to myself.

"Just a few hours, then I'll be back. Call me if anything changes."

"I will. Now go."

Jenny runs her hands through her hair, then walks over to the other side of the room and collects her coat and handbag. She gives one last look at Kai and gives me a small smile before turning to leave with Tim in tow.

Finally. Alone.

I remove my coat and close the door to Kai's room, strolling over to his bed to take the seat that Jenny just vacated. I take Kai's palm in my hand and watch every breath that leaves his body.

"You come back to me now, sweetheart. We have things to discuss. Your bad behavior, for one. Being stabbed won't get you out of being punished."

Beep, beep, beep. The sounds start to feel like a relaxing melody, my shoulders relax but my mind won't quit.

"They'll never bother you again. I got rid of them. For you. I'd do worse to protect you, Kai. From this moment on you will not leave my side."

Beep, beep, beep.

I roam my eyes over his chest and abdomen, noticing something is missing. My marks. My branding. I bet he missed it when he left. While I can't do anything to his chest or stomach, you know, because he was stabbed, there is one place I can reclaim his body. I stand and move to the other side of the bed and pull down the sheets until that hot as fuck tattoo comes into view. Needing a taste more than I need to breathe, I lower my mouth and suck on the thorns of the rose, suckling at his skin, drinking up his sweetness. My teeth gently bite down and the monitor to his heart increases in pace. I move away and lick where a bruise now forms, pleased with how it looks. Hopefully when he wakes he'll feel it.

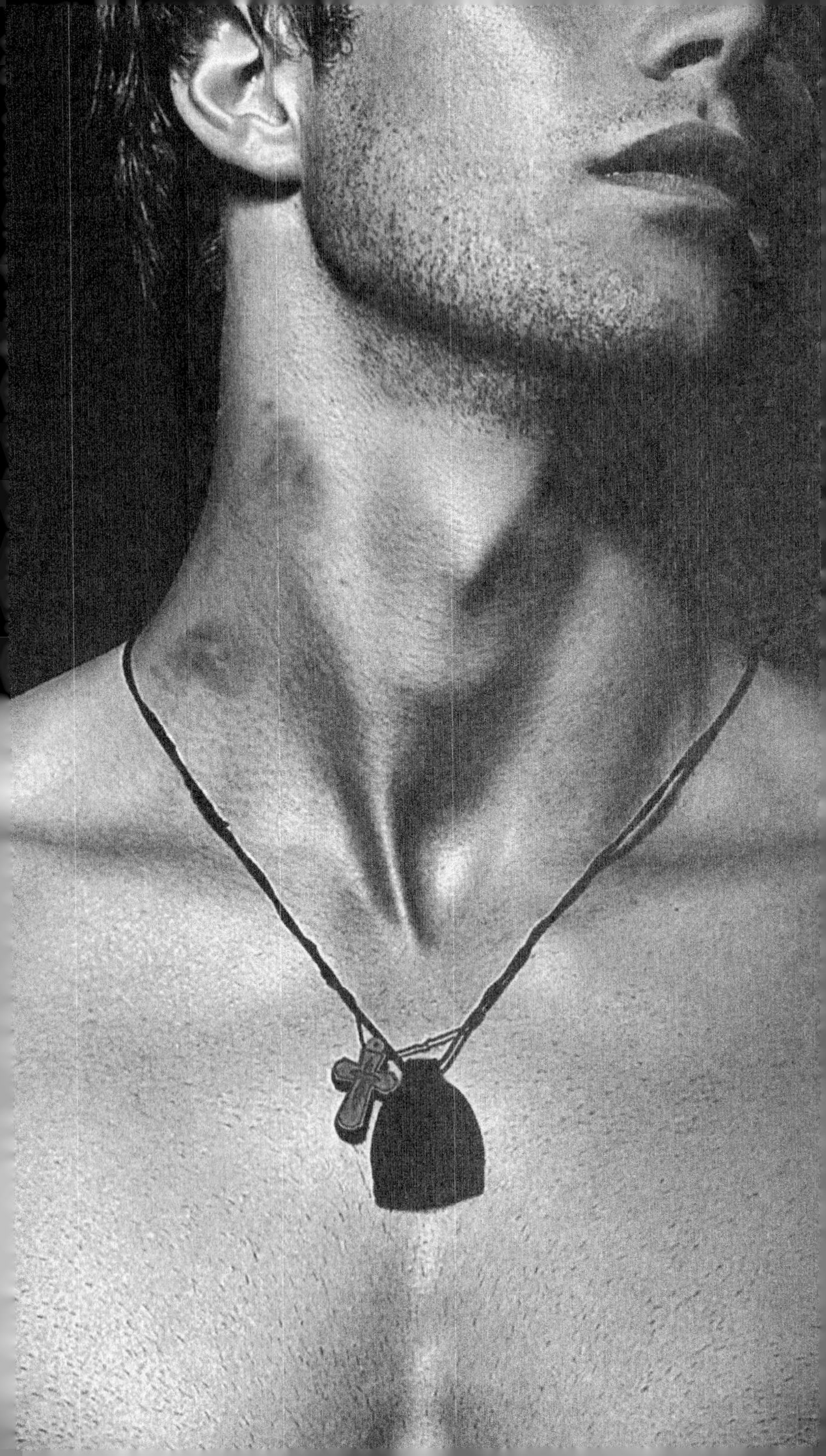

CHAPTER 44
KAI

I'm so thirsty. My head hurts. My stomach hurts.

Water. I need water.

What's that beeping noise? And that smell...it smells like antibacterial agents. That's not what my room smells like. *I miss Jules's smell.*

Fuck, I hurt all over. My heavy eyes slowly open and panic sets in. A hospital room. Oh no. The pain in my stomach intensifies, and I squeeze my eyes shut to try and calm my breathing, but the deeper I breathe, the more it hurts.

Opening my eyes again, I turn my head to the side and see Jules asleep in a chair. *Jules.* I look down at my body, noticing the bandages and IVs connected to me and the stabbing comes rushing back to me. Zac and Jez. I thought I was dead. I go to speak to Jules, but my throat is dry and sore, making my voice croaky and quiet.

"Jules," I say, trying to make my voice louder. I'm in so much pain, and so thirsty.

"Jules!" I rasp out, and that makes him flinch. He rubs his eyes before opening them, and upon seeing me he jumps up out of the seat and dashes over to me, grabbing my face in the palms of his big hands.

"Kai, fuck, you're awake."

"Hurts...water," I whisper.

"Let me go get a doctor or nurse," he says, before running out into the corridor. Not even a minute later, a nurse returns with him and checks me over.

"He said he's in pain and wants some water," Jules says.

The middle-aged brunette takes my vitals and smiles at me. Her smile is of kindness and warmth. It's been a while since I've seen such a thing.

"Nice to have you back, Kai. I'll top up your pain meds, but you can only have ice chips for now, at least until the doctor has checked you over, which should be soon," she says.

"I'll go get some. I need to text your mom," Jules says.

"Is she here?" I ask.

"Yeah, she was with you last night, but I sent her home to get some rest. I'll be back in a minute."

I nod, and let my head fall back onto the pillow. Every inch of me aches like I've completed a forty-eight-hour Pilates class. Before Jules has a chance to come back, a tall skinny doctor with glasses walks in with another nurse, inspects my wound, and goes over my medical notes.

"It's looking good, Kai. No sign of infection so far, or any further internal bleeding. We completed a blood transfusion on you when you arrived. You've got a little way to go in healing, but you're incredibly lucky," he says.

"When can I go home?"

"No chance of that yet, young man. Let's see how you're doing in a couple of days. Then we can discuss it further. Now, on a scale of one to ten, how's the pain?"

"The nurse just gave me some more pain medication, so I'm at a four. It's bearable. I'm really thirsty."

"You can have some water, but not a lot. Always a risk for complications after the surgery."

"Okay."

"I'll be back this afternoon to check on you again. Try to rest, and not aggravate your stab wound."

"I will."

"I'll make sure he sticks to the plan, doc," Jules says, walking back into the room with a cup of ice chips in one hand and a coffee in the other. I could kill for a coffee.

"See that you do," the doctor says before he leaves the room.

Jules prowls over to me, eyes focused on mine, and I want to squirm. Now that I'm hooked up to monitors, I can't hide his effect on me and my racing heart.

"Excited to see me, Kai?" he says as he places his coffee on the bedside table, and sits on the edge of the bed, level with my chest with the cups of ice chips.

"I'm sorry," I say in a hushed voice.

Jules takes one of the ice chips in between his fingers and guides it to my mouth. I'm so parched.

"Open," he says, voice low and commanding, and his sight set on my lips.

I open my mouth and he gently pushes in the ice chip and rubs it along my tongue and lips before leaving it in my mouth. The heart monitor can't hide how happy I am that he's here. I suck slowly on the chip, letting the ice-cold water numb my mouth and ease the dryness.

He repeats the process and feeds me another two chips before placing the cup next to his cup of coffee.

"I'm not happy, Kai. You've got a lot of explaining to do."

I move my legs in the bed, unable to stop the fidgeting under his scrutiny. As I move, a tenderness where my tattoo is lights me up from the inside. The ache is a familiar and comforting sensation.

"What's wrong? Do you need more pain meds?"

"No, it's just, my thigh feels tender. Did I injure my leg?"

Jules smirks and lowers his mouth to my ear. His breath tickles my lobe before he speaks.

"No. I did it last night. It didn't look right, you not having my marks on you. I knew you missed it. Missed the soreness from my mouth."

Holy shit. If I wasn't in so much discomfort and doped up with medication, I'd kiss him right now. Jules has other ideas, as he places languid kisses down the side of my neck.

"You had me worried, Kai. I lost myself. Don't you ever fucking do that to me again. Do you understand?" he growls into my neck as he gently nibbles and licks the skin. I swallow hard at his words. The lies eventually caught up with me, but at least I was the only one to get hurt.

"I promise."

"You're coming back with me after they've released you. No arguments."

"You gonna force me, Jules?" I say, unable to stop the slight pant to my words. My stomach is hurting like a bitch, but arousal is determined to make an appearance as the idea of him going all King Kong gets my blood pumping like nothing else.

"I'm gonna be doing a lot of things to you when we get back."

I don't doubt his words. Jules is a controlling asshole, and it may now become worse since all this shit happened. Actually, I'm surprised he hasn't interrogated me about who did this.

"Aren't you gonna ask me who did this to me?"

"I already know. Zac and Jez."

My mouth hangs open. How the hell did he know that?

"How...how did you know?"

"They'd been stalking your mom on and off since you left, but she thought nothing of it. You know, considering you didn't tell any of us that they threatened you if you returned. Apart from Seb."

The warning in Jules's voice makes me tremble to my core. He's pissed. I lied.

"Zac told me before…you know. But, why didn't she say anything?"

"She didn't want you worrying. I'm more interested in why you hid what was going on and what on earth you were thinking going back there? Why didn't you come to me? But you felt okay talking to Seb?"

I look away from him as I can't stand the judgement. He's right.

"Seb talked to me at a low point, and it just all came out. I didn't mean to say anything. I was so upset after overhearing you and Dima that I needed to get away from you, so I just kinda thought they wouldn't know I was home. I was too hurt by you."

"I didn't do anything, Kai. You're so impulsive, reacting to only part of a conversation. I'm not fucking happy that you question my loyalty to you. I'm pissed you felt you could talk to Seb and not me and purposefully hide what was going on."

"I'm sorry."

Jules lets out a long sigh, a sound of defeat.

"Everything will be fine now. They'll never harm you again."

I swing my head back to face him at those words. The movement makes me moan out in pain as it aggravates my injury.

"Calm down. The doctor told you to be careful."

"I know what he fucking said."

A large hand crushes my throat as my body screams.

"Just because you're in the hospital, doesn't mean that attitude will fly, sweetheart," he says, and fuck, does the threatening tone do shit to me.

"What did you do, Jules?" I ask as he removes his meaty hand.

"You really wanna know?"

I look into those icy blues, and I can see the darkness, the crazy depths of vengeance that he took pleasure in. I thought it would anger me, disgust me. But...why am I eager to know? Eager to know how far he'd go for me?

"Every detail," I whisper, and Jules moves closer to my mouth.

"You've been spending too much time with Aaron," he says before kissing me. A kiss full of ownership and love. I want him so much.

"What the hell are you doing?" a loud female shrill screams. Fuck. It's Mom. Jules pulls away and shocks the hell out of me by smiling at me.

"Time for the truth to come out, because I ain't hiding or leaving you."

Fuck. Well, if that didn't make my heart somersault then I don't know what would.

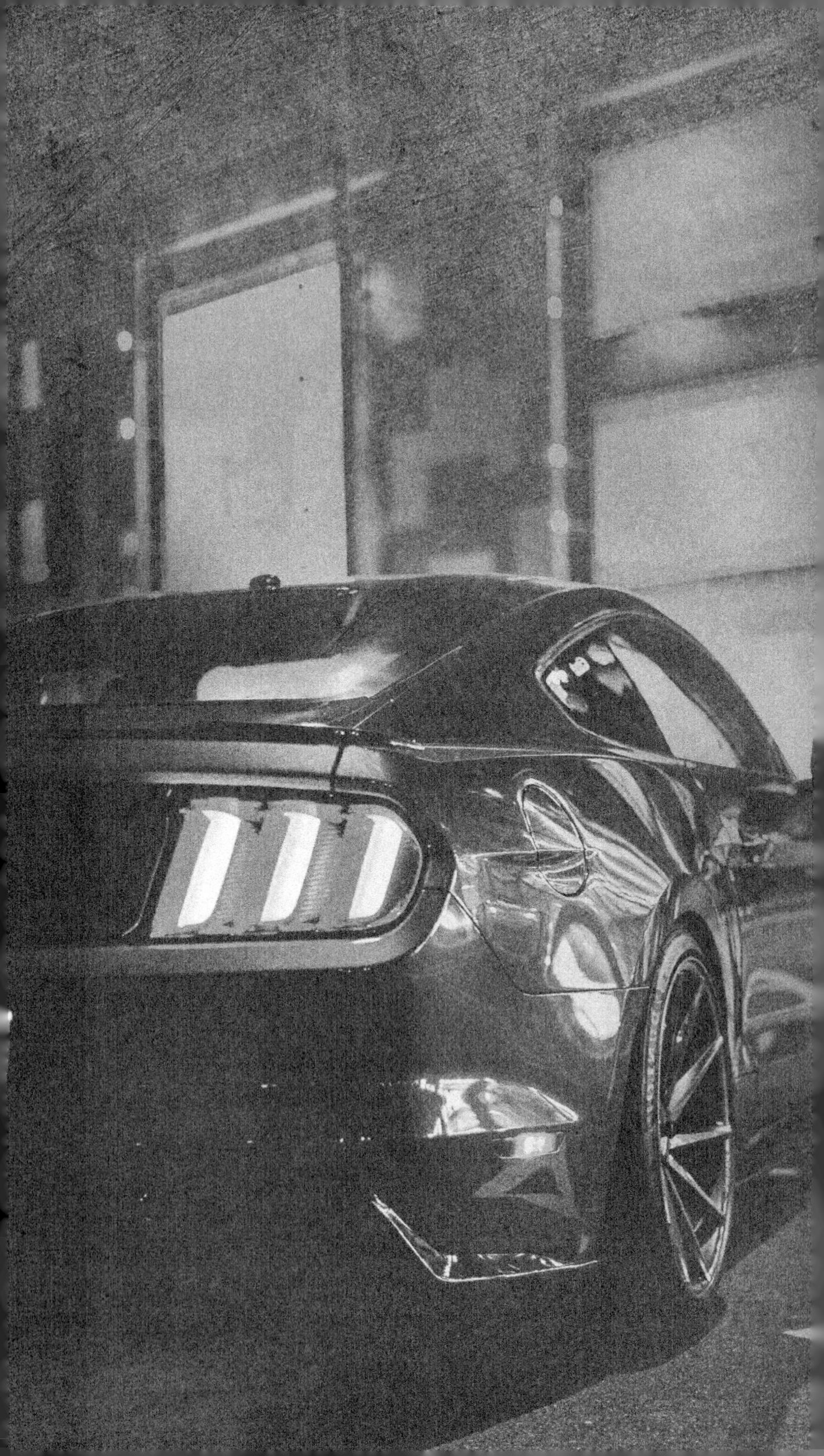

CHAPTER 45
Jules

"Get your hands off him, Jules," Jenny shouts at me as she runs over, like she is protecting Kai from a madman.

"No," I say as I stand up from the bed next to Kai and hold his hand in mine.

Jenny goes to smack me in the face when I catch her hand mid-air.

"I'd be very careful of who you raise your hand to," I say. This is a non-negotiable situation. She can be upset, hurt even. But that's her shit to sort through, Kai is my only priority.

"Take your hands off me," she snarls. I push her hand away and she stumbles back slightly. She looks down at Kai, who is very quiet, and moves to the other side of the bed to take him in her arms.

"Mom, careful. It hurts," he says, pulling away from her and clutching at his stomach.

"Sorry, honey. I'm just so happy to see you awake and talking. How's the pain?"

"I'm managing."

"Jules, I want you to leave," Jenny says.

"No. I'm not going anywhere," I say, standing tall and crossing my arms across my chest.

"He's my son!"

"You're being hysterical. He's an adult."

"You can't touch him. It's sick. Kai, did he force you?"

"What? No! Mom, I don't want him to leave. But there are things we want to explain," he says as his head falls back into the pillow. His eyes are droopy, exhaustion taking over.

"I don't want to hear any of it. I want him gone, Kai. Or I'll make security get rid of him."

"No you won't. I'm an adult patient and I get to say who stays. I want him here, Mom."

"I don't need to listen to this. I'll wait outside. You're obviously so doped up on medication that you don't know what you're saying."

"Don't patronize him."

"And don't you tell me how to treat my boy. My baby who you barely know."

"I know him better than you, Jenny, and I will correct how you treat him if I think it's unfair. Let him rest. He's been stabbed, if you hadn't noticed."

"You son of a bitch."

"That title fits. I am the son of a bitch."

"Can you two stop? Please. I'm tired and in pain, and you're not helping," Kai says, his voice gentle as he loses the battle to keep his eyes open. I run my hands through his hair where he snuggles against the touch.

"Sleep, sweetheart. I'll be here when you wake up."

I swear he purrs like a kitten as he falls asleep with my hands in his hair. He's so fucking beautiful. Jenny is evil eyeing me so hard, I'm expecting to be set alight from the hate she's projecting. But I really don't give a fuck. Nothing and no one will come between us.

"I can't believe you'd do this to me. You've groomed him or something. This isn't natural. You're his uncle. It's sick, is what it is."

"You can put as many spins on this as you want to justify your feelings, but he ain't my nephew. We share no blood, not even the same surname. I was hardly in his life. You can make it as perverted as you want, but it won't change. Kai is mine and he's coming back with me. Nothing you do will change that."

Jenny stands in shock, a tear escapes her left eye, her eyes like saucers. Devastation written all over her face.

"Always have to have your own way. Selfish as a child, and selfish as an adult. I'll find a way to keep you away from him. He's too good for you."

I laugh, unable to contain how stupid those words are. She's no idea what she's talking about. Still bitter and resentful about a situation that I had no part in. I was a child when she got pregnant with Kai and I'm sick of her bitchy ass blaming me for a fantasy relationship with our parents that I never had because of her. But that's an argument for another day, and as we've learned, no threat should be treated as idle. I glance over at Kai's sleeping form, my feelings solidifying more, and my need to possess him is overwhelming.

I move over to Jenny, a foot between us, and I lower my mouth to her ear.

"I'd be careful with the threats, Jenny. You don't know me. Now, I'm gonna leave you with Kai for an hour so you can have some time together, and that's the last time you'll be alone with him. Make it count."

I walk away, out of the room, and notice Tim sitting in the waiting area, looking at his phone. He looks up at me as I approach and pockets his phone as I get closer.

"Jules. How is he?"

"In pain and tired, but it looks good. Any news on who did it to him?"

"I think you already know. I've looked into your friends. Don't play me for a fool, Jules. Where are they?"

"Who?"

"You fucking know who. We can't locate Jez and Zac. They just so happened to disappear on your first night in town when you go AWOL. A coincidence? I think not."

"No idea what you're talking about."

"Liar."

"You have your opinion. I would put that mind to better use and go comfort Jenny."

"I thought you said he was okay?"

"He is, but Jenny hasn't taken the news well that Kai's my man."

"My god, this family is out of their mind."

"Yep. Be good for you to remember that," I say as I grin and walk away. He has nothing on me, no matter how hard he digs.

Needing some air, I head outside, letting the sharp bursts of wind cut across my skin like shards of ice.

I can't wait to get Kai home.

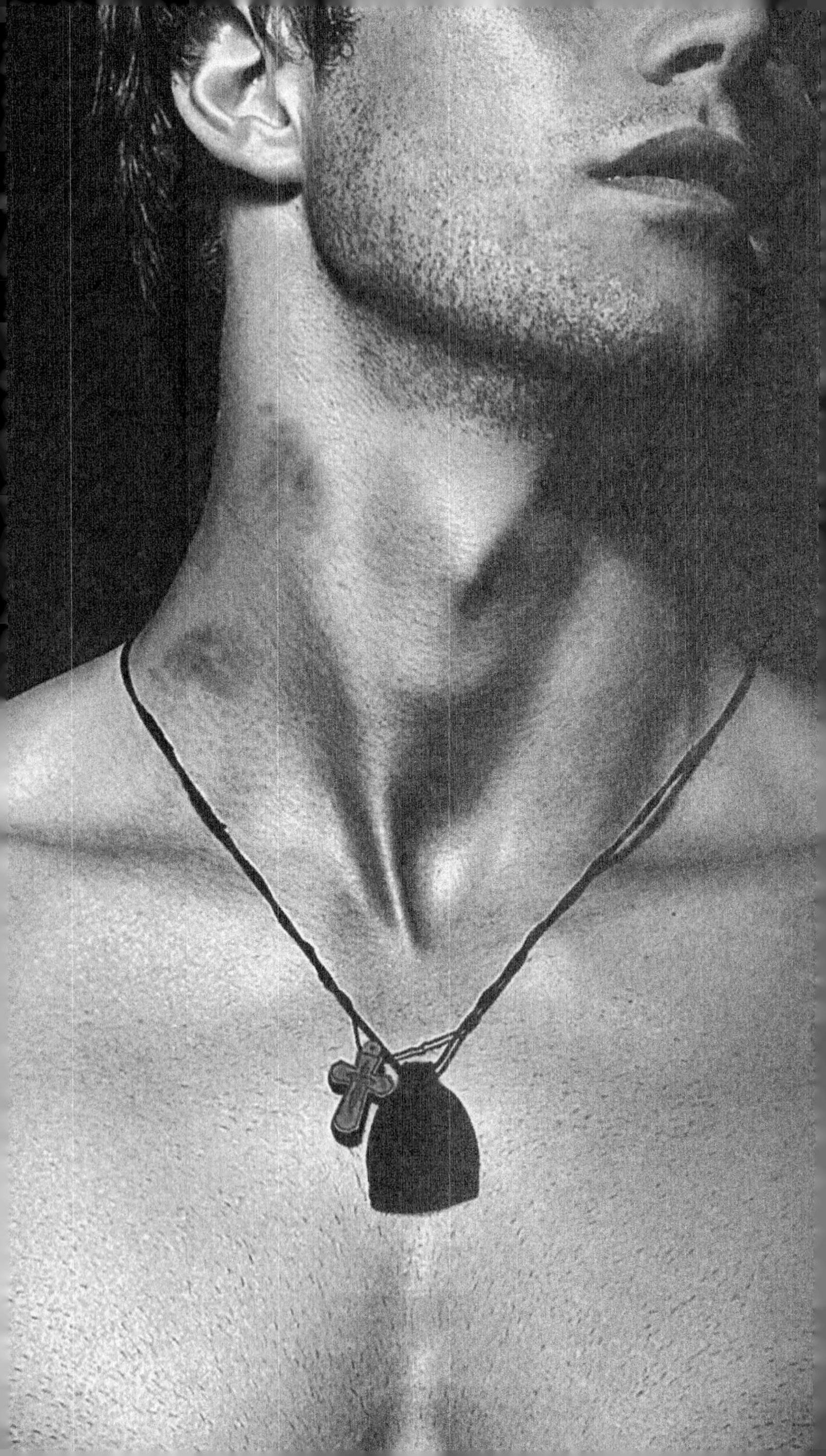

CHAPTER 46
KAI

"Kai, I need you to wake up so I can do your observations," a voice says, pulling me out of a peaceful slumber. I hate it, because the pain that disappeared in sleep comes back in full force.

"Sorry, you can go back to sleep when I'm done. How's the pain?" the nurse asks.

"It's starting to hurt more."

"Okay. We'll take a look and change the dressing, then I'll talk to the doctor about increasing your pain meds."

"How long was I asleep for?"

"Just over an hour," my mom's voice jolts me fully from being dozy. I turn my head and see her sitting in the chair. Where's Jules? The nurse starts to remove my bandage and inspects the wound. I can't bring myself to look at it, so I stay focused on my mom.

"Before you ask, he's taken a walk," she says, her tone firm with a hint of disgust.

I hiss as the nurse places the new bandage onto my wound. She obviously senses the tension as she gives me a smile full of pity before leaving the room.

"How long have you been with him?"

"It's been building since we left home. If you're asking how long we've been fucking, only a few weeks."

"Don't speak to me like that, Kai. I'm your mother."

"Why not? It's all you care about."

She scoffs and flicks her long black hair over her shoulder.

"I care about the fact Jules took advantage of you. You can't possibly think this will work or be accepted."

I close my eyes and take several deep breaths to control my building frustration.

"I don't really care what anyone thinks, Mom. Including you," I say on an exhausted sigh.

"How can you say that to me?"

I snap my head to the side to face her, bewildered by how she can be so self focused right now.

"Because I nearly died yesterday, so forgive me if this doesn't seem as important. It's only made me realize how much I love him and want to be with him. I'm sorry if that makes you upset, but it's reality."

"Why did you come home if everything was so great? Did you fight?"

"It was a misunderstanding. You wouldn't understand."

"You're so naive, Kai. I thought you had more sense than being this selfish."

"I'd watch your fucking tone when you talk to him," Jules bellows as he fills the room with his dominating presence. Tim follows in behind him, but I can't take my eyes off Jules. The hero I wanted is standing in front of me to rescue me like he does in my dreams. I'm so fucked up.

"Hey, don't talk to Jenny like that," Tim says, putting his hand on Jules's chest. Not the best idea.

"This ain't your business and take your fucking hand off me before I move it myself," Jules snarls. I can see what Aaron meant about how hot it is when your man fights for you.

"Can you all, please, just stop," I say as loud as I can, all eyes turning onto me.

"Mom, Tim, I think you should both leave."

"I'm not going anywhere! I won't allow this, Kai. Who'll take care of you when you get out of the hospital?"

"I'm going back with Jules."

"Over my dead fucking body," she shouts, and Tim stands behind her, placing his hands on her shoulders.

"That can be arranged," Jules threatens.

"I'd watch it, Jules. Just because I'm off duty, doesn't mean I can't have you taken in," Tim says, narrowing his eyes on Jules.

"You do that and I'll report you for harassment. I'm serious. You both need to stay out of my business. I'm not a minor. I'm an adult of sound mind, and I want you both to leave. If you hadn't noticed, I'm supposed to be resting, and you're making it impossible."

"You're right. I'm sorry, honey. I'll keep quiet."

"I want you to go. I need to sleep. Let's just start again tomorrow when everyone has calmed down," I say pleadingly. Jules certainly picks his moment to come over and place a kiss on my lips before he sits in the chair beside me with a childish grin on his face.

"I can take a hint. You know you can call if you need anything. Come on, Tim." And here I thought I was the child. They both stomp off and finally, the room mellows out.

Jules runs his hands through my hair, a move that I'm starting to become addicted to. I feel special, cherished and safe.

"Sleep, Kai. I'll be here when you wake up."

"Mm-kay," I say before I drift off.

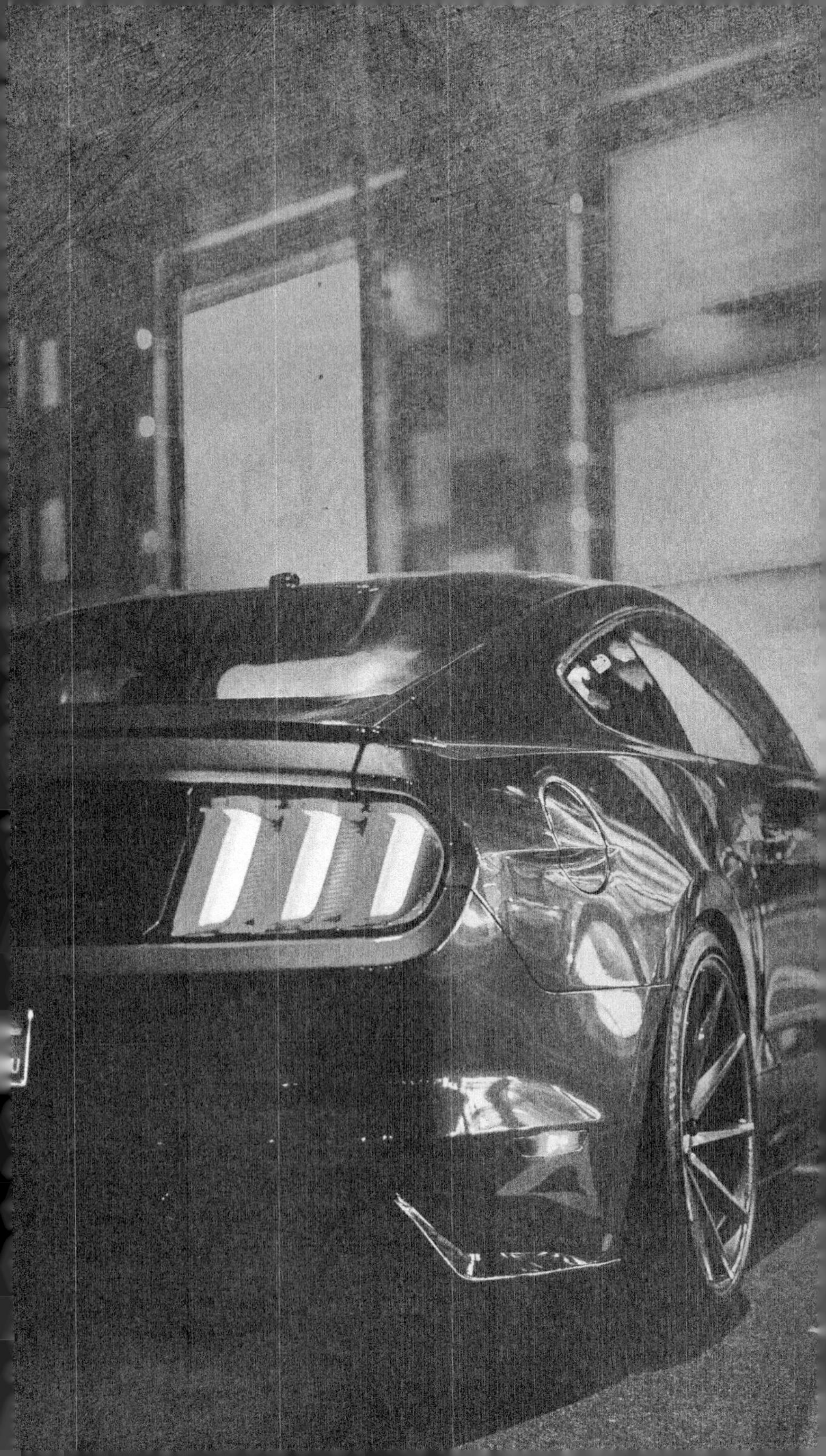

CHAPTER 47
JULES

Kai has been asleep for a few hours now, but I can't seem to shut my brain off to let myself rest. My body is automatically programmed to watch over him. Protect him. I thought he would back away from me when his mom found out about us, but he stood his ground. While Kai isn't someone who will ever get on board with the physical side of our job, his confidence has grown since he left home. He doubts himself so much, but he doesn't realize just how strong he is. He knows who he is and what he wants, and it's beyond fucking sexy.

The door to Kai's room opens, and I turn to see Lev walk in, but he remains close to the door, so I get up and move over to him.

"Hey," I say.

"How's he doing?"

"Good. Should be released in a week or two if all goes well. Where's Ivan?"

"Back at the hotel. I forgot how much he loves to talk."

That makes me chuckle. Lev's idea of hell is having to be social.

"We're gonna have to head back tomorrow, D needs us."

"You know I'm not coming?"

"Do I look fucking dumb to you? Of course I know," he says, rolling his eyes.

"My car's at Jenny's. Could you drop me over there in the morning so I can collect it?"

"Yeah. You gonna tell her about you and Kai?"

"She already knows. Walked in on us earlier, screamed at us and threatened us, then left."

"Fuck her, then."

"I don't give a shit. As long as she and that nosy fucking Tim stay away, we'll have no problems."

"We can always dispose of him."

"I'll keep an eye on him for now. Have you heard anything about Carlos's guys clearing up our mess?"

"Haven't you heard? You should look at the local news. Apparently, a stolen car belonging to another local gang was found at the bottom of a ravine. Exploded into a fireball. Will take a while to identify who was in the car," Lev says with a smirk.

"Carlos is full of surprises."

"I'm definitely having a chat with him when I get back. He's always been a mysterious fucker."

"Wish I'd had longer with them," I say as I look over at Kai.

"It's never enough, especially when it's personal. You did good though."

"Thanks."

"I'm out. I'll drop by in the morning to take you over to your sister's."

'She ain't my sister."

"Fair enough," he says with a shrug, and leaves without another word.

I move back over to Kai and take my place in the most uncomfortable chair in the world and try to relax.

"Are you sure you want to go over to Mom's tomorrow?" Kai mumbles with his eyes still closed.

"I thought you were asleep. Listening in on conversations again?"

"Yep. You weren't exactly quiet."

"Go back to sleep, Kai."

"So you did kill them?" he whispers and looks up at me with those pretty innocent blue eyes.

"I did."

"When I'm better, I want you to tell me everything. How you did it. What they said."

"Kinky fucker."

"No. Just in love. Do you love me, Jules?"

"I think the trail of bodies should answer that."

"It does, but I need to hear it."

I stand and hover over Kai, clutching his face in my hands and leaning down over his lips, never breaking eye contact.

"I love you. I will torture, kill, and destroy anyone in my way when it comes to you. Never forget it."

"What have you done to me, Jules? That should not sound as romantic as it does."

I laugh, because I knew this would happen. Something about the Kozlov family converts you to look at the world differently. Crazy being the new normal, and I wouldn't change it.

"It's not a bad thing. Embrace it, Kai. Because you're going nowhere. Where do you belong?"

"With you?"

"Who owns you?"

"You."

"That's right. I refuse to live without you, Kai. And I'll never let you live without me. It's a done deal with us."

"Jules stop, you're getting me hard," Kai groans and I silence him with a kiss. Sealing our souls together to never part.

It's the following morning, and while Kai is having an examination by the doctors, Lev and Ivan have picked me up to take me to Jenny's, to collect my car that Kai stole. There better not be a scratch on my baby.

"You heard anything from the police?" Lev asks.

"No. They turned up at the hospital when Kai was sedated, but said they'd be back. I guarantee Tim will be eager to try and involve us somehow."

"Ohh let me hurt him, Lev. I can't stand the fucker. I want to try new shit out on my tattoo gun," Ivan says from the front seat.

"As much as I'd love to see that, you know we can't do anything here. Not unless he came on our turf. Everyone will notice a cop missing in a town like this."

"I'm hoping he won't be a problem once we leave," I say.

"All people are a problem," Lev says as he pulls onto my sister's street and parks outside her house. My car is in the driveway and doesn't look like she's come to any harm.

"You got the keys?" Lev asks as he turns off the engine.

"No. Kai said he left them in the hallway. Plus I need to get his clothes."

"Get him some new shit. You know she won't let you take any of his stuff, Jules. Just get your car and leave," Lev says, and he's right.

"Good idea. Oh shit, here we go," I say as I see Jenny come outside with Tim following.

"Does he live here?" Ivan asks.

"I bet he wants to."

Lev and Ivan go to get out of the car too, which I won't argue with.

"What are you doing here? Wait...is Kai okay?" Jenny asks, her scowl changing to worry.

"He's fine. Just here to collect my car, Kai said he left my keys on the hallway table."

"Does that mean you're leaving?" Jenny asks with a lilt of hope that I'm leaving Kai.

"If you mean am I leaving Kai, then no. Can you get me my keys? Please."

"You know the police are going by the hospital this afternoon to question Kai? I think maybe you should leave your car here. Don't want you running off anywhere," Tim says.

"Why would Jules run off?" Jenny asks Tim.

"These guys that Kai has been working for are criminals, Jenny. I think they had something to do with it," he says.

"What! Jules, is this true?"

"You know we had nothing to do with Kai's stabbing, you fucking moron. Have you found who did it yet? Or are you still too busy trying to fuck Jenny? Gotta say, your police here suck."

Lev and Ivan move in closer behind me and Jenny takes a step back, her eyes flicking back and forth between them. I really don't understand where Tim's misplaced arrogance comes from. Maybe everyone around here has kissed his ass for so long, he believes he has a power, and maybe he does. But not with us.

"I suggest one of you goes inside and gets Jules's keys, otherwise I'll get them myself, and you don't want that," Lev says. The edge his voice carries is something I've heard so many times before he lashes out. He'll have no problem bundling them both up and driving them back to Grinston with him.

"Or what? You have no authority here. You're just the regular scumbag crooks who think money can buy them anything. That won't work around here," Tim says to Lev. Everyone freezes to the spot in those few seconds that feel like hours. Tim even looks shocked at his own words. Too late for him to take them back now. As fast as a bolt of lightning, Lev has Tim pinned against the side of the house. Lev is significantly larger than Tim, who is unable to get himself out of Lev's grip.

"You listen to me, you washed up piece of shit. I could have you in the back of my car and take you somewhere where nobody would hear your screams as I remove the skin off your bones. But I won't. Yet. Your pathetic little threats are starting to annoy me, and nobody wants that. So either shut the fuck up, and move on with your life, or I will personally make sure it's a life of hell."

"Jules, tell him to let him go, please don't hurt him," Jenny cries, grabbing my arm.

"No, you should've thought about that before you decided to try to play like the big boys. Get me my fucking keys," I say to her, pulling away from her touch. She runs off inside and I look back to Lev and Tim.

"You're not above the law," Tim says, his voice more unsure than he was a few minutes ago.

"I am. You can try to take us on, though. How's your daughter getting on at college?" Lev asks, and I raise my eyebrows at his words. How did he know about that?

"What?"

"Your daughter, Callie. She's a pretty little thing isn't she? I bet she gets a lot of attention, especially when she runs around in those tight little shorts she wears," Lev says, grinning at Tim's reaction. I think Tim may have gone into shock.

"How do you know about my daughter? If you touch her...."

"You'll what? More empty threats. You'll do nothing because you're gonna go on about your life. But just remember, we know everything about you. Including precious little Callie."

Jenny comes back out as Lev moves away from Tim, who is seconds away from collapsing onto the ground. Jenny passes me my keys and I head over to my car. I've been away from Kai for too long.

"You're all monsters," Jenny says as she goes over to hold Tim, who has become mute.

"Yeah we are. Always keep one eye open, baby," Ivan says as he winks at Jenny and jogs back over to the car. Lev follows and gives me a nod.

"Check in with me later about the cops," Lev says.

"I will," I say. I get into my car and pay no attention to Jenny and Tim as I drive away toward my future.

Arriving back at the hospital, I come to a halt when I approach Kai's room and hear other voices. I walk in and notice two cops standing on either side of Kai's bed, one with a notebook and the other guy, who I remember as baldy cop from when I collected Kai from the police station, standing over Kai's bed with his arms crossed, asking questions. Tim said they were arriving this afternoon, sly fuckers.

"Can I help you?" the cop that isn't baldy says. I'd say this guy is mid fifties. A full head of gray hair and stubble to match. A guy that looks like he can take care of himself.

"He's fine, that's Jules," Kai says with a hint of pink to his cheeks. Is he unsure what to refer to me as? How fucking cute.

"I'm his boyfriend," I say. I walk closer, not at all intimidated like they would hope I would be. I push in front of baldy and give Kai a kiss before moving to the chair and taking a seat.

"Anyway, Kai, do you have any idea who could've done this to you?"

Kai quickly glances at me, unsure of what to answer.

"No, like I said, their faces were covered. They just walked into the house, and when they saw me they stabbed me and ran out," Kai says, and I want to smile. The lie falling so easily from that talented mouth.

"Unfortunately without any weapon or witnesses, it's like looking for a needle in a haystack," baldy says.

"What happens now?" I ask. Gray cop assesses me, no doubt making judgement off of my appearance.

"We can only keep following up any possible leads. None of the neighbors saw anything, and without a description of even a car? We just have to hope someone will come forward with information," gray guy says.

"You have my card if you think of anything that might help catch these guys, Kai. Just look after yourself," baldy says.

"I will. Thanks."

Both cops leave without any further questions, and I smile as I grab Kai for a kiss.

"Well done, sweetheart," I say as I kiss down his neck. He moans as I lap at his gorgeous soft skin, pushing his neck further into my mouth. I know what he wants. But he has to ask.

"Feeling needy?" I say.

"Yes. I miss the bruises, Jules. Please. I need your mark. I need to feel you on me all the time."

I latch my lips onto his neck below his ear and suck as hard as I can.

"Ah fuck! Yes...more," he moans long and low as I bite and suck all down the left side of his neck until I reach his collarbone. He tastes so fucking good. I muse over the idea of breaking the skin and lapping up his blood, how fucking sweet it would taste.

I pull back and run my finger down the path of hickeys I've just placed, and he groans again at the sensation. My little pain whore.

"Fucking beautiful. When we get home, I'm gonna decorate that hot little body of yours in my marks. You'll never live another day without it."

"I want nothing more."

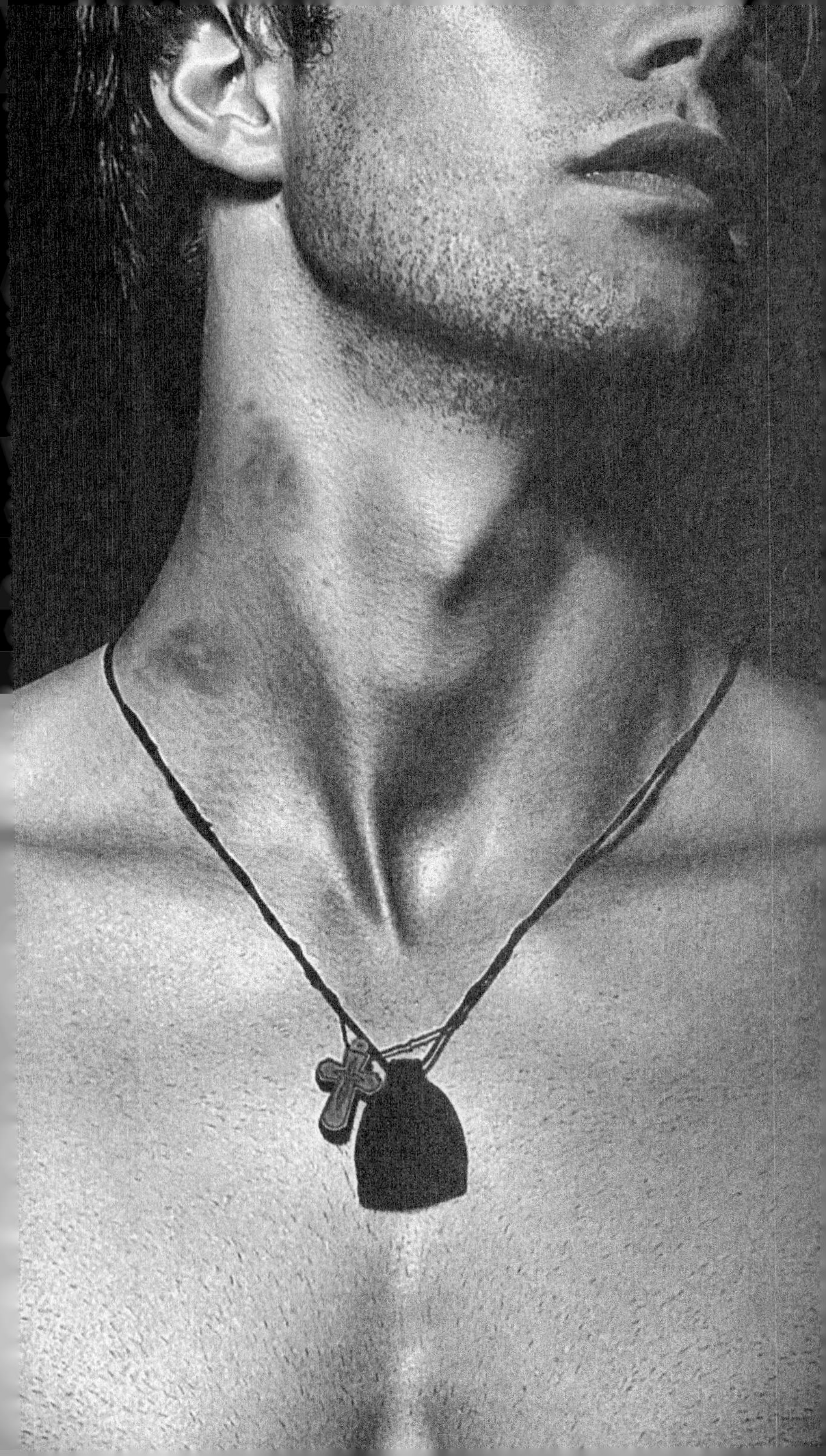

CHAPTER 48
KAI

Today is the day I finally get to leave the hospital. Two weeks with no privacy, constantly being prodded and questioned, and being persistently horny, has me all excited to go home. I'm still a little tender from where I was stabbed, but the scar is healing nicely, according to doctors, and I'm off the pain meds. The nurses were a little alarmed when they saw the sudden array of bruising on my neck and thighs, thinking something was wrong. Jules not so subtly explained what they were and I haven't been able to stop blushing since. Mom hasn't tried visiting, but has texted me daily to see how I am. She won't come near me if Jules is here, and that's her choice. I'm never pushing him away again. He's my heart and lungs. My life. I don't want to live if it's not with him. Unhealthy? Hell fucking yes. But I don't care. As long as I have him around me I don't need anyone or anything else. For the first time in years, I'm strong, I believe in who I am and what I want. I'm not ashamed of us or what we are. To have the ability to finally do what makes me happy and not to worry about the other shit is so damn liberating, and I can't wait to start life with Jules properly.

"Ready to go?"

I look over at Jules, and fuck, it takes all my energy not to pounce on him. He's looking extra damn hot today. Dressed all in black. Black jeans, black sweater, all finished off with the dick melting leather jacket.

"Stop looking at me like that, unless you want me to fuck you in front of the nurses."

"I can't help it. I'm horny."

Jules grabs me and pulls me into his body. My cock has been hard nearly all day every day with him around, so I don't try to hide it anymore.

"Hmm, sounds like my pretty little whore is back and looking for a good fucking. Is that what you want, to lay back while I make you feel good?" he growls into my ear and I can't stop the whine that leaves my mouth.

"Please don't call me that in public."

Jules chuckles and kisses down my neck, sucking gently over the bruise that already decorates my skin, making the throb from the soreness travel down to my cock.

"Why? That's what you are, my pretty pillow whore."

"Stop! It makes me all fuzzy when you call me that and I don't want anyone knowing that part of me. Only you."

"As you wish. Let's get your gorgeous ass home. Aaron and Seb are getting on my nerves with all the texting asking when you're getting home."

"Really?"

"Yes. I encourage you to spend more time with Seb, I don't want you morphing into a stabby version of Aaron."

I laugh at that. The boys have been great, they've both texted me every day and it's a nice feeling. That someone gives a shit and is excited to see me again.

"What about Dima?"

'Don't worry about him. He told me to bring you back. I'm sure it's all gonna be fine, and if not, we'll leave."

And boy does that send a wave of contentment over me. He's with me in everything.

"You're right. Let's get out of here."

In the new clothes Jules has bought me because he decided to leave my other stuff at my mom's, we don't have anything to carry. A huge gust of cold air hits my face as we walk out of the hospital, and I inhale the air until it chills my lungs, because let's face it, I'm lucky I'm walking out of here alive, and I plan to enjoy every second life gives me.

"Kai!" my mom's voice shouts out as she runs over to us. This is the first time in my life I don't know how to act with her. She's my mom, but not the mom I thought she was. The decision of what to do is taken out of my hands as she ignores Jules and hugs me tightly.

"I was hoping to see you. Can we talk? Alone?"

Jules snorts behind me but says nothing.

"You can say whatever you want to say in front of Jules, I want him here."

"It isn't a lot to ask to have a private conversation. Surely you can bear to be apart, unless he won't let you."

"Mom. Stop it."

"I've got your room ready. You can come home and I'll take care of you. Tim said he can help find you a job, a fresh start."

"I have a job. And a partner."

"You're being stubborn and childish, Kai."

"Childish? You're the one who is ignoring Jules like he isn't here, and refusing to listen because you're not getting your own way. You wanted me to leave and start a new life, and I did."

"He's manipulated you, Kai. How can you not see how immoral and perverted this all is? And don't tell me you're safe in that job. Tim said you're working with criminals. How can I let my son live that life? How can you let 'him' convince you that's a good life?"

"For the hundredth time. I'm. An. Adult!"

"Did he tell you how they threatened us at my home? How his boss threatened to hurt Tim's daughter?"

No he didn't. I look over my shoulder at Jules and he just shrugs.

"That's just how Lev is," I say. Which is true, as I doubt it was unprovoked.

"I don't believe this. What's happened to you, Kai?"

"I'm awake. I'm alive and see things for what they are. I doubt Lev did that without something to provoke him, which we all know Tim has done since I got hurt."

"Tim is a good man."

"I'm sure he is, Mom, and I will always appreciate how he's helped me, and I hope he makes you happy, whether you're friends or more. But I'm happy with Jules and I'm finished having this discussion. I don't want to lose you, Mom," I say, and I genuinely mean it. I can accept that she doesn't agree with me and Jules, but she doesn't have to cut me from her life because of it.

Mom moves until she stands in front of Jules. Disdain and repulsion masks her face. I feel guilty that I've come between them, but I'm too selfish to dwell on it. I want him for myself.

"You got what you wanted, as always. No different from the spoiled little shit who could do no wrong."

"Shut the fuck up, Jenny. You don't know what you're talking about."

"Don't I? I bet you had it made when I was tossed on the street, pregnant and scared."

Jules pushes his face into Jenny's and grabs her by the wrist.

"You know nothing. They hardly bothered with me after they kicked you out. I couldn't look at them with how they treated you. I was abandoned by the parents I lived with and lost my big sister. You have a large ego for someone who lives under the guise of being oppressed. I was on the streets, dealing at seventeen to look after myself before my bosses offered me a home and a job, only to then have to bury both your dad and my mom without any help from you. Take your pity story and choke on it.

Stop punishing your son and get over it. But you and me? We're done."

I'm dumbfounded. That's the most vulnerable and open I've ever seen Jules. Mom never explained too much about life before me and I never asked. Jules lets go of my mom and moves to my other side and holds my hand in his. My mom follows the move and looks between us. I think she was as astounded by that declaration than I was.

"You know where I am, Kai, if you need me and when this falls apart. Love you honey," she says, and pecks me on the cheek before walking away.

"Jules," I start to say, but he stops me.

"No more talk about it. That chapter of my life is done and I said what needed to be said. Let's go home."

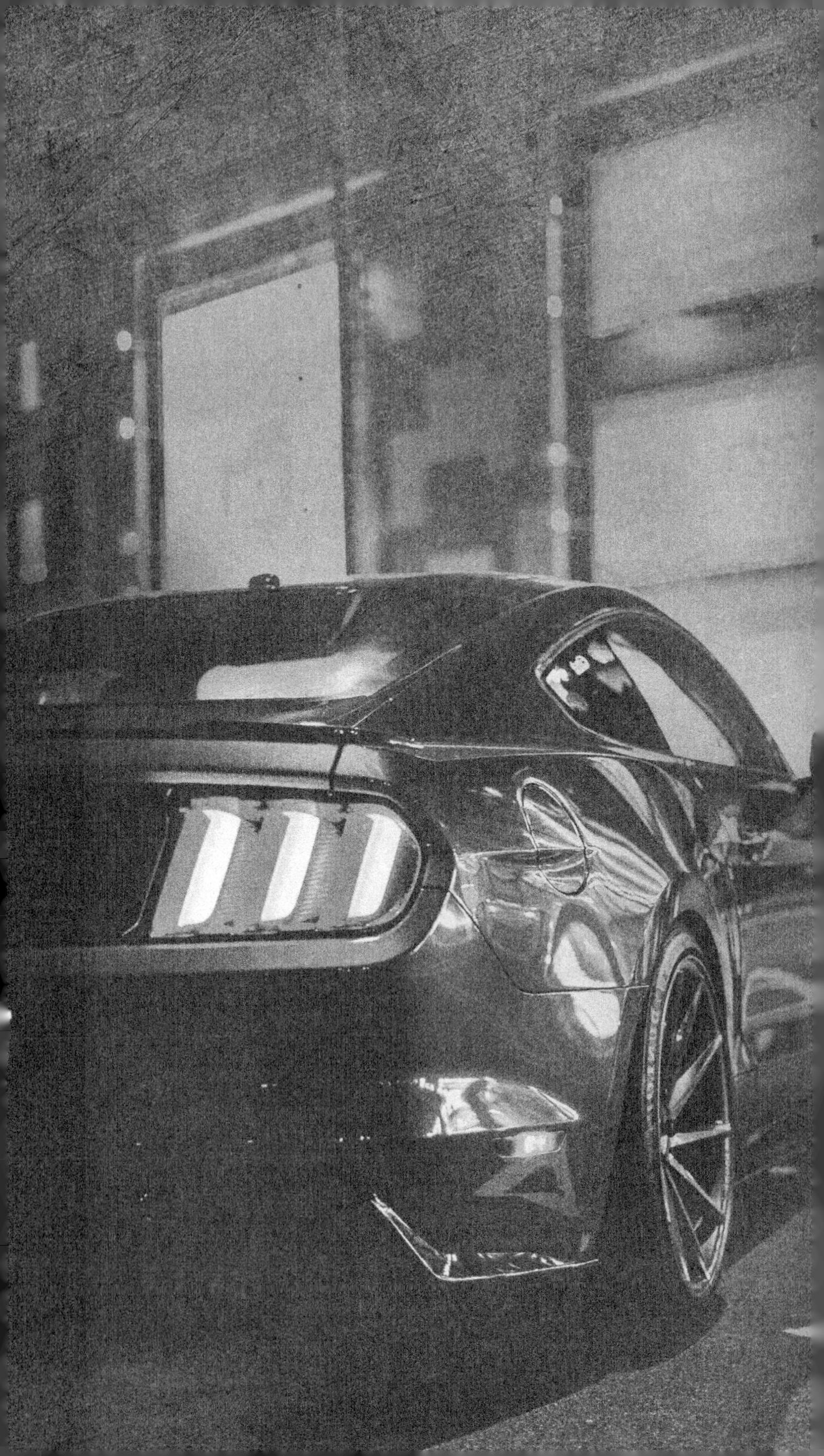

CHAPTER 49
JULES

Thank fuck we're home. Four hours on the road because of traffic was the last thing we needed, as Kai has been uncomfortable. He said he was fine, but I watched him out of the corner of my eye, wincing when he moved.

"Do you need a hand out of the car?" I ask. I should be dead on the spot with the look of annoyance on his face.

"I'm just achy. Not an invalid."

"I see it hasn't affected your attitude."

"It's the effect you have on me, you annoying asshole."

I walk over to his side of the car and open the door.

"Keep it up. I don't plan on going gentle on you. The more snarky you are, the harder I'll go on you," I say, and the cheeky little shit stands out of the car and faces me head on.

"The harder the better," he says, and if it weren't for Aaron and Seb who are jogging over to us like excited spaniels, I'd pick him up in my arms and take him to bed.

"Kai, so happy you're back, man," Seb says, grabbing Kai into a bear hug.

"Can I see the scar?" Aaron asks as Seb releases Kai.

"Uh yeah," Kai says, about to take off his jacket.

"No," I say.

"Why?" Aaron asks, completely confused.

Lev and Dima appear at the door and start to walk over. Fucking hell, I wasn't expecting such a welcome party.

"Lev, tell your man to back away."

"No. I'm not giving him attention today, he's been a fucking asshole since I got home," Lev says, avoiding eye contact with Aaron, who is on the verge of producing steam from his nostrils as he stares Lev down.

"I don't need you. Kai's here now."

"Fucking watch it, doe. I ain't in no mood for your games."

"And Kai is not here for you to play with, Aaron. He needs to rest."

"I do?" he asks.

"No, Jules wants to fuck him," Dima says as Seb smacks him in the chest.

"What? It's true. If you'd been in the hospital I'd be like a beast in heat."

"How charming," Seb mumbles.

"You saying you don't like my attention, beautiful?" Dima says, clutching Seb's hips from behind, and Seb melts into him.

"I never said that."

"Can we go inside? It ain't getting any fucking warmer out here," Lev moans, stomping off back into the house with Aaron running after him.

"I know you two lovebirds want to be alone, but we need to talk first," Dima says, and I grab Kai's hand and pull him along with me, following Dima back into the house, making his way to the office. As we walk inside, Lev joins us and closes the door, before we all take a seat.

"When you're feeling ready, Kai, Lev has suggested that you take on dealing with the books for the club and bar. Simon vouched for you. You won't have to take part in the messier side of things, unless of course, you change your mind."

"Oh, thanks. I don't think I'll change my mind, but I'm definitely up for the other work. Thanks, and I'm sorry for bringing trouble."

"It happens, Seb and Aaron did the same thing. It's like a fucking ritual," Lev says, and I have to agree.

"Does this mean you're staying?" Dima says, now focused on me.

"Yes."

"Good. The architect we've hired is visiting tomorrow afternoon to go over plans for the properties in the back. I assume you'll be wanting to live together?" Dima says.

"Yep."

"Jules, you can start back tomorrow as we need you at the bar. Take advantage," Lev says.

"Who made you the fucking boss?" Dima snarls at Lev. Here we go again.

"Shut up, D."

"No, I'm the fucking boss of this family and I give the orders, not you. You're second in command, brother. Not first. I make the decisions."

"Okay, Princess."

"Call me that name a-fucking-gain."

"Princess."

Dima lurches over at Lev, who laughs as they tussle like a couple of kids.

"Fuck off, you two," Lev laughs as he pushes Dima off him. I don't have to be told twice. Grabbing Kai by the arm, I drag him away, eager to get him all to myself.

We pass Aaron and Seb in the hallway but I don't stop, I'm too keyed up.

"Kai, do you wanna…" Seb starts to ask but I continue to pull him along.

"He'll catch up with you tomorrow!" I shout over my shoulder. Aaron cackles like a creepy fucking witch in the distance. We make it outside and walk down the garden path to our home. Si better not be around, because I'm not in the mood for chit-chat. Luckily, the house is empty as we walk down the corridor toward my room, or should I say our room. He's not sleeping away from me ever again.

"Slow down, Jules," Kai laughs as we walk inside my bedroom, and I lock the door behind us. I crowd up against Kai until his back hits the wall.

"No slowing down. You've put me through hell these past few weeks. Time for you to pay up."

"Pay up? I didn't plan on getting stabbed, Jules."

"But you left me. Doubted me then put yourself in harm's way. I'm owed a debt, and I'm cashing in. Strip, and make it fucking fast."

"Fuck, I've missed your demanding voice."

I walk over to the window and lean up against it, my arms crossed over my chest, and watch the show in front of me. My hard dick is pushing so tightly against the zipper of my jeans, I wonder if it'll bust through the material. Kai keeps his eyes on me as he drops his coat to the floor and removes each shoe, tossing them to the side. He then holds the bottom of his sweater and slowly pulls it up over his head. His beautiful smooth chest on display and the golden hue to his skin has me dying for a taste. My eyes of course drift over the long scar on his stomach. It's not as inflamed and raised as it was before, but it will be a constant reminder of how I almost lost him.

"Does it repulse you?" Kai asks, looking down at his scar.

"No. I think it makes you even more beautiful. It tells me you're strong, and a survivor. Does it hurt?"

"Not really, only when you put pressure on it, it gets a little sore."

"Got it. I promise not to hurt you there. Now, remove your pants. I want you bare, sweetheart."

With shaking hands, he undoes his jeans and pushes them down to his ankles to remove them from his legs, followed by the quick removal of his underwear. That beautiful thick dick bounces on his abs, as wanton for touch as I am.

"Lay on your back in the center of the bed," I say, and he walks over to the bed, climbing on all fours, giving me a perfect view of my prized possession. He turns and flops on his back, awaiting my next move.

I stand at the base of the bed and scan my eyes over every inch of his supple body, so delectable. Ripe for the taking. I remove my clothes as quickly as I can, my dick screaming to be set free.

"Open your legs for me, sweetheart."

Kai parts his legs, a whimper leaves him, he's on the verge of despair as he shivers all over, holding on to his sanity, trying not to let go and bitch at me to just fuck him and get on with it. But tonight, I will savor him and punish him by not giving him what he wants. I always keep my promises. I move to the bedside table and grab the lube, dropping the bottle onto the bed. Crawling onto the mattress, I lay my upper body in between his legs and start to kiss his shin bone, I leave open mouth kisses and kitten licks on his flesh, before moving up towards his knees. I kiss around the knee, taking little bites, causing him to gasp at the small stings. Then I head toward my goal, that tattoo. I lick a long path from knee to thigh, until I reach the base of the rose and bite down. Hard. Kai yells out, which then morphs into a long moan as I start to suck around the rest of the rose, alternating from kiss to suck, over and over.

"Fuck Jules, I love it when you bite me."

"Me too. I want to mark you permanently here. My teeth marks and bruises to be with you forever."

"I want that too."

A rumble of possessiveness leaves my mouth, and I almost lose control of the battle to take this slow. I kiss up further to his hairless groin and suckle on the flesh around his sharp V and pubic bone. He arches under me, pushing himself into my face, begging for more. And more I give him, creating a pattern of hickeys from one hip bone to the other, creating a bruise belt that looks so fucking hot, I want to cum all over it. Kai is losing himself into a panting, fidgeting mess. Begging and begging.

"Oh please Jules, suck me hard, fuck me, please. I need you."

"Soon."

"Ugh, Jules! Don't piss me off. I need to cum, just fucking fuck me, you fucker!"

I grab his balls in my hand and tug hard.

"Ow! What the hell?"

"Did you forget yourself? Remind me again, who is in charge?"

"Fine. You are."

"Good. Now shut the hell up and let your man make you feel good. Just lie back and be the little pillow whore you love to be."

To my glee, he does as he's told, and I go back to the job at hand. I kiss further up to his nipple on the non-injured side of his body and swirl my tongue around his tight little bud. After a few sloppy swipes of my tongue, I suck the bud into my mouth and drink that little peak of sweetness up. As Kai gets louder, I bite down until a burst of copper hits my tongue, the little drop of blood awakening my body in ways it has never been awoken before.

"Fuck! I love it when you do that."

I move up his body until I'm at his neck, where I run my tongue over his prominent Adam's apple. So fucking tasty. Needing a kiss before I get started, I clutch his hair in my hands and push my mouth onto his, getting lost in his mouth, his passionate tongue fucking, the flavors that are all Kai, burst on my tongue, heightening this sexual experience to explosive levels.

I break the kiss and smile down at Kai's blissed out face. He's so responsive and it doesn't take much for him to get to this stage, which is amazing for my ego.

"Want me to fuck that little hole? You ready to welcome me home?"

"Oh god, yes, yes," he mumbles.

I move back down his body until I'm in between his thighs, and I move both legs over my shoulders, giving me an open and perfect view of his hole. Welcome home to me.

I can't hang on for much longer, so I dive in head first and push my tongue into his tight as fuck channel, forcing myself past the first muscle as he clenches around me. Kai is so loud now I can't even hear my own thoughts. I lick and thrust and soak his ass until it drips with saliva. Reaching out to find the bottle of lube on the bed, I cover my fingers in it before pushing one finger into his ass and locating his p-spot on the first try.

"Oh shit! Harder, yes, right there. Fuck, fuck I'm gonna cum," he groans as I assault his ass with my thick fingers, enjoying the sounds of his cries with the squelching of the lube. I need to get inside him, this is too damn erotic.

"Gotta fuck you, Kai. I can't be gentle."

"I don't want you to be."

I position myself in between his legs while on my knees, and he spreads his thighs like the whore of my dreams. I slick up my cock and throw my lube bottle on the floor, not giving a shit if it spills. I line up my cock with his gaping hole, and look at him, waiting to see what his answer will be to my unsaid question.

"Yes. Choke me, I miss the feeling."

I hold his throat with both hands as he grasps at the wrists to hold on.

"Tap my arms twice if you want me to stop."

"Okay."

With one push of my hips, I slide back home inside him and nearly howl at how fucking amazing it feels. His ass is so warm and snug, it's difficult to move at first, as his ass clings onto me, afraid I'll leave.

"What are you waiting for? Fuck me, fuck me good," he rasps as my hands squeeze a little tighter while I fuck him with long steady thrusts. The headboard rattles against the wall. Kai is so loud I think the night animals can hear his version of the mating call, and I just stare down at this gorgeous man, overjoyed that this is our life.

"Harder, Jules, I'm no princess, I can take it," he says with all the snark.

"My whore wants a pounding? Hold on."

I pound into him at a rate that has definitely not happened to me before. I wonder if it hurts, but looking at the drunken state of lust that Kai is in right now, and the obscene noises he makes, I think he's managing fine.

"I'm gonna cum, Jules. You're hitting my prostate so fucking good, make me cum," he says, pleading. My orgasm builds and just as I feel it about to spill over, I squeeze his neck harder until his face turns red. As soon as he starts to gasp for air, his eyes roll back and he cums like a water fountain, spraying that delicious seed all over himself. Of course the sight triggers my own orgasm, flooding his ass with weeks of stocked up cum, filling him to the brim. I remove my hands from his neck and try to relax my breathing as I'm depleted of any energy. Fucking Kai is hard work, but the best work. I roll over to lie next to him, and he scoots in close, his body becoming limp as his rapidly beating heart slows to normal. I watch as he strokes his throat with his fingers, a small smile on his face.

"That feel good?"

"Yes. I've missed it so much. Never let me go that long without your markings again."

"You really enjoy the pain of it, don't you?"

"It's not just that. The tenderness makes me feel secure, it's like being in armor. That your mark protects me in some way. I know it sounds dumb."

"Nothing you say sounds dumb, and I've got no issue keeping those bruises on you for the world to see."

He leans back and looks at me from beneath his thick lashes, he smiles, showcasing that sexy-ass dimple.

"I love you."

"I love you too."

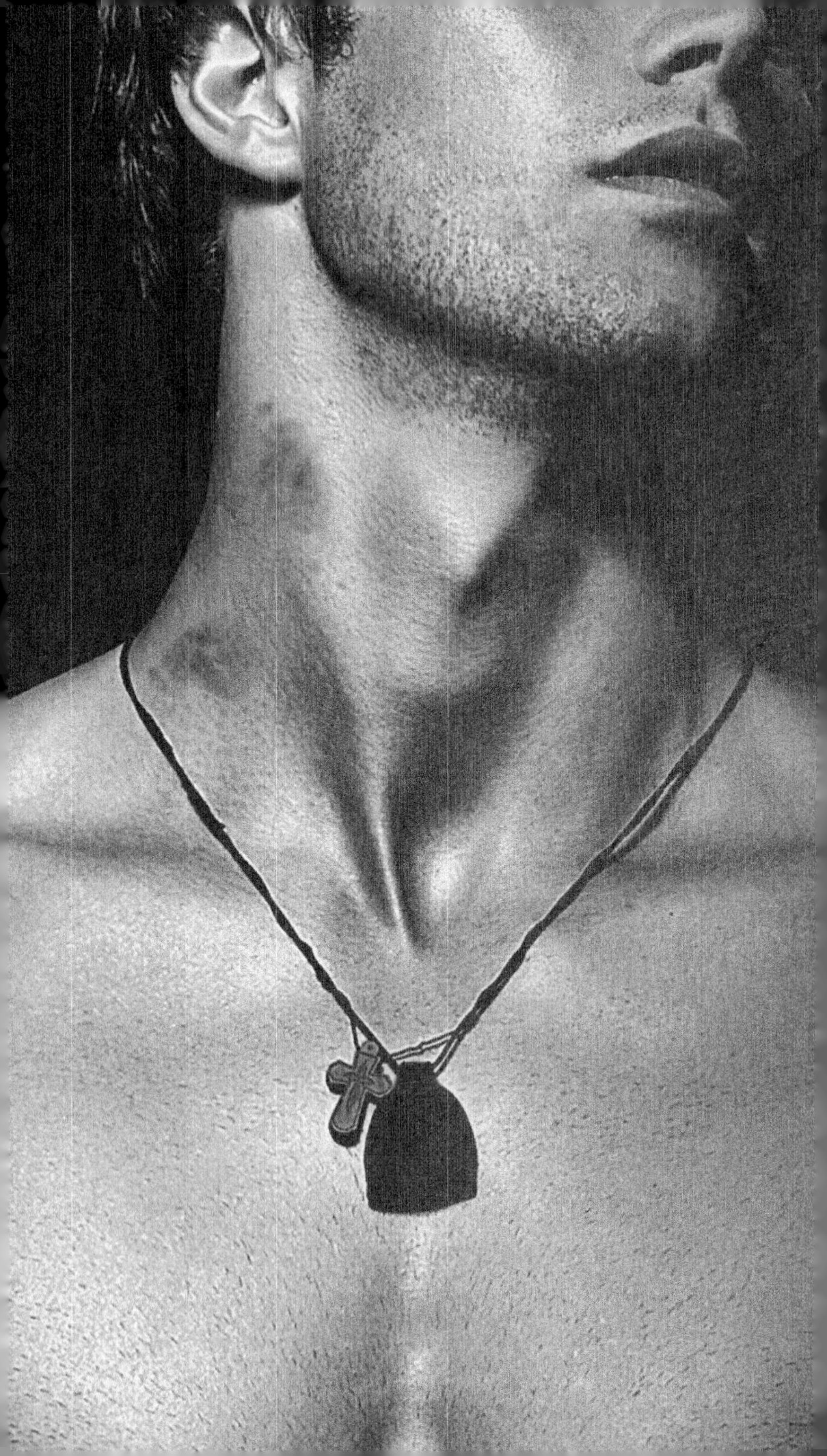

CHAPTER 50
KAI

I've been back home for three days now, and I'm so freakin' happy I could burst into song. Today I'm going back to work, because sitting around waiting for Jules is driving me insane. I wish I could work with him, but Dima has forbidden it unless necessary. Prick. Not that I'd call him that to his face. Dressed and ready for the day, I walk out into our kitchen where Jules and Simon are chatting. My man is so damn sexy. I can't believe I ever did life without him. He's my solar eclipse. Everything else in life gets shut out when he's around me. Okay, I can see why Dima has split us up for work.

"Hey Kai," Si says as I walk further into the kitchen.

"Hey. What's the plan for today?" I ask as Jules pulls me into his side while he finishes his slice of toast.

"We're hanging back today. The architect is arriving to meet with Lev and D this morning, and he wants us there."

"I'll see you guys over at the main house, gotta go speak to Lev," Simon says, seemingly distracted as he puts his coffee mug in the sink and walks out of the front door.

"Is he okay?" I ask. Simon's mood appeared off this morning.

"I think Carlos was goading him last night at the club. I'm just waiting for the fireworks between those two."

"It'll be fun to watch. You know, I was thinking, after hearing you speak to Mom the other day, I never realized you had a different last name. She never spoke about our grandparents, so, what is it?"

"It's Moore."

"Jules Moore. Huh. Sounds so proper."

"I prefer Kai Moore. We need to get on that."

"Get on that?"

"Yeah, you should have my surname. You're mine and this is the final step."

My heart stops, literally stops at the insinuation.

"Hold on, do you want to get married?"

"Yeah. I'd thought you would've worked that out by now."

"No, why would I?"

"You need to pay more attention, Kai"

I laugh at the casualness of this, just an assumption that this is where we're headed, and I love it.

"Sure."

"Good, now let's go before the brothers start throwing a fit."

As we enter the main house, everyone is congregated in the large kitchen. I spy Ivan over near the door and slip away from Jules to have a chat with him.

"Hey Ivan, can I ask for a favor?"

"What is it?"

"I know you have a tattoo gun, Jules mentioned it."

"Ahh did he tell you what I did to your friends with it?"

Yes he did, and I still feel queasy from it. But I rode his dick like a cowboy at the lengths he went to for me. I'm getting distracted.

"Yeah but that's not why I'm asking. You can do tattoos for real, right?"

"Yep. Why, you want a piece?"

"I do and I want it to be a surprise, can you do it later?"

"That should be okay, meet me at the club office tonight and I'll do it."

"Thanks Ivan."

The buzzer to the gate alerts us to the architect's arrival, and I follow Dima and Lev out into the hallway with Ivan, while the others remain in the kitchen. I open the large front door to witness a tall, lithe, gorgeous man in a suit walk up towards us with a large satchel over his right shoulder and carrying what appears to be blueprints with his hands. His hair is styled like a model, brown and thick. He looks like he's in a commercial or something, the guy is hot as fuck.

"Holy shit, is this the architect?" Ivan says from behind me.

"Put your dick away, Ivan. I don't want the drama," Dima says.

"Sorry, can't help you there. He's fucking hot. I can't wait for him to be working under me," Ivan says, his voice low and growly. Uh-oh, poor guy.

"I bet he's straight," Lev says as the guy gets closer.

"That's even hotter. Love a good challenge," Ivan says, even more determined.

The guy walks up to us on the doorstep and introduces himself.

"Hi. I'm here to see Dima Kozlov? I'm Tyler Blackford, Senior Architect from Lexington."

"I'm Dima, and it's nice to meet you," Dima says, and shakes Tyler's hand.

"Tyler. That's a great name," Ivan says as he strides forward, towering over the guy with his hand out for Tyler to shake.

"I'm Ivan. Can't wait to be working with you," he says, and keeps Tyler's hand in his as he shakes it. Tyler's eyes widen as he takes in how huge Ivan is and gives him a small smile. He looks petrified.

"Come on, Tyler. Let's go to my office so we can start," Dima says.

"Sounds good," Tyler says, following Dima and Lev to the office. He looks over his shoulder where Ivan's eyes are laser focused on his ass, and walks faster out of sight.

"You've freaked him out," I say to Ivan, who grins at me like the cat that got the cream.

"Oh I plan to do a lot worse," Ivan says, winking at me before following the guys down to the office. He wasn't invited to the meeting, but it appears Ivan just does what he wants. That Tyler guy won't know what hit him. Let's hope he's married with a family so that Ivan will leave him alone.

"What are you smiling about?" Jules says as he comes up behind me, placing his hands around my waist and sucking on the back of my neck, causing a small moan to leave my lips.

"Ivan, he's set his sights on the architect."

Jules laughs.

"What's so funny?"

"Let's just say you never want Ivan's attention in that way, It never ends well."

"He won't hurt him, will he?"

"No, but he won't leave him alone, probably stalk him and break him down until he submits. Ivan loves to hunt."

"That doesn't sound good."

"No, but it's not our business. I know you like Ivan, but don't be fooled by the nice guy persona. He's worse than Lev and D put together."

"Kai, stop smooching with Jules. We gotta go," Simon says as he walks by us, jogging out of the house. Someone is in a pissy mood.

"I want you to text me when you get there," Jules says.

"Why?"

"Just do it. If you don't, I'll only come find you."

"Still a controlling asshole."

"For you only."

It's later in the day and I'm more tired than I thought I'd be, especially after seeing Ivan for him to do my tattoo. He was very excited when he saw what I wanted, but he stuck to his word and kept quiet. I'm now lying in my boxers on Jules's bed, waiting for him to see what I did for him. And me.

"I want to come home every night to you on the bed like this, waiting for me," he says as he walks into the bedroom. I have no problem with that request. I hope he likes my surprise, both my surprises. Not only the tattoo, but I've prepped myself to ride his cock. Ever since Ivan finished it I've been so turned on at the thought of Jules's reaction.

"I have a gift for you."

"Oh yeah?"

"Here." I let my thighs fall open and he looks down and spots the tattoo under the rose on my thigh. I had Ivan tattoo over the teeth marks Jules left. I wanted them branded into my skin so the stamp of his ownership remains on me forever.

"You had my teeth marks tattooed, sweetheart? Who did it?"

"Ivan."

"Ivan saw you like this?"

"Don't get jealous. I want you. No one else. Do you like it?"

"Like it? I fucking love it. We should tattoo all my marks on your skin."

"No, I only want them from you."

Jules's hands move up to my throat to caress the marks he left there from our choking session the other day, and I let myself enjoy the feeling, only slightly disappointed they aren't as sore as they were.

"I have one more surprise."

"Show me," he whispers in my ear as his clothed body covers my semi naked one. I guide his hand down to my boxers for him to take them off, which he does. As he covers my body again with his I wrap my legs around his waist, and guide his hand to my open and willing hole, where he pushes two fingers in and I groan at the burn.

"Holy shit, you prepared yourself for me? You need my cock that bad?"

"Yes. I wanna ride you, make you feel good."

Jules jumps off the bed and undresses at an impressive speed before lying on his back, stroking his cock, looking at me like I'm the most beautiful thing in the world.

"What ya waiting for? Hop on, Kai."

Straddling Jules's hips, I line him up with my hole and sink down onto his perfect cock. We both groan at the sensation, it never gets old. Taking control, I bounce on that dick until I see stars as Jules pinches my nipples until we both climax in unison. Bonded as one. Jules is mine as much as I'm his.

Finally, I belong.

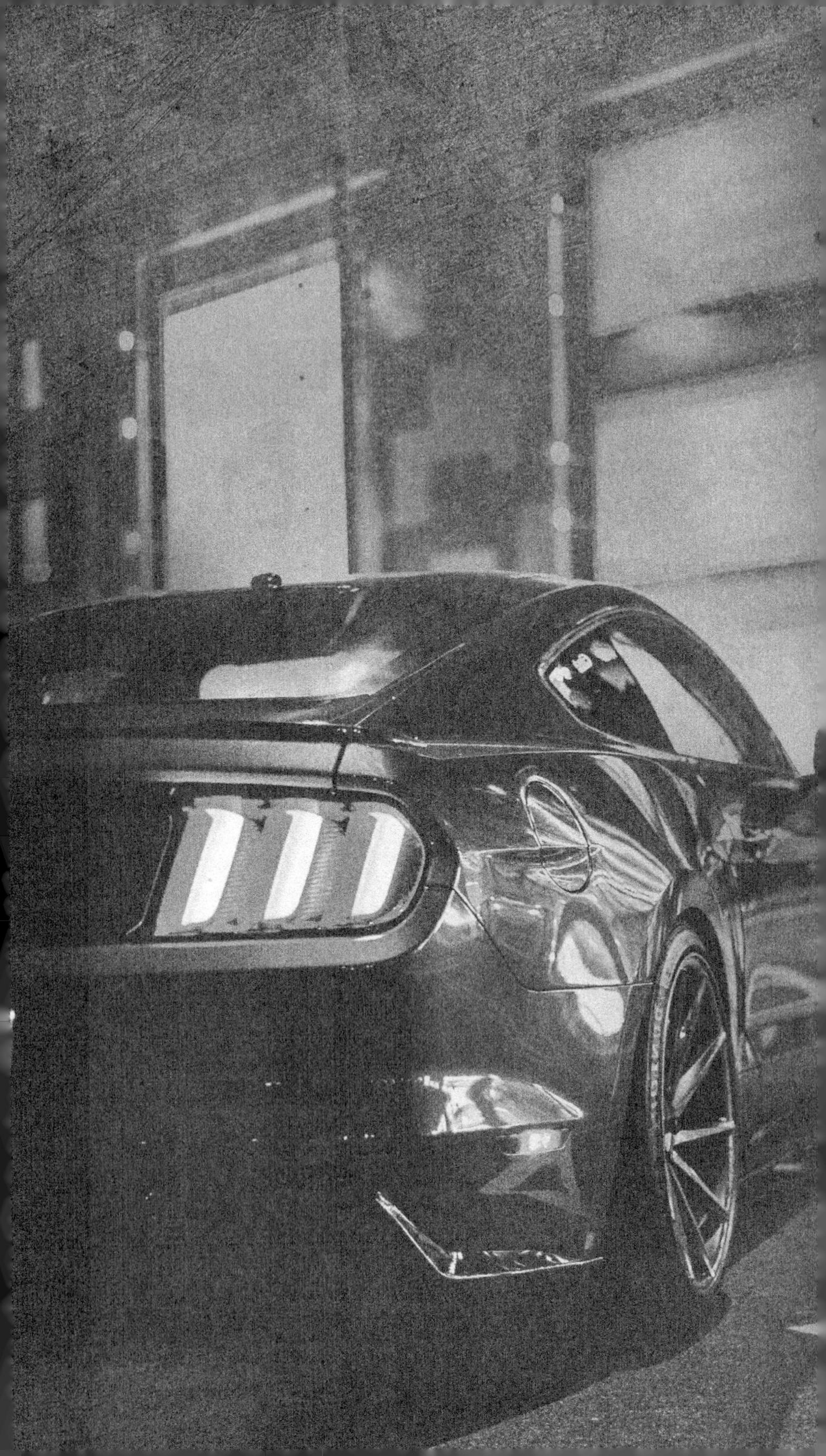

CHAPTER 51

Jules

It's been two weeks since Kai was released from the hospital, and things have now gotten into a good rhythm. He's enjoying work and I'm not going fucking crazy every ten minutes about where he is or what he's doing. That's because he checks in with me every day and also shares his location. I may have emotionally manipulated him with the stabbing in order to get him to comply with my stalking, but it calms the beast. Things are also back to normal with Dima and Seb after what happened. When Kai got home, it was a new page, and nothing needed to be said. We were all relieved he was alive and home. The only thing that makes me on edge is the amount of time Kai spends with Aaron. They talk a lot together in hushed conversations and it freaks me the fuck out. Aaron brings out that paranoia in anyone he meets.

"Morning," Kai says to me as he comes out of the bathroom in just a towel. His body covered in my marks that

I rebranded on him yesterday. It's become a ritual that I would hate to live without. He has a huge smile on his face, that fucking dimple out in full effect, and I'm so tempted to drag him back to bed.

"Morning. Why are you smiling like that?"

"Would you prefer me to be a grumpy asshole like you?"

"Watch it, Kai."

"Don't growl at me like that. I'm already late meeting Si."

"You can relax this weekend, D has given us time off."

"Time off? Since when?"

"Since I booked the courthouse."

Kai doesn't respond at first. With how rigid he's gone, you might think he'd turned into a mannequin.

"Kai?"

"Wait. Courthouse?"

"You knew we were getting hitched."

"Errr, that's news to me."

"I said you would have my surname."

"Yes you said that but you never proposed, you only hinted at getting married," he says, totally bewildered by my thinking.

"Why do I need to propose?"

"Oh my god, you really are a neanderthal," he says, moving over to me where I still lay on the bed, and straddling me.

"Yep. Then I'll whisk you away to my cave."

"Sounds fucking perfect to me," he says, before kissing me with the sweetest of kisses I've ever received. Sappy fucker. I slap his ass to get him to move, otherwise I'll be inside him again.

"Up. There is stuff I need to do today."

"Fine, fine," he moans, as he gets up and walks away to get dressed. When he leaves the room, I grab my phone from the bedside table and bring up Jenny's contact details. I know Kai is happy, but I can sense he misses his mom. There may be no going back for me and Jenny, but I want Kai to have her in his life still. To know he doesn't have to choose. That is, if she sees it that way.

I press call and expect for it to go to voicemail, which it does. The beep sounds and I leave a message that I hope will make her come around.

"Jenny, it's me. Jules. I'm calling for Kai. We're getting hitched this weekend, and while I don't give a shit what you think, I know Kai misses you. While we'll never see eye to eye on this, don't cut your son off. He needs his mom and I'm sure you need him. Don't let your issue with me come between you. Call him. Come over and see him. Whatever suits."

Without saying goodbye, I end the call and breathe a sigh of relief. That part of my life is done, but I know I've done all I can to give Kai everything he wishes, even when he doesn't articulate what that is.

After I've dressed, I walk out into the kitchen to hear laughter between Simon and Kai. Call me stupid but I still get irked at anyone who makes him laugh.

"What are you guys laughing about?"

"Ivan. You should see what he's putting that Tyler guy through."

"Tyler?"

"The architect," Kai says.

"Ivan is going all out for a piece of that guy," Simon laughs, and I smile. Ivan will not let that guy escape.

"I gotta get over to Lev. See ya later," I say, before giving Kai a kiss and leaving to head over to the main house.

When I locate Lev in the hallway of the mansion, he's typing a message on his phone with a frown on his face.

"Everything okay?" I ask.

"Fucking Aaron, being a pain. Why the hell did I get involved with the fucker?"

"Because you're a psycho who loves the challenge."

"That must be it. Anyway, told Kai the news?"

"Yeah."

"Why are you getting married? It's all so fucking cringe."

"I want him as mine in all ways, this is the final step. Why? Don't you want to get married?"

Lev looks at me like I'm mentally unwell and a stranger to him.

"What the fuck do you think? Can you imagine?"

"Yeah. I can imagine some satanic ritual with blood swapping knowing you two," I say, not totally joking.

"Please don't give him any ideas or you won't make it to your own wedding. Can't believe I have to go to another wedding this year," he says, walking out of the front door as I follow.

"I called Jenny."

"Why the fuck you do that?"

"For Kai. Just to give her a chance to make it up to him."

"Better you than me, she's a fucking headache."

I laugh at his dramatics, but he ain't wrong.

It's late in the afternoon and we're finally back home after a long day of shipment issues that me and Lev had to deal with. I part ways with him as soon as we get back, and go straight back to the guards's house. I cannot wait until we get our own homes. I need some privacy with Kai.

As I walk inside, I see Kai sitting slumped on the sofa in the living room.

"Kai? What's wrong?"

He looks up at me, his baby blues glassy and bright.

"Mom called."

Oh shit. I wasn't expecting her to respond.

"Yeah, What did she say?"

"She wants to meet up halfway. Talk. You called her and told her about the wedding?"

"She needed to see what she's missing out on. I had to give it one last chance for you."

"I'm meeting her tomorrow. I need you to know I'll always pick you, Jules."

"It's not about choosing. We can both be in your life without dealing with each other. As long as you know me and your mom are done, then I want you to have whatever kind of relationship you can with her."

Kai walks over to me and wraps his arms around my neck and buries his nose into my shoulder.

"Thank you," he says, and nothing more needs to be said.

The next day, I'm pacing around the house. I've worked out for an hour with Lev, done some work at the club, and now I'm wearing a hole into the kitchen floor, waiting for Kai to come home. He's been gone most of the day, and I'm anxious, because I really hope she gave him a chance. I hear the front door unlock and rush around to greet Kai.

"How'd it go?" I ask him as he removes his shoes.

"Wow, can you let me get through the door first?"

"Kai..."

"It went well. She apologized for how she acted. She still doesn't agree, or as she put it, 'condone' what we're doing, but she won't mention it again and we'll just go from there.

"Good. You okay with that?"

Kai grabs my face and kisses me softly.

"Very happy. It's a huge weight to be lifted, Jules. I love you so much. Thank you."

"Love you too."

Finally, the start of our lives together can begin. Fuck anyone who doesn't like it. I couldn't give a shit.

AFTERWORD

I hope you enjoyed Jules and Kai's story! While I love writing stories that are dark, this story has a slight difference as Jules does display feelings. While my family of psycho's have their weird ways of showing affection, Jules is more of a morally corrupted guy who is a result of neglect emotionally and physically. Kai brought out that softer side of him, and it just felt right for them to have the soft and hard sides in their relationship. Kai and Jules's issues all stem from Jules and Jenny's parents neglecting her when she needed them, and it had a domino effect, ultimately ripping the family apart. Even years later, Jenny's underlying resentment and jealousy over Jules still exists as strongly as it did when she was abandoned. I wanted to highlight that when issues are left unresolved for years, the destructive effect it has on future family and the mental strain can make the idea of mending those relationships impossible. Jules was a child and had his own struggles with his parents when Jenny was thrown out of the house and is an unfair target. I wanted to show how things are not always as they seem, and jealousy like this, that's so con- suming, stops any logical thinking and seeing the bigger picture. Jenny and Jules do love each other, but words cut deep, and life takes its toll. Are they too far down the line to repair their relationship now that Jules is with Kai? We will have to see how the following two books play out, but I have some hope, as long as Tim keeps his nose out!

Kai is definitely my sweet baby, that I felt protective of. He got stuck in a cycle and absorbed all the negativity from his mother's past that had a damaging effect on him. His low moods and feeling of not being wanted were so real to him. So when Jules turns up again, he throws himself straight into anything that makes him feel good. The hick- ey kink was cathartic for him in some ways; the sore feeling reassured him of Jules's want for him when they weren't together. It's not a healthy habit, and of course, therapy would be a good option, but the norm does not exist in this world of the Kozlovs, and it works for them.

Tyler and Ivan are next; Ivan is the craziest guy I think I've written, all I can say is poor Tyler. Get ready for some dark shenanigans in that book.

Then there is Simon and Carlos's book. Their book will be my darkest to date and I cannot wait to share them. The hate and passion between those two have me all giddy!

ACKNOWLEDGEMENTS

This new series has been fun and daunting. I would like to thank a few for their contributions.

My alpha readers, Amy V. and Sadie, I love you both so much. Thank you for reading, listening to my concerns, and being honest with your input. You both have been with me every step of the way, even before I started writing, and I hope you will both stick with me, as I couldn't do this without either of you.

Jen, Thank you so much for editing and proofreading this book. Your input was invaluable, and I cannot wait to work with you on future books.

Jordan – My PA and dear friend, thank you for all you do and for listening to me complain and doubt myself sometimes. You always manage to perk me up, and I'm thankful to have you on this journey with me.

My beta readers – Jordan and Danielle. You're the best, and thanks for reading so quickly! Thanks for cheerleading me every step of the way.

Katelyn (Design by Kage), you are so talented and kind. I cannot thank you enough for the beautiful covers and formatting you have done for me. You're stuck with me now!

Amber (insertclevername__here), thank you for brainstorming names with me for Aaron's switchblade! We had fun discussing that, and I really appreciate you.

Julia – I had to mention you as you are you. Gahhh!! Love ya!

To all my ARC readers and street team. I value you all so much, and seeing your reactions to Jules and Kai has been a joy. You're the best team I could ask for!

To every reader, thank you for taking a chance on me. It makes me so happy to see people reading my stories, and I love the messages of support and love. Thank you for making a dream come true.

Syn x

ALSO BY SYN

Tied To You
Kill for You
Craving the Chase

Printed in Great Britain
by Amazon